Storrington nodded. "I do believe that Bellamy bears looking at in the Candover matter."

"Will you help me? Will you tell the Bow Street runners to investigate him?"

"I don't see how I can do that without revealing how you found the information." He placed a slight stress on the word "you," warning her that his forbearance towards her ambiguous situation went only so far. "I'll poke about and see what I can find out. At the very least I should be able to discover if he was in Brighton, or anywhere nearby, at the time of the poisoning."

Jacobin barely refrained from casting her arms round his neck and kissing him again. It was so wonderful to have someone on her side, to feel she wasn't completely alone anymore.

He grinned down at her, his facial expression less guarded than any she'd seen him wear. "I have a feeling I'll regret this," he said, but his words had no bite. "We'll probably end up together in Newgate prison. I just hope they'll allow you to provide the meals."

Romances by **Miranda Neville**

NEVER RESIST TEMPTATION

Never Resist Temptation

MIRANDA NEVILLE

AVON

An Imprint of HarperCollins*Publishers*

AVON BOOKS
An Imprint of HarperCollins*Publishers*
10 East 53rd Street
New York, New York 10022-5299

Copyright © 2009 by Miranda Neville
ISBN 978-0-06-171591-4
www.avonromance.com

First Avon Books paperback printing: March 2009

Avon Trademark Reg. U.S. Pat. Off. and in Other Countries, Marca Registrada, Hecho en U.S.A.
HarperCollins® is a registered trademark of HarperCollins Publishers.

Printed in the U.S.A.

10 9 8 7 6 5 4 3 2 1

To Kathy, Sophia and Susan,
without whom . . .

Acknowledgments

Thanks to my fabulous critique partners and beta readers—Susan, Kathy, Sophia, Cathy, and Madame Sophie. To my wonderful agent, Meredith Bernstein. To Esi Sogah and all the brilliant people at Avon, for guiding me through the publication progress. And to my daughter Becca for being a drama queen.

Prologue

Cards are war, in disguise of a sport.

Charles Lamb

London, 1816

Nothing in Anthony's upbringing or experience had taught him the proper etiquette for taking delivery of a woman won in a card game. Had his prize been a courtesan, his imagination might have been adequate to the occasion. But this girl—what was her name? something outlandish like Robina or Jacinta— was the niece of a baron, the blood relation of the man he'd defeated at piquet. However awkward he might feel under the circumstances, Anthony consoled himself with the reflection that it must be far worse for the uncle.

Good. Candover's discomfort was his goal. And he intended to make sure it greatly increased by the time he had finished with him.

"Lord Candover, my lord," announced the butler, who had been told to show the visitors directly to the library.

The old debauchee was alone and wore a furtive look that clashed with his gold-embroidered purple waistcoat. Candover must have decided the correct protocol was to leave the girl in the carriage. Just as well, perhaps. What the devil would the servants think if she were delivered like a parcel and abandoned in his respectable household? Anthony could imagine the tittle-tattle. And though gossip was certainly his goal, he'd prefer to control it until he'd made up his mind what form it should take.

"Candover," he said with a polite bow. "I take it you're here to settle our bet."

"Storrington." Candover returned Anthony's courtesy with a creak of corsets. Then he cleared his throat but said nothing more. His face darkened to an unbecoming puce, and perspiration glistened on his forehead.

As Anthony covertly observed his distress, Candover's eyes shifted to a tray of drinks on the marbled-topped rosewood table in the center of the room. Anthony toyed with the notion of ignoring the hint. He knew everything about Candover's habits, including just how long he usually went without alcoholic stimulation. Not very long. Spirits and sweets were addictions the man never resisted, as testified by his complexion and his girth. Anthony tamped down his hatred and rage. Time enough to reveal himself to his enemy when victory was complete.

Like a courteous host he walked over to the table and picked up a decanter. "Brandy?" Without waiting for a reply he poured a generous measure.

Candover seized the offered glass, tipped back his head, and drained it. A few drops of spirit dribbled from the corner of his flaccid mouth, down his chin, and onto his protruding belly.

"About our bet . . ." he began, then faltered. "I can't meet the terms." He looked away to avoid Anthony's eye.

Anthony was surprised that Candover owned scruples enough to regret his shocking wager. He'd been eager to offer his niece as Anthony's mistress in an effort to recoup a loss of ten thousand pounds, had goaded Anthony to accept the terms. Anthony forced himself to remain as unemotional as he always did at the piquet table. With Candover the game didn't end when the last card was played.

"Might I suggest, Candover," he said with gentle reproach, the tone he might take with an erring friend, "that you shouldn't have wagered something you weren't prepared to part with. Not, of course, that I don't understand your reluctance to part with your niece."

"Reluctance, be damned," Candover growled. "I've never reneged on a debt of honor in my life. You could have the girl and be welcome to her if I could deliver her. But I can't. The chit ran away."

"Dear me," Anthony murmured, enjoying Candover's embarrassment. "Do you mean she wasn't willing to come to me?"

"Willing or not, she'd do as I ordered." Candover's temper, never easy, was fraying at the edges. "But the bitch ran off with my cook, my French pastry cook. Eloped in the night! Damn it," he shouted in an explosion of ire, "I'll never find a hand with pastry like Jean-Luc."

"I regret the loss of your cook, Candover." Anthony found it difficult to keep his features impassive. "And of your niece too, of course. Do you need a few days to arrange your affairs before settling with me?"

"If you'd be good enough to wait," Candover replied, "I'd be grateful. It'll take me a day or two to raise ten thousand."

"Twenty thousand," Anthony reminded him quietly. "Twenty thousand. If you recall you were already down ten when you staked your niece against your previous losses."

Candover gulped. "Twenty it is, Storrington."

"A most unfortunate run of bad luck. Take your time." Anthony positively oozed false sympathy. "Shall we say one week?"

Inwardly he exulted. Twenty thousand was a vast sum, difficult for any man to raise in such a short time, even one in better financial health than Candover. It might well be enough to tip him over the edge into utter insolvency. At the least his enemy would endure a miserable seven days attempting to meet his debt of honor.

Revenge was most definitely a dish best eaten cold.

Chapter 1

<u>**Rose Bavarian Cream**</u>

Strip the petals off about thirty freshly picked roses and put them, with a pinch of cochineal grains, into clarified boiling sugar syrup. Cover, and when it has become just warm, add isinglass. Strain the mixture through muslin and set on ice. When it begins to set, fold in whipped cream.

Antonin Carême

Three months later

Jacob Léon muttered a French word inappropriate for polite company. It was, however, the kind of language heard often in the kitchens of the Royal Pavilion at Brighton. Especially on a day when the Prince Regent was giving an important dinner and the staff was under pressure to prepare dozens of dishes.

Mrs. Underwood, the supervisor of confectionery, swept into the frigid pastry room and sneered at the young French pastry cook.

"Why aren't you working, Léon?" she demanded. "We've a banquet. Or did you maybe forget?"

Jacob Léon suppressed an insolent retort. There were suppressed sniggers from the other cooks in the big chamber, and Jacob knew that they—and Mrs. Underwood herself—were enjoying the supervisor's sarcasm. Her long nose had been out of joint since Antonin Carême, the most famous *pâtissier* in all of Europe, had taken command of the Prince Regent's kitchens. Carême didn't approve of professional female cooks and failed to treat Mrs. Underwood with the respect she deserved for her ten years in the royal service. Although Jacob had sympathy for the woman's position—more than she would have suspected—he wished she wouldn't use him as a whipping boy for her resentment.

Most of the royal staff disliked him too, because he was French. And it didn't help that he was on the short side, with effeminate features and no trace of a beard. To retain their respect he made sure his language—in both English and French—exceeded any of theirs in the depth and variety of its profanity. But this was not the moment for swearing, or for the cocky attitude he adopted to keep bullies at bay.

"The recipe for rose Bavarian cream," he explained. "Someone's mixed up the quantities again. I've made this dish a hundred times and I can tell the proportions are wrong. Someone translated French ounces to English ones without making the adjustment."

He shuddered to think what would have happened if he'd ruined the rose cream and wasted those costly blooms. Mrs. Underwood would love an excuse to toss him out. Even more than most in domestic service, Jacob needed to keep his job. Desperately.

"I can send Charlie to fetch Maître Carême's book and look up the correct quantities." He glanced at the skinny kitchen boy who was shivering in the ice-cooled room.

"Finish it quickly," said Mrs. Underwood with an impatient sniff. "You're wanted in the small confectionery room."

"Why?" Jacob was surprised to be summoned to Carême's own domain, and a little alarmed. Since Carême had hired him as an assistant pastry cook, he'd had little direct contact with the great man.

Mrs. Underwood looked as though she'd swallowed something nasty. "Mr. Carême has come down with a fever. He cannot work today."

Jacob gasped. "*Les pièces montées!* They are not finished."

"We are all well aware of that fact. Mr. Carême has directed that *you* will complete them."

It was midnight by the time Jacob reached his small room in the servants' quarters. His shoulders ached from the painstaking task of decorating architectural monuments constructed from almond paste. Absurdly, to Jacob's mind, these elaborate productions were not intended to be eaten, but rather to decorate the buffet table and astonish diners with the virtuosity of the chef. Maître Carême had been working on them for several days, but there had been hours of labor left on an *ermitage russe* to compliment the evening's guest of honor, the Russian ambassador. Using dyed icing, Jacob transformed the miniature version of a supposedly humble thatched wooden building into an exotic retreat, colored in pale green and yellow and resting on orange rocks that sprouted moss and, oddly enough, a palm tree.

Once these *extraordinaires*, as Carême dubbed his masterpieces, had been safely stowed in the ice room, Jacob had to turn around and assist in the final production and serving of the meal. Chaos was barely kept at bay, despite the fact the Pavilion boasted a huge kitchen, designed to the most exacting modern standards, for serving a prince who loved to eat. Even with a small army of kitchen and dining room staff, the serving of oysters, hors d'oeuvres, three different soups, two fish dishes, three roasts, six entrées, several vegetable entremets, and no fewer than eight choices of dessert was not to be achieved without dangerously fraying tempers and a good deal of cursing in several languages.

The heat from the charcoal grills and huge ovens had been almost unbearable after a day spent in the frigid temperatures of the confectionery room. Now alone, Jacob sighed with relief as he removed his double-breasted chef's coat and the padding he wore beneath it.

Within minutes the pudgy cook was transformed into a slender girl.

She longed to unwind the tightly wound linen cloth that constricted her small breasts. But she wasn't yet ready to be Jacobin de Chastelux, the identity she would resume only when she retired to her narrow bed. Too enervated to sleep, she craved cool sea breezes. Quickly she donned the breeches, coat, and boots that made her look like a well-bred youth. She deftly tied a linen cloth around her neck, and even through her fatigue spared a glance of appreciation for the dapper young man in the tiny looking glass. She reflected on the irony that she was better dressed as a lowly cook than she'd been as a young lady from a wealthy family. Tying her unruly chestnut hair in a neat queue, she put on her hat and set off with a quiet swagger and a jaunty air.

On a cool November evening Jacobin had the Steyne almost to herself on the short walk to the seashore and back. But as she approached the servants' entrance to the Pavilion, she noticed a figure waiting nearby. Something about him struck her as familiar. Stopping, she examined the man cautiously. There was only one person in Brighton who was likely to recognize her. Lord Candover had attended this evening's dinner, but he'd never stand out in the cold. He wouldn't set foot outside until his well-warmed carriage was ready to receive him. Besides, this man was short and slightly built. Jacobin waited until the man turned his head and one of the lamps caught his features.

Edgar. What was Edgar doing in Brighton? He rarely left Hurst Park.

Her heartbeat accelerated. He mustn't see her. She couldn't even keep her head down and hope to pass as an anonymous stranger. It was all too possible that Edgar would recognize her clothes, since only three months earlier they'd belonged to him. To be fair, she supposed they still did. She certainly hadn't obtained his permission before helping herself to them.

Jacobin withdrew among some of the heaps of stone and building equipment that littered the area around the unfinished palace. The cold bit through the wool of her coat, and she felt exhaustion overtake her. Curse Edgar. She couldn't stay here all night. She crept out from her hiding place and turned sharply in the opposite direction, practically running to the far corner of Castle Square. Straight into trouble.

"Wot 'ave we here?" demanded a drunken voice as she almost collided with a group of three men. "'Ere's a pretty lad."

From their clothing Jacobin deduced the trio were laborers employed on the renovations. From their state of inebriation she concluded that it was payday and she'd interrupted a celebration.

"I'm sorry, sir," she said pacifically. "I didn't mean to disturb you gentlemen."

They all roared with laughter. One man's eyes bulged like marbles from a filthy and unshaven face. He was the largest of the three and apparently their spokesman.

"Gen'lemen, are we?" he mocked. "Don't 'e speak

nicely, this one. D'you reckon 'e's a *gen'leman* too? I don't think so. I think this one would like to be a *lady*."

Zut! How could this drunken oaf have seen through her disguise?

"Look, lads," the man continued. "I think we've caught ourselves a molly boy."

"Disgustin'!" commented one of the others, and the third grunted his agreement.

"What would one of your kind be doin' out here in the middle of the night, I wonder. Lookin' for trade with one of the nobs with the same unnatcheral 'abits?"

It was a relief they thought her merely an effeminate boy, but their intentions seemed far from friendly. She prepared to run.

"No yer don't." A meaty hand encircled her upper arm, and the overpowering smell of stale onions mixed with gin assaulted her nose. She struggled, but liquor hadn't affected Bulgy Eyes's strength.

"What do you say, lads?" he asked his friends, digging his fingers into Jacobin's flesh. "Let's get the young gen'leman ready for 'is next customer. Pull off them fancy britches, then 'Is Lordship won't have to look too hard for his bumhole."

Jacobin didn't want to even think about what would happen when they discovered she was female.

The Earl of Storrington dismissed his carriage at the entrance to the Pavilion. He preferred to walk the short distance to the Old Ship Inn and let the breeze dissipate the annoyance of a wasted evening. He was beginning to wonder whether his careful cultivation of Prinny was worth the past three months he'd spent in the regent's circle. He'd come no closer to luring Candover into another game of cards. All he seemed to achieve was a succession of achingly long and ridiculously elaborate meals like the one just served in the prince's seaside pleasure palace. There'd been enough rich, overgarnished dishes to feed a multitude. Little wonder he needed a walk.

Somehow Candover had scraped together the twenty thousand pounds he'd lost after the girl eloped with the French cook. And now he stubbornly refused to sit down with Anthony at the piquet table again.

A commotion ahead pulled him out of his frustrated musing. In the dimly lit street he could make out a figure lying on the ground, under attack by three men.

He didn't like to see such unfair odds, so his first impulse was to launch himself into the fray. A mill with a group of ruffians would be just the thing to appease his irritation. But Anthony, who took pride in possessing the logical mind of a mathematician, disdained impulsive actions. He recollected that he was unarmed, and the wise option would be to avoid the scene and go for help. Negotiating a compromise between inclination and common sense, he embarked on a third course: bluff. He lengthened his gait, and as he came closer he could see that the victim was slight, only a youth, but flailing his arms, gamely resisting the efforts of the others to—good Lord—remove his breeches.

"Stop that!" he shouted.

The attackers looked up. One of them, a dirty brute with protruding eyes, looked assessingly at the earl, probably trying to decide how much damage he and his fellow bullies would sustain in a brawl. Anthony's fists clenched with anticipation of inflicting a good deal of damage. Confidence leached out of the lout's expression as he contemplated the earl's well-muscled six feet, two inches. That was the trouble with spending hours in the boxing saloon. Only an idiot wanted to pick a fight with you. Alas, this man wasn't an idiot.

"Just havin' a bit of fun, me lord," he cajoled. "Caught this nancy boy lurkin' round the prince's house. Thought we'd give 'im a scare like."

The boy on the ground thrashed about at the man's accusation, but was held fast to the ground by two of his captors. "I'm not a nancy and I wasn't doing anything," he gasped, winded by his struggle.

"I suggest the three of you leave, immediately," Anthony said, regretfully abandoning visions of combat and falling back on his usual persona of haughty aristocrat. "If you get out of my sight now, I may forget that I saw you and be unable to report you to the magistrate."

Casting reluctant backward looks at the youth, the three took themselves off up North Street. Storrington turned to the boy, who was now on hands and knees, trying to get up. A glance was enough to see that the lad's clothing was of superior quality, his style that of a gentleman. A very young gentleman who had no business being in the streets at such an hour.

"What are you doing out so late, and alone?" he asked, offering a hand.

Brown eyes gazed up at him. He could see why the boy's looks had attracted attention. His face was delicately handsome, saved from girlishness only by a firm jaw.

"I thank you, sir, for your intervention." The boy was still short of breath and having difficulty standing, so Storrington seized his hand and tugged him to his feet. The lad lost his balance and fell against him, forcing the earl to clasp him round the waist lest they both tumble to the ground.

A curious shiver passed through Anthony's body. He looked at the youth with alarm. Good God, he'd never felt that way about a boy. Almost a sexual frisson.

Hastily he dropped his arms and stepped backward so quickly that the youngster lost his balance again and stumbled forward. Anthony reached out a hand to ward him off and felt a slender shoulder through the fine wool jacket, sending a shiver of awareness up his arm. Appalled, he snatched it back. A surprisingly light body crashed against his chest, and he found himself inhaling a faint, sweet scent from a cluster of curls that tickled his nose. There was nothing for it but to remain still, suffering the same discomforting physical reaction, until the boy had regained his equilibrium.

Anthony dismissed his initial intention of seeing the boy home safely. Not when he found himself looking at a pair of lips and noticing that they were plump, rosy, and sensually curved.

"It's nothing," he said gruffly. "Get along now, be careful, and don't wander the streets of Brighton at night again."

The boy scampered off, and Anthony resisted the urge to watch where he went.

The devil! What was the matter with him? Almost two years without a woman, without even wanting a woman. It seemed that the Almighty, or some other power, was playing a joke on him.

Chapter 2

The morning after a banquet was a pleasant change from the fevered activity of the event. Some of the mountains of leftover food could be reused for the evening's meal, but there was still a healthy surplus. Starting early in the morning, servants from other Brighton households appeared at the back door with dishes to be filled. With so few members of the *ton* in Brighton in November, the demand was less than in summer, when the kitchens of fashionable households drove up prices with their lust for luxurious scraps from the royal table. Nevertheless, the cooks were kept busy apportioning out the uneaten remains.

A particular china serving dish made Jacobin grimace. She recognized the Candover crest as she filled it with the rose-flavored Bavarian cream she'd made the previous morning. She was well aware that it was one of Lord Candover's favorite puddings. Apparently his passion for the dish wasn't shared by others; it had been returned almost untouched to the ice room the previous night.

A summons to the main kitchen interrupted the lazy tenor of the day. As the confectionery staff hurried into the great chamber, the rumor traveled through the ranks that the Prince Regent was making one of his periodic visits to the magnificent domestic offices that were among the wonders of the Pavilion. The senior cooks ordered everyone to make sure they wore clean uniforms before they lined up, like soldiers in a regiment, for royal inspection. Jacobin blessed the fact that her jacket had survived the morning without a stain. There was no time to find a private spot to change.

A more pressing worry arose when she heard that His Highness was accompanied by the Russian ambassador and several other gentlemen. She pulled the floppy crown of her toque around, so it would at least partly cover her face, then slipped into the back row behind a pair of particularly tall fellows. If Candover were among the visitors he probably wouldn't notice one among dozens of similarly garbed cooks, but it didn't hurt to take precautions. Perhaps the Earl of Storrington would come too; she knew he'd also been one of the dinner guests.

The regent walked in with a thin man wearing a foreign order, presumably the ambassador, followed by about half a dozen others. Though Jacobin couldn't be certain, she didn't think Candover was among the cluster of men in the prince's entourage. Her uncle was likely still in bed, sleeping off the three bottles of claret that were his minimum daily intake. She was wondering if one of the overweight exquisites, each rivaling their prince as dedicated trenchermen, was Storrington, when she noticed a tall man bringing up the rear.

His relative youth, good looks, and muscular form set him apart from the rest of the royal cronies, as did the restrained manner of his dress. He was plainly garbed in a dark green morning coat over a matching waistcoat, the cut of these garments as fine as that of his buff pantaloons and as impeccable as his perfectly arranged white neck linen. Light brown hair was arranged in a windswept style, but without the disorderly excess she had seen in some dandies on the strut during the fashionable hour in Hyde Park. Instead the tousled locks made a pleasant counterbalance to the severity of his clothing. From her vantage point at the far end of the kitchen she couldn't have described the color of his eyes or the details of his features, but she had no trouble recognizing him. He was her rescuer from the previous night.

She stared at him like a village idiot, oblivious for a moment of Candover, Storrington, or the Prince Regent himself.

The prince was asking for Carême. "The ambassador wishes to compliment him on the excellence of last night's dinner," he explained to the head sauce cook, who bent almost double in his effort to acknowledge the supreme honor of such attention.

"Alas, Your Highness, Maître Carême is indisposed," the cook explained. "He has a fever."

"Not caused by the travails of last night, I trust?" inquired the prince graciously.

No indeed, the cook elaborated. Monsieur Carême had been in his bed since yesterday morning.

Expressing his astonishment that the dinner had been so well executed, the prince congratulated the kitchen staff on their success without the guidance of their leader.

"I am disappointed," said the ambassador. "I hoped to convey the regards of my master, Tsar Alexander, who enjoyed Monsieur Carême's services in Paris last year. Also, I wished to thank him for the compliment of including a Russian *confit* in the presentation last night. Doubtless the charming *ermitage* was created before Monsieur Carême was taken ill."

"True, Your Excellency, but the finishing touches were supplied in the morning by one of the confectionary staff."

"Ah," said the ambassador. "Perhaps in the absence of the master I may compliment his capable deputy."

The sauce cook bowed. "Of course, Your Excellency." He turned to Mrs. Underwood, who stood behind him. "It was Léon, I believe, who completed the *pièce montée*. Where is he?"

Looking less than enchanted, Mrs. Underwood sent out the word for Léon to appear. Jacobin hesitated to emerge from the protection of the two tall roast cooks who stood in front of her, but one of the footmen spotted her and pointed her out. She felt the curious eyes of the entire staff on her as she made her way across the cavernous chamber to the regent's group.

Keeping her head low in feigned humility, she managed to examine the group of gentlemen, her heart in her mouth as she wondered what on earth she would do if her uncle was present. Her confidence rose as she failed to find him; she straightened her stance and found herself meeting the eyes of her rescuer. They were gray-blue, and their alerted expression left her in no doubt that he'd recognized her. At closer quarters she realized what she'd been too agitated to see the previous night: he was an exceedingly good-looking man. But his appearance was marred by the cold arrogance of his mien. Under his steely gaze, lacking any trace of warmth or humor, the flutter in her stomach engendered by his looks subsided to a dull resentment. What had she done to make him regard her as though she were a bothersome insect? It wasn't her fault she'd been attacked by those marauding drunks.

Having reached the visiting dignitaries, she turned her attention to the regent. Under other circumstances she would have enjoyed the opportunity to view England's ruling prince at close quarters. He was tall and imposing, bulky of course, but impressively dressed and coiffed. Anyway, she was hardly in a position to criticize his avoirdupois, given the substantial false belly bulging under her linen jacket. She thrust her shoulders back and tilted her chin before sweeping into an extravagant bow. She couldn't help a thrill of pride that her skills were receiving such lofty recognition.

"This is Jacob Léon," said the sauce cook. "He came to us a few months ago. I believe he was trained in Paris."

"My compliments on the hermitage," said the ambassador, speaking in French. "A magnificent piece of work, although," he added with a smile, "palm trees are not often found in Russia."

"Thank you, Your Excellency," Jacobin replied in the same language. It felt good to converse in French, and she could relax now she was sure Candover wasn't in the visiting party. "I added only a few finishing touches. Most of the praise must go to Monsieur Carême." Thus she tactfully dismissed hours of painful work. She couldn't afford to offend Carême by having it reported she was stealing his glory.

"You are very young for such responsibility. Where did you learn your skills?"

"I was apprentice to a former colleague of Monsieur Carême," Jacobin replied, "a cook who worked at the maître's shop in the Rue de la Paix. I have been fortunate, even at second hand, to learn some of the master's extraordinary skill."

"Very good, very good," interrupted the regent, sounding impatient. "Very well done, young man. Your master will be pleased with you, I have no doubt." He turned to the head sauce cook. "I shall have my own physician attend Carême." Then, doubtless considering his lesser servants sufficiently honored, he drew the ambassador's attention to the construction of the kitchen and the vast central steam table, capable of keeping forty platters of food hot at the same time.

Jacobin feared she had now drawn the interest of the entire staff and the envy of many. Given the intrigues and resentments that were rife in the prince's kitchens, her rise to prominence would cause more problems than not. In her situation it would be safer to relapse into obscurity. As soon as she could, she escaped out to the kitchen court to share a tankard of ale with young Charlie and Dick Johnson. Dick was an amiable member of the confectionery staff, who didn't hold "Jacob's" Frenchness against him. Right now he was more interested in his potential windfall from the sale of the food surplus than in Jacob Léon's sudden notoriety.

"I wonder how much we'll get from this morning's work," he mused, blowing a smoke ring from a cheroot, filched by one of the footmen from the post-dinner detritus of the dining room. "Let's hope the head cook doesn't rise from his bed and snaffle the lot."

With Carême still indisposed, the kitchen staff was particularly cheerful that morning, for the earnings from the surplus food would be distributed to the staff according to the long-established system of entitlements. Not least among the grudges held by the Prince Regent's staff against the French chef was Carême's habit of making his own deals for the sale of food and retaining the income for himself.

"*Mon Dieu*, it doesn't seem fair," Jacobin agreed, "if it is indeed true that his salary is two thousand guineas. *Quelle richesse!*"

Charlie's eyes looked ready to pop at the notion of such wealth. "Wot would you do with two thousand yellow boys, Jake?"

Jacobin laughed and rumpled the boy's hair. "I don't know, Charlie. Maybe drink a bottle of wine every day? The good stuff, not the filth they serve to the staff."

"One! I'd drink two! And get meself a fine coach and 'orses and drive round all day like a nob."

"I'd marry Alice Tomkins," averred Dick, who was consistently ignored by the prettiest kitchen maid. "She'd be all arsey-varsey for me if I was rich. And I'd get out of here and buy me a cottage in the country."

"Not me," Jacobin countered. "I'd go to London and open a pastry shop, and all the fashionable households would buy from me, instead of Gunter's."

"You could do it, Jake," said Charlie. "Your pastries are the best in the kitchen."

"And how would you know that?" she asked. "None of the others let you pinch samples like I do."

"I know," Charlie said stubbornly. "And now His Highness knows too. Soon you'll be as famous as Mr. Carême."

In her more optimistic moments she indeed harbored such grandiose ambitions. And when realism intruded, her goal was more modest: to have enough money to resume her own identity and live comfortably without the grueling work of being in service. With a small shop in London she could enjoy some of the pleasures of town life. Her years in the country had been damnably dull compared to her girlhood in Paris.

But two thousand guineas were unlikely to come in her direction. All the more reason to hope a few shillings from this morning's trade would supplement her wage of thirty pounds a year.

Their comfortable ruminations on wealth were interrupted by the arrival of a stranger, a servant but not a member of the royal staff. From his clothing he appeared to be a groom rather than an indoor servant.

"I'm looking for a French cook," the man said. "Can you tell me where to find"—he referred to a slip of paper—"Jacob Léon."

"I am Léon," said Jacobin in surprise. "What do you want of me?"

"I've come to offer you a job," said the man. "My master is looking for a new pastry cook and he's heard you're a good one. Heard you can cook as well as Carême."

Jacobin laughed. "Hardly, monsieur. Your master must have heard that I finished some of Monsieur Carême's work in his absence."

"But you can make those fancy French pastries the nobs are mad for?" the man persisted.

"I am an excellent pastry cook," Jacobin acknowledged proudly. "Is your master a connoisseur of such cuisine?"

The man looked uncomfortable. "I don't know about a connersewer, but he likes puddings and he needs a good cook. He told me to offer you eighty pounds a year."

Jacobin pursed her lips and nodded appreciatively. That was a princely salary, and would let her save for her shop much faster. For the first time since escaping her uncle's house, she glimpsed a future with possibilities beyond the boundaries of her imagination. Perhaps it was a good thing Candover and Storrington had engaged in their immoral wager. Without it she'd never have left the safe but confining dead end of life as her uncle's despised dependent.

"That is generous, monsieur," she said, visions of golden guineas dancing in her head. "Tell me, what is the name of your master who loves pastry so much?"

"Bless me, did I forget to tell you? My master is the Earl of Storrington, and I am Jem Webster, his groom."

Chapter 3

It had seemed a brilliant idea, Anthony thought as he finished breakfast in his private parlor at the Old Ship Inn. To hire Jacob Léon. Candover's weakness for sweets was well-known, and he'd been without a first-rate pastry cook since the last man eloped with the niece. If he wasn't mistaken, word that young Léon had stepped in for Carême when the master was ill would soon get around the Prince Regent's circle. He'd be besieged by offers, and Candover would be at the head of the line. If Léon was working for Anthony, his services could be used to lure Candover into another card game.

Too bad the young man had refused, but Anthony wasn't giving up yet. He'd sent Jem down to the Pavilion again this morning to sweeten his previous offer. He wondered if the young cook was aware that the Earl of Storrington was the man who'd saved him from those louts two nights ago. If he didn't know it, perhaps he should. Gratitude might persuade him to leave Carême where money had proved ineffective. Should Jem fail again, Anthony supposed he'd better make the approach in person, but he hoped it wouldn't come to that.

Anthony felt a visceral reluctance to have any direct contact with the young man. He hadn't forgotten the strange attraction he'd felt when he'd helped him up from the ground, and it embarrassed him. He'd recognized the face when Léon had spoken with Count Lieven, the Russian ambassador. At first he'd only seen an anonymous plump cook, thick around the middle with a protruding belly that testified to his enjoyment of his own confections. Only when he'd examined the young man more carefully had he connected the refined features and glowing dark eyes with the youth he'd rescued.

Odd, really. When he'd held the boy to save him from falling he hadn't felt at all fat.

The door opened and Webster entered the room.

"Back already, Jem?" Anthony asked. "I didn't expect you for hours. Did you manage to speak to Léon? What did he say to one hundred guineas a year?"

"I didn't see him at all, m'lord. Things are all at sixes and sevens at the palace kitchens and the news is all over town. Thought I'd better get back and tell you."

Anthony looked at the groom with interest. Jem Webster was a stolid man, not given to high drama.

"Lord Candover's been poisoned."

Anthony leaped to his feet. "Good God! Is he dead?"

"No, and they say he'll live. There was something in a dish he had for dinner last night but he was took ill right away, after only a bite, and his valet called a doctor. They say he'll pull through."

Anthony paced up and down, assessing the effect of these tidings on his plans.

"You said the palace was upset. I can see why His Highness would be concerned, but the household? Why would such news disturb the kitchens?"

"Because the pudding came from there. It was left over from the dinner the other night. Lord Candover's cook bought it from the royal kitchen."

Jacobin was close to panic. The staff was in an uproar at the rumor that Lord Candover had been poisoned by a dish purchased from the Pavilion kitchen. The regent was said to be outraged and demanding a full investigation. The local magistrate was already interviewing the senior cooks, and it wouldn't be long before he received assistance from London. The prince had sent posthaste for Bow Street runners to come and turn the kitchen staff inside out and upside down.

Her disguise would never survive concentrated scrutiny, and scrutiny she would receive as the cook who'd prepared the poisoned dessert, even if no one remembered that it was she who had actually filled Candover's dish with the rose cream. Once they identified her as a female it would be only a matter of time before they knew she was Candover's niece. His estranged niece. They'd rush her to the gallows and never bother to look further for the would-be murderer.

She wished she'd accepted Storrington's offer and left

Brighton already. Why did it have to be Storrington? How worse than ironic that her only offer of employment, her sole chance of escape, came from a man as wicked as the uncle whose house she'd fled. The prospect of placing herself in his power terrified her. But not as much as execution for attempted murder.

Given the confusion in the kitchens, it was easy to escape to her own room, where she gathered her meager worldly possessions into a bundle. She sat on the bed, took a deep breath, and considered her options.

Flight. It was the first, last and only choice available to her, and the farther the better. If she could get to France, Jean-Luc would take care of her, but she had barely enough money to pay for passage across the Channel. She didn't even know whether he was in Paris. It might take her weeks to track him down, and she'd need something to live on in the meantime. She needed a place to hide, a way of earning more money. Her quarter's salary from the royal household, due in a few weeks, would have to be abandoned.

It wouldn't be many more hours before every lawman in southeast England was searching for a young Frenchman. But they wouldn't be looking for an Englishwoman.

The bare bones of a plan began to form in her mind.

But why did it have to be Storrington?

Shown into the Earl of Storrington's private parlor at the Old Ship Inn, Jacobin almost fell over.

"My lord," she said, and managed a deep bow. She hoped her voice hadn't come out in a squeak, belying her masculine attire.

Shock at discovering that Storrington was the man who'd saved her from the drunken workmen bloomed into relief that her uncle's piquet opponent wasn't the elderly roué she'd expected. Quite the contrary.

Perhaps her plan to place her female self in his employ wasn't as risky as she feared. This man had saved her from the drunken workmen, an act that required some courage and at least a modicum of altruism.

Surveying him more closely than had been possible from the back row of cooks in the royal kitchen, she judged that the earl was in his mid-thirties and no less attractive than he'd seemed before. He lounged at ease in an armchair, one elegant booted leg crossed over the other, looking at her down a finely chiseled, slightly aquiline nose. He seemed to be examining the white linen jacket and apron of her uniform.

His unsmiling gaze roused a prickly warmth in her face and a strange tightness in her bound breasts. Sternly she reminded herself that he'd gambled for the favors of a woman he'd never met, without knowing if she was willing. The shameful thought drifted through the back of her mind that with this man her fate might not have been entirely terrible.

Having finished his perusal of her clothing, he looked up, but without making eye contact. "Mr. Léon. Does your presence mean that you have changed your mind and decided to accept my offer of employment?"

"Is the position still open?" she asked.

"It is, and I shall be pleased if you accept it." He spoke without warmth and sounded anything but gratified. The expression on his face was one of distaste, almost as though he found Jacob Léon disgusting.

"I hope I am not presuming, my lord, but I came to you because I am able to recommend another *pâtissier* who has a similar training to my own and is equally skilled."

Storrington frowned. "I had hoped to acquire your services after your triumph at the Pavilion. Who is this other cook."

"Rather, my lord, I should say *pâtissière*. She is my cousin."

Jacobin thought she caught an arrested look on the earl's face, but only for a moment. His expression returned to aristocratic indifference.

"A female? Is she French too?"

"Half French, my lord. Our mothers were sisters but her father was English. She speaks much better English than I."

Storrington raised his eyebrows. "Your own command of the language is excellent. How long have you been in this country?"

"A few years," Jacobin replied noncommittally. "*Ma cousine* speaks without the accent."

"You worked at Carême's shop, I gathered from your conversation with Count Lieven. Was your cousin also employed there?"

Jacobin decided not to correct his misconception.

"We had the same teacher, who was a senior cook there. Like me, Jane is competent in all aspects of the art of *pâtisserie* and confectionary. Tell me your favorite dishes and I will describe how we both make them."

"I'm not interested in the details of your trade, only in the results." His tone was dismissive, but she had the odd impression he was playing cat-and-mouse with her. A sharp glint in his eyes belied the indifferent drawl of his voice. He stood up suddenly, and crossed the distance between them in three strides. Once again he stared at her white linen jacket, as though he found the uniform fascinating.

"Will you see my cousin?" she asked, to distract his attention from her chest. Besides, she was eager to get down to business. "And would you offer the same salary?"

From his superior height he gazed into her eyes, and her heart raced. With anxiety about his answer, she told herself. It had nothing to do with the faint masculine scent or the warmth emanating from his muscular frame as he towered over her.

Without any softening of his steely expression, he raised his hands and calmly began to unbutton her jacket. She shivered when his fingers brushed her breasts, even through jacket, shirt, and the several layers of linen she used to flatten them. Shocked into frozen silence, she merely stared as he pushed the unbuttoned coat from her shoulders, then carefully untied the strips of cloth that held her cotton wadding "belly" in place. When she was left only in shirt and breeches, he took a step backward and looked her up and down. She was horribly conscious that the bindings around her breasts diminished, but did not level, them.

He looked up, and for the first time she saw a gleam of humor in his eyes and the hint of a smile on his lips.

"Cousin Jane, I presume."

Two hours later Anthony suspected he had taken leave of his senses. Why else would he be bowling along the road from Brighton to Storrington Hall, sharing his carriage with his newest employee, Jane Castle, a possibly murderous female pastry cook?

So dizzying had been his relief when he realized that the latest object of his attraction was not, in fact, male, he had swallowed the explanation for her charade with unwonted credulity.

It was, he supposed, a reasonable narrative.

Jane Castle had applied for work at the Pavilion disguised as a youth because the great Carême refused to hire women. She feared the investigation into the poisoning of one of the regent's friends would lead to the exposure of her sex and the loss of her job. Impulsively she had decided to accept Storrington's offer of employment, but in her own guise.

"I regret that I tried to deceive you, my lord." She had shaken her head, and a few bright chestnut curls came loose from a ribbon tying them back. "Had I known who you were, that you were my kind rescuer, I would have trusted to your sense of justice and thrown myself on your mercy from the beginning."

She had clasped her hands to her breasts, which managed to heave quite effectively, despite the fact that they were obviously constrained by some kind of binding, and sighed, her whole body seeming to plead for forgiveness and acceptance. Jane Castle had a dramatic streak that would have graced the stage at Drury Lane. He'd rather desperately wanted to laugh. Among other things.

Instead he'd sent her out of the room to change into feminine clothing. The urge to indulge in further examination of her underpinnings was becoming acute. He really, really wanted to remove her shirt and whatever else was underneath and discover the precise size and shape of her breasts.

And he'd decided to engage her services as pastry cook. Without references. He'd even agreed to pay Jane Castle the same outrageous salary he'd offered "Jacob Léon," absurd since female servants always earned much less than their male counterparts. And agreed to some conditions of employment that would likely induce fits in his secretary and his steward, who usually took care of such negotiations.

And ruled that she travel in his own carriage instead of in the baggage vehicle with his valet.

He peered at her out of the corner of his eye. She sat primly across from him, dressed in a sensible cloak and bonnet over a plain gray gown, very suitable for a superior servant. She didn't look nearly as enticing as she had in breeches, but it made no difference. He vividly recalled the feel of her slight waist when he'd prevented her from falling. And the slender but delectable curves revealed that morning when he'd removed her jacket and that ridiculous padding. He should have let her squeeze into the other carriage with the trunks. That unusual sweet scent, which he thought he'd now identified as vanilla, was wafting faintly from her side of the carriage. Being penned in a confined space with her was creating havoc with the usual orderly working of his brain.

His surreptitious glance had been intercepted. "My lord?" Huge brown eyes widened in question.

He cleared his throat. "Er, tell me about your upbringing. Were your parents in service?" He suspected not, since she spoke English perfectly in a well-bred accent with just an occasional—and attractive—Gallic roll.

"Neither of them were *pâtissier*s," she said, not exactly answering the question. "I was apprenticed to a cook after they died."

"When was that?"

"When I was twelve. My father first and soon afterward my mother."

"I'm sorry," he replied. "I lost my own mother when I was five." And wondered why he'd said that. He rarely spoke of his mother, and never to strangers.

"In which part of France did you live?" he continued hastily.

"Always in Paris."

"Hm, during eventful times."

"I was born the year of the Terror."

"And did your parents approve of guillotining aristocrats?"

Her gloved hands were clenched into fists. The firm jaw, which he'd once thought masculine but now gave her face character, was thrust forward. Pale winter afternoon light filtered through the carriage window and illuminated a small but distinct indentation—more than a dimple, perhaps a shallow cleft—in her chin.

"No!" She turned full face to him. She glowed with passion. "*Absolument non!* My father was a man of peace. He approved of the principles of the Revolution but he never wished for anyone to die."

"Liberty, equality, and fraternity," Anthony said ironically.

"And what's wrong with that?" Jane asked fiercely. "Can you tell me what is wrong with such principles?"

"Not a thing, save that they are impossible to achieve. You only have to look at the career of Napoleon Bonaparte to see where your revolutionary ideals got you."

She sighed. "I can't argue with that. My father always mistrusted Bonaparte. He died soon after his coronation as emperor, and it's my belief that it was the final death of the Revolution that killed him." The fire had faded from her eyes, leaving a look of great sadness.

"I'm sorry," he said again. "You must miss him very much." He was beginning to wonder about her father. What kind of Englishman settled in France, and apparently remained there, even when the countries were at war?

"Your father was a man of education?" he probed.

"He was well educated for his station in life." Miss Castle's tone was unconfiding and her features had set into a guarded neutrality. But he noticed again that her hands were clenched hard enough to cause her pain. He found himself more and more curious about her.

"Were you also well educated? Did you expect something better in life than to enter service as a cook?"

"I am quite content with my situation," she replied evasively. "I am devoted to my craft. In fact, if you don't mind, my lord, I would like to take this opportunity to ask you about your requirements. What are your favorite dishes?"

Anthony would rather be talking about her background. It hadn't occurred to him when posing as a lover of sweets that he would actually be expected to show knowledge of the subject.

"I'm not very good with names," he demurred. "Especially French names. I was never very good at French." This last fact at least was true. He had his own reasons to despise all things French, including the language, and he'd deliberately neglected that part of his schooling.

"What do you like to eat for breakfast?" she asked.

He shrugged. "The usual things, I suppose. Beef, ham, eggs sometimes. Toast." He brightened up. "Toast. I like bread."

Jane looked puzzled. "I was not aware that baking bread would be one of my duties."

Anthony had very little idea of the division of labor below stairs. His butler and housekeeper saw to those details. Come to think of it, he was completely ignorant of the duties of a pastry cook.

"Why don't you tell me some of the things you make best and I'll tell you if I like them," he improvised.

Miss Castle looked at him a little oddly, but appeared to give his idea some consideration.

"Do you enjoy Nesselrode pudding? It's one of His Highness the Prince Regent's favorite dishes."

"Remind me what's in it." It was doubtless some vilely rich concoction if Prinny adored it.

"Chestnuts, cream, eggs, raisins, maraschino brandy."

Gad, he thought, it sounded disgusting. He must come up with a pudding he liked.

"Gooseberry fool. I've always enjoyed that." He had too. In the nursery.

"Very English," commented his high-priced Paris-trained *pâtissière*. "Hardly something you'd need to hire me to make."

He racked his brains. He'd never had much of a sweet tooth and now he couldn't for the life of him remember a single pudding, even one he *didn't* like. He closed his eyes for a moment and envisaged a sumptuous buffet at a banquet.

Aha. What the devil were those things called?

He opened his eyes in triumph. "You know what I really like, Miss Castle? Those little puffy things. Can you make puffy things?"

What in heaven does the man want with a French pastry cook? Jacobin wondered, as it became obvious that Lord Storrington, far from being a "connoisseur" of continental *pâtisserie*, was a total ignoramus on the subject. She'd think he was engaging her for quite a different position if he hadn't tried to hire her before he knew she was a woman. She wasn't unaware that, were his intentions dishonorable, he might have preferred her as a man. But though he'd conducted himself perfectly correctly since removing her jacket, she'd intercepted a glance or two that went beyond what was appropriate for a nobleman toward a cook. Confined as her life had been at Hurst, she hadn't reached the age of twenty-three without learning to spot male appreciation. This particular gentleman didn't prefer boys.

She didn't know exactly what he wanted from her, but she seriously doubted it was dessert. Much against her better judgment she found his admiration . . . stirring.

Little puffy things indeed. She'd give him little puffy things. She'd whip up a batch as soon as she got settled into her new pastry room and find out whether he'd actually eat them.

Despite the perils of her situation, she couldn't help enjoying their conversation. She found herself liking this rather dour man when he'd become flustered under her interrogation about his confectionary tastes. She got a glimpse of the man under the exterior shell of the unflappable nobleman, arrogantly confident of his own power. When he'd discovered her sex he'd shown just a glimmer of a smile, one she'd like to see repeated.

"*Ah, les petites choses bouffies,*" she said airily, daring to tease him a little. "One of the greatest challenges of the *pâtissier*'s art. Not every cook possesses the necessary finesse. They require the utmost lightness of hand. But fortunately for yourself, my lord, you have hired the right person. I can promise you little puffy things like you've never tasted before,"

Her employer gave her a hard look. "You misspeak. Did no one ever explain to you, Miss Castle, that one of the first requisites of a successful life in service is to address your master with respect."

Jacobin threw back her head and summoned the expression of blazing creativity she had observed in the eyes of Germaine de Staël when her father had taken her to the novelist's Paris salon.

"Ah! Monsieur," she exclaimed in a pronounced French accent. "It is you who misspeak. I am no servant. I am an *artiste*!"

For a moment she thought she'd gone too far, that she'd jeopardized her position, her future, possibly her very life.

Then his features relaxed and the Earl of Storrington laughed.

Chapter 4

Lord Candover's butler accepted the presence of a Bow Street runner in his master's Brighton house without surprise. Given what Tom Hawkins had already learned about the nature of Candover's mode of living, the servant was probably used to irregular occurrences.

"I'd like to speak to Lord Candover," Hawkins said, hooking his thumbs into the pockets of his scarlet waistcoat.

"His Lordship is not receiving. You had better speak to Mr. Edgar." The butler led the runner into small reception room.

"Mr. Hawkins, sir," he announced.

"Ah, the runner, no doubt," said the occupant of the room. "I am Edgar Candover, Lord Candover's cousin."

"Thomas Hawkins, at your service. I am investigating Lord Candover's attempted murder at the request of His Highness the Prince Regent."

Edgar Candover was a slight man of below average height. His features were undistinguished, and the only impression he gave was one of colorless anonymity.

Even his age was uncertain, though he couldn't be above thirty. He could have been any gentleman anywhere. Yet as Hawkins examined him, he noted that the man had aspirations to dandyism, his clothing plain but well cut and of superior quality. A chased-silver fob watch hung from his waistcoat.

"It's a terrible thing," Candover said, wringing his hands. "I can't believe anyone would wish to murder my cousin. I feel sure it's all a terrible mistake."

"The physician was certain that the symptoms were of aconite poisoning, not an ingredient usually found in food."

"No indeed," Candover replied. "Thank heavens his valet was at hand."

"Saved his life, so I hear."

"My cousin ate a single spoonful of the affected dish and was taken ill immediately. His valet acted quickly and called a physician."

"I'll have more questions for you later, but first I'd like to speak to Lord Candover, as soon as possible."

Candover's eyes filled with concern. "I don't think it would be wise today, Mr. Hawkins. He's very weak. Tomorrow perhaps. In the meantime I will be happy to assist you."

Hawkins asked the obvious question, expecting the indignation that it always aroused. "Who stands to gain from Lord Candover's death? Who inherits the title and estate?"

Edgar Candover seemed undisturbed. "Although not a close relation, I am the heir to the barony. My cousin never married and he only had a sister, who died some years ago. The estate is unentailed and I have no idea who is named in his will. I assume it is myself, but he has never told me so."

"Is the fortune a large one?"

"I have been acting as His Lordship's steward for nine years. The estate is in reasonable health, though my uncle has lavish tastes. If you would prefer to receive details from someone other than myself I can refer you to my cousin's solicitor in Guildford."

So apparently Edgar Candover was the one to benefit most from Candover's death, Hawkins thought. He didn't seem worried about his situation, though Hawkins wouldn't accept that alone as a sign of innocence.

"Are you familiar with a young French cook by name Jacob Léon?" he asked, observing Candover closely for any reaction.

Candover shook his head. "Should I be?"

"He was employed as a pastry cook at the Pavilion and disappeared from Brighton yesterday. No one has seen him since the news of your cousin's poisoning spread through the servants' quarters." Leon's location was of crucial concern to Hawkins. None of the kitchen staff appeared to know where he came from. He had been hired directly by the head cook, Carême, who was in the grip of a fever and unable to answer any questions.

"Why would a French cook in the employ of the Prince Regent wish to kill my cousin?" Candover asked, sounding bewildered.

"That's what we'd all like to know, isn't it, Mr. Candover."

Leaving the Bow Street runner to interview Lord Candover's valet, Edgar went upstairs to his cousin's bedchamber.

Lord Candover sprawled whalelike in his huge bed, propped up by a mountain of pillows so that he could, against doctor's orders, drink brandy in comfort. His valet had commented to the butler that it was most likely the pickled state of his stomach that enabled him to survive the poison.

"What's the news, my boy?" he asked Edgar, sounding surprisingly cheerful. "Do they know yet who tried to do me in?"

"As your heir I'm the prime suspect," Edgar replied.

"Nonsense, nonsense, you'd never think of such a thing, even if you had the means. What an absurd suggestion. But I heard the rumor that a cook is missing from the Pavilion, the same one who completed Carême's work for the dinner. Pity, I was hoping to hire the boy, but I suppose I shouldn't if he's a poisoner."

"I wish you wouldn't jest about such things, cousin."

"You're too scrupulous, Edgar. Why should he want to kill me, anyway? Perhaps he'll appear again and I can get him to work for me. I miss Jean-Luc." Candover sighed, reflecting on his lost *pâtissier*. "Come to think of it, that rose cream reminded me of Jean-Luc. It was prepared just the way he used to. My favorite dish."

He sipped some more brandy. "What was his name?"

"Who?" Edgar asked.

"The cook. The one that ran away." Candover reached over and selected a tartlet from a plate on the bedside table. Not even a brush with death could dull his passion for pastries. He examined it critically. Since Jean-Luc's departure he constantly complained about the quality of the sweets produced in his kitchen.

"Jacob Léon."

"Funny that," Candover mused. "You don't think it could have been Jacobin, do you? The similarity in name, you know. That bitch would love to kill me."

"You're imagining things," Edgar said soothingly. "How could Jacobin get a job as a cook at the Pavilion and keep it? She doesn't have the training. She's in Paris with Jean-Luc, and Jean-Luc is working for the Duc de Clermont-Ferrand."

"Damn his eyes, and damn hers too," the older man growled, spitting a shower of crumbs onto his barrel of a chest. "And refill my glass."

Edgar left Candover to the enjoyment of his brandy, his pastry, and his spleen. He needed to find Jacobin. Fast.

Chapter 5

J acobin's doubts about her new job were confirmed
   when she saw her working quarters, or rather lack
of such. The kitchens at Storrington Hall were spacious,
well equipped, and fully staffed. There was no vacancy
for a specialist in *pâtisserie*, because no such position
had ever existed.

As for the cook, Mrs. Simpson, she reminded Jacobin
of a plumper version of her old enemy Mrs. Underwood
at the Pavilion.

"I don't know what's got into His Lordship's head,"
remarked the cook with an indignant sniff when presented with Jane Castle's arrival. "He's always been
quite satisfied with my puddings, just like his father
before him. Apple tart, fruit fools, and Christmas
pudding in season. Good English fare. That's all we've
ever served here."

Jacobin sighed inwardly. It was too much to hope for
the kind of friendly acceptance she'd enjoyed among her
uncle's servants. Still, she had no intention of allowing
the woman to bully her.

"I don't know anything about that, Mrs. Simpson,"

she said firmly. "But Lord Storrington has engaged my services as a *pâtissière* and *confectionère*. Please be good enough to show me to the pastry room."

"Dear me, Miss Castle! We don't have any place like *that* here." From the cook's scornful tone, Jacobin might have asked to be shown to a brothel. "There's a marble slab over there"—she indicated a corner of the kitchen—"I use for rolling out dough."

"That's not good enough," Jacobin replied. "I must have my own room where the temperature can be kept cold enough for pastries and jellies."

"You'll have to ask Mr. Simpson. Now if you'll excuse me, I've dinner to get on the table in two hours, thanks to His Lordship arriving unexpected."

"Mr. Simpson?"

"He's the butler," the cook replied. "And my husband."

Jacobin kept a rein on her ever volatile temper and decided a temporary retreat was in order. "I will get out of your way then, madame."

She left the kitchen and went to inspect the rest of the offices. She found an ample ice closet and guessed that a plentiful supply of ice would be forthcoming. Storrington Hall's location—like that of the Brighton Pavilion—near the chalk downs provided perfect conditions for the storage of ice year-round. Not far from the main kitchen there was a small unused pantry that could easily be equipped as a pastry room.

Diverted by the sound of a visitor at the back door, demanding to see the head cook, Jacobin drew closer to the half-closed door of her pantry.

The steps of the under servant who'd opened the door retreated to the kitchen. After some indecipherable, but clearly irritated, speech, heavier footsteps approached the back door, and Jacobin heard Mrs. Simpson asking the visitor his business.

"I'm inquiring if there's a new pastry cook been hired on here." The voice was one of a superior servant.

"What's that to you?" Jacobin now had reason to be grateful for Mrs. Simpson's suspicious nature.

"I'm trying to a find a cook named Jacob Léon, a young Frenchman," the voice continued. "I've heard reports he's taken service in a household near Brighton."

Zut, Jacobin thought, how could they have tracked her down so quickly?

"We don't have any Frenchies here," said Mrs. Simpson firmly. "And no male cooks neither. His Lordship's new pastry cook is an Englishwoman, just like I am."

"What's her name?" The inquiry was relentless.

"You want to know anything else, you go to the steward. Or to His Lordship. Come back here and I'll give you what for, snooping around His Lordship's kitchens like this."

Jacobin's confidence, on the rebound since Storrington had agreed to employ her without a lot of difficult questions, seeped away. It was bad enough to face the political quicksands of her new position without investigators dogging her footsteps. She needed to keep this job until the furor over Candover's attempted murder had subsided. Or until they found the real culprit. She hoped the authorities—for she had little doubt it must be the representative of a magistrate or of Bow Street who pursued her—were searching all over Sussex rather than having specific information linking her to Storrington.

Loath to face interrogation by the cook, as soon as the coast was clear she slipped out the back door for a walk in the grounds.

The damp winter chill, stiffened by a purposeful breeze, cut through her worn cloak and echoed the cold fear in her heart. She longed desperately for an ally. At her uncle's house she'd at least been surrounded by friendly servants. Below stairs she'd found a family. Not one capable of replacing her doting parents, whose love and attention had made her childhood an endless summer of warmth and safety. But her welcome in the servants' hall had comforted her when she was reeling with grief at the loss of both father and mother within a few months, and alleviated the cruelty and neglect dealt her by her uncle and guardian.

She missed the trivial daily gossip of life below stairs at Hurst Park. She missed the kindly cook who had shown her how to roll out pie crust. She even missed Edgar, her dull but amiable cousin who hadn't treated her unkindly. Most of all she missed Jean-Luc.

Since Jean-Luc Clèves had taken command of Candover's kitchen when she was sixteen, he had been her closest friend. He'd reminded her of her childhood in France and taught her to cook. And he'd helped her escape from Hurst.

There was no one to help her now. She, who rarely cried, felt the prickle of tears. Ever since her father's death she'd had to look after herself. As an eleven-year-old girl Jacobin had propped up her heartbroken mother and arranged their escape from Napoleon's France. Orphaned soon afterward, she'd suffered years of living with Candover's hatred, months in the regent's kitchens in constant fear of being unmasked, and now she was on the run because of a crime she hadn't committed. A rising sob tore at her breast, and she succumbed to waves of fear, loneliness, and a desperate anger at the injustice of her situation.

For the first time in months she consciously recalled the events that had led to her departure from her uncle Candover's house.

It was a rare occasion when Jacobin was summoned to her uncle's presence. In eleven years at the Candover estate she could probably count the number of times on the fingers of her two hands—and without needing the thumbs. Experience told her this encounter would be unpleasant.

She hurried upstairs from the kitchen to tidy her hair and smooth out the creases in her gown created by apron strings securely bound at the waist. At least at this hour of the morning her dress was still clean; several hours in the pastry kitchen would find it dusted with flour and smeared with butter, despite the protection of the large linen cook's apron. She'd prefer to face Candover looking like the well-bred young lady she was supposed to be, little as he honored her position.

Her mind raced over the possible cause of his displeasure. Although he was usually content to ignore her existence, he seemed to feel the periodic need to berate the niece he'd given houseroom since she was eleven years old.

In a tiny corner of her mind, Jacobin couldn't help hoping that for once he'd show her an iota of kindness, a small indication that he regarded his sister's only child with anything but loathing.

She knocked softly at the library door. Candover didn't trouble to rise when she entered at his curt command. Trying to gauge his mood, she eyed him cautiously. A darkly shadowed chin and the state of his dress told to expect nothing good. At nine-thirty on a Hampshire morning he was slumped in an armchair, still in evening clothes. That meant he'd driven from London by night and was likely still foxed. Sober he was merely cold; drunk he could be vicious.

"There you are." He looked at her through bloodshot eyes that held a curious gleam, an expression that seemed almost triumphant. "You're to go and pack. You're leaving today."

He was throwing her out.

"Why?" It was the only thought she could utter.

"I have found a position for you." His slack lips curled nastily.

A position? For a moment Jacobin was glad. Glad to get away from Hurst Park and out of her uncle's power. But relief gave way to suspicion as she considered what kind of position he meant. It seemed unlikely that anyone would hire her as a governess. Although more than capable of fulfilling the academic requirements of such a post, she was—thanks to Candover—without the feminine accomplishments that gently bred parents expected their daughters to master. Latin, Greek, and a thorough acquaintance with French intellectual thought were not useful qualifications for a young woman seeking employment.

"What kind of position?" she asked.

He gave a crack of laughter. "On your back!"

She wasn't too naïve to understand the inference.

"Lord Storrington is taking you," Candover continued. "I had nothing left to wager, so I staked you instead. And lost."

"He wants to marry me?" Jacobin inquired cautiously, unwilling to believe in the more obvious meaning of his words.

Candover's laughter was ugly and without humor. "Marriage? To a worthless French slut? You flatter yourself. You'll be lucky if he sets you up as his mistress instead of taking a quick tumble and throwing you into the gutter as you deserve."

"*Non! Jamais!*" she cried, breaking into her native French as tended to happen when her emotions were kindled. "*C'est infâme, vil. Vous n'êtes qu'un macquereau immonde.*"

Her uncle hated her speaking French, though he understood the language well enough.

"Call me a dirty pimp, by all means," he sneered. "Knowing such names merely proves what you deserve.

You're no better than a whore so you might as well be one."

"I am of age," she said carefully, reverting to English. "You can't make me do it. You can throw me out of your house but you can't control my actions. I'd rather starve than agree to such a disgusting arrangement." Beneath a veneer of calm, panic churned. Without a penny to her name and deprived of even her uncle's unloving protection, her future was precarious.

Candover rose to his feet. His body was grotesquely swollen despite the corsets that strove to confine his massive belly. He lumbered toward her and took her arm in a painful grip.

"You could leave here and go to hell your own way—if you could escape me. No, my dear niece"—his sneer intensified—"I promised you to Storrington and I'm a man of my word. A gentleman never reneges on a wager."

Jacobin spat in his face. "Some gentleman! My father was a gentleman. You are a filthy pig," she hissed.

Tightening his hold on her arm, he raised his other hand and slapped her face, hard. "Give me—or your new master—any trouble and I'll sell you to a bordello. At least I'd get a few hundred pounds for you and be rid of your accursed presence to boot."

Her uncle's eyes were filled with a kind of madness beyond anger and inebriation. Jacobin wanted to cry out her hurt, to ask why Candover found his closest living relative a curse, but she wouldn't give him the satisfaction of seeing her cower.

Nursing her stinging cheek, she managed to retort through a rising tide of terror, "You can't force me. There's no slavery in England."

"See this bell rope?" he said, reaching for the tapestry pull. "One ring and my valet will come. He knows you've been—difficult—and is prepared to tie you up and escort you to my carriage. After that you will be driven to London and delivered to Lord Storrington— unless you would prefer the other place I mentioned."

Her choice was bleak: a liaison with Storrington— doubtless another dissipated member of the regent's set— or forced prostitution of an even more terrifying kind.

"Why?" she demanded in a whisper, unable to maintain her defiance. "Why would you do this to your sister's child? My mother loved you."

Tramping aimlessly through the park at Storrington, Jacobin sobbed out her loneliness and grief. She was so tired of being strong. She wanted to be home in France. She wanted her parents back.

Candover's face had reflected only hatred as he reached for the brandy glass that was never far away, even at that hour of the morning.

"You are *his* child," he had said.

Why had Candover loathed her father? Auguste de Chastelux had been a hard man to hate. Handsome and brilliant, Auguste had possessed a rare charm that drew everyone he encountered. Her mother Felicity had loved him devotedly and he had been the center of Jacobin's life for her first eleven years.

She realized now that her father's love for her mother had never equaled Felicity's for him. On some level Jacobin had always known that Auguste's deepest devotion was for her, his only child. Yet Auguste had been a kind and attentive husband, and Jacobin did not believe he'd been unfaithful. It couldn't have been neglect or cruelty toward his wife that made his brother-in-law hate him.

Besides, nothing she knew of her uncle led her to suspect he'd mind if his sister was mistreated. Really, she thought savagely, given what an unpleasant man he was, she wasn't surprised someone wished to kill him. But not her. However much she loathed and resented her uncle, she was her father's child, and Auguste had deplored violence.

As her sobs subsided, she thrust Candover from her mind. Her fit of tears had made her feel better, calmer. Her natural optimism reasserted itself as she took stock of her surroundings. Even in November the grounds at Storrington were beautiful. The path she followed took her up a gentle rise through an extensive stand of rhododendrons. As she emerged on the other side the landscape opened up to reveal a valley with a small lake. At one end the lake was fed by a swift stream, and a rustic watermill took advantage of the race. A decorative stone bridge crossed the stream leading to the far side of the water. And at the other end stood a two-story building of plaster and timber in a French country style.

The scene was strangely familiar, yet Jacobin had never been here before. She stood and gazed at the buildings for several minutes, something plucking at her memory. Then she gave a gasp of recognition. It wasn't quite the same but very similar. Just on a smaller scale. She'd heard the place endlessly described by her mother and seen drawings of it. She'd even visited it once. It was almost as though her yearning for her native land had been answered.

"*L'hameau de la reine,*" she said out loud. "The queen's hamlet."

"Quite so," said a deep voice behind her, causing her to start. "Queen Marie Antoinette's folly, the model village where she played at shepherdess while her subjects starved."

Storrington must have come up behind her while she stared at this little piece of France in the middle of Sussex. He stood beside her, quite at ease, dressed in casual country attire of buckskin breeches under a warm, knee-length coat. He went hatless, so the fashionable disorder of his hair had been exacerbated by the attentions of the wind. His eyes, appearing more blue than gray in the subdued autumnal landscape, shone from a face glowing with exercise. Her heart gave a little jump as they exchanged glances, then she looked away. But it wasn't in her nature to be demure or to let a falsehood go unchallenged.

"She never pretended to be a shepherdess, my lord. That was a canard invented by the queen's enemies."

"As a daughter of the Revolution," he said, "I would expect you to be eager to believe anything ill of the French royal family."

Jacobin shook her head. "I hope my opinions would

never blind me to the truth. And in this case you are quite mistaken. I have nothing against the poor queen. And my mother admired her greatly."

"Mine too," the earl said, sounding surprised. "In fact I was named after her."

"Is your name Marie-Antoine, then?"

"Certainly not," Storrington replied. "I am English, and Englishmen are not named Mary. My father would have had a palpitation at the very notion. My Christian name is Anthony."

"The house here is very like *la maison de la reine* at the queen's hamlet, yet somewhat smaller, I believe."

The earl looked at her curiously. "Did you ever visit it? The original I mean, at Versailles."

"I grew up hearing about it from my mother. It was she who told me the queen enjoyed visiting the farm and using its produce at her table, but she never did the work herself. I went there just once, as a child, when it was turned into a restaurant after the Revolution. It was rather sad, I think."

"Was your mother in service to the queen? Is that how she came to visit the hamlet? I understand that only the privileged few were invited there."

"My mother was with another lady who was visiting the queen," Jacobin replied, regretting she'd said so much. It was a joy to speak of France, to recall happier days. And it didn't hurt that a very attractive man was listening to her with rapt concentration and regarding her with a fascinated gaze. Her attention-starved soul blossomed in the sun of Lord Storrington's interest. She fought an urge to confide in him, to share her troubles with a sympathetic ear.

Sympathetic! There must be windmills in her head to forget, even for a minute, his own role in her plight. It was vital she not give away her identity and reveal her connection to Candover. She shouldn't have let herself be carried away and speak so much of her mother.

"How do you come to have the Queen of France's village in this English park?" she asked.

A flicker of sadness passed over Storrington's face. For a moment he appeared vulnerable and very human.

"My mother loved France." His voice was smooth, and Jacobin wondered if she'd imagined his distress. "As I said before, she admired the queen. The mill was already here and my father built the Queen's House to please her. To try and make her happy."

"And did it?" she inquired, not daring to ask why the late Lady Storrington should have been unhappy.

"No. She died not very long afterward." His voice was matter-of-fact, but the expression on his face was forlorn.

"You miss your mother, don't you? Tell me about her," she said gently.

Once again his willingness to confide in her surprised Anthony. She was still dressed in the drabbest of gray gowns, but she had a face that couldn't look gray under any circumstances and possessed an exotic cast that spoke of her French blood: wide, brandy-brown eyes with thick dark lashes; flawless skin two shades darker than the typical English complexion; a perfectly straight and symmetrical nose; plump, curving lips; the small but determined chin decorated with that intriguing cleft. Chestnut brown curls that fluttered in the wind topped it all off.

He was attracted to her, of course, which was why he had, against his better judgment, pursued her through the park. And there was something more. Something about his newest employee elicited his trust.

"My mother was the most delightful person in the world. When I was very young she'd fetch me from the nursery and we'd go on picnics. She took me bathing in the lake here and played hide-and-seek. She'd tell me stories, and she would laugh and laugh." He felt his heart squeeze tight with mingled pain and pleasure at the recollection of those lost halcyon days.

"What happened?" she whispered, standing close to him. Her eyes were huge and glowed with sympathy. He could drown in their chocolate depths.

"I don't know," he said bleakly. "My father took her to France after my sister was born, and when they returned she was different. I don't think she ever smiled again." He turned away from her and stared unseeing at the hamlet. He could feel the weight of incipient tears behind his eyes. Instinctively his shoulders hunched and his head dropped to hide his grief.

Damn it, where had this sudden weakness come from? He was never sentimental. He faced life as he found it and did what needed to be done.

"It was a long time ago," he said, stiffening his spine. He wanted to reject Jane Castle's compassion. He didn't need it. "There's no point dwelling on it."

Forcing his emotions into the deep recesses of his mind where they belonged, he made his voice as unyielding as his stance. "I was going to summon you later to discuss a house party I am planning. We might as well do that now. I want my guests to enjoy the best confections you can produce."

She gave him a look that, he feared, meant she wasn't fooled by his change of subject and knew exactly how affected he had been. But she didn't say anything. How could she? She was only a servant, after all.

"Certainly, my lord," she answered agreeably. "What dishes would you like me to make?" The wicked glint in her eye told him she wasn't letting him off entirely. She was well aware he had no idea how to answer that particular question.

He waved his hand dismissively. "I leave that for you to decide, Miss Castle. Earn your princely salary and impress my guests."

She tilted her head proudly. "I assure you, my lord, I can impress anyone."

He had the urge to ruffle her composure, to repay her for the turmoil in his heart caused by speaking of his mother.

"One of the guests will be a particular connoisseur of your art, a lover of confectionary on a par with the Prince Regent," he said. "Lord Candover."

He watched closely for her reaction and wasn't disappointed. She blanched.

Chapter 6

"**A**nthony," croaked the dying man, reaching out feebly to his son.

Anthony stood at his father's bed and took the offered hand. The long fingers, so like his own in shape and size, were cool and paper-dry. They felt desperately frail in contrast to the warmth and vigor of his own.

His father was dying. The physician said it wouldn't be much longer now. The old earl had sent the doctor, nurse, and his younger offspring out of the room, leaving him alone with his heir. The wasting disease that had sapped his vitality over the past months left him without strength, but Anthony sensed rather than felt his father tug him closer. He leaned over the bed so that the old man could look him full in the face. The dull blue eyes stared at him intensely.

"Catherine," the earl murmured. Anthony wondered if he had been mistaken for his mother. He'd always been the image of her, a masculine version of the beauty who had dazzled London society in her heyday. He waited, saying nothing.

"Catherine," his father repeated. "I loved her."

Anthony knew that. His father had never recovered from her death. Ever an undemonstrative man, he had completely withdrawn into himself after the loss of his wife.

"I loved her," the earl continued, "but she was never the same after France."

Anguish pierced his father's customary dry tones, and Anthony wanted to offer comfort.

"I loved Mama too, Father," he said. "She was sad, but she still loved us."

"No!" exclaimed the earl. "She never loved me again. He took her away from me and then he stole her. And she died."

Anthony tried to make sense of what his father was saying. His mother had drowned. It had been an accident.

"What are you saying, Father? Mama never had another man. She was faithful to you." Anthony couldn't bear to think otherwise.

The earl continued. "I must tell you." The strain of speech was evident but some great need gave him the force to tell his tale. "She fell in love with him in France, and things were never the same. Then, that night, she left me to join him. There was a storm. She died."

Anthony's throat clenched. Even had he found the words he couldn't have uttered them. The knowledge of his mother's infidelity shook him to the core. He felt his father's pain, but even more he felt his own. She'd left *him*. He wanted to roar out his hurt. He'd like to kill the man who'd ruined his life.

"Who?" The single word was all he could articulate.

He was scarcely aware now of his father clutching his hand. His own rage consumed him.

"Who!" he cried, the need to know the truth releasing his vocal cords from bondage.

"The letter . . ." His father's voice was now only a whisper. Anthony had to lower his ear to the dying man's lips to hear the words. "The letter came . . . and she left."

"Whose letter?" Anthony was wild for the truth. "Who was it, Father? The name! Give me the name."

"The letter came from Candover . . ."

The earl rose from his supine position and thrust back the covers. He left the bed and stood up, all sign of weakness gone. He stood as tall and straight as he'd ever been and shook his fist in the air above his head.

"Avenge me," he cried. His voice was young and vigorous. "My son, you must avenge me."

Anthony awoke in a sweat, as he always did when he had the dream. He couldn't count how many times it had come to him since his father's death. It was always the same. And it was always exactly like his father's last minutes. Until the end.

"The letter came from Candover . . ." had been his father's last words. His life slipped away as spoke them.

Only in the dream did he call for revenge. Yet sometimes Anthony found it hard to credit that his father had not risen from his sickbed like that. It always seemed so vivid, so true. And his demand seemed so just.

Jacobin couldn't get her mind off her employer.

He'd looked so bleak, dismissing his mother's death as something that happened a long time ago, when it was obvious that her loss scarred his soul to this day. She'd wanted to hold his head to her breast and stroke the improbably windswept locks; to soothe the faint lines at the juncture of the brow, lines of care and worry; and then she wanted to make him laugh and laugh as he recalled his mother doing. To make him laugh until the marks of trouble were erased and the corners of his eyes and mouth crinkled with enjoyment.

These were foolish thoughts. There couldn't ever be anything between her and the Earl of Storrington, and she shouldn't want there to be. She mustn't forget that he was her enemy, a man who'd won her at a game of cards. For all she knew, if he discovered her identity he might believe he held some kind of *droit de seigneur* over her. She didn't know how Candover had settled his bet with Storrington after her disappearance, or what either man would do if they realized who and where she was.

And Candover was expected at Storrington Hall. She'd have to keep out of his way. If he found her here it would be much too convenient for him to hand her over to the earl on the proverbial silver platter.

She'd like to think Storrington would refuse the offering, but a core of common sense told her not to rely on her instinct. Or on her wishes rather. She was in danger of seeing Storrington as a knight in shining armor based on nothing but a superficial attraction to his appearance and a hint of vulnerability in his personality. She didn't really know much about him, and what she did know wasn't encouraging: he was a gambler; he was a friend of her far-from-trustworthy uncle; and he'd hired her as a cook for an unknown reason that had nothing to do with a taste for pastry.

If she were wise she'd give Storrington a wide berth. She had no reason to trust him.

Her sleep in the small bedroom in the upper reaches of the great house was disturbed. She awoke in pitch darkness and knew there was no chance of regaining unconsciousness. She might as well begin to earn her living while the kitchen was free of the antagonistic presence of Mrs. Simpson. Since she'd be alone, she could dress for comfort. She reached for the breeches and jacket that had been her uniform at the Brighton Pavilion.

The delicate business of kneading chilled butter into the yeast-flour mixture soothed Jacobin's jangled nerves. With the heel of her hand she repeatedly smeared the sticky mixture over the cool marble slab until the dough was fluffy and could be set aside in a basin for its first rising in a warmer part of the kitchen. She'd better not catch Mrs. Simpson touching it.

Philosophically, she'd decided to set aside the dangers and ambiguities of her situation and try to make herself indispensable in her new position. Maybe Storrington had no personal need for a first-rate pastry cook, but she vowed she'd change his mind. She guessed the earl wasn't overly fond of sweet things. But she could show him that breakfast offered greater refinements than toasted English bread. Her lip curled scornfully. Wait till he'd tried her brioche.

Because *pâte à brioche* had to rise three times over several hours, she wouldn't be able to serve it to her employer that morning, if he kept anything resembling country hours. Of course he might be like her uncle, who never rose before noon. But, despite his undoubted elegance, there was an energy about Storrington that made her doubt he was a slug-a-bed.

She had no intention of waiting another day to impress him. She stoked up the fire in the thankfully modern kitchen range and set water to boil.

A pool of light illuminated the work surface and the new cook's hands. She cracked an egg into the pot on the table and did something vigorous with a wooden spoon for perhaps half a minute. Then she picked up another egg and repeated the motion. Anthony admired the fluid way she handled the eggs with her left hand alone, while beating briskly with her right. He had no idea what she was doing, but he suspected it was more difficult than it looked. There was something reassuringly competent about Jane Castle.

He didn't know what, in his wakeful state, had brought him to the kitchen in the wee hours of the morning. He doubted he'd set foot in the place since he was a hungry boy scrounging a forbidden bite to stave off the pangs of hunger between meals. His usual territory during sleepless nights was the main floor of the mansion, the expansive, elegantly furnished rooms inhabited by generations of Storrs. There was no particular reason that tonight's wanderings had brought him to the utilitarian depths of the house. A faint light had drawn him to the kitchen, a room that should be dark and empty. Instead he found the object of far too many of his thoughts.

It was interesting that she had recognized his mother's French folly. It seemed unusual, to say the least, that a pastry cook would be so familiar with the Queen of France's rustic retreat. A mystery surrounded Jane Castle, formerly known as Jacob Léon, that went beyond her recent change of sex. Given the circumstances of that change she was quite possibly involved in a murder, but Anthony was hard put to believe it. There was something so warm about her, so alive. He didn't want to see her as an agent of death. Her eyes reflected a spirit that made him want to laugh, to set aside duty, to enjoy life in a way that had eluded him for years—for almost as long as he could remember.

Thrusting his hands into the pockets of his velvet dressing robe, he leaned against the doorjamb and watched Jane Castle, wondering why she was at work at this unearthly hour.

She leaned over to peer into the pot, and Anthony lost interest in that question because he'd found the answer to another. He'd wondered about the shape and size of her bosom, and now he knew. The upper part of her body was outlined by the wall lamp beside the table. Small, sweet curves were delineated through the muslin shift that was all she wore on top.

Whatever whim had brought him here, it was an excellent one.

She hadn't noticed him. His fascinated eyes gazed at the uptilted breasts, each crowned by a delicately pointed nipple, firm and peaked as though aroused.

Anthony shied away from that particular thought; it too nearly matched his own state. Unmistakably, things were stirring down below. He pulled on the sash of his robe to make sure it was secure. On second thought, maybe this wasn't such a good idea.

She spun around to face him, her mouth opening in a moue of surprise. The wooden spoon clacked onto the marble table as her hand covered her lips, eyes widened with shock. She stood motionless and silent for a long delicious moment during which dusky areolas were visible through the white shift. Then, with a gasp, she crossed her arms protectively across her chest.

"My lord, I didn't expect to see you here—now. I didn't think to see anyone at this hour." She glanced over to a chair a few yards away where her cook's jacket had been tossed. It was warm in the kitchen, Anthony realized, aside from any heat being generated for other reasons. He held up a restraining hand.

"Don't change your attire on my account, Miss Castle. If you are comfortable as you are, please remain so."

She gave him a suspicious look, as well she might, given that his eyes kept wandering between her upper torso and the alluring curve of hips and thighs clad in snug breeches. With an effort he fixed them on her face. The lamplight glowed through her chestnut hair, casting a fiery aura around her head and making her look like a slightly grumpy angel. To distract her from the idea of donning additional clothing, he looked around the dimly lit room with an intense—and entirely feigned—interest.

"It's been years since I've been in here," he remarked. "I couldn't sleep and noticed the light. Are these the normal hours of a pastry cook?"

His casual speech seemed to dispel her embarrassment. She shrugged and turned back to her work, taking up the dropped spoon again.

"I don't usually start this early, but since your staff seemed quite unprepared for my arrival, there isn't a suitable place for me to work. I thought I'd cook a few things before anyone was stirring." She gave him an impudent look. "You've never had a *pâtisserie* specialist before, have you?"

It was time to get the upper hand here, Anthony decided. He wasn't going to suffer another of her impertinent interrogations into his tastes.

"As it happens, no," he said coolly. "You are a new addition to the household because I am making some changes in my way of life." He had no intention of making any further explanation to this servant. Her job was to follow orders and collect her exorbitant salary.

The woman was irrepressible.

"Excellent," she said, a wide smile lighting up her whole face. "You are to be married?"

Well, that was as good an excuse as any. "It is time that I should. I have responsibilities to my position."

"May I be so bold as to wish you and *milady* every joy?"

"Well I'm not actually betrothed . . . yet."

She looked as though this was the most delightful piece of news and she'd like nothing better than to sit down for a friendly chat about his nuptials. He found it exceedingly irritating. The spoon clattered to the table again, and she spun around and flitted over to the range.

"Sit down," she said.

Irrepressible and bossy, by God.

"I'll make you some tea, then in a little while you can have a first taste of my cooking."

This definitely wasn't a good idea, he thought. He should be putting her in her place. A friendly chat in the middle of the night, alone, with a much too attractive female servant was completely inappropriate. He never encouraged undue familiarity from his staff. But instead of taking a haughty leave, he found himself sitting down at the big pine kitchen table while she fussed around with a teapot and lit another lamp to place beside him. The tea, in a thick earthenware cup, was strong and tasty, and he felt an unwonted sense of well-being.

Once he was served she returned to her corner. He watched her spoon the contents of her pot into a triangular cloth bag.

"What are you making?"

She cast him a quizzical look, her head cocked to one side, then returned to her task. "I think I'll let it be a surprise." She squeezed blobs of thick pale yellow paste through a hole at the bottom of the bag onto a metal tray, which she then carried over to the stove. She opened the oven door and casually thrust her bare arm into the heat.

"Be careful," he said in alarm, prepared to leap up and save her from being burned alive.

"I'm just checking that the oven is hot enough." She laughed. "If it were dangerous there wouldn't be many cooks left."

Once she'd put the tray into the oven, she came over to the table, sat down beside him, and poured herself a cup of tea.

"Tell me about your lady," she invited. "Is it an arranged marriage?"

"Well," he hedged, "I don't actually have anyone in mind yet. In fact I shall be doing some entertaining in London so that I can meet some suitable young women." He'd only just thought of it, but it was a good plan. News of a dinner party—with a spectacular display of desserts—would reach Candover's ears. The trap needed to be baited.

"You've never married, Miss Castle," he remarked. She was certainly attractive enough to find a husband.

She gave her characteristic shrug, which he labeled in the back of his mind as typically French. "Had my parents lived they would have arranged a match. Now, who knows?"

Anthony's curiosity was caught again. He was aware that arranged marriages were still the norm in France, more so than in England, among the upper orders. He didn't know if it was also true of other classes.

"Arranged marriages are no longer fashionable in this country," he said. "It is thought better for a couple to be well acquainted and have some affection for each other."

"No doubt that is true," she rejoined, "but is it any more a guarantee of eventual happiness than marriage to a partner carefully selected by one's family?"

He considered his own parents. He believed that it been a love match, at first. But the love had become one-sided and brought neither partner long-term joy. He shied away from the thought. The emotions engendered by his recurrent dream were too raw.

"Was your parents' marriage arranged?" he asked.

"Yes."

"And were they happy together?"

He detected a momentary guarded look before she replied. "I believe that both were satisfied with the arrangement." A careful response that begged further questions.

"So you would have been content with your family's choice?"

She shrugged again. "Perhaps. More enlightened parents—and my father was certainly such—would never force a daughter into marriage without consultation."

"But your father was English, after all."

She seemed about to argue with him, then thought better of it. Instead she rose from her seat and went over to the stove.

Zut. This was dangerous, Jacobin thought. She'd nearly contradicted him and revealed that her father was French. It was hard to keep her story straight. Whenever she conversed with this man she tended to forget her masquerade, to speak without reserve or dissimulation. To be Jacobin de Chastelux.

She busied herself setting water and sugar to heat on the range, then looked for vanilla. She was pleased to find a supply of castor sugar already infused with vanilla beans. Mrs. Simpson might be difficult, but she ran an efficient kitchen.

She peered at Lord Storrington through her lashes. He was the epitome of informal masculine grace in his full-length claret velvet robe. Her mind recoiled from speculation about what he might be wearing beneath it. She eyed her jacket, which she'd taken off when the fire heated the room. Accustomed to working in frigid confectionery kitchens, she'd quickly become uncomfortably warm. But putting another garment on now would draw attention to her state of dishabille. It wasn't as though her shift was particularly indecent. It was made of sturdy muslin, she thought optimistically.

Giving the syrup a good stir, she decided not to initiate further conversation. Any form of intimacy with Lord Storrington would be unwise or worse.

Apparently he didn't have the same compunction.

"Have you ever been in love, Miss Castle?"

Had he really asked that? It seemed so unlike the cool aristocrat she was acquainted with. She turned to examine him. He seemed oblivious that he'd said anything untoward. He looked at her with an air of disinterested curiosity that might be inspired by a question about the weather. She wanted to jolt his complacency.

"Yes, I have," she replied, looking him full in the eye. "Once. But it didn't end well."

"What happened?" He cocked his head forward with an intent look.

"Our feelings were not the same. It ended." She infused her tone with subdued tragedy and summoned moisture to her eyes by dwelling on sad thoughts of maimed Parisian beggars and the hungry-eyed cats that haunted the Luxembourg Gardens. It was a trick she'd learned as a child and often put to good use when bending her doting parents to her will. To make sure he noticed her tears, she moved closer to the table.

She expected him to be embarrassed; instead he stood and took her hand.

"I'm sorry," he said softly. "I've distressed you with my questions. Please forgive me."

His hand cradling hers felt large and firm and warm. She looked down and noted the contrast between his well-manicured nails and her own fingers, which were roughened by work and bore several tiny scars from cuts and burns, the inevitable bounty of the cook. His regret sounded genuine, and she was ashamed of her manipulation.

"It doesn't matter. Don't think anything of it." She meant to smile reassuringly, but met his eyes. Dark gray in the dim light, they held sympathy and a warmer emotion she didn't want to identify. Breathless, she could only stand there, captured by his gaze and feeling a flush suffuse her cheeks. She wasn't much given to blushing, and the sensation was alien. She wasn't sure she liked it.

The aroma of baking roused her from a confused silence.

"The oven," she muttered, retracting her hand and hurrying to the range. As she removed the tray from the oven she could still sense the pressure of his fingers gliding over hers as she'd pulled away.

He followed her to the stove and looked over her shoulder. She could feel his warm breath at her ear, mingling with the steam arising from the tray of pastries.

"Little puffy things," he said, his voice husky and amused.

Chapter 7

He'd followed her without conscious volition. The withdrawal of her hand seemed an unbearable loss, and he was driven to regain her proximity, her touch, the feel of her skin against his. But when he saw what she was cooking, the purely physical need to be near her was enhanced by a tug on his emotions. She was making something she believed he liked. The fact that she had risen in the middle of the night to prepare whatever those things were called made him feel . . . cared for. Which was absurd since she was, after all, a servant hired to cater to his tastes.

"May I have one?" he asked, reaching out.

As she put the tray down on top of the cast-iron range she lightly slapped his hand aside.

"Not yet. They're too hot. You'll burn yourself. Besides, they're not ready."

On a mischievous impulse he tried to reach around her to grab one of the pastry puffs. She turned and stood in front of the tray, hands on her hips, a forbidding frown creasing her brow, belied by a glint of laughter in her glance.

"Please," he asked, moving close to crowd her. She was tall for a woman, but with only a few inches of space between them the advantage of his height was exaggerated. She had to tip her head up to meet him eye to eye, and there was something about the stubborn set of her dimpled chin that made him gleeful.

"Please," he repeated, like a small boy begging for sweets. In a lightning move he tried to sidestep her to snatch one of the delectably scented golden puffs. She was too quick for him and seized his marauding arm in a surprisingly strong grasp.

"*Non, méchant*," she said. "You are very naughty, my lord. Now go and sit down again and wait. They'll be ready soon enough."

For the moment he gave in and obeyed her. From his seat at the kitchen table he kept her under surveillance, pondering another attack. She gave a pot on the stove a good stir, then poured cream from a jug into a bowl on the table, a few feet from where he sat. Then his mind emptied of any notion of stealing pastry.

With a contraption that resembled a small stiff broom, she briskly whipped the cream. Through the sleeve of her shift he could see the taut muscles of her right arm at work. But what riveted his attention was once again the outline of her unconfined breasts. They gently jiggled as she moved, begging him to place his hands around them and discover if they were as firm and shapely as they appeared. The sight deadened his brain and had quite the opposite effect on his nether regions. It wasn't the first time since he'd met Jane Castle that he was tempted to end a long dry period without a woman. But it was the first time he'd seriously considered doing something about it.

He stared as though mesmerized as the cream rose thick and fluffy in the bowl and she deftly sifted and beat in sugar. Then she gave the mixture a final stir and took a dollop from the whisk on her forefinger. Momentarily distracted from her breasts, his eyes followed the finger as she inserted it between perfectly bowed red lips and sucked it clean. Mentally he moaned.

Perhaps the noise wasn't just mental. She looked at him curiously. Apparently she saw nothing amiss and smiled in a friendly manner.

"Nearly there," she said. "Are you hungry?"

"Yes," he said hoarsely, unable to utter another word. He stopped noticing what she was doing. He was aware only of her body and her lips and a desperate need to possess her. The tiled floor of the kitchen was an unwelcoming surface for dalliance. Eyes momentarily distracted from the focus of his lust—why hadn't he realized before that breeches were such alluring garments on a female?—he considered the table. As large as a good-sized bed. Not as comfortable but with distinct possibilities. He imagined laying Jane Castle down on it, and found the vision more than pleasing. He fixed his glance on the object of his hunger and awaited his opportunity.

Her voice interrupted his planning. "Just a minute or two for the caramel to cool, then we can eat."

The matter-of-fact tone acted on his fevered yearning. Not like cold water—it would take an entire bathful of the stuff to do that—but perhaps like a cool shower of rain. *What the hell are you thinking?* he asked himself. Seducing a servant in a kitchen was very far from his usual sexual modus operandi. Past liaisons had been conducted in opulent love nests with well-paid courtesans. If he had any sense he'd stand up and keep walking, without looking back until he reached the safety of his own rooms.

Staggering uncomfortably to his feet, he again tightened the sash of his robe.

"It's late," he said brusquely. "I should go back upstairs."

"Oh no!" she objected. "You must have a taste before you go. They're at their best when fresh from the oven."

Jacobin wasn't going to let him leave without sampling her pastry. It would be wiser to let him go. She'd had enough experience evading the advances of backdoor visitors at her uncle's house to suspect that his intentions were seductive. But her professional mettle had been aroused.

She picked up one of the cream-filled puffs in its glossy caramel cloak and stood in front of him. He swayed backward, refusing the proffered morsel. With reckless audacity she moved closer and placed it to his lips. He took a bite, and her fascinated eyes followed the motion of his stubbled jaw and exposed throat as he consumed it. She could almost taste it with him: the light, spongy pastry for texture; the richness of the cream; the darker, more intense sweetness of the caramelized sugar, taken from the fire at the very brink of burning.

"Delicious. I can see you haven't exaggerated your talents." His lips parted in demand, so she popped the rest of the puff between them, removing her fingers just before they were captured by his closing mouth.

"I'm glad you're satisfied."

These artless words—or perhaps the perfection of her pastry—seemed to affect his voice. "What are these things really called?" he croaked, staring at her so intently her very bones quivered.

"In French they are profiteroles. Little puffs made from *pâte à chou* and filled with *crème chantilly. Chou* is also the French word for 'cabbage.' *Petit chou*—'little cabbage'—is an endearment often used toward children."

She was babbling, she knew. Anything to take her mind off the nearness of a large male clothed in a dressing gown and who knew what, or how little, else. Something, perhaps the scent of his skin, indefinable and enticing, had scrambled her brain.

"Do you want another?" she asked huskily. He nodded and popped one in his mouth, concentrating on the rich little wisp. She helped herself to one too. She bit carelessly and the inevitable happened: cream spewed from the overstuffed puff over her lips and chin. She could even feel a small cold blob on the tip of her nose.

Now she had all his attention.

"You've made a mess," he chided. "Let me help you."

Arms encircled her waist, and she felt a tongue delicately lick the end of her nose.

"Mm, sweet," he murmured, then lowered his mouth to gather the remainder of the chantilly from her lips. Her tongue, engaged on the same mission, clashed with his, and his heat, mingling with the cool cream, was not unpleasant.

Quite the contrary.

She had to admit to herself that she'd wanted to kiss the Earl of Storrington. The reality was even better than her unconscious anticipation. Thought vanished into a vanilla haze as he deepened the embrace, plundering her mouth and drawing her body to his chest. It was unlike any kiss she'd ever experienced. She responded fervently, pulling his head closer with eager hands that laced through his hair and traced the shape of his skull.

His hands were busy too, massaging her back through the muslin shift, then descending to press her against him. She could feel his erection, alarmingly hard, but apprehension disappeared in a sensual wave, powerful enough to submerge any doubts. Her inarticulate mind reveled in contradictory sensations of delicious danger and a safety such as she'd rarely felt in years.

"Sweetness," he murmured against her mouth, then renewed his assault. She didn't know whether it was an endearment or a comment on the cream. Neither did she care. All she knew was that this was where she was meant to be, what she'd been born to do.

Now his face was buried in her neck, kissing and

nipping the sensitive skin and sending lightning darts throughout her body that focused in a sweet, hot ache between her thighs.

"You feel so good," he whispered. Large hands were pulling at the shift tucked into her breeches.

"Yes!" she urged, yearning for those hands to find her bare skin. "*Oui, mon chou.*"

Why had he stopped? She wanted him to touch her *now*.

His arms hung at his sides as he drew back. He looked stricken.

"I'm sorry, so sorry. I shouldn't have done that. It shouldn't have happened." Turning from her, he hurried to the door.

"I'm sorry," he repeated as he left.

Chapter 8

T welve hours later Anthony was in London. He'd escaped the kitchen like a fugitive hare and hardly stopped until he reached his Brook Street house. Even there the harriers snapped at his feet; his lust for Jane Castle had led to several sleepless hours in bed and continued to torment him during the hours of his hastily arranged journey. Jem Webster might grumble at the inconvenient turnaround, but it was worth every silent and not-so-subtle reproach aimed at him by the head groom. Only when ensconced at his desk in the library of the Storrington town house did he feel at ease.

He must put the previous night's scene behind him, and—God knows—lay off the pastry. The sweetness had robbed him of his wits. It was good to be back in town and turn all his attention to the business that really mattered: completing his plan of vengeance against Candover. He'd think no more about Jane Castle and her golden chestnut curls, her glowing eyes, her lithe feminine body, the taste of her apricot lips . . .

Ah, Jane! A less aptly named woman he'd never met. Not a plain English rose but everything exotic: an orchid, silk damask, perfume of Arabia, sauternes, Turkish delight . . .

And a respectable young woman in his service.

He refused to think about what had saved him from committing an unpardonable indiscretion: the memory of his mother feeding him sweets and calling him her *petit chou*.

He took up his pen and settled to the unwelcome task of writing to his sister.

Lady Kitty Thornley, along with her young daughter, Catherine, received him in the drawing room of the comfortable house that she and her husband had rented every season since their marriage.

"I thought you'd be in Brighton, Anthony, since you've become so attached to the Prince Regent's set."

Anthony tried to suppress the twitch of irritation that was often spawned by his sister's pronouncements. He always sensed subtle criticism of his activities.

"I'm hardly an intimate of Prinny's, Kitty," he said in a level tone. "I merely spent a few days in Brighton and attended his dinner in honor of Count Lieven. I was surprised to hear you were in London at this time of year. I gather Walter didn't accompany you."

Lady Kitty's response might, in one of less ruthless elegance, be called a snort. "Leave Leicestershire during hunting season? Never! Nothing would drag him and the boys away. Not even week after week of appalling weather. But Cat and I decided to escape the rain and come up to London for some shopping."

"What did you do about servants?" The Thornleys always brought their household with them to London.

"Left most of them at home. Cat and I can manage with simple meals and very little attention." She smiled at the girl who was seated at a Pembroke table working on a drawing.

Anthony felt a recurrence of the guilt that had plagued him when he'd first received word of Kitty's unseasonable London trip. He had a large house and could easily offer room to any or all of his sister's family. He just couldn't abide the thought of having her there for several weeks. She doubtless resented his lack of generosity. The house had, after all, once been one of her homes, and she'd made her debut and been married from it.

Catherine fixed her eight-year-old eyes on Anthony. "Mama said she'd take me to Grafton House this morning, Uncle Anthony. We're going to buy Christmas presents for Papa and John and George. Do you think, Mama, that there will still be time?"

Oddly enough Anthony didn't mind this hinted reproach, much more overt than any Cat's mother had aimed at him. He was fond of his niece, and of both her brothers. He grinned at her.

"My apologies, Cat, for disturbing your plans. I'll try and conduct my business with your mother quickly so you can get on with your outing."

"What business?" Kitty cut in. "I'm curious about why you're here."

"I wish to give a dinner party and would like you to act as hostess."

Kitty seemed pleased. In repose she wasn't a particularly pretty woman. Unlike her brothers she took after her father; her appearance was distinguished rather than comely. It occurred to Anthony that she'd been pale and dejected, but now her face lit up and she looked quite handsome.

"What fun! Of course there aren't many people in town now, but with so little going on everyone will be delighted to come. Who do you wish to ask? How many? And how soon?"

Anthony held up a hand in protest. "One question at a time, please! I have a few suggestions for the guest list but I need your help too. You know better than I of any unmarried girls who might be available."

"Anthony!" Kitty leaped to her feet in ecstasy. "Girls? Don't tell me you're finally going to look for a wife."

Again he fought irritation. Kitty had been haranguing him for years about his single state, and he hated to give her the satisfaction of seeing him change his stance.

"I'm not unmindful of my duty," he said stiffly. "It's been long enough since our father died, and I am aware that I must see to the succession. Invite two or three young ladies—though not too young, I beg you. And please be tactful about it."

"You may leave it to me. No one will suspect a thing. In fact it might be better if I give the impression that this is my party and you are being kind enough to let me hold it in your house."

Out of habit Anthony looked for the hidden barb in this suggestion, but couldn't find one. Kitty seemed perfectly genuine in her wish to be helpful. Too helpful in fact.

"Whatever you think is best, Kitty. You know the capacity of the house. Do you think you could manage it in a week or so?"

She considered the matter before nodding her agreement. "I don't see why not. But Gunter's must be contacted at once for the sweets. We won't get an impressive display without enough notice."

"There's no need to order from Gunter's." When it came to the point he found himself reluctant to talk about Jane Castle. But this was, after all, the whole point of hiring her. "I've employed a pastry cook. French trained and as good as any in London."

"Why on earth?" Kitty demanded in astonishment. "You hate puddings!"

"Not all of them," he replied, "and it's quite the mode now to have French pastry cooks."

"My dear brother! When did you ever trouble about *the mode*?"

He raised his eyebrows. "Are you accusing me of being unfashionable?"

Kitty snorted again. "Hardly. But you've usually preferred to set fashion rather than follow it."

That sounded almost like a compliment from his sister. How singular.

"Whatever the reason," he said with more warmth than he'd felt since the conversation began, "I have hired the woman. She's at Storrington now, but I'll send for her at once and you can arrange the menu with her and the cook."

He tried not to feel pleased about the prospect of having Jane Castle under the same roof again. He'd do better to leave his female relations to their own affairs and go to his club. There, no doubt, he'd find the latest news on Candover's health.

Tom Hawkins had never investigated a crime against a member of the nobility before. After a week he began to feel a measure of sympathy for the would-be murderer. Lord Candover's associates tended to regard the Bow Street runner's questioning in the light of a personal affront. At least one bloated peer seemed to feel the impertinence of the inquiry was on a par with the crime itself. He'd treated Hawkins as though he were no better than the assassin he was trying to track. Hawkins had an Englishman's healthy scorn for all things French, but there were moments when it crossed his mind that the froggies might have had something when they started stringing up their aristocrats.

Thinking of the French brought to mind the one break he'd received in the case. When the Prince Regent's fancy French chef, Monsieur Antonin Carême, had finally risen from his sickbed he'd revealed that the missing cook, Jacob Léon, had been hired on a recommendation from a former colleague: Jean-Luc Clèves, lately employed by none other than Lord Candover.

Coincidence? Tom Hawkins didn't believe in coincidence. But this promising lead was blocked by the fact that Jean-Luc Clèves was currently at some unknown location in France. Even with the cooperation of the English embassy in Paris, it could take weeks to find and question him.

In Hawkins's opinion there was something havey-cavey about the way Clèves had left Candover's employ. Lord Candover had been devilish cagey on the subject, and his servants, who'd worked with the man, were as tight-lipped as their master.

Which left Hawkins with only one alternative: to find Jacob Léon.

A young cook, a friend of the missing man, told him that someone had offered Léon a job the day of the attempted poisoning but claimed he didn't know who. Hawkins was inclined to believe him. Dick Johnson lacked both the head and the stomach for deception. But the kitchen boy Charlie was another matter. Charlie's knowing eyes gleamed with sincerity as he denied all knowledge of Léon's whereabouts. Hawkins didn't trust the young varmint for a minute.

Jacobin regarded herself as thoroughly level-headed, imbued with Gallic pragmatism, her attitudes and decisions based firmly in reality.

But she knew she had a tendency to be just the teeniest bit impetuous. There were unfortunate moments when she acted without thinking, and too often those actions got her into trouble. Oddly enough it was her sentimental English mother who had deplored this proclivity as a child, begging her to look before she leaped. Felicity had been mortified when the six-year-old Jacobin had been overcome with the urge to bounce on Madame Récamier's chaise longue, and spilled her chocolate on the upholstery. Her adoring father had merely laughed. He did so again when she asked the voluble Germaine de Staël why she talked so much.

"She only posed the question everyone else in Paris wanted to," Auguste had assured his embarrassed wife.

Every time Jacobin was punished by her uncle for some transgression, she'd sworn she'd never again give him an excuse to abuse her. But, although they came less frequently as she grew up, there were instances when a desire to do something took hold of her and she had no will to resist the urge

Like feeding a profiterole to Lord Storrington.

What had she been thinking?

The answer to that was easy. Intellect had nothing to do with it, only impulse. He had refused to eat her pastry, and she was determined that he would. Everything afterward had followed as a result of her shocking urge to feed her employer. Recollecting the event in tranquillity—well, at least in a semblance of such—she was appalled. Surely not even her father would have laughed. Certainly not about the kiss.

Never again, she told herself, however much she'd enjoyed it.

First there was the basic stupidity of a servant encouraging advances from the master of the house. Was she to end up ruined and *enceinte*? She'd always despised women who foolishly let themselves be used that way.

Then there was her own particular situation. As a fugitive from the law, the last thing she should do was draw any special attention to herself. Not to mention Storrington's behavior with regard to that infamous wager. If that wasn't enough reason to distrust him, he was apparently also the kind of libertine who dallied with his servants.

Not that he'd dallied long. He'd run out of the kitchen as though pursued by man-eating dogs. Really, it was quite annoying.

Having snatched a couple of hours' rest in her comfortless room in the servants' wing, Jacobin descended to the kitchens resolved to avoid the earl. It turned out to be easier than she'd thought. He'd left for London.

Her lovely brioche went untasted and ended up with the pig swill. Mrs. Simpson made it clear that such foreign muck wasn't going to be served in any servants' hall of hers, and she spurned Jacobin's offer to contribute to the household meals.

"His Lordship may do as he wishes," she said icily, "but I'm in charge of feeding the staff."

"Very well, but please don't hesitate to ask if you need assistance." Jacobin had decided there was no point further antagonizing the cook. "I'll go and speak to Mr. Simpson about getting my pastry room arranged."

With some reluctance the butler, who clearly resided firmly under the thumb of his surly spouse, said he'd speak to His Lordship's steward about setting up the unused pantry for her. Which left Jacobin with nothing to do but wander aimlessly around the park in unpleasantly dank weather.

In negotiating the terms of her employment with Storrington, she'd insisted on an hour free a day. Life in the Prince Regent's household had left her little time for exercise and reflection. Now she had nothing to do except exercise and reflect. Her feet developed chilblains from treading soggy paths, and she'd rather be busy than spend any more time worrying about her problems. And trying not to think about her employer, his enthralling attention, and his dazzling kisses. She'd give a good deal to be back in Brighton constructing a *charlotte russe* for the regent's dinner.

A couple of days later she was returning from another dreary walk, wistfully recalling the fun she'd had in the Hurst Park kitchens with Jean-Luc and her friends among Candover's staff. The servants at Storrington barely spoke to her. She sensed that most of them might have been friendly enough, but chose to take their cue from the Simpsons, both of whom continued to treat her with hostility. As she approached the kitchen court she caught sight of a familiar figure and thoughtlessly cried out with joy.

"Charlie! What are you doing here?"

The boy turned, and his eyes were bigger than an owl's.

"Blimey, Jake. You've turned into a girl!"

"*Zut.*" Jacobin assumed her French accent. "Would you believe I'm in disguise?"

Charlie looked her over from head to toe.

"No," he said baldly. "I reckon not. I reckon you was in disguise before. You're a girl all right." He grinned happily. "I'd love to see Underwood's face if she knew you was a girl all this time."

"She mustn't know, Charlie," Jacobin said. "Please don't tell anyone."

"I wouldn't peach on you, Jake." He frowned. "What's your name anyway? I can't call you Jake."

"Oh, please do, Charlie. I miss being Jake. I missed you. Tell me all the kitchen gossip. How did you find me? How did you get here? *Why* are you here?"

Charlie cast his eyes heavenward. "You really are a girl, aren't yer? Put on a skirt and you're gabby as a peep of chickens. I came to warn you. There's people lookin' fer yer. Why'd yer run away? Everyone thinks you tried to off that lord."

"I didn't," Jacobin assured him. "But I was afraid they'd find out I was female and I'd get the sack. I swear I had nothing to do with the poison."

Charlie displayed a shocking lack of concern about her possibly murderous career. "Can't say I care if you did, Jake. If you tried to kill him I'm sure there was a good reason. But I thought I'd better tip you the wink to keep hugger-mugger."

"Is it the runners?"

"Them, yes. And some other cove. Came pokin' around the kitchen askin' questions."

"How did you know I was here?" she asked anxiously. "Does anyone else know?"

"I was there when Lord Storrington's man offered you a job. I guessed you might have decided to take it after all."

"Oh Lord, Charlie! Dick was with us that day. Does he know I'm here too?" She fought panic. Dick wouldn't wish to harm her, but neither was he the sharpest knife in the Pavilion's *batterie de cuisine*. Creditable prevarication was beyond his skill.

"Dick told the runner you'd had an offer but 'e didn't hear who it was." The boy tapped his forehead cagily. "Wot 'e don't know 'e can't tell."

"Someone's already been here looking for me. Luckily they don't know I'm a girl. But I can't stay hiding here for the rest of my life. Whatever shall I do?"

"Well, Jake, if you didn't try to off the nob, someone did. Reckon they won't stop looking for you till they find the right man."

Jacobin groaned. "And they won't even trouble to look if they think Jacob Léon is guilty."

Charlie nodded his agreement with this gloomy assessment. "Seems to me you're goin' to have to look yerself."

Chapter 9

Apricot Tartlets

Put four ounces of sugar, two glasses of water, and twelve ripe apricots cut in halves into a middle-sized saucepan, and set them on the fire to boil; when the apricots have thrown up a dozen bubbles, take them out with a fork and peel off the skins. Boil the liquid until reduced to a rather thick syrup. Now make half a pound of flour into a fine paste and roll it out to a little more than one-half of an inch thick. Cut it with a round paste-cutter, of two inches in diameter, into twenty-four circles. Lodge the circles in twenty-four small tartlet molds, then take small strips of paste, one by one, and after rolling them between your fingers and the board, twist them into a kind of screw by rolling one end to the right and the other to the left; then lightly wet the rim of the tartlets and place one of the screws round it; egg the screws only, and put in each tartlet a little pounded sugar, and on this half an apricot with its flat side downward. Put your tartlets in a hot oven, and when the bottoms of them have acquired a fine yellow color, take them out, and put on each of them half a spoonful of the syrup, placing in the middle half a kernel of an apricot.

Antonin Carême

A pricots cost a fortune in November. Jacobin had no idea what hothouse had produced the flawless specimens she had discovered at a stall in Covent Garden, but surmised that the fruit was the product of an aristocratic estate. Whether the owner was aware that his gardener was selling off the surplus she neither knew nor cared. The order had come down to the Brook Street kitchen that no expense was to be spared in creating sweets that would make Lord Storrington's dinner party the talk of London.

"They smell good," commented the doyenne of Storrington's London staff. Mrs. Smith was a jovial soul, in marked contrast to her Sussex counterpart. Unlike the irritable Mrs. Simpson, she greeted Jacobin's arrival from the country with an expansive welcome.

"I have quite enough to do making a dozen dishes for this dinner party without mucking around with pastries and sweets," she said comfortably. "His Lordship's gone for weeks, then suddenly he's invited two dozen for dinner with only a week's notice. Not that I'm not glad of it. It's about time there was a bit of life in this house. His Lordship's kept himself to himself since his previous Lordship died."

"He's been observing the mourning period, I daresay," Jacobin suggested.

"There's mourning and mourning," Mrs. Smith said disapprovingly. "There's no need for a young man like that to give up all his enjoyment. You'd think he'd inherited his late father's—God bless him—character along with his title. The old lord was a good man, and no one who worked for him would say otherwise, but he wasn't much for entertaining. Kept himself down in the country except when Lady Kitty was making her come-out."

Jacobin had heard about Storrington's sister. She expected to meet Lady Kitty later in the day to gain approval for the dinner menu. She was not surprised that the earl had delegated that particular task, recalling his bafflement under interrogation about his taste in desserts. Jacobin tried not to care that in the two days since her arrival in Upper Brook Street, she hadn't so much as set eyes on the master of the house.

"If the previous earl didn't like London, I'm surprised he maintained a full staff in both places," she observed.

"Lord Storrs—as his present Lordship was then—spent most of his time here," Mrs. Smith explained.

"He used to get up to all sorts of malarkey." The cook's tone was one of deep approval. Clearly she didn't subscribe to the school of thought that felt sprigs of the nobility should behave with restraint and responsibility. "He used to give all sorts of dinners here; bachelor dinners, you understand. There's no one better to cook for than a lot of young men. They know how to enjoy a woman's cooking."

"No ladies?" Jacobin asked with deceptive innocence. She hadn't missed the cook's emphasis on the word *bachelor*.

"Not the kind of ladies we ought to mention." Mrs. Smith's repressive tone was belied by a twinkle in her eye. "Oh well! Boys will be boys."

Before Jacobin could probe further into this fascinating aspect of the reserved Storrington's character, a new arrival in the kitchen distracted the cook.

"Smithy, the love of my life!"

Mrs. Smith emerged from the embrace of a young man who bore a startling resemblance to the master of the house. He wore a splendid military uniform of dark blue with scarlet facings and an expression of frank mischief. Otherwise he could have been Storrington ten years earlier.

"None of your nonsense, Master James," said the cook, her plump cheeks glowing pink with pleasure.

A waft of almandine scent drew Jacobin's attention to the oven. Heavens! The tarts had better not be burned. Just because she'd been given carte blanche didn't make it acceptable to waste those ruinously expensive apri-

cots. She laid the tray of hot tartlets on the table and
carefully examined the underside of one—thankfully it
had achieved the exact shade of yellow demanded by
the maître's recipe. A hand snaked around from behind
and reached for the pastries. Jacobin slapped it aside
just in time.

"Stop that!" she ordered, pivoting to greet a laughing face and a pair of unrepentant blue eyes.

"My, my, what have we here?" asked the young man
appreciatively, and he wasn't looking at the tartlets. "I
don't believe we've met."

Jacobin placed her back against the table to block marauding incursions and bobbed a perfunctory curtsy.

"I'm Jane Castle and those tarts aren't for you. I don't
have time to make more," she said sternly. "Besides, I
doubt I'd find any more apricots in the market."

"I am delighted to meet you, Jane Castle. I perceive
that you are as precious as an apricot in November. I'll
give you a kiss in exchange for one."

While having no intention of agreeing to this brazen
suggestion, Jacobin was hard put not to smile. The
young officer was clearly a born charmer. She kept her
expression stern.

"Is that supposed to be an irresistible offer?"

He shrugged ruefully. "I thought so, but I see I was
wrong. You are a cruel and heartless woman, not like
Smithy. *She* has never refused me a treat, not since I
was a scrap of a lad." He glanced at the cook, who was
regarding him with indulgent fondness, then turned his
dancing eyes back to Jacobin.

"You won't get the better of me, Miss Castle. If I can't steal your pastries by foul means I'll resort to fair, by taking tea with my brother." Waving carelessly at the denizens of the kitchen, he sauntered out of the room.

"I didn't know His Lordship had a brother," Jacobin remarked. "He looks a good deal younger."

"Master James—Captain Storrs I should say—is ten years younger than the master."

"I had no idea," Jacobin commented with interest, "that Lord Storrington's father had married again. Did his second wife die also? How tragic!"

"Oh no!" replied the cook. "The old lord was only wed the once. Her Ladyship gave him three children— His Lordship, Lady Kitty, and Master James. Poor little mite was only two at the time of the accident."

"For some reason I thought she'd died earlier." Jacobin frowned. She was positive Lord Storrington said he'd lost his mother when he was five. "What kind of accident?"

"Her Ladyship was drowned in the millrace at Storrington Hall. There was a terrible storm."

"She was alone? And out in foul weather?" On the face of it, it was an odd story, a thought confirmed by a shuttered expression falling on the cook's open countenance.

"We don't like to talk about it," Mrs. Smith said flatly. "I was only a kitchen maid on the estate then, but I remember it to this day, all of us do. The master was never the same again."

She no doubt meant the former earl, but Jacobin

wondered if the same could be said of the title's present incumbent.

"The captain seems quite—forward." She tried to put her question delicately. "Do the female staff have any trouble with him?"

Mrs. Smith merely laughed. "Dear me, no! That kissing offer wasn't serious. Pay no attention to his nonsense. It's all in fun." She looked earnestly at Jacobin. "You're a pretty girl but you have nothing to fear here. This is a respectable household, and the captain would never lay a finger on one of the servants. Not His Lordship neither."

Considering that His Lordship had laid rather more than a finger on her a few days earlier, Jacobin found the statement less than entirely convincing.

"Who's that beauty you've got stashed away in the kitchen?"

Anthony usually greeted his brother with pleasure, particularly when he hadn't seen him in several weeks, but James's opening question raised his hackles.

"I trust you know better than to begin an intrigue with a servant in this house?" he asked brusquely.

James looked astonished. "Whoa there, Tony old boy! Who said anything about an intrigue? I merely stopped in to see Smithy and discovered this ravishing female. Forgive me for having eyes!"

Anthony clenched his hands together where they were concealed from view behind his desk and made a conscious effort to calm down. There was no reason to take offense at James's casual reference to Jane Castle. It wasn't his brother's fault he had a guilty conscience where that particular servant was concerned.

"Sorry, James." He leaned back in his chair, and waved a hand expansively at a wing chair on the other side of the desk. "Take a seat and tell me how you are."

"You know what, Tony? You need a woman. How long ago did you give Rosa her congé? Must be two years. You've become a bloody monk. Abstinence isn't good for the temper."

Perhaps James was right. Maybe this whole unsuitable attraction to Jane Castle was a sign that his libido, depressingly dormant since his father's death, was making a reappearance.

"Rosa was a luscious piece," James went on. "I never could understand why you broke with her."

Neither could Anthony, specifically. "You know women. Leave them before they leave you. They always do in the end and it saves a lot of grief in the long run if you end it first."

His brother snorted. "And when, exactly, did any woman leave you? It must have been when I was still in the nursery because I certainly can't recall it happening. To my knowledge you've left a string of fashionable impures heartbroken."

Anthony didn't want to discuss his inner feelings about women with James, or anyone else for that matter, but he couldn't leave a statement like that unchallenged. "Heartbroken! Not in a thousand years.

The only thing I've ever hurt by leaving a woman is her purse, and then not badly. I hope you know me better than to believe I'm in the habit of abandoning my mistresses to the gutter."

"And I was looking forward to seeing you today but I can see you're in a devilish mood. I'd better leave."

Anthony could see he'd upset his brother. He didn't know why he was so irritable but he needed to get a grip on his temper. "Ignore me, James. It must be the weather. Sit down and have a drink, for God's sake."

The library in Upper Brook Street was Anthony's favorite room in the house and one that invited masculine informality. Soon the brothers were lounging comfortably with their feet up and ankles crossed on the desk between them, nursing glasses of the best French brandy imported by their father thirty years earlier.

James was not long to be distracted from the subject of the new pastry cook. He didn't fail to twit his big brother about his lack of a sweet tooth. Anthony, who was getting tired of defending himself against the charge of Insufficient Fondness for Puddings, explained how he had come to hire the woman.

"So you see," he concluded, "It turned out that Jacob Léon, French cook, was really English, female, and named Jane Castle."

"You're mad," interjected his brother bluntly. "The woman may be a poisoner. Has it occurred to you that you might wake up dead one fine morning?"

"Nonsense," Anthony replied. "First, she likely had nothing to do with Candover's poisoning. Her need to maintain her disguise seems a perfectly good reason for her to leave the prince's kitchen." Ignoring James's look of skepticism, he counted out his arguments on his fingers.

"Second, even if she did, for some bizarre reason, try to murder Candover—and I'm hard-pressed to discern a motive—it doesn't follow that she would wish to do the same to me. Before I offered her a job she didn't know me from Adam. And third"—he spoke over James's grunt of derision—"she doesn't seem the criminal type."

James's face wore an expression of mingled disbelief and resignation. "It's your decision, Tony, but I'm glad she wouldn't let me steal a tartlet from her. I might be writhing in agony on the floor even now. I hope your precious dinner party doesn't end with half of London dead. Has Candover been invited?"

"As far as I know he's still in Brighton. But I'm counting on the news of a spectacular display of desserts to reach his ears. I thought I'd invite him down to Storrington for a few days. Once I've got him there he won't be able to resist another game of piquet."

"I still find it strange that he's avoided a rematch for so long," said James. "Given his usual luck at piquet, you'd think he'd be raring to recoup the twenty thousand he had to pay you."

Anthony frowned. "I don't know where he got the money. As far as I've been able to discover he didn't sell anything to raise the ready. It bothers me that he has resources I know nothing about. Ruining him may be harder than I thought. But I'll do it in the end. I must."

"Just don't do anything foolish," James said, his tone unusually grave. "You know how I felt about playing cards for the man's niece. I still don't understand why you accepted that bet, Tony."

Anthony wasn't sure himself. Had he been told about another man making such a wager, he'd have been shocked, even disgusted. But when Candover made the offer, and then mentioned his mother, he'd been overcome by rage. He now knew exactly what people meant when they referred to "seeing red." He'd seen it. Even thinking about that moment shook him to the soul and made him ready to do anything—anything—to revenge himself on the man who'd destroyed his family. Sometimes it frightened him to think of what he might do to achieve his goal.

"I wish you'd give it up," James said. "The whole business is making you behave strangely. You haven't been near your mathematical friends in two years. Completely abandoned your investigations in that area. I might think they're outlandish, but they used to give you pleasure."

"Not true. I've made an extensive study of the probabilities of card games. Why else do you think I always win?"

James looked disgusted. "It'd be healthier if you'd branch out in a new direction. Why don't you take in a meeting of the Royal Society and catch up on new discoveries? Better yet, have some fun. Take a new mistress. Or find a wife and fill your nursery. That's what Father would have wanted. I'm certain he wouldn't approve of this fixation on revenge."

James didn't know about the recurring dream, which Anthony had never confided to a living soul. And he couldn't remember their mother. Although always a supportive brother, he didn't share the urgent need to settle the score with their mother's seducer.

Further discussion was cut off by the entrance of the butler announcing Lady Kitty Thornley, followed by the energetic entrance of the lady herself.

"James!" she cried happily as her brothers struggled to their feet to greet her. "I haven't seen you this age!"

"I managed to escape for two weeks at Melton, but the miserable weather drove me back to the dubious delights of guarding Carlton House."

"I'm glad you'll be here for Anthony's dinner party. I've got too many girls." She looked about her and wrinkled her nose in distaste. "Really, there's nowhere to sit in this room. Foley, we'll take tea in the blue room."

The brothers reluctantly abandoned the manly comforts of wood paneling, leather furniture, books, and strong spirits for the more refined confines of the drawing room. Once ensconced behind the tea tray with her male relations perched decorously on a pair of blue silk-upholstered bergères, Kitty beamed happily. Her irritated elder brother was about to make a caustic comment about managing females and uncomfortable furniture when he was distracted by the mention of a well-known name.

"I've just come from Countess Lieven's," Kitty said, "and she has news about the Brighton poisoning."

Anthony leaned forward. "Of Candover?" he asked.

"Yes, of Candover. Who else?" Kitty turned to James. "You may not have heard, since you just returned to town, but a week ago Lord Candover was poisoned in Brighton, with aconite in a Bavarian cream served at the Pavilion. Can you imagine the scandal? Lieven says Prinny is quite beside himself."

"Is he dead?" James asked, pretending ignorance of the event. "Candover, I mean, not Prinny. I'd have heard if he'd kicked the bucket."

Treating such levity with the disdain it deserved, Kitty continued with her story. "Candover is expected to make a full recovery, but the really interesting thing is that it seems the poisoner was actually employed as a cook in the prince's kitchen. Can you believe it? The whole royal family might have been murdered!"

"That seems unlikely," Anthony interjected sardonically, "given that most of them aren't on speaking, let alone dining, terms with Prinny."

Kitty refused to be sidetracked. "This young cook, a protégé of Carême himself, disappeared without trace the next day. A Frenchman, you know. Countess Lieven says Bow Street suspect Bonapartist involvement."

James delivered a discreet sidelong glance of concern at his brother. For the first time it occurred to Anthony that by harboring Jane Castle he might be getting himself into trouble. Yet he still couldn't believe her guilty of the crime. And to suggest she might be in league with sympathizers of the exiled Bonaparte was absurd. She herself had expressed her loathing for the tyrant, hadn't she? Rather than feeling suspicious of his mysterious cook, his sentiments were quite protective. The realization hit him forcibly: should Candover's attacker not be discovered, Jane Castle's position was parlous.

Kitty interrupted his thoughts. "I suppose I'd better see this new cook of yours about the menu for Wednesday. Unless you have anyone to add, I believe our final number will be twenty."

Anthony wrenched his mind back to concrete matters. Not that he gave a damn who was coming to the party. The sole purpose of the occasion was as a vehicle to demonstrate Jane Castle's talents as a confectioner.

"I have invited six young unmarried ladies for you to meet," Kitty continued. Having almost forgotten that he was supposed to be seeking a bride, Anthony was unprepared for James's startled whistle.

"Young ladies?" he jeered. "Don't tell me you're entering the marriage market, Tony?"

"I have to do it sometime," replied his brother defensively. "And Kitty has *kindly* agreed to present a few candidates to me." This with a baleful glance at his sister, who looked unbearably smug.

"Six perfectly eligible young ladies," Kitty continued triumphantly, "despite the fact that London is almost empty. The Misses Baring, Lady Sophia Wortley, Miss Mannering, and—oh yes—the Bellamys. They have a daughter and a niece they will be presenting this spring."

"Debutantes, Kitty? I said not too young." Anything to deflate Kitty's annoying complacency.

"Not debutantes, Anthony, with the exception of

Miss Bellamy. The niece is a few years older and making her bow late."

James had a different objection. "The Bellamys!" he exclaimed in disgust. "Chauncey Bellamy is the biggest prig in London and Lady Caroline the biggest prude. I can't think, Kitty, why anyone would want to sit down to eat with them, let alone marry one of them."

Anthony had a reason for not joining, as he normally would, James's twitting of their sister. He cast his brother a minatory frown. "They are, after all, almost our next-door neighbors in London. And I daresay the girls are charming."

Kitty looked a little surprised at his acquiescence. "I'm glad to find you so open-minded," she said with approval. "May I pour you more tea before I meet your new cook? I may as well go down to the kitchen and speak to Mrs. Smith at the same time."

Once Kitty had left the room, with Anthony's reminder to "make sure the menu was as fancy as possible," James reiterated his disgust at having to sit down to dine with the tedious Bellamys.

"You forget, James," Anthony responded, "or maybe you never knew, that Chauncey Bellamy was in Paris." Kitty knew nothing of their mother's love affair, their father's deathbed revelation, or of Anthony's plan for revenge. James was his brother's sole confidant, the only person he trusted.

"I don't believe for a moment that Mama could have been in love with that bag of wind!" James expostulated.

"No," Anthony agreed, "he was only eighteen at the time, making his grand tour. But he was in Paris at the right date and he might know something. I shall be able to question him over port, and the evening won't be wasted."

"How could the evening be wasted when you have six—excuse me, *five* since one is too young—luscious potential brides to look over?"

"For God's sake! You make me sound like a bloated Eastern potentate. I had to give Kitty a reason why I was giving this infernal dinner."

"She means well, you know, Tony," James said soberly. "Kitty's a good soul. I wish you could get along better with her."

Anthony didn't. But he and James had never seen eye-to-eye on their sister.

"Are you having doubts about Candover?" James asked. "Do you think Bellamy might have some different information?"

"I have no doubts at all," Anthony replied firmly. "But I want to have as complete a picture as possible of our parents' trip to Paris in 1786, and Bellamy may be able to sketch in a few details. I expect that if Bellamy has anything relevant to contribute, it will only confirm the connection between Mama and Candover."

Chapter 10

<u>Pièce Montée</u>

A Basket of Spun Sugar. The basket has a base of confectioner's paste surrounded by a border made of madeleines. Make meringues shaped in ovals like half of an egg. Fill the meringues with crème plombiére, *iced cream,* fromage bavarois, *or whipped cream, and fit them together in pairs along the flat side. The effect is of a basket of eggs.*

Antonin Carême

Jacobin had welcomed Storrington's summons to London, despite the danger that she might be recognized in the city. Charlie's visit had brought home the uncomfortable truth that the authorities investigating Candover's attempted murder were focusing on Jacob

Léon. Since they weren't looking for the true culprit, they weren't likely to unmask him.

Candover's poisoning was the talk of the Mayfair servants' halls. Jacobin had little trouble establishing that her uncle remained in Brighton, but was expected to return to London soon. The first place to start the investigation was her uncle's house. She needed to visit the servants there immediately, if only she could escape from the preparations for Storrington's dinner that were consuming his entire staff. If she had to work this hard all the time, the noble earl was going to get his money's worth.

She finally completed the basket of spun sugar that was to form the central *pièce montée* of the dinner.

"I'm stiff all over," she informed the sympathetic Mrs. Smith as she drew on her drab cloak and headed for the back door. "I need to go out for a walk. Make sure no one touches that basket. It's surrounded with ice and must be handled with the utmost care or the threads of sugar will snap."

She spoke no more than the truth. Shaping the intricate basketwork had taken the best part of a day. Her head felt numb from hours of concentration, and her shoulder and arm muscles ached from the labor, which required minute control and tedious repetition. And all this performed in an icy pantry. The lords and ladies who enjoyed the frivolous fruits of the *pâtissier*'s art had no idea of the backbreaking effort that went into their creation.

Recent rain had made it damp underfoot, but watery

sunshine filtered into the mews as she made her way
north. She stopped to breathe deeply. Even the grimy
city air felt good after the long morning's work. A groom
backed a pair of grays out onto the cobblestones and
hitched them to a smart curricle. While Jacobin idly
admired the royal blue paintwork, picked out with gold,
and the rippling flanks of the splendidly fit horses, Lord
Storrington entered the mews and greeted the servant.

Jacobin hadn't set eyes on him since their abruptly
terminated scene in the Storrington Hall kitchen, and
she'd missed him. She had no trouble identifying the
feelings provoked by the powerful but graceful figure
dressed in a multicaped driving coat and gleaming
boots. Suddenly she felt short of breath. Something
tightened beneath her breastbone and descended to the
pit of her stomach.

Desire. It had been lurking below the surface of her
consciousness since the first moment she'd seen Storrington. When she'd been floored by the Brighton bullies, outnumbered and helpless on the cold night street,
he'd appeared like a guardian angel . . . no, that was too
mild an image . . . like a hero, to dismiss her tormenters
with an arrogant hint of his power. Hurt at her uncle's
neglect crystallized into a despairing rage that he had
deprived her of the right to aspire to such a man on
equal terms. Instead she'd been treated as a possession,
a chattel to be carelessly lost over a game of cards.

The earl saw her as nothing but a servant, to be trifled
with but never taken seriously. At least as his servant he
apparently had some respect for her person. What if he

knew her true identity? She'd like to think well enough of Storrington that he wouldn't take advantage of her helplessness. But she knew little of the man, and her judgment was tarnished by her attraction to him. Her fear of his reaction dispelled any slight impulse toward confession.

Perhaps sensing her gaze, Storrington turned from examining the horses and looked over his shoulder in her direction. Their eyes held for a few seconds, then he swung all the way around and bowed to her, an obeisance such as he might afford a lady of his own rank. Jacobin returned the gesture, not with a maidservant's bob, but in the correct manner taught her by her mother, as though she were being presented at a fashionable entertainment. And without her thinking about it, her curtsy was of the depth due to an equal rather than a social superior.

Then the moment passed and the earl was climbing into his equipage and Jacobin continued her journey out of the mews. For some reason the encounter raised her spirits.

"Now you sit down right there and have a nice cup of tea and a piece of my lemon cake, Miss Jacobin, and tell Cookie all about it."

Jacobin accepted the soothing beverage and even more comforting sympathy from the elderly woman who'd been the closest thing she'd had to a mother since her own died. Neither Candover nor Edgar was in residence at her uncle's London house, just a quarter of an hour's walk from Upper Brook Street. That meant that she was safe from an encounter with their personal servants; no other member of the staff would ever betray her. Two of the maids joined them at the kitchen table. For the first time in months she felt truly at ease. She was among friends.

"I'm very well, Cookie," she said, "and I have an excellent new position."

"I don't like to see you in service," Cook said with a frown. "It isn't fitting. I hope it's a respectable household with no single gentlemen."

Jacobin had already decided not to reveal her exact whereabouts; it was better for her uncle's servants not to know, so they wouldn't be put into the position of lying to their employer. She shuddered to think what Cookie would have to say about the noble Earl of Storrington and his flirtatious younger brother.

"Very respectable, Cookie. Well run and the staff are friendly. You needn't worry about me."

"Does Mr. Edgar know where you are?" asked Rosie, one of the housemaids.

"No," Jacobin answered, "and please don't tell him you've seen me."

"He's been that worried about you," Rosie said. "Can't I at least tell him you're safe."

"Better not," Cookie interrupted. "You can't trust Mr. Edgar not to tell His Lordship everything."

Jacobin smiled at the crestfallen maid. "I'm perfectly safe, Rosie, and in an excellent household. Why, I'm even managing to have a little fun in London."

Naturally Cookie and Rosie wanted to know all about *that*.

"I'm going to a public ball the day after tomorrow with one of my new friends. I'm so excited. I've never been to a dance."

"Disgraceful!" Cookie exclaimed. "Your precious uncle should have seen to you being presented proper like a young lady should, instead of letting you hobnob with the grooms and kitchen maids."

Jacobin smiled at her affectionately. "But then I wouldn't have had such good friends, like you, Cookie, and Rosie and Lily and Peter and everyone at Hurst. And I'd never have known Jean-Luc either and I'd have hated to miss that!"

Cookie smiled. The handsome Frenchman had always been a favorite of hers.

"Have you heard from Jean-Luc?" Jacobin asked.

"He wrote to me when he reached France, the rascal, to let me know you were safe. Lord, I do miss that piece of French sauce. His Lordship never stops complaining about my puddings."

"That's unfair! You may not have Jean-Luc's training, but no one make meringues like you." Jacobin reached for a slice of cake and took a bite. "Mmm . . . delicious. Or cakes. Uncle Candover doesn't know how lucky he is to have you."

"He just goes on and on about this fancy French dish and that. The sooner he gets himself a new pastry cook, the better. Finally get a bit of peace around here."

"I heard he was taken ill in Brighton," Jacobin mentioned casually. "Rumor said he was poisoned."

Cook sniffed. "That's what they say, though what with the amount His Lordship eats and drinks I don't see how they could tell. It's a miracle he doesn't get a stomach upset every day of the week. But whoever's in charge thinks someone tried to kill him. We've had Bow Street runners bothering the staff with a lot of impertinent questions. One of them was here again only the day before yesterday asking about Jean-Luc. Seemed to think he might have something to do with it."

"Jean-Luc?" Jacobin asked. "He's been in France for months. Why would they suspect him?"

"Something to do with a friend of Jean-Luc's who they think might have done it. The man wanted to know why Jean-Luc left us."

"You didn't tell him about me, did you?" Jacobin asked. She didn't want the Bow Street runner to even begin to make a connection between Jacobin de Chastelux and Jacob Léon.

"Of course I didn't and neither did anyone else. None of his business. The very idea!"

The very idea of what, Jacobin wasn't certain. But the occasional obscurity of Cookie's utterances was equaled by the steadfastness of her loyalty.

"Do you know any reason why someone might kill my uncle?" Jacobin held her breath. If anything untoward had occurred in the house, Cookie would know about it.

"Well!" Cookie leaned in with a conspiratorial

air. "There was something odd happened about three months ago."

That didn't sound promising: too long ago. Still, any information was better than the blank page Jacobin had now. She made an encouraging noise.

Cookie, none too reluctant to gossip, lowered her voice confidentially. "I shouldn't say this, but Peter overheard His Lordship have a right donnybrook with a visitor, a Mr. Chauncey Bellamy."

"Really?" Jacobin didn't have to feign fascination at this piece of news. Peter, the first footman, was a notorious eavesdropper and kept the household informed of goings-on upstairs where the more discreet butler might hold his tongue. "Did he know what they quarreled about?"

"Peter didn't hear that—he didn't arrive until after they started yelling at each other."

"Who is this Bellamy?"

"Not one of His Lordship's friends. Called here once or twice over the years, but I hear he's very respectable. Peter said Mr. Bellamy was roaring angry. Threatened to thrash His Lordship."

Chapter 11

<u>Gâteau de Mille Feuilles pour
Grosse Pièce Ordinaire</u>

Sixteen circles of puff pastry (cooked) in circles of six to eight inches, a hole of two-inch diameter removed from center of each. Leave one whole. Glaze. When cold make a tower, sandwiching them together with apricot marmalade, red currant jelly alternating. Cover the completed tower with egg whites beaten with sugar and strew with sugar. Make a small clear flame at the mouth of the oven, and hold your cake before it, but at the distance of a foot, turning it gently all the time. Ornament the whole circle of pastry with small meringues and decorate with apple or currant jelly and a rosette. At the moment of serving fill the inside of the tower with vanilla-flavored whipped cream and put the lid on top.

Antonin Carême

"What do you think of the earl?" Miss Lavinia Bellamy examined the fair curls clustered at her temples and fluffed them up with anxious fingers. The ladies had withdrawn at the conclusion of dinner, leaving the gentlemen to their wine, and been shown to a bedroom on the second floor by their hostess. It was, Lady Kitty explained, the chamber she'd occupied during her two seasons. It was well equipped with every kind of looking glass for the critical assessment and maintenance of a debutante's toilette. Most of the women had completed their repairs, leaving the two Bellamy girls the sole occupants of the room.

From her perch in the sewing room that adjoined the bedroom Jacobin wished the pair would hurry up and leave. She'd come here to change into masculine attire, and time was short if she was to execute her plan safely.

"He's certainly handsome enough," replied the other girl, Lavinia's older cousin. Susan Bellamy's voice was mature and poised in contrast to that of her companion, whose ever-present giggle was an indication that childhood had barely been left behind. "But he seems a little distracted. I think I prefer a gentleman who shows more interest when he converses. His brother has far more address and is just as handsome."

"What fustian!" Miss Lavinia said dismissively. "Captain Storrs is a younger son. He may be better company than his brother, but there is no comparison."

"Are you setting your cap at Storrington, then?" inquired Miss Susan. "You were certainly making up to him. He must be thirty-five if he's a day, and according to Aunt Caroline has never shown the least inclination to marry."

Jacobin felt quite indignant on Lord Storrington's behalf. Perhaps it wasn't such a great thing to be a rich nobleman if it meant being pursued by idiot chits interested only in your money and title.

On second thought, she decided, Storrington could take care of himself. The truth was she envied these young ladies, who could sit in the dining room and chat and flirt and eat delicious food. Unlike Jacobin, who was merely awarded the dubious honor of preparing part of the meal. At least her dishes had returned to the kitchen in ruins, proof that the confections had found favor with the guests.

"It's odd, you know," Miss Lavinia continued. "When he was Lord Storrs the earl had quite a reputation. I hear there were all sorts of shocking parties in this house."

"Lavinia! That's servants' gossip. Stop at once."

Go on, Jacobin urged silently, wanting to discover more about the younger, jollier Storrington already hinted at by his cook.

"In any case, since his father's death Lord Storrington has obviously decided to be as stuffy and dull as Mama and Papa." From her tone, Miss Lavinia didn't think this was a good thing. "Mind you, Mama might not like the match above half, given what happened to the earl's mother."

She lowered her voice confidentially, and Jacobin had to strain to hear what was being said.

"Aunt Mary said she was quite mad and ran off with a *lover*."

"Really! Lavinia!" Jacobin pictured Miss Susan throwing up her hands in despair. "You'll be kept indoors for a week if my aunt catches you. But seriously, I can't imagine why she should have doubts about a man simply because his mother died in an accident when he was quite young. Even if the circumstances were scandalous, I can't see how she can blame the son."

"Oh, you know Mama. She's the highest stickler. But I believe she'll have to adjust. If she disapproves of every gentleman with a relative who has done something doubtful, neither of us will ever get married." She giggled. "I believe I may try for Storrington. It might be worth being married to an old man to be a countess."

Old man! The chit was out of her mind. Nothing Jacobin had seen suggested Storrington was too old for anything.

She began to dislike Miss Lavinia Bellamy. Just as well, since her plan for the rest of the evening was to prove the girl's father guilty of attempted murder.

It was a damn dull dinner party. Kitty's notion of "not too young" when it applied to marriageable ladies turned out to be "over eighteen but under twenty-two." The younger Bellamy girl, who didn't even meet that criterion, was quite a saucy piece and persisted in trying to engage him in flirtation, which both amused him and made him feel old. The niece, Miss Susan Bellamy was better: handsome rather than pretty, and possessed of some intelligence and wit.

"Nice girl," muttered James as the ladies withdrew from the dining room. His brother had been seated next to Miss Susan, lucky man. Anthony had to endure the utter tedium of Lady Caroline Bellamy's conversation. As the daughter of a duke the woman was higher in the instep than a French-heeled shoe and just as uncomfortable. There was no escape. The woman would have been fatally insulted if not given the place of honor at her host's right.

Now it was time to see if the male half of the couple had anything interesting to say. Objectively of course, there was no chance that the Honorable Chauncey would have anything to contribute that wouldn't send the average man into a stupor. But Anthony retained a faint trace of optimism that reminiscing about his far-off—and dare he hope misspent?—youth in the wicked city of Paris would breathe life into the corpse.

It didn't.

"I spent a short time there," Bellamy said stiffly, as though it was distasteful for him to have to admit he'd ever set foot within one hundred miles of the French capital. "I was very young and I don't recall coming across your late parents. I wasn't there long enough to mix in society."

"I suppose you were busy enjoying the architectural marvels of Paris?"

"My late father, like many of his era, thought it essential to my education to see Italy, France, and some of the

German principalities. If one thing good came from the recent wars, it was putting an end to such travels. Our sons are safer in England. Sending impressionable youth among foreigners can only lead to them wandering into error."

Anthony tried to envision Bellamy wandering into error, but his imagination wasn't up to the task.

"Did you ever come across Candover there?" he asked, on the chance that he might get something useful from one final line of inquiry.

The effect was immediate. Bellamy's face turned puce and wore an expression of extreme distaste, mixed with something stronger. Rage? Fear?

"I am acquainted with Lord Candover," he said, "but his is not an association I would care to pursue. Without wishing to speak ill of the Prince Regent . . ."

Why the hell not? Anthony thought. *Everyone else does.*

". . . I cannot approve of the caliber of man with whom he prefers to surround himself. And Candover is one of the very worst. A worthless gambler and drunkard."

Bellamy's attitude put a damper on the normal post-prandial male congeniality. They didn't linger long over their port before joining the ladies in the drawing room. The minute the gentlemen came in, Miss Lavinia Bellamy made a beeline for Anthony and fluttered her eyelashes.

'Struth, thought Anthony in horror. *The girl's setting her cap at me, and she can't be a day over seventeen.*

"Lord Storrington!" She giggled. "My mama and

Lady Kitty have come up with such a scheme. Do, pray, say you'll agree."

"Lavinia!" called her mother repressively. "Such forwardness is unbecoming. Let Lady Kitty speak."

Though Anthony's instinct was to depress any ideas the pretty little chit was developing—and certainly to foil any plan of Kitty's—he found his dislike of the odious Lady Caroline took precedence. Besides, Lavinia looked quite crestfallen at her mother's snub, so he gallantly stepped in to save her. He took Lady Caroline's hand, bowed over it, and gave her his most charming smile.

"I'm sure any scheme that you and Kitty could come up with would be quite delightful," he lied. "I am agog to discover what joys you have in store for us."

Lady Caroline's thin lips stretched into a narrow smile.

"Lady Kitty has persuaded me," she said, "much against my better judgment, to join her at the public ball at the Argyll Rooms tomorrow night with you and Captain Storrs as our protectors."

He'd certainly walked into that pit with eyes open.

"How very broadminded of you, Lady Caroline. Not every mother cares to expose her daughters in such an environment." That, he hoped, would put a stop to that. Although it wasn't unheard of for well-bred girls to attend such events, it wasn't the Bellamys' usual cup of tea. From the woman's dyspeptic expression he could see that the charge of broadmindedness had hit home. For a few seconds the issue lay in the balance, but came down firmly on the side of snatching an earl for her daughter.

"With London so thin of company, my girls haven't

even had the chance to dance at an informal ball. Lady Kitty has persuaded me that it will give them the opportunity to gain confidence dancing in public."

Anthony made one last attempt to save himself. "Such admirable condescension! Such liberality to be ready to occupy the same dance floor as one's servants!" If that didn't do it, nothing would.

It didn't.

"I know that your presence, and that of their father and Captain Storrs, will guard the young ladies from any impertinences by members of the lower orders."

Anthony had nothing left to do but accept his fate and resign himself to an evening dancing attendance on a pair of children in a public ballroom. At least it could hardly be as tiresome as his own party.

The guests apparently agreed with his assessment of the entertainment and took their leave at an embarrassingly early hour. And Kitty, the witch, left with all the others instead of waiting decently so that her brother could tell her what he thought of her meddling. Even James pleaded a late engagement, leaving Anthony alone with his own thoughts.

In one way at least the dinner had succeeded beyond expectations. Jane Castle had performed superbly and the desserts caused a sensation. The centerpiece of a fantastic basket filled with egg-shaped meringues had elicited gasps of admiration from his guests, as had a tower of crispy pastry stuffed with cream. He himself had consumed a couple of those puffy things and raised his glass in a silent toast to the cook.

He had no doubt that word of his brilliant new cook would spread around the *ton* like news of an indiscretion at Almack's. Candover would be wild to taste her offerings. If nothing else lured him to the piquet table with Anthony, the prospect of gaining Jane Castle's services would.

The thought of using the lovely cook as a stake in a card game caused him a momentary pang of unease. She was alone in the world and in trouble, suspected of murder and a fugitive from the law. It occurred to him that she showed remarkable courage and deserved his protection. His mind drifted to the circumstances of another young woman. He preferred not to think about Candover's niece, about why she'd fled. Had elopement with Candover's cook really been her choice, or had she been desperate to avoid him? He'd never have harmed her, but she couldn't know that. His conscience stabbed him. He was responsible in part for a young lady being adrift in a harsh world. He hoped she was safe.

His misgivings were soothed by the reflection that Jane Castle's position was quite different. Her services as a cook would be at stake, not her sexual favors. Cooking was her profession. What did it matter whom she served?

Besides, he had no intention of losing. No, indeed. Candover would once again succumb to Anthony's superior skill and lose a fortune he couldn't afford.

But, damn it, where did he raise the twenty thousand last time?

The image of Jane Castle's beautiful face lingered in his mind. He really ought to thank her for her efforts tonight. He stopped himself in the act of reaching for the

bellpull to summon her. At this hour she was probably
abed. Tomorrow would be much more suitable. Or
better yet a message by way of the butler. Staying away
from such an attractive female servant was the only
sensible thing to do.

To aid this worthy resolution he stepped outside into
the garden behind the house. The weather had turned
cold, and a full moon illuminated the neighboring
houses, even through the smoky town haze. He shivered
in his black evening coat of superfine wool, but the mild
discomfort didn't succeed in diverting his thoughts.

Jane Castle didn't really conduct herself like a servant.
Her manner toward him, even setting aside the matter of
that disturbing kiss, was more that of an equal. Those
remarkable brown eyes had the habit of meeting his
boldly, and the chin with its intriguing cleft was proudly
assertive. Perhaps that's why he'd found himself bowing
to her in the mews a day or two earlier.

It had been an awkward moment, their first encounter since embracing in the kitchen at Storrington. He'd
meant to treat her, when he couldn't avoid her, with cool
propriety and set their association on a proper footing.
But instead of a "Good day, Jane," or even a pleasant
nod such as he might afford anyone else in his service,
he'd greeted her like a passing duchess in Hyde Park. And
she'd responded in kind. That was no servant's curtsy.

He had to face the unpleasant truth that his pastry
cook might not be who she purported to be. There was
something irregular about Jane Castle. If that was even
her name.

Chapter 12

Tracking down Mr. Chauncey Bellamy had been ridiculously easy. A casual inquiry in the kitchen revealed that the gentleman's London house lay a mere two doors down on Upper Brook Street from Storrington's. Without raising suspicion, Jacobin had managed to gather a fair amount of information about the habits of the Bellamys and their staff.

On the night of the dinner party she was putting the finishing touches to a sensational *mille-feuilles* tower, gleaned from Maître Carême's *Le Pâtissier Royal*, when the kitchen chatter revealed that the guests dining upstairs included the entire Bellamy family.

It seemed like fate. Jacobin decided to strike at once when she knew they were occupied for the evening.

She lost some time outwaiting the young Bellamy ladies in the sewing room, but even so, she calculated she would have at least two hours before the Bellamys went home. Surely there would be music, conversation, and even cards in the drawing room to occupy the company.

Once she reached the garden without detection, it was the work of a minute to pull herself up and over the wall into the garden of the empty house next door and to repeat the climb into the Bellamy property. Waiting crouched in the shrubbery, she shivered with cold, but her information had been correct. Before long the Bellamy's butler emerged to light up a cigar and take his evening stroll. As soon as the man reached the bottom of the garden, well away from the back door, Jacobin slipped from her hiding place and silently entered the house.

Her heart raced with fear but also with a mad exhilaration. She stood motionless in the passage, straining her ears for the sound of any human activity. All was quiet. As she'd expected, with the family out for the evening, all the servants had retired save the butler. She walked stealthily into the hall, then examined the ground-floor rooms, one by one.

She had no idea what she was looking for, or even if there was anything to find. Only the convenient proximity of the house had made her undertake anything so foolhardy. She forced herself to slow down, rather than rush through the house at random. Impulse having driven her this far, it was time to use her brain.

What might she find to prove a connection between Candover and Bellamy? A portrait, perhaps. But if there was a family connection, that would be simple to discover elsewhere. Something small and incriminating. Papers. A letter. She needed to find Chauncey Bellamy's desk.

The house was lit, though dimly, and she quickly discovered there was nothing resembling a desk in the dining room or morning room. She'd have to go upstairs. In one sense this was good. She'd be less likely to be heard by the butler once he reentered the house. In this weather she couldn't expect him to take a prolonged constitutional. She ascended the darkened staircase on tiptoe, cursing under her breath at a creak from one of the risers about halfway up.

A drawing room: nothing there. A music room: the Bellamys' taste was for plain and unadorned furnishing—nothing but a pianoforte, a harp, and a few uncomfortable-looking chairs. Under other circumstances Jacobin might have found such barrenness dispiriting, but she could only be grateful that it made her search easier. Neither did the family appear to care much for literature; there were almost no books in the house. Good. In the novels she'd read, important papers were often secreted within the pages of books, and she wouldn't fancy searching a library of several thousand volumes.

One more door to open. She sent up a fervent prayer that Bellamy didn't conduct his business in his own rooms. If she had to go up to the bedroom floor, she'd be close to the servants' quarters and in danger of disturbing them.

She found treasure! Or rather a library. Not a very large library, thank God. There were perhaps a few hundred books in a glass-doored breakfront bookcase. A warm fire blazed in the hearth and a tray of drinks stood on a side table. The seating was more inviting than she'd seen elsewhere in the house. She guessed this was the room used by the family when they were alone in the evening and had been prepared in case they wished to take refreshment after their evening engagement. And against one wall was a desk. Not a lady's escritoire but a substantial masculine desk.

In seconds she began opening drawers. The room was brightly illuminated, fortunately so since the windows gave onto the garden. The curtains looked thick, but any change in the lighting might attract the attention of the butler. She had no trouble reading thick wads of letters and bills. She skimmed through them rapidly, fighting feelings of guilt. She suppressed her scruples. If there was nothing relevant she would forget what she'd seen. If she found proof of Bellamy's culpability in Candover's attack, then he deserved to be spied on.

The papers confirmed Bellamy's reputation as a dull man. Most of the letters concerned the business of his estate and investments. Alas, nothing struck her as significant. Such personal correspondence as existed was from relatives, and concerned children, visits, and the state of the writers' health: the mundane stuff of daily life, so fascinating for those involved and so tedious to the outsider. The bills were unsurprising save perhaps in their modesty. Clearly Bellamy was not given to undue extravagance.

By the time she reached the bottom of the pile, the sense of optimism that had launched the evening's adventure had evaporated. What was she doing here, she wondered, pawing through the banalities of a stranger's life? And with the deadening of hope came an appalled realization of her peril.

The consequences of being caught here were terrible. Even being found breaking into a gentleman's house could lead to imprisonment and transportation. Once the authorities discovered her identity, the hangman's noose threatened. She couldn't count on Storrington's continued protection if he got wind of this little escapade. Every impulse told her to get out at once.

But the house remained quiet and she steeled herself to remain and finish the job. She perspired under her wool coat, from the heat of the blazing fire and from fear. She shrugged out of the garment, then pulled a thick ledger from the last drawer.

The volume contained three or four years' worth of household and personal accounts. The script was neat and the letters commonly formed, save for oddly idiosyncratic curlicues on the descenders, as though the penman possessed some core of rebellion or artistry that emerged only in his handwriting. Her heart now thumping so hard she feared it would awaken the dead, Jacobin forced herself to apply logic to the final task. Candover and Bellamy had quarreled three months ago, so she would start by looking at entries around that date.

She found it immediately and could scarcely believe her luck. The sum leaped from the page for the simple reason that it was so much larger than any other.

Before she could digest the significance of the discovery and look further, she heard the front door open and the sound of voices in the hall. Hastily replacing the ledger and shutting the drawers, she snatched up her coat and dashed over to the window and behind the curtain, which luckily covered a narrow window seat.

Please don't let them come in here.

Her luck had run out. Footsteps ascended the stairs, and the voices came nearer.

"We'll take tea in the library."

Jacobin shoved up the sash and scrambled out onto the window ledge. She could hear the library door open, and the voices became distinct.

"I think I'll drink a little sherry to warm me on this cold night. How about you, my dear?"

Nothing like the cold he'd feel once they came into the room and realized the window was open.

"I think you had enough to drink after dinner." The peevish female response came from inside the library.

Clinging to the lintel with trembling fingers, Jacobin took a deep breath and moved one hand to the top of the sash. She managed to push it down. Silence. She'd escaped just in time.

But hardly to safety. She was perched on a six-inch-wide ledge a dozen feet from the ground, her face jammed against cold glass, holding on to frigid stone with the tips of her fingers. Added to that it was freezing cold. Her coat slipped from her arm into the garden below, and an icy breeze caught her midriff on one side. Gingerly she lowered a hand to pull down her shirt, which had come loose from the waistband of her breeches.

The shirt had caught in the side of the thoroughly closed window.

Oh God, she begged fervently and with more sincerity than her prayers had possessed since childhood. *Get me out of here.*

She couldn't imagine how the deity would manage it.

Anthony strode along the narrow path to the end of the garden and turned when something caught his eye a couple of houses away. Someone was clinging to the stone architrave of an upper window. That was Bellamy's house, wasn't it? And seemingly in the act of being burgled. He meant to go indoors and order a servant to summon the watch, when something about the felon tugged at his mind. Even with her face to the wall he recognized the slim feminine figure in breeches and a white shirt that shone in the hazy moonlight.

It couldn't be. Even Jane Castle wouldn't be so insane.

How the hell was she going to get down from there without breaking every bone in her body?

In three seconds Anthony was scaling the garden wall.

"Jane," he called softly, standing in the Bellamy garden just below her unstable perch. "Drop down and I'll catch you."

"I'm stuck. My shirt's caught in the window." The normally confident voice broke on a sob.

"It's all right," he whispered soothingly. "I'll get you down." He didn't know how, but he had to prevent her from crying aloud and rousing the Bellamys. "How badly is it caught? Pull it gently. I'll catch you if you fall."

It must have taken enormous courage for her to release one hand from her tenuous grasp on the lintel, but she did it. Anthony held his breath as she grasped the linen and gave it a firm tug. He sensed rather than heard her sigh of relief echo his own when the cloth came loose.

"Well done! Now, do you think you can grasp the top of the sash and hang from it? You should be low enough that I can grab your legs."

She nodded, and one by one her hands followed his directions. Then—sensible girl—she knelt on the ledge before letting her body hang all the way down. The distance was less than he'd estimated, and with raised arms he grasped her waist. As soon as his hand touched bare flesh she shot upward out of his grip, lifting herself so that her chest was level with her hands on the sash.

'Struth, the woman was strong. He wasn't sure *he* could do that!

"Jane," he hissed reprovingly. "This is no time for modesty."

"Your hands are cold."

"You'll just have to put up with it." Nevertheless he breathed on them and rubbed them together—she was right, they were cold—before returning them to her waist. This time she didn't flinch.

"Now let go, I have you."

NEVER RESIST TEMPTATION 137

It wasn't a flawless dismount, though it could have been worse. They both remained on their feet, but a lurch as she hit the ground knocked a stone pot he'd failed to notice on the dark ground. To Anthony's ears it cracked like a fifty-gun salute.

"Let's get out of here!" he murmured, snatching her hand.

Leaving the garden wasn't as easy as entering. The neighbors had a conveniently placed bench against the wall, but the Bellamy side offered nothing but ten feet of sheer brickwork. Anthony swung her up by the waist and she pulled herself up and over the other side. Lucky she had those muscles. He was glad to find, as he followed her, that his were in equally good condition.

They collapsed onto the bench in the deserted garden, panting with exertion and relief. Anthony had an absurd urge to laugh and found himself shaking like a madman, silent chuckles rocking his chest. He hadn't done anything so foolish, so exhilarating—so much fun—since the days of his misspent youth. Jane Castle was worth every penny of her outrageous salary in entertainment value alone.

Impulsively he swung an arm around her shoulders and found that she too was trembling with mirth. Registering on some level that their escape had gone unnoticed and all was quiet next door, he exhaled a huge belly laugh, and for a couple of minutes they clung to each other, cackling like a pair of deranged hens.

Another sensation invaded his consciousness. She wasn't wearing anything under her shirt.

His hand stroked a well-defined shoulder blade and tentatively crept lower and around her side, seeking her breast. She must surely be cold. That quivering wasn't all laughter. In a smooth move he hoisted her onto his lap, opened his coat, drew it around her, and held her tightly in his arms. Just for warmth, of course.

Her unbound breasts pressed against his waistcoat, and her heartbeat seemed to match his own. A faint scent of vanilla warmed the wintry redolence of decaying vegetation and frozen earth. She raised her head from his shoulder, but it was too dark to see her expression. Neither did he know who made the first move. Perhaps it was a simultaneous advance.

Her lips were soft and warm. Initially the kiss spoke of companionship and mutual appreciation. But not for long. She opened up to him, and he was lost in a sweet, shadowy retreat where only the two of them existed. A gentle tattoo pulsated in his chest. It felt like joy

Tentative at first, her response intensified into hunger for the feast. They kissed for who knew how long, and he was content with the fruit of her lips, the honeyed tongue, the rich confection of her mouth. Not that he wouldn't have taken more. His whole body tingled with knowledge of her nearness. But he made no gesture of increased intimacy. Jane Castle's kisses were enough, for now at least, to make him entirely happy.

It was she who changed things. Somehow she'd unbuttoned his silk brocade waistcoat so that the warmth of their bodies melded with only two layers of linen between them. The definition of her breasts against his chest sent a sharp message of desire to his nether regions and awoke him from his blissful trance.

There was no more excuse for trifling with Jane Castle than there ever had been. She was still his servant. Reluctantly he withdrew his embrace and lifted her from his knees, placing her once more beside him on the bench.

Jane Castle had some explaining to do.

Out of the *poêle*, into the *four*.

Except the sauté pan had been a freezing nightmare and the oven was a warm, delicious haven. Jacobin would happily have gone on kissing Storrington all night.

Once again he'd come to her rescue. The contrast between the black despair of her situation on the Bellamys' window ledge and the paradise of his embrace banished all fear. All she wanted was to be as close to him as physically possible. Her mind was incapable of considering the consequences of the evening's business. The enchantment of his arms and mouth was everything.

Sadly he didn't feel the same way. She found herself bereft of his heat and unceremoniously dumped onto a cold bench. The sudden physical chill—and the chill of rejection—made her shudder.

He shrugged off his coat and threw it around her.

"You'll need it," she demurred as he thrust her arms into the sleeves.

"I have my waistcoat," he said gruffly, and buttoned her up to the chin, like a child. Her hands drowned in the sleeves of the garment, much too large for her slender figure. The fine wool with its silk lining was soft as a petal and smelled faintly of wood smoke and tobacco and a masculine soap.

He rebuttoned his waistcoat. Heavens, she'd undone it herself. Now that she'd come to her senses she couldn't believe her audacity. She felt deeply humiliated that she'd thrown herself at him but he hadn't wanted her. And just when he'd gallantly saved her from a terrible pickle, instead of letting her tumble to injury or death, or calling the watch, which would have been the sensible thing for a respectable, law-abiding peer to do. And still could.

"Now, Jane Castle." He was no longer touching her but sat sideways and eyed her severely. As he spoke she could see his breath in the night air and feel it tickling her ear. "Why don't you tell me what you were doing and why I shouldn't turn you right over to the watch?"

But his tone, though stern, was not hostile. She gazed at him, and as far as she could tell in the scanty light, he didn't look unsympathetic. Nor should he, she thought with returning confidence. No one had forced him to come to her aid and no one had forced him to kiss her.

With a touch of rebellious impertinence, she answered his second question with just a hint of a query in her tone. "Because you kissed me?"

She wasn't sure that was strictly correct. She might have kissed him first, but he'd definitely participated.

"True. And I shouldn't have. Once again I must apologize." He looked grim. "But I must insist on knowing why I find my pastry cook clinging to the wall of my neighbor's house late at night."

There wasn't any point to further prevarication.

"My lord," she began, taking a deep breath and clutching his coat around her. "I am wanted for attempted murder."

He took this dramatic statement calmly. "I know. I heard the investigation was concentrated on the search for one Jacob Léon, a missing cook." After a pause for consideration he continued. "I rather think it was a mistake for you to have fled. Even had you lost your position when your sex was revealed, you could doubtless have found a new one. It'll be difficult now to persuade anyone of your innocence. Given tonight's events I can see that you are given to rash impulses."

Unable to reveal the real reason for her flight, she could hardly argue with his assessment. Ignoring the just accusation of impulsiveness, she stood up and flung out her arms in agitation. Thinking about the injustice of her situation, she didn't have to feign indignation.

"*Exactement*. They won't look for the real villain because they are sure I am guilty. So I have to find out who poisoned Lord Candover. I must help myself."

"And where, may I ask, does the Bellamy family come in? Do you have some notion that Chauncey Bellamy tried to kill Candover, or perhaps Lady Caroline? God knows her personality is poisonous enough."

Jacobin waved aside Storrington's note of sarcastic disbelief.

"Yes! And I think I'm right. Three months ago Mr.

Bellamy had a furious quarrel with Candover and threatened to kill him."

Storrington raised his eyebrows. "And whence came this fascinating information?"

She tapped her nose knowingly. "We servants have our sources."

He laughed shortly and without humor. "And so you do. And on the basis of this nugget of gossip you decided to burgle Bellamy's house."

"Yes."

"You're crazy!" He leaped to his feet and towered over her, a furious glower creasing his forehead. "Do you have any idea what would have happened to you if I hadn't come along and seen you trying to climb in that window?"

"I wasn't climbing in," she said. "I was leaving, and I would have been perfectly safe if they hadn't left your house so soon. It must have been a dreadfully dull party that the guests left so early. If *I* were a hostess I'd make sure people were enjoying themselves enough to stay till a decent hour."

He looked ready to burst with irritation. "That's neither here nor there. The fact is, you took an intolerable risk with little or no chance of finding anything." His voice rose to a shout. "What were you thinking?"

Although when she was sitting in Bellamy's library her own thoughts had been identical, Jacobin was irked by his high-handed attitude, and she refused to give an inch. "As it happens," she said with a superior smirk, "it was well worth it. I found something very interesting."

"About Bellamy? He's nothing but a stuffed shirt."

"What would you think if I told you he lost twenty thousand pounds to Candover at piquet?"

That got his attention. "The devil! Twenty thousand, you say. Are you sure?"

"It was there in his accounts book. Candover. Piquet. Twenty thousand pounds. About three months ago."

Storrington was now pacing, hands behind his back and his head bowed as though in deep thought.

"It's important, yes?" she pursued. "To lose such a sum must surely be a motive for hatred."

"Perhaps," he replied, frowning. "It seems so unlike Bellamy. He's such a model of dreary respectability, and notorious for his disapproval of gambling and cards. I've never seen him play so much as a game of penny whist."

"So he wanted to keep it a secret! It makes perfect sense."

Storrington nodded. "He'd certainly want to keep it from his wife. If I'm not mistaken she's the master in that household. It was a brilliant match for him. Her father's the Duke of Wensleydale, and the whole family are ardent evangelicals. Very worthy people of course, supporters of Wilberforce. But not likely to tolerate such a huge slip from the straight and narrow."

Enthusiastic as she was about this line of reasoning, Jacobin couldn't help seeing a flaw. "If he wanted to keep it from his wife, why would he record it so openly in his accounts?"

"I don't know, but I do believe that Bellamy bears looking at in the Candover matter."

"Will you help me? Will you tell the Bow Street runners to investigate him?"

"I don't see how I can do that without revealing how you found the information." He placed a slight stress on the word *you*, a warning that his forbearance toward her ambiguous situation went only so far. "I'll poke about and see what I can find out. At the very least I should be able to discover if he was in Brighton, or anywhere nearby, at the time of the poisoning."

Jacobin barely refrained from casting her arms round his neck and kissing him again. It was so wonderful to have someone on her side, to feel she wasn't completely alone anymore.

He grinned down at her, his facial expression less guarded than any she'd seen him wear. "I have a feeling I'll regret this," he said, but his words had no bite. "We'll probably end up together in a cell in Newgate. I just hope they'll allow you to provide the meals."

She thought she'd melt. Not only was he kind and helpful and a wonderfully timely rescuer of maidens in distress, not only was he madly handsome and an incredible kisser, but he even had a sense of humor.

His next words reminded her that he was also an arrogant, domineering beast. "I'm sending you back to the country tomorrow."

"No!" she gasped. "I can't find out anything there."

"Yes," he said firmly. "You'll be safe there. Anyone might recognize you in town."

"Not tomorrow!" she begged. "I'm going out with Lucy. We have the evening off."

"Lucy the housemaid?" he asked carelessly. "I suppose you won't come to much harm with her. Very well, the next day. You can travel down with my baggage. I don't need you here now. I won't be entertaining again until I have guests at Storrington."

She was glad he'd said that. She'd needed the reminder that to him she belonged firmly in the servants' hall, and his offer of help was likely no more than he'd offer any of his dependents.

Come to think of it, it was all his fault she was in this mess. If he hadn't gambled with her uncle with her person as a stake, she'd be comfortably in the kitchen at Hurst Park, cooking with Jean-Luc, and have never set eyes on him.

Chapter 13

L ucy reverently unfolded the dress from its wrappings. The deep rose silk, the color of raspberries lightened by a modest dollop of rich cream, glowed in the cramped and unadorned attic room that the two young women shared in the Earl of Storrington's London house.

"Are you sure you want to let me wear this?" Jacobin asked. "I can't believe you don't want it yourself."

It was the most beautiful gown Jacobin had ever seen. That wasn't saying much of course. She'd long since grown out of clothes she'd worn when she and her mother had fled France. Since then the housekeeper at Hurst had eked Jacobin's garments out of the servants' clothing allowance; her dresses had been uniformly practical and just as drab.

Lucy gave her a quizzical look. "As though it would fit me!" she exclaimed. "The cloth is too fine for me to risk altering. Besides, it's not the kind of thing I have any use for. I'm saving it, and one day I'll sell it for a pretty penny."

Jacobin saw her point. She was a good six inches taller than the diminutive housemaid. Attired in a simple muslin, Lucy looked exactly what she was: a pretty servant—from a superior household, but a servant nonetheless—dressed in her best for an evening out.

"It doesn't look as though it's ever been worn," Jacobin remarked, holding the dress against her figure and kicking out with one leg to admire the way the fabric draped the limb.

"It never was. Lady Kitty's aunt wouldn't let her wear it. Said it wasn't suitable for a young girl. So she gave it to me." Lucy had served as Lady Kitty's personal maid when the earl's sister was making her debut.

Jacobin surrendered to temptation. As soon as she put on the gown she saw just why Lady Kitty's chaperone had objected to it. The neckline wasn't indecently low, despite showing more of Jacobin's breasts than she'd ever displayed in her life, nor was the trimming too lavish for a young girl. Aside from some ruching at the bodice and three bands of self-trim around the hem, the dress was quite severely cut. But the way the supple silk clung to her body made it much too sophisticated for an eighteen-year-old.

Odd, really, that she knew that. She must have paid more attention to her mother's lectures than she'd thought. Dreaming of the day she would present her daughter to society, Felicity de Chastelux had tried to prepare Jacobin to be an English debutante—when she could lure her ungrateful daughter from the more lively company of her adored and indulgent father.

"It's beautiful, Lucy. I'll take the greatest care of it."

The two of them crept down to the spare bedroom to check their toilettes in the long cheval glass. Jacobin thought she looked splendid, from her hair, arranged by Lucy in a cluster of curls on top of her head, to her toes sheathed in brand-new slippers. She'd slipped out to Oxford Street that morning to squander some of her savings on them, together with a pair of silk stockings and—wicked indulgence—silk garters to match the dress.

She couldn't help wishing that Storrington could see her now, dressed neither as a servant nor as a youth. Not the garters of course.

It was the third time Anthony had danced with Lavinia Bellamy and he feared she was getting the wrong idea. At a public ball in such a small party there was no help for it. He'd danced twice with her cousin too, once with Kitty, and once, an experience he hoped wouldn't be repeated, with Lady Caroline. Even if the girl weren't young enough to be his daughter and didn't remind him strongly of his niece, Cat, he'd rather be strung up by his thumbs than have Lady Caroline as a mother-in-law.

The Argyll Rooms were packed with a diverse miscellany of high and low society, mostly the latter, and were full to the point of discomfort. It seemed that every denizen of London with a shilling or two to spare had decided to go dancing that night. It was for the most part a well-behaved crowd. Quite dull really, and not worthy of the revolted diatribe on the distressing habits of the great unwashed he'd had to endure from Lavinia's mother.

Listening to the girl's chatter with half an ear, he was making a turn in the country dance when he almost stopped dead and caused a collision. He glimpsed a vision in deep rose performing the same maneuver in the parallel set.

Recovering his poise, he took advantage of a respite from the demands of the country dance to inspect his impossible pastry cook. Regal as a duchess and as seductive as the highest of flyers, she looked good enough to eat and utterly unlike any servant he'd ever seen.

Where the hell did she get that gown? He'd always found women in red attractive. On Jane Castle that color, whatever it was called, sent a rush of blood to his head and heat to his loins. The way the skirts clung to her body left little more to the imagination than those damn breeches of hers; the upper part of the gown left considerably less. The glorious array of shoulder and bosom made his hands itch to touch, caress, and disrobe . . . He wondered if he could find an excuse to leave Kitty's dreary party and dance with her. That would give Lady Caroline something to complain about.

Who the devil was she dancing with, anyhow? Some London lover perhaps. He hadn't forgotten she'd told him she'd once been in love and it had ended badly. The man must have been a dolt.

He craned his neck to see her partner and gave an explosion of laughter that made Lavinia, standing decorously opposite him in the dance line, scrutinize him sharply.

Jane Castle was dancing with his footman.

Joseph had doubtless been deputed to escort Jane and Lucy the housemaid on their evening jaunt. He was big enough to scare off any predatory attention, and owned an unfailing willingness to perform the kind of mindless errands that made him an exemplar of his position. He'd come to Storrington from Lethbridge House, preferring a bachelor household to the demands of the notoriously lascivious duchess whose advances, Anthony guessed, had completely baffled him. For Joseph had the face and body of an Adonis and the brain of a mentally deficient rabbit.

It was possible that Jane Castle would find Joseph's attributes appealing, but Anthony doubted it. He hoped she was enjoying herself.

Jacobin would have preferred a partner with more conversation. On the other hand Joseph accepted her rudimentary dancing skills without comment, reacting to her frequent missteps with his customary witless geniality. She and Lucy—they had giggled hysterically when the butler ordered the footman to escort them to the ball—took turns dancing with him and rolled their eyes at each other between sets. Lucy danced with a few men who presented themselves to the girls, but Jacobin had declined such invitations, not feeling confident enough to entrust herself to an unfamiliar person on the dance floor. When alone she fended off enterprising strangers, surveyed the crowded scene, and kept a mildly anxious eye out for anyone who might recognize her. Unlikely, given her limited acquaintance and the throng of bodies squeezed into the assembly rooms.

She would have liked to have a partner besides the gormless Joseph. Her awkwardness on the dance floor was yet another consequence of her uncle's ill treatment. It was pathetic that she'd reached the age of twenty-three before attending a ball.

She almost vaulted skyward when a hand touched her shoulder.

"Jacobin?" said a familiar voice.

"Edgar!" She sprang around and looked in consternation at her second cousin.

"Jacobin," he repeated. "Where have you been? I've been so worried about you."

"What are you doing in London, Edgar?" she demanded warily. "You never come here."

"I've come to meet your uncle. He's arriving from Brighton tomorrow. But never mind that. Are you well? Where are you living?" His mild face wore a look of grave concern, matching the earnest tone of his interrogation.

Jacobin had nothing against Edgar, but could she trust him? He'd always been pleasant enough to her and done nothing to warrant her dislike. But neither, as far as she knew, had he ever intervened with Candover on her behalf. As Candover's nearest male relation and the steward of the Hurst estate, he lived in the house. But while Jacobin had been confined to the nursery and then, once she reached adulthood, been left to fend for herself in the household, Edgar had the status of an honored member of the family. He had his own horses and personal servant, dressed well—as she could attest, having helped herself to some of his clothing—and was her uncle's trusted companion and confidant whenever the master was at his country house.

"I'm well," she said, her tone reserved. "There's no need to worry about me."

"I thought you'd returned to France with Jean-Luc. What are you doing in London? You shouldn't have left Hurst. It's not safe for a young woman to be out in the world alone."

That was too much. "So I was better off under the 'protection' of my uncle?" she inquired sarcastically. "Thank you very much, but I've done better on my own."

A couple heading for the dance floor jostled her and she moved out of the way. Following, Edgar seized her arm and steered her to the edge of the room. With one hand on the wall behind her, he loomed over her, as much as a bare two-inch advantage in height allowed, his pale eyes close to her face and glinting with sincerity.

"Was it so bad?" he asked. "I don't know why he doesn't like you, but you were at least warm and fed."

"Yes indeed," she said angrily, "and a useful stake at cards when he ran short of cash."

"Whatever do you mean?"

"You didn't know?" she asked. "Why I ran away?

Candover's so-called protection was to lose me in a card game. I was to be a whore to one of his gambling cronies." She felt outraged all over again. If Storrington were to appear now she'd give him a chilly reception.

Edgar looked shocked. "You should have come to me for help. I would never have let him use you so."

"I had no reason to think you'd help. To be blunt, Edgar, you never showed any concern for my position at Hurst. For all I knew, you'd help my uncle tie me up and bundle me into the carriage."

"I'm hurt you'd think such a thing of me," he protested, raising a hand to her shoulder. "I'd have protected you in the best way I could. By marrying you."

Jacobin was astonished. She'd never had any reason to believe Edgar held any tender feelings for her, anything stronger than mild liking. Suspiciously scanning his face, she couldn't detect symptoms of extraordinary passion.

"I still can," he continued. "Marry me, Jacobin, and I'll look after you forever. You must know how I've felt about you, ever since I first came to Hurst."

"I don't believe this!"

"Don't you know how beautiful you are? But you never looked at me. Only at Jean-Luc. You preferred a common French cook!"

Jacobin bristled. "Whatever Jean-Luc is, he most certainly isn't common."

"I'm sorry, Jacobin. It's just that I was always jealous of him. I love you!"

Edgar's declaration, intensely delivered in his reedy

voice, evoked gratitude seasoned with a strong dash of irritation. Deprived of familial affection since her mother's death, Jacobin was touched by her cousin's feelings—if they were genuine. He'd certainly never given her a hint of them before. Or offered her help when she most needed it.

But to be fair, even if he exaggerated when he spoke of love, he offered her something of value: to defy Candover, his patron, to protect a penniless and powerless cousin. She shuddered to think what her uncle would do if Edgar told him of their engagement.

Perhaps die of an apoplexy, she thought with some hope and no charity.

And the thought of Candover dying made her see why Edgar's offer, on the face of it the solution to all her problems, came too late. If she came out of hiding now she'd be instantly arrested and there was nothing he could do about it.

She examined his face, trying to gauge his dependability. His watery blue eyes, rimmed with straw-colored lashes, protruded slightly. She'd never noticed before. And his mouth, pale like the rest of him, was damp and sagged at the corners. His forehead shone with a light film of sweat. A hint of attraction, perhaps lust, glinted in his normally opaque gaze. She thought about kissing him and repressed a shudder. Especially when the vision of another face, another kiss, flashed through her consciousness.

"Will you marry me, Jacobin?" Edgar asked again.

The anxiety in his tone made her feel guilty. But she

found she didn't trust him enough to confide her difficulties. He might believe she was responsible for poisoning her uncle and turn her over to the authorities.

"Thank you, Edgar," she said gently. "I'm grateful for your affection but I cannot accept your offer." When he would have protested she laid a discouraging hand on his narrow chest. "I don't feel the same way about you, you see, but I'm too fond of you to expose you to my uncle's wrath. What would you do if he repudiated you? I know you have little fortune of your own."

"We could manage without him," he argued. "One day I'll inherit his title and estates, and in the meantime I could bring him round. He's fond of me, you know."

"I do know, and he must remain that way, for your sake." Suddenly she felt very alone and blinked back a tear.

"I can't think why you'd want to marry someone who stole your best clothes," she said with a tremulous attempt at humor. "I apologize for that."

"That isn't important," he said. "I'm glad you could make use of them."

Perhaps he did care for her. It made her all the sorrier that she no longer possessed his fine tailored coat, which she'd lost when she fled over the wall of the Bellamys' garden. When she'd crept out early the next morning, it had disappeared.

"At least let me know where you're living." He leaned in, crowding her against the wall. Some strong but unreadable emotion fortified his gaze. His body was tense.

She squirmed with momentary alarm and peered over his shoulder, looking for Joseph. But the music told her that he was still on the dance floor with Lucy. "Please, Edgar, you're too close. People will notice."

He drew back and relaxed. Inoffensive and unthreatening once more. She must have imagined anything more.

"I'd like to know that you are safe," he said, "and be able to see you sometimes."

"I think it better if you don't know where I am. Then you won't be hiding anything from my uncle."

"Please, Jacobin. I worry about you constantly. I must know you are well. Perhaps I can make you change your mind."

"I'll write to you sometimes, to let you know I'm well. And if I need help. It's good to see you again, Edgar."

She meant it. It was good to know she had another haven other than the dangerous protection of the Earl of Storrington.

Observing her in close conversation with a well-dressed man, clearly a gentleman, put Anthony into a state of fury.

There was no reason, of course, that Jane Castle shouldn't have such an acquaintance in London. But the way the man stood so near to her, leaning over intimately as they talked, suggested more than a casual relationship.

Surely that wasn't the kind of fellow she was attracted

to? He was barely an inch taller than she was, and even from a distance his pitifully puny physique was obvious.

Had she shown any indication of distress, Anthony would have marched over without hesitation and sent the stranger about his business, preferably with a bloody nose. But she seemed quite happy, even giving the bounder a kiss on the cheek when they parted.

He leaned against the wall and fumed, able to devote his full attention to his displeasure by the temporary withdrawal of the Bellamy ladies to the retiring room. Not for long. Kitty joined him, disturbing his solitude and exacerbating his irritation.

Earlier in the evening James had remarked on their sister's lack of spirit. Anthony's only reply was that Kitty had better be enjoying this ghastly event since she'd dragged them to it and *he* certainly wasn't enjoying himself.

But James was right, he realized. Kitty did seem dejected. If he were a good brother he'd get her to confide the source of her distress and try to relieve it. He never sensed such reluctance dealing with James. He'd always felt profound affection and a comparable sense of responsibility for the welfare of his younger brother, even to the point of preventing him from purchasing his commission until Bonaparte was safely tucked away on the island of Elba. Of course the villain had escaped, and Anthony had lived through torments until James emerged from the Waterloo bloodbath unscathed.

But he'd never felt such concern for his sister. Kitty had always been so damn happy. He didn't know why he found the fact annoying.

Ignoring her, he strained to see if he could spot Jane Castle, who had rejoined her companions after parting from that damn stranger. He caught a glimpse of dark rose silk through the crowd when Kitty gasped. Looking around, he saw a familiar figure threading his way toward them. A tall man with an agreeable rather than handsome face, he had a muscular build and the neat but unstylish mode of dress that proclaimed the country gentleman with a passion for sports.

Thornley. What the devil was his brother-in-law doing here? And not alone either. Walter Thornley was accompanied by a woman, whose elbow he held as he guided her through the crowd. A tall lady about the same age as Kitty, gowned in deep lavender velvet that suited her dark coloring. Her handsome face was graced with glowing gray eyes and a rosy, healthful complexion.

Kitty, by contrast, was pale as death.

"My dear!" boomed Thornley, unaware of his wife's distress. "Look who I have with me. Marabel had to see her man of business so I decided to escort her to London. When they told us at Mount Street you were here, we changed into evening gear and came to surprise you." He gave his wife a hearty buss on the cheek and beamed at her.

"A surprise, indeed," Kitty responded stiffly. "How lovely to see you, Marabel," she added, and kissed the woman on both cheeks with all the enthusiasm she might greet a hedgehog.

Wondering what was going on, Anthony shook hands

with his brother-in-law and was presented to Lady Morrison, a country neighbor of the Thornleys. Thornley, oblivious of the fact that Kitty was less than thrilled to see them, chatted on about what they'd all do together in town. Lady Morrison seemed less confident and kept darting anxious glances at her reluctant hostess.

"It's lovely to see you both," Kitty interrupted. "But we are, after all, at a ball. Anthony just asked me to dance with him, and that's not an opportunity I'm likely to miss." She grasped him by the arm and dragged him toward the dance floor.

"Slow down, Kitty," Anthony protested. "Suppose you tell me what's got you up in the boughs." So much for not involving himself in his sister's affairs. He had a notion he was about to hear all about them.

"How could he?" Kitty raged. "I've never been so humiliated in my life."

"Are you telling me that Walter is having a . . . liaison . . . with Lady Morrison? Walter?" he asked incredulously. Kitty's husband, though not the most thrilling chap in the world, was thoroughly solid and had always appeared to adore his more dashing wife. "You're cracked. He worships you."

To his alarm, Kitty was on the verge of tears. Appalled at the idea of coping with feminine hysterics in a public place, Anthony hauled her off into a corner and prayed no one could see them. "Now," he said, throwing a brotherly arm around her shoulder, "what makes you think old Walter is playing you false?"

"Oh Anthony!" Kitty wailed. "I'm so unhappy.

Marabel used to be a good friend of mine, and her husband, Sir Francis, was Walter's favorite hunting crony. But then Francis died and now Walter likes her better than he likes me."

"I'm quite sure that's not true—"

"It is!" Kitty interrupted. "Walter goes to their house nearly every day, helping her with the lawyers and the estate."

"I don't see anything so bad in looking after a friend's widow."

"I told myself that, but it's been a year now, and surely she doesn't still need him. And it's not just that." Kitty's voice was fierce. "She likes all the things he does. Horses and riding and country things. She never wants to give parties or go to town or the other things I like and Walter hates. She never buys too many new gowns or refurbishes her drawing room. She and Walter are perfectly suited."

"If Walter objects to your level of expenditure," Anthony said coldly, "he should remember that your marriage portion was generous enough to support it. Not to mention that his own fortune is more than adequate." An idea struck him. "Walter hasn't been losing money, has he? Taken up gambling, or playing the exchange?"

"No, I'm sure he hasn't. But he got so angry with me when I recovered all the drawing room chairs in tapestry. But I had to. The straw-colored satin was hideous."

Anthony was beginning to get the idea. "How old was the satin?"

"Six months old. But truly, Anthony. It had to go. You'd have hated it."

He felt a twinge of sympathy for the man, having his drawing room turned upside down twice in a year. But it didn't seem enough to drive him into the arms of another woman. He could think of something that might, but his mind absolutely cringed at the notion of interrogating his sister about the intimacies of her marriage.

"I'll tell you one thing, Kitty. Walter said he'd brought Lady Morrison to stay in your house. A gentleman would never bring his mistress under the same roof as his wife."

"What does it matter?" Kitty said despondently. "Even if she's not his mistress, he wishes she was and that's just as bad. He doesn't love me anymore and it's all my fault."

"Why don't you talk to him about it? Ask him."

Kitty threw him a look of scorn that reassured him that at least her spirits weren't totally depressed. "A lot of good that would do. Whatever his feelings for Marabel, he'd just tell me not to be silly and I'd be no farther forward."

Anthony couldn't argue with that. It was exactly what he'd do under the circumstances. Without a clue how to help his sister he felt useless. "What would you like me to do?" he asked.

"Why, nothing," Kitty replied in surprise. "There's nothing you can do. But thank you for listening to me. I feel a little better."

No question. Women were completely incomprehensible.

"Now," she said, straightening her back, "there's someone I'd like to speak to here. Will you escort me, please?"

The surprise of being accosted by Lady Kitty Thornley was nothing to the shock of seeing Storrington. Despite the crush, Jacobin couldn't believe she hadn't been aware of his presence. A glow of pleasure warmed her body at the realization that he could see her in the beautiful rose dress.

The beautiful dress that had been made for his sister. Who was standing in front of her.

"Miss Castle," Lady Kitty said graciously. "When I saw you I had to come and congratulate you on the splendid dishes you made for last night's dinner. The sugar basket of eggs was a sensation, and I'd like to get the recipe for your pastry tower for my own cook."

Jacobin acknowledged the compliment gracefully. Perhaps Lady Kitty hadn't recognized the gown.

"And may I say," Lady Kitty continued, "that you look wonderful in that gown. I remember it well. I loved the color so much but my strict aunt wouldn't let me wear it."

Jacobin could sense Storrington's stir of interest at this exchange. Darting a sideways glance at him, she saw him examining the garment with intensity, or more specifically the area of her chest that was left exposed by it. *Mon Dieu*, she loved to look at him. And the expression on his perfect face made her feel hot down to the tips of her toes. She wished she owned a fan.

"Would Your Ladyship like it back now?" Jacobin asked, wrenching her attention back to Lady Kitty. Lucy would be disappointed but she felt she had to offer.

"Lord, no! I gave it to Lucy. Besides," she added with an air of mischief. "I had a dozen such made up just as soon as I was married and away from my aunt."

"I'm very grateful, my lady," said Jacobin, "to have the chance to wear such a beautiful garment."

"There is something you could do for me. A favor."

"Anything, my lady." Jacobin wondered what on earth this elegant creature could want from her.

"When you return to Storrington, would you go and visit Nurse Bell and take her a treat. She was always fond of sweets."

"Nurse Bell?"

"Yes, our old nurse. She lives in a cottage on the estate."

"I'd be delighted. Is there some confection she particularly enjoys?"

"Chocolate cake, perhaps. She was always fond of chocolate, wasn't she, Anthony?" Lady Kitty turned to her brother, whose face had become an expressionless mask.

"I don't remember," he said curtly. "If you say Nurse Bell enjoys chocolate you're no doubt correct."

Really, Jacobin thought, what was there about chocolate cake to put the man in a taking? When it came to *pâtisserie* there was no pleasing him.

Chapter 14

Anthony hoped Lord Hugo Hartley could provide the final piece in the puzzle. Considering he'd waited for months for an audience with the old gentleman, his mind should have been fully occupied with the coming interview. But all Anthony could think about was a certain pastry cook and how enticing she'd looked in that cast-off gown of Kitty's. And how she'd look even better out of it. And how unfair it was that his sense of honor wouldn't let him compete for her charms against that stunted stranger she'd met at the Argyll Rooms.

Well! He'd queered his game, at least. Jane Castle was in his baggage coach on her way back to Storrington and unable to respond to the advances of any dubious suitors who might present themselves. And, since he wasn't there to save her from the consequences of her own folly, hopefully unable to embark on any more harebrained adventures. He wasn't certain whether, in the feudal past, earls had the right to lock up their servants, but it sounded like a practice worth reviving.

A butler admitted him to the narrow-fronted brick house in Bruton Street and showed him upstairs to a beautifully furnished sitting room. Though he was anxious to greet his host, it was a pleasure to wait in surroundings appointed by a man famous for taste and acuity in the acquisition of objects of art. Lord Hugo came in as Anthony admired an exquisite side table inlaid with several different woods.

He didn't know Lord Hugo well, but had easily recognized him in a Gainsborough portrait hanging over the fireplace. The tall, slender figure was unchanged, though now clad in the austere fashion of the day rather than the flamboyant pink satin of the portrait. Instead of powdered hair worn long and held back in a queue, the old man sported a fashionable crop, still thick and now naturally white. Dark eyes had lost their youthful brilliance but the aquiline nose was unmistakable. He walked carefully into the room, posture erect but maintained with the help of an ebony cane chased with silver. A manservant hovered at his elbow, but let his master make his own way to a wing chair, only offering an arm as the frail old man lowered himself into the seat. An attempt to place a rug over ancient knees was waved aside with the graceful sweep of a hand as pale and crumpled as old parchment.

"May I offer you something to drink, Lord Storrington? A glass of Burgundy, perhaps. Or tea." His light baritone voice was steady and imbued with a timbre of aristocratic courtesy that spoke of centuries of civility. Anthony had the feeling that he was in the presence of the epitome of noblesse oblige. He refused refreshment, and the servant withdrew.

"I'm sorry to have kept you waiting so long for this call," Lord Hugo said. "As one nears one's eightieth birthday one tends to suffer from troublesome ailments." He placed one long-fingered hand over the other on his knees and examined his visitor's face with a still-keen gaze. "I'm sure I'm not the first to have remarked on your extraordinary resemblance to your mother."

Anthony bowed his assent from his seat a few feet away. There was something about Lord Hugo that made him instinctively mimic the older man's courtly gravity. "Not the first, Lord Hugo. Did you know her well? As you know, I wish to ask you about my parents."

"I was well acquainted with her," Lord Hugo replied thoughtfully, "for a number of years. But she was not, I believe, a lady anyone knew well. Despite her famous charm and vivacity there was always a reserve in her bearing that precluded intimate friendship. And something beneath her gaiety, an undercurrent of darkness." Anthony was fascinated. Not one of his mother's contemporaries had described her manners as anything but open and confiding. Before her withdrawal from society. Before Paris.

"When Catherine made her appearance she dazzled everyone," Lord Hugo continued. "She could have married anyone. There were at least two dukes at her feet, but she settled on your father. A sensible choice, I think. Your father was a solid man, reliable and kind. One wouldn't have expected a young girl to have shown such good judgment."

Lord Hugo would have been in a position to assess his mother's suitors. A boyhood friend of the king, whose exact contemporary he was, he had been a fixture in London society since the beginning of George III's reign.

"Do you think she loved him?" Anthony asked. He was hesitant to speak of such intimate matters, but something about Lord Hugo's air of kindly understanding invited frankness. He suspected the old gentleman had been the recipient of many confidences over the years. Who knew what secrets lay sheltered behind those perceptive eyes?

"It was my observation that there was great affection between the two of them," Hartley replied, "but I would also have to say that Storrington's sentiments exceeded hers. There were hidden depths there, but any profound ardor—and I'm by no means certain it existed—was not directed toward her husband."

Poor Papa, Anthony thought. It was just as he'd always thought. But one thing he was certain of was that his mother had loved *him*, and without reserve, until she changed. After Paris.

Taking a deep breath, he broached the reason for his visit. "I want to ask you about Paris in 1786. My father took my mother there for a holiday, to celebrate my sister's birth. He spoke to me of it on his deathbed, and I've been attempting to find out what I can about their time there."

"Ah, Paris! I spent the spring there that year, the last time I was there. Such wonderful times. We were quite oblivious of the tragedy to come. I suppose a less shallow man than I would have been aware of the troubles in France, but I only saw the beauty, the gaiety, the elegance of the French court." Lord Hugo's eyes regained some of their youthful glint. "To us stuffy English, Paris was an enchanted island of wit and liberality."

"Do you think my mother found it so?"

"I don't recall her behaving with any less than her usual animation. The queen took a fancy to her, I remember. Dear Marie Antoinette. Such a charming, vivacious woman. And unlike so many, she appreciated the same qualities in others of her own sex. She invited your parents to the Petit Trianon—a great honor."

"My mother spoke of that visit. It was important to her."

"I was there too. It was a magical day. We toured the queen's little hamlet. An absurd conceit but a delightful place. The farm animals were kept at sufficient distance to remain picturesque." Lord Hugo wrinkled his nose in a gesture of distaste, and Anthony recalled that he was relentlessly urban in his habits. Rumor had it that he hadn't stepped out of the bounds of Mayfair and St. James in twenty years.

Enjoyably evocative as these recollections were, Anthony steered the subject back to his own investigation. "Were there many other English in Paris that year?"

"There were always English in Paris."

"Do you remember who was there at the same time

as my parents?" Anthony waited on tenterhooks for details that would confirm or deny Candover's guilt.

Lord Hugo sighed happily and settled into reminiscence. "The Duke of Dorset was ambassador then. Let me try and recall the parties at the embassy. There were always a few sprigs of nobility stopping by during their grand tours." He rattled off a few names.

"What about Chauncey Bellamy?" Anthony asked, on the chance that Lord Hugo might have some knowledge that would help Jane Castle. He wasn't the only one with something to investigate.

"Bellamy?" For a moment a slightly wary look crossed Hartley's features but then they relaxed into benign indifference. "I'm not sure if I recall him there. He must have been very young."

"He was," Anthony pursued, "and making the tour. He dined with me recently and told me he'd been in Paris briefly."

"Then no doubt he was," the other said. "I may even have met him there but I don't recall."

Anthony had the impression his host wasn't being frank with him about Bellamy. And the most obvious reason for such discretion seemed incredible.

For Lord Hugo, despite his impregnable position in society by reason of his birth and personal charm, was widely suspected of a preference for his own sex. Not that anyone ever mentioned the fact. To accuse someone out loud of a capital offense would be insufferably gauche. Yet somehow Anthony had always known that Hartley preferred the company of other men. He supposed at some time in the past someone had referred to the matter obliquely and it had settled into his consciousness. Lord Hugo had never been the subject of a tittle of scandal. His tastes were just a fact that everyone knew and nobody spoke of. Everyone except King George III, he amended mentally. The family-minded king was ardently opposed to toleration of any kind of sexual irregularity.

The notion that the preposterously dull and respectable Chauncey Bellamy might share Lord Hugo's tendencies was an idea he set aside for later consideration. Now he had an important question to pose.

"What about Candover?" he asked, not letting his tone reveal how deep was his interest in the answer. "Did you know him in Paris?"

"Candover." Lord Hugo's voice expressed mild distaste. "Yes, he was there."

"What was he like then?"

"Quite an attractive man, not that you'd know it to see him now. He's let his looks go completely in the last twenty years." The disapproval in his voice was now undisguised. "He had charm enough, I suppose. But he was always a tiresome character with a habit of poking his nose where it was none of his business to be."

"Why was he in Paris?" Anthony asked casually. "Was his visit purely for enjoyment?"

"He was trying to marry off his sister. Succeeded too, though he had to sweeten the pot to get de Chastelux to accept her. Rather a poor creature Felicity Candover, but once she set eyes on Auguste de Chastelux she had to have him, and she managed it too, with her brother's help. Now there was a beautiful man."

Anthony wasn't much interested in Candover's brother-in-law, but he courteously allowed the old gentleman to continue.

"Auguste was of excellent family but without a sou to his name. He had to marry money. The French always do, of course, but for Auguste it was essential. I don't think I've ever met a man whose wit and intelligence matched his looks to such an extraordinary degree. Marie Antoinette adored him, despite his revolutionary sympathies. He was there, with the Candovers, that day at the Trianon. They must have been invited for his sake."

"So my parents met Candover that day," Anthony interjected. It was the first concrete confirmation that his mother and Candover had met in Paris.

"Yes. I seem to recall that Candover was one of Catherine's court. I doubt she found him impressive."

Anthony smiled grimly. Despite sixty years observing society, Lord Hugo wasn't infallible.

"It's an odd thing," Lord Hugo continued, clinging to his previous train of thought, "but I was thinking about Auguste just the other day. Lieven was here and told me he'd seen a cook at the Pavilion who was the very image of de Chastelux. Said that cleft chin was unmistakable."

Chapter 15

Small Chocolate Cakes

When cold fill with pastry cream, mixed with two ounces of chocolate, prepared with vanilla. Then put three ounces of fine sugar, with three ounces of chocolate, and half of the white of an egg in a small tureen. Stir this for some minutes with a silver spoon, and then cover the tops and sides of the cakes with it, leveling it at the same time with the blade of a knife.

Antonin Carême

*S*he's a beauty. Looks like her father. He was the handsomest man in France.

At the time Anthony hadn't paid much attention to the words Candover used to persuade him to accept the wager. He hadn't been interested in Candover's niece, or her appearance. He'd been consumed by his own vengeful rage.

Lord Hugo's courtly accents formed a low hum in the background of his tumultuous thoughts. "Lieven wondered if he could have been a by-blow, though I don't remember that Auguste was much of a womanizer. Too obsessed with politics. But Lieven said this boy could have been Auguste returned to life."

Anthony felt like he'd been punched in the gut.

Surely it was too much of a coincidence. But perhaps not. Given Candover's employment of a French pastry cook and his niece's affair with the cook, it made sense that the niece would end up working for Carême. Hadn't she said she'd been taught by a pupil of the famous Frenchman? No doubt that detail of her story was true.

Anthony never afterward remembered how he dredged up the good manners to take leave of Lord Hugo. He could only hope he'd said everything proper. Neither was he aware of the short journey home. He sped into the library; pulled his file of information on Candover from a desk drawer; shuffled through the papers detailing Candover's personal and financial affairs. Here it was.

Felicity Candover, married in Paris in 1786 to Auguste de Chastelux, who died in 1804. Felicity died in England in 1805. One daughter, born 1793, Jacobin Léonie de Chastelux.

Jacob Léon. Jane Castle.

She wasn't called Jane. He was glad. She'd never seemed like a Jane to him. Jacobin suited her much better: uncommon, even a little exotic, an old English name with intriguing overtones of French revolutionary fervor. He had no difficulty thinking of her as Jacobin. The name settled into his consciousness.

No wonder she'd run away from the Brighton Pavilion. If the runners discovered her relationship to Candover they'd be after her like a pack of hungry wolves. His brain shied away from the fact that they might be justified in doing so.

It was *she* he'd won in that infamous piquet game. Unconsciously ashamed of the impulse that had made him accept Candover's terms, he'd scarcely considered the young woman who'd been used as a gaming piece. Now he faced the cold heartlessness of the wager and tried to imagine Jacobin's feelings when she learned her person had been offered as a stake, to be turned over as the sexual plaything of a stranger.

You can do whatever you like with her. Have her as your mistress. Anthony remembered Candover's callous words. He wasn't surprised Jacobin had flown the coop. The woman he'd come to know had too much spirit to accede to such treatment. He was glad for her sake that she had the French cook to escape with. He wondered what had happened to the man, her lover; why he'd left her.

If he had Jacobin in his bed he wouldn't willingly abandon her. The kisses they'd shared told him she'd be a mistress of uncommon passion.

A surge of triumph made his head buzz and his body itch with anticipation. She wasn't an untouchable member of the servant class. She wasn't a respectable unmarried lady. There was nothing to stop him having her.

"Lady Kitty has always been so thoughtful, always remembers me at Christmas."

Jacobin was settled by a blazing fire in Nurse Bell's cozy little cottage. The old woman was the very picture of what Jacobin imagined an English nurse to be: white-haired and apple-cheeked, with a sweet smile and just a touch of acid on her tongue. A woman who wouldn't have taken any nonsense from her charges.

She poured Jacobin a cup of tea and handed her the plate of chocolate cakes. With nothing to do in the Storrington Hall kitchen as long as its master was absent, Jacobin had remembered Lady Kitty's commission and tracked down her old nurse with the promised treats. It gave her something to do besides worry about the Bow Street runners, wonder about Chauncey Bellamy, and try not to think about her employer and his disturbing kisses.

"I'm sure she calls on you too," Jacobin said, "when she is visiting her brother."

Nurse Bell pursed her lips. "Which isn't often. Not often enough to my way of thinking. Lady Kitty and Lord Storrs—His Lordship I should say now—were never close."

"How odd," Jacobin remarked. "Lady Kitty seems

such a charming woman. How could anyone dislike her?"

"It goes back to when they were children and their mother's illness. Do you know about that?"

"I know she died in an accident, that's all. Was she unwell for a long time?"

"It was a strange illness. His Lordship was five when Lady Kitty was born. Their poor mother, she'd lost two in pregnancy in between and had a difficult time."

"It's a sad thing." Jacobin nodded wisely. "My mother too lost a child. I was the only one that lived."

"After Lady Kitty's birth Her Ladyship was a little down—I wasn't here then but so I was told. His Lordship, the old lord," the nurse continued, "took his wife to Paris to cheer her up. But it wasn't a success. When she came home she went into a deep melancholy and never recovered."

"When I first met Lord Storrington he told me he'd lost his mother when he was five. I was surprised to learn she'd lived much longer."

"Poor little boy, he didn't know what to make of it. Suddenly his mother had no time for him whilst before, I hear, she doted on him, lavished him with love and attention."

"And Lady Kitty was just an infant," Jacobin prompted. "He must have connected his mother's withdrawal with her arrival."

The older woman nodded. "Something else happened too, the reason I came to Storrington. Nurse Taylor was in charge of the nursery then. Then one day, just after she came back from France, Her Ladyship turned her off, just like that. No reason that I ever heard to believe Taylor wasn't a good nurse. So the poor boy lost his nurse just when his mother was behaving so strangely. I never met such a bewildered child as I found when I came to take up the post."

"I'm sure you were a loving nurse too."

"I did my best but he was hard to console. Didn't want to have anything to do with me at first." She sighed. "I was busy with the baby and couldn't give him all my attention. It'll always be on my conscience that I didn't do enough for him, when he'd been abandoned by his mother and his nurse, both."

"So he always resented Lady Kitty?"

"I'm afraid so. Not that he was unkind to her, mind you. He was always a good boy. But he never warmed up to her like a brother should."

"Perhaps he didn't like her because she was a girl," Jacobin suggested. "Me, I don't know much about brothers, or sisters either, but I've heard little boys don't think much of females."

"That comes later," replied Nurse Bell with a hint of an impish grin. "And I daresay you're right and that was part of it. He doted on Master James as soon as he came along and the brothers have always been close." She smiled more broadly. "Master James was always a charmer. Lady Kitty loved him too, and his father."

"And all this time their mother was—how did you put it?—melancholy?"

"Always! Another seven or eight years it was before she died and never a happy day, hardly a smile on her face. His Lordship tried everything to cheer her, buying her gifts, building that farmhouse in the grounds just like the French queen had, but she scarcely noticed it. Just sat in her rooms, day after day, staring out of the window."

"And she paid no attention to her children?"

"It might have been better that way. But sometimes she seemed to get better and she'd come and take them from the nursery, especially Lord Storrs. She'd take him out to play in the garden, or on a picnic, and he'd be happy as a lark. But it didn't last. Just as suddenly as she'd cheered up, she'd fall back into gloom and she'd push the boy away from her and send him back to me. I used to dread those moments because he'd be so upset. Those were the times I had trouble with him."

"What about his father? Was he good to the children?"

"Well, you know gentlemen. They don't concern themselves much with nursery business."

Jacobin didn't know. Her own father had indulged her completely. He had supervised her education himself and taken her everywhere with him. As a small child she attended the salons of revolutionary Paris, playing on the drawing floors of Mesdames Récamier and de Staël, even of Josephine Bonaparte, as the politics of the Directoire and later the Consulat were debated. She'd sat on Talleyrand's lap and played cards with the young Beauharnais, Josephine's children.

Life in the Storrington nursery, as portrayed by Nurse Bell, sounded like a foreign country, and a cold one.

She was coming back through the park and crossing the bridge close to the little hamlet when she saw Lord Storrington walking on the other side of the small lake. Instead of ignoring her, as she half expected, he waved.

"I've been looking for you," he said as they drew closer. "You never seem to be in the kitchen."

"I have time off for exercise according to the terms of my contract," she said coolly. "And I didn't know I was needed. I wasn't even aware you'd returned from London." She dropped a belated curtsy. "My lord."

He removed his hat and added to the disorder of his windswept coiffure by running a hand through his locks. Unexpectedly he smiled, and looked devastatingly handsome. A lurching sensation disturbed her insides.

"There's no need to be touchy," he said, still smiling. "I asked for you and they told me you'd left on an errand."

"Yes, I was taking some cakes to Nurse Bell at Lady Kitty's request."

"That's right, I remember." He didn't ask after the old woman. "I need to speak to you."

Jacobin shrugged. "We're speaking."

"Not here. It's too cold. Come into the Queen's House."

A nasty wind bit through her cloak in the dull late afternoon light. She was glad to follow his gesture and precede him through the rustic door of the folly. He'd removed a key from his pocket to unlock it. She wondered if he always carried it with him or whether he'd planned to enter the building, which gave no sign of recent occupation: the furnishings were covered with sheets, the surfaces dusty, and the atmosphere damp with neglect. The house was small, much smaller than the original at Versailles. The ground floor appeared to consist of not much more than one large room.

He swept away a dust sheet to reveal a gilt canopy sofa in the Louis XVI style, upholstered in pale blue satin.

"Do sit down, please," he said, then frowned. "Maybe we should light the fire." He looked at her in such a way that when he said *we*, he really meant that she, Jacobin, should attend to the matter.

If there was one thing Jacobin had learned in years in the servants' hall, it was that sensible servants don't do other people's work. It was the path to neither reward nor respect. She knew her place and didn't intend to budge from it. Cooks didn't light fires.

She ignored his unspoken suggestion and, though he raised his eyebrows a trifle, he seemed to accept that if anyone was going to make this place warm it would have to be he. Dry wood and some crumbly-looking kindling were stacked next to the fireplace. He piled a few logs on the grate, balanced sticks of kindling on top, and set the tinder to them. Flames flared up, casting a welcome glow in the dusky room. Storrington held out his hands toward the warmth.

From her perch on the sofa Jacobin watched and waited, suppressing her grin. Poor man, it wouldn't do to show her amusement. As the flames faded away he looked adorably puzzled, then prodded the sorry structure with a poker.

She took pity on him. It wasn't his fault he'd been raised in a position of privilege. "Let me do it," she said. "The kindling needs to go underneath." Soon the dry wood was blazing and began to dispel the frigidity of the room.

"Why did you wish to speak to me?" she asked. He settled beside her on the blue sofa. She was acutely conscious of his tall frame, of the faint scent of soap or toilet water cutting through an outdoors smell, of his muscular thighs, displayed when his great coat fell open, just a few inches from her own. She found his proximity both thrilling and disturbing.

"Do you have any news of Mr. Bellamy?" she asked, clenching her knees to put some distance between them without making the movement obvious. "I believe those were his daughters you were squiring at the Argyll Rooms. Are you going to marry one of them? If so, I'm afraid you won't want to pin a crime on their father."

Who was to say he didn't like them young, foolish, and uppity? She fully expected one of his haughty setdowns at this piece of impertinence. Instead she was rewarded with a smile that made her heart thump.

"Daughter and niece, actually," he corrected. "And yes, I did manage to find out that Bellamy was in London the night of Candover's poisoning."

"Oh," Jacobin said in disappointment.

"Not that it's worth much," Storrington continued. "It would take a more thorough investigation to see if he had a chance to make the journey to Brighton and back in the course of the day. And there are always hirelings to undertake unpleasant tasks."

"Like murder, you mean?"

"Like murder."

"Thank you." Jacobin turned to him impulsively and laid a hand over his larger one, which was resting on his thigh. "Thank you for not dismissing my idea completely."

"I might have," Storrington admitted, "but by chance I found out something else about Bellamy. Or got a hint, at least. A hint of something so embarrassing that I can easily see him open to blackmail."

"*Mon Dieu*, what?" she asked in rising excitement.

He seemed loath to continue and hemmed and hawed for a moment or two before picking his words carefully.

"Something someone said to me indicated, perhaps, that it's just possible that Bellamy might—how can I put this?—not much care for women."

Jacobin, ready to wriggle with frustration during this mealymouthed recitation, nodded knowingly. "A molly, yes?"

"You know about such things?" he asked in surprise.

"Of course. The night you helped me in Brighton. Those men who were attacking me—that's what they thought I was. Who told you Bellamy was like that?"

"An acquaintance. And as I said, it was just a hint. But I will look further into both matters."

On one level Anthony was attending to the conversation about Bellamy. On another he throbbed with awareness of her proximity.

He didn't want to think about Lord Hugo now, and his other revelation. He didn't want to think about Jacobin's identity in case he revealed that he knew it. What he wanted to think about was the woman at his side. Her hand was sending waves of heat through his own to his thigh, heat that suffused his body and filled him with ideas about leading her to the bedroom upstairs. It would be cold but he'd soon warm them up.

She gazed up at him, her eyes glowing with gratitude. "Thank you. Oh, thank you," she repeated.

Time to make his move, now she was so pleased with him. He lowered his head and brushed his lips across hers.

"Oh," she murmured, but she didn't withdraw. He leaned closer, covering her slightly open mouth with his own, and breathed in soft warmth. Before he could go further she pulled back, though her hand remained on his.

"This is not proper, my lord." But her husky voice belied the statement, or at least suggested that impropriety wasn't troubling her overmuch.

He put his arms around her, drew her close, and kissed her thoroughly.

It was an excellent kiss. Jacobin's kisses were like her cooking: sweet, intriguingly textured, subtly flavored.

But he wanted more. He ached to touch every inch of her, to taste warm skin he knew would be as lush and silken as cream. He pushed aside her cloak and found her breast. Even through her sturdy gown he could feel it tightening, straining for his touch. He heard himself moan with desire.

Her arms were now about his neck and she was kissing him back with her warm mouth and lissome tongue. Then she stopped and drew back a couple of inches.

"I am a servant," she whispered. "There can be nothing between us. We have to stop."

He leaned against the back of the sofa and pulled her close. His chest heaved with exertion or excitement, and her head, resting against his upper body, reflected the movement.

"I want you," he said. "So much. I want you as my mistress. And I think perhaps you want me too." A nipple, pressing through God knew how many layers of cloth, was communicating with his caressing fingers.

"I do," she admitted in a small voice. "But I'm not sure I want to be a mistress. What does it mean?"

He couldn't help laughing.

"Not that," she said, raising her head and pummeling his arm with a playful fist. "I know it means I would share your bed. But what else does it mean? Would I still work as your cook?"

"If you wanted. Perhaps you'd like to cook just for me. Little puffy things," he whispered into her ear, running his tongue around the tender whorls for good measure. He rather thought she was purring. "I'd find you a house in London, perhaps one on the estate too. You'd have clothes, jewels, a carriage, anything you wanted. I'm quite rich, you know."

She frowned. What did she want? Whatever it was, he was ready to offer it, and more.

"I'd make sure you had enough money to take care of yourself if we parted. And I'd take care of any children, make sure they were educated and provided for."

She was now definitely unhappy. "I don't think I'd like to have children like that," she said. "They'd be bastards, and that's not nice for children."

"There are ways of ensuring that there are no children."

"Really? I had no idea!" She was more naïve than he'd thought. She'd been lucky to have avoided pregnancy with her precious lover, the cook.

He didn't want to think about the damn cook.

"Please," he whispered, inhaling the faint scent of vanilla that always hung about her. "Please, J-Jane, I'll make it good for you, I swear."

She felt herself weakening, succumbing to the promise of his warm breath, his hand stroking her breast, the melting heat between her legs.

"What if I say no?" she asked, desperately. "Will you throw me out?"

"Never. If this happens between us, it will be because we both want it. If you say no, you can go on as you were before, cooking those delicious confections."

"Which you appreciate so much." The attempt at humor came reflexively. Her mind dwelt on the clean, masculine scent of him and the weight of his hand sending shivers through her belly and his soft hair tickling her temple.

"I'm appreciating them more every day." His voice was dark and velvety against her ear. Irresistible.

"And you'd still help me find the one who poisoned Lord Candover?"

"Of course. I gave my word."

She wanted to say yes. Every instinct urged her to trust him. Yet she tried to be wise, to think the matter through. For once in her life not to act on impulse. Resting her cheek against the lapel of his coat didn't help. His nearness flooded every sense, driving out rational thought.

She was going to say no. He was astonished at the dread and anxiety he experienced as he anticipated her response. He didn't believe he'd ever desired a woman as much. She twisted her neck to examine his face, her eyes big with apprehension. After a moment or two their expression softened, sending a rush of heat to his chest.

"You'd make sure there is no child?"

"I promise."

Why not? she asked herself. What—or who—was she saving herself for? She could never now make the alliance her parents would have planned for her. Who would want a lady who'd disguised herself as a man and earned her living as a cook? Though untouched, she was already ruined in the eyes of decent society. There was no place for her there. She'd long ago faced the fact that life wasn't fair.

And she suspected making love with Lord Storrington would be the most exciting, pleasurable thing that had ever happened to her.

She took a deep breath.

"Very well, I will share your bed. As for the rest? The houses, the clothes, and such, we shall see."

He gave a little grunt of triumph and swept her into his embrace. Quickly she found herself on her back and his hands were meshed in her hair, holding her head still as he ravished her mouth with kisses. Giddy with pleasure, she met his tongue thrust for thrust with her own, reveling in his taste, his scent, and the weight of his body on hers. Burrowing through his heavy topcoat and jacket she pushed her arms around him, sensing his racing heartbeat even through his winter waistcoat. She ached to feel his firm-muscled flesh through skin and nothing else.

And soon she would. She gave herself up to the heady moment and the promise of even better things.

Whoever had made the sofa—for King Louis himself or a member of his court—had designed it for sitting. Storrington cursed softly when, wrestling to remove her cloak, his elbow banged against the ornate carved wood of the backrest. Jacobin became aware that this was no feather bed.

He rolled off her and perched on the edge of the seat beside her recumbent body.

"This is a damn uncomfortable piece of furniture."

She giggled. "So what do we do now?"

"I'm tempted to take you upstairs straightaway," he said. "There's a bedroom. But it'll be cold and this place is depressing." He looked with disfavor at the neglected room.

"I think it's beautiful," she demurred. "It just needs to be cleaned. But perhaps it reminds you of your mother, since it was her retreat."

"No. She hardly ever came here." He laughed without humor. "My father spent a fortune on it, and on the furnishings, all valuable French pieces, because he thought it'd make her happy, but she didn't care."

She'd pulled herself up and sat next to him again, companionably curling her arm round his. "It seems such a waste."

"It is a waste," he said suddenly, smiling down at her. "And if you like it then let's make use of it. I'll have it cleaned up and we can use it. It wouldn't do for us to meet at the house, anyway. While you're still employed here we don't want the other servants to know of our liaison. It would be difficult for you."

He was right, she realized. The Simpsons, butler and cook, were hostile enough, and the rest of the staff took their cue from them. She shied away from the word he'd used: *liaison*. Somehow it sounded tawdry.

"We'll have supper here tomorrow." His face was now alive with enthusiasm, making him seem younger and infinitely attractive and terrifyingly dear. "Go to the gatehouse and I'll send a carriage for you. Only Jem will know, and you can trust him to keep his mouth shut."

"You're sure you don't want to just run upstairs in the cold?" Jacobin asked. To her amazement she now felt enough at ease with the situation to be saucy.

Hands on her shoulders he kissed her, close-mouthed but with a promise of greater pleasures. "Anticipation heightens the appetite. As a cook you should know that."

Chapter 16

Souper à Deux: Menu

Turtle soup
Cold pheasant in a white sauce
Lobster mayonnaise with asparagus
Braised mushrooms
Potatoes à la lyonnaise

However often she looked at her two shabby gowns, neither became remotely suitable for a romantic tryst. What was she going to wear?

As she examined her meager wardrobe, Jacobin's mood approached panic. Her stomach fluttered with nerves and growled with hunger. She'd hardly eaten a bite at the servants' dinner, too keyed up to fancy the plain but hearty fare served in the servants' hall. Besides, she'd be eating later.

The kitchen buzzed with the news that His Lordship was taking supper at the Queen's House; he'd never done such a thing before. The cleaning staff had been run off their feet and complained vociferously about the work they'd had putting the place in order in a single day. Equally extensive was the speculation about who would be joining him there. The scarcely veiled innuendos of the male staff were enough to make Jacobin profoundly grateful that her participation in tonight's entertainment was a secret.

She knew the menu for the evening. And then there was dessert. Jacobin had been busy that afternoon. His Lordship had made a special request. And then . . .

Afraid her courage would fail her, she tried not to think too much about afterward. She preferred to think about lobster, which a groom had been dispatched to the coast to fetch. She hadn't tasted it in years. Such delicacies were reserved for the master of the house at Hurst Park.

She kept telling herself that she wanted what would happen tonight. That it was her own decision, freely made, to give herself like this. Yet it was far from the romantic—and post-nuptial—bedding of her youthful dreams. How shocked her mother would be. She'd always wanted Jacobin to be a proper English lady. Well, she thought defiantly, if her mother hadn't wanted her to become a mistress—hateful word—then she shouldn't have died and left her to the untender mercies of her abysmal brother. Her father would have understood her decision. He never cast judgment on others.

And she was going to enjoy *it*. From everything she'd

heard about *the act* from the servants' gossip at Hurst, it
was most agreeable once you got used to it. She wouldn't
think about the maids' horror stories about blood and
pain the first time. Old wives' tales, no doubt.

By the time the discreet Jem Webster deposited her at
the door of the Queen's House she was on the verge of
bolting. Then Storrington greeted her at the door, and
she remembered why she'd said yes. Her heart pounded
in a way she hadn't experienced since her sixteen-year-
old self had first set eyes on Jean-Luc. And even the
handsome Frenchman had never looked as gorgeous as
Storrington in black trousers, a cream silk waistcoat
figured in silver, and an evening coat of dusty burgundy
that seemed to intensify the subterranean gray of his
eyes. Eyes that were gazing at her in unalloyed admiration, despite her tatty cloak.

With a brave flourish she untied the strings and
swung it off to reveal her best clothes.

Anthony's eyes nearly popped out of his head. She
wore her breeches and a linen shirt and tall shiny
boots and looked good enough to eat. Luckily women
weren't in the habit of dressing thus—at least women
built like her. They'd never manage to cross the street
unravished.

"I don't own a gown suitable for the occasion," she
said with an air of defiance.

His mouth felt dry. "It's entirely suitable." It was
too gauche—or too early—to admit that what he really
wanted was to get her out of that costume as soon as
possible and discover if the feminine reality underneath

matched the promise of those figure-hugging masculine garments. Not that he had much doubt. Always partial to long slim legs on a woman, he discovered that male attire revealed their existence without having to wait and get under her skirts.

"I have something for you that will enhance this delightful fashion." He opened a box on a side table and picked up the result of a quick expedition to Rundell and Bridge, his last stop before he left London. A much more expensive one than any he'd made before. Confident, he awaited her reaction to the impressive diamond and emerald necklace. And was disappointed.

True, her eyes glinted for a moment, then faded to uncertainty.

"I don't believe this is *comme il faut*." She'd never seen such beautiful jewels, but such a lavish present sat badly with her. She'd rather have had something modest, or nothing at all. It made her feel . . . bought. A hint of arrogance in his stance as he held the necklace up irked her.

"Everything is *comme il faut* between lovers." Now his expression held nothing but warm admiration and even a tinge of anxiety. His low voice sent shivers down her spine. "I saw it and it made me think of you. So beautiful, and so much fire."

She was softening but didn't want to let it go without giving him an intimation of her feelings. "You must have been very sure of me, to spend so much money."

"I wasn't sure," he said quietly. "I hoped."

He should have guessed she wouldn't react like the

average ladybird, who would have crowed with plea-sure and snatched up the opulent gift without more ado. Jacobin's unpredictability was no small part of her appeal. Her prickliness boosted his confidence in the decision not to reveal his knowledge of her identity. He knew she'd be furious if she found out, so he'd just have to make sure she didn't.

Not that he was entirely comfortable. He *ought* to tell her he knew she was Jacobin de Chastelux, not Jane Castle. But his motives were pure—in one sense of the word. He wanted her to come to him freely, without feeling she owed him her body for reasons of obliga-tion, gratitude, or any other emotion save desire. Once their relationship progressed, and she learned to trust him, she would no doubt tell him herself, and he'd feign decent surprise. So he ignored the niggling conscience that accused him of specious rationalization and listened to the part of him that wanted her badly. Immediately.

"Won't you try it on?" he asked, removing the neck-lace from its velvet nest. "Let me."

She turned and lifted her neat queue of hair, tied at the back with a black ribbon. Working the clasp he in-haled her scent, clean, warm, and slightly soapy with that faint hint of vanilla. Below her hairline light fuzz gave way to the slender arc of her neck. As he pressed his lips to her nape, he found the skin as silken to the touch as it looked. Taking her by the shoulders, he steered her to the gilt-framed mirror over the mantelpiece.

"Look," he murmured from behind. "Perfection. You could start a fashion."

The odd disparity between her beautiful face, set off by a small fortune in precious stones, and the masculine severity of her clothing was extraordinarily erotic. She stared at herself in the mirror, then at him, their eyes meeting in the glass. Her lips curved into a perfect bow. "Thank you. I should like to wear it tonight. It makes me feel more dressed."

"Shall we sup?" he asked, offering his arm and imagining her less dressed. Food first. They'd both need their strength for later. He led her over to a small table where supper was waiting.

"I sent Jem home and thought we'd serve ourselves. It'll be more enjoyable to be alone." He poured champagne for them both and asked her to serve the soup, which was keeping warm over a lamp.

He wondered what they should talk about. He'd noticed her looking with interest at the furnishings in the house. His father had spared no expense in finding pieces his wife might enjoy.

"Does this room make you think of home?" he asked. "All the furniture is French and some pieces are said to be of royal provenance. My father bought them at auction from French émigrés." He recounted the history of some of the objects in the room, then frowned.

"That piece." He pointed to a desk between two tall windows. "I don't know why it's here. My mother had it in her sitting room. My father must have had it moved here. Anyway, it was built by a cabinetmaker who worked for Queen Marie Antoinette."

"Very beautiful," she replied. "And much finer, of course, than anything my family owned."

He repressed a smile. Jacobin de Chastelux must know about such things. Or maybe not. She would have been born at the height of the revolutionary Terror, and he had no idea how such aristocrats as had survived Madame Guillotine lived. He'd be interested to ask her about it. Instead he had to pretend she was Jane Castle, a cook.

He couldn't bring himself to call her Jane. He needed a nickname, or perhaps an endearment.

"Sweetheart," he said, trying it on for size. "Darling." Better. "Could you give me some of that lobster?"

She raised her eyebrows as she handed him a plate.

"Don't you like such names?" he teased. "Would you prefer me to speak to you in French?"

"Your French isn't very good, is it?"

It was true, though he didn't particularly like being told as much. "What makes you think that?"

She started to gabble in very fast French, and he didn't understand a word of it.

"Very well, I admit it," he interrupted with a raised hand to stop the flow. "I neglected that portion of my studies. How did you know?"

"You misunderstood something I said to Count Lieven in the Pavilion kitchen."

"Really? What?"

"I don't recall now," she said evasively, flicking a speck of mayonnaise from the side of her mouth with her tongue.

Like hell she didn't. No doubt some detail about her fictitious career. "What did you say to me just now?"

"It's not important," she said shortly. "Why didn't you like learning French? Don't you like the French?"

He shrugged, which was answer enough, and sipped his wine. "I like *you* and that's what matters. Would you prefer me to address you by some French endearment? You'll have to teach me some."

She cocked her head with a naughty smile, and he wondered what was coming.

"*Ma biche, mon lapin, mon poulet, ma puce,*" she recited.

"I understand *mon poulet*—'my chicken,' isn't it? But not the others. What do they mean? *Biche* doesn't sound polite."

"It's just a female deer. A doe. Isn't that pretty?"

"*Ma biche,*" he repeated. "And the others?"

"*Un lapin* is a rabbit *and une puce* is a flea."

"A flea! That's not very romantic. Tell me some more."

"*Mon trésor. Mon coeur.*" He understood those ones and approved, especially when spoken with Jacobin's seductive inflection.

"*Ma mie,*" she purred. He watched, riveted, as she raised a spear of asparagus to her luscious mouth.

"What does that mean?" he asked hoarsely.

"The *mie* is the soft inside of a loaf of bread."

"You're quite strange, you French. Animals. A flea, for heaven's sake! And now an obscure culinary term. Appropriate for a cook, I suppose."

She piled a plate with pheasant and potatoes for him and didn't answer. Truth to tell, she felt skittish again. Ever since her arrival there'd been moments of awkwardness. For one thing, she was a little irked that he seemed to expect her to serve him all his food. In an intimate supper she'd have thought he could have shared the labor, instead of just keeping their glasses plied with champagne, the one task apparently not beneath his male aristocratic dignity. That last reference to her being a cook wounded her *amour propre*. Surely between lovers there should be nothing of the master/servant?

And there was his attitude toward the French. True, England had been at war with France for many years, but that was all over now. And they were sitting in a building modeled after a French house, filled with French furniture, drinking French champagne, and eating French food. Conveniently forgetting that she was half English, had lived in the country half her life, and spoke the language without a trace of an accent, that she'd loathed Napoleon and rejoiced in his downfall, Jacobin perversely decided that in disparaging the French he slighted her.

But what disturbed her most was an undercurrent of frustration that she was living a charade. Her disguised identity made for a fundamental dishonesty in their connection. Between lovers, even illicit lovers, there should be ease and openness. Instead she had to watch every word to maintain her mask.

Then he smiled at her, with affection surely, and

something else, something scorching hot that melted her dissatisfaction. Pushing aside his plate, he leaned across the table and took her hand.

"*Ma biche*—my deer—" he said, meeting her eyes in a sizzling exchange. "Shall we *remove* the *dessert* upstairs."

She loved the play on the English and French words for the course that was the last to be served before the end of the meal. How could she resist a witty man?

Chapter 17

It was a beautiful bed with a canopy of yellow satin swags, and curtains and counterpane in broad stripes of a rose satin and floral toile that reminded her of her mother's bedroom in Paris. Next to the bed, on a table, sat a dark blue and gold dish that looked like Sèvres, piled high with profiteroles in a pyramid. She'd wondered where they'd got to. He'd planned it, right down to the little puffy things.

The lighting was low, only a handful of candles, but not low enough that she—and he—wouldn't be clearly visible. Everything she'd ever heard led her to believe they'd be naked.

She swallowed, balancing sensations of terror and excitement. What was she doing with this imposing figure of masculine beauty who stood next to her, searing her with his gaze? The heat in his stormy-sea eyes, now devoid of any hauteur, set her heart thrumming. How could she, with her purely theoretical knowledge of lovemaking, hope to please him? The defiance that had brought her this far was seeping away, and an urge to run niggled the back of her mind.

"What would you like to do now?" she asked in what she hoped was a casual tone, too proud to let her intimidation show.

"Guess," he said wickedly, stripping off his coat and throwing it onto the floor in a way that would give his valet fits. He examined her meticulously, his gaze ranging from the tip of her head, lingering over her breasts in her linen shirt, scanning her breeches, and coming to rest on her riding boots, freshly polished that morning.

"I like the boots," he continued. "I'd like to see you in them, and nothing else."

That sounded positively depraved. And quite stirring.

"But for now, I think they should come off." Guiding her down to sit on the bed, he knelt before her and pulled one off.

"Silk stockings?" he asked with an appreciative twinkle, caressing her calf through the hose and shooting blissful tingles up her leg. "You are always surprising, my chicken."

Once he'd attended to the boots he shed his own footwear and his waistcoat, which joined his coat on the floor, and sat beside her on the bed. "Will you help me with my neck cloth, my rabbit?"

Apparently he found it tremendously amusing to go through the whole menagerie of endearments—in English. Actually, it was funny. The names she'd learned from her nurse sounded absurd, yet also touching, in prosaic Anglo-Saxon.

The starched linen cloth hit the floor. "Thank you, my flea."

Impulsively she pushed aside the plackets of his shirt to reveal his neck. It was beautiful, the sinews finely etched.

"Fleas bite." Acting on instinct, she leaned in and gave his flesh a sharp nip, just at the vee of his collarbone.

The effect was electrifying. In two seconds she was flat on her back being kissed breathless.

"You're a naughty little treasure," he said, mockingly stern, when he finally came up for air.

She liked this game. Besides, she didn't know what to call him. She didn't like to address him as Anthony, as his sister had, without invitation. And she wasn't going to "my lord" him when they were rolling around on a bed. It pleased her that he didn't call her Jane.

"I apologize, my bread crumb."

He gave her a look that told her he thought this riposte was feeble, as indeed it was, but they'd run out of animals. Anyway, she was too busy thinking about the fact that his fingers were at the buttons of her breeches, which he tugged off, along with her cotton drawers.

"More surprises," he said happily when he saw the rose satin garters tied just above her knees.

She'd anticipated this moment when she put them on, determined to make use of her only feminine adornments. Kneeling next to her, he ran his fingers over the satin ribbons, then bent to bestow a warm kiss on each inner thigh, just where the stockings gave way to sensitive skin. She twitched with alarm as his hair tickled her farther up, so close to her private place. Thankfully he didn't seem aware of her fright, perhaps because it was accompanied by a little sigh of pleasure.

She settled back against the pillows, now clad only in her knee-length shirt, stockings, and garters, while he stood to remove his clothing. Hers was an excellent vantage point to admire the well-defined musculature of his chest, lightly sprinkled with golden brown hair, and shapely calves, uncovered as shirt, stockings, and trousers were cast aside. But when his hands grasped the waistband of his drawers, she felt too shy to look and instead fixed her eyes on a painting that hung on the wall opposite the bed.

An ornate gilt frame surrounded a faux-pastoral confection showing a young girl in a simple rustic-style gown, which happened to be made of pink silk and trimmed with lashings of lace. She languished on a swing in a wild garden, featuring a profusion of flowers that Jacobin was reasonably sure never bloomed at the same time in any country she'd ever heard of. In one corner an equally well-dressed country lad peeped at the glimpse of ankle revealed by the maiden as she swung, one frivolous high-heeled slipper barely clinging to her toes.

"I think that must be a Boucher," she said, suddenly anxious for conversation to dispel her tension and forgetting that she was supposed to belong to a class that knew nothing of such frivolities.

His glance followed hers. "That picture? Silly, isn't it?"

"I think it's charming." She kept her eyes fixed on it, to avoid looking at an incredibly tall, lean, and utterly naked male body.

"I'm glad you like it." She heard the bed creak as he stretched out beside her. She continued to stare at the girl in the swing, but her mind was transfixed by what she couldn't help noticing out of the corner of her eye. That *it*, his male member, was erect and alarmingly large. She felt a big hand stroking her breast through her linen shirt and his teeth nipping gently at her ear. Both things felt so good that she relaxed a little.

"What's a *boucher*?" he asked. "I like it when you explain French to me. You're much prettier than any of my teachers."

"Boucher was the name of the painter, but it also means 'butcher.'" Now his tongue, warm and moist, was playing deep inside the ear, for some reason sensitizing every inch of her body and making her skin ache for his touch. "*Bouche* means 'mouth'" she babbled, shivering as his hand pushed under her garment and painted lazy whorls with his fingers over both breasts. "And *une bouchée* is a mouthful."

"Mmm." His *bouche* was too busy for coherent speech.

Conversation had failed to distract him, so she tried another tack. Reaching over to the plate next to the bed, she selected a profiterole and offered it to him, nudging him with her shoulder.

"Here. *Une bouchée pour toi.*"

"Feed me," he begged huskily, and took the whole

puff into his mouth along with her forefinger and thumb and sucked on them before letting them go and swallowing the airy confection. "Tell me, what did you think when I sent the message asking you to prepare little puffy things for tonight?"

"That it wasn't very polite to invite me to supper and then expect me to provide dessert."

His fingers were now teasing her nipples, creating blissful sensations there and lower down, between her thighs. "We'll both be providing dessert tonight." He withdrew his hand, eliciting a moue of protest.

"I think you're overdressed," he said, and rapidly she found herself as naked as he was, between the twinkling gems at her throat and the satin frivolities at her knees. Shy, she clenched her knees together, but he didn't seem to notice; his attention was fixed on her breasts.

"I wondered what color your nipples were," he said in a mesmerizing whisper. "Pink, like wild strawberries. And what are strawberries without cream?" And taking a profiterole he squeezed the little pastry and adorned the tips of her breasts with the whipped cream filling, then sucked it off, first one side and then the other. The contrast between the cool cream and the heat of his mouth aroused her feminine mounds to an almost painful excitement and dispelled any embarrassment.

Jacobin, a fast learner, snatched another cream puff and did the same to him, licking the vanilla-sweetened *crème chantilly* from the flat copper disks on his chest, fascinated by the hardness of the little peaks. Sensing his heart beat faster and his chest heave at her ministra-

tions gave her a feeling of power. *She* was causing this
excitement.

He chuckled when, with a peep of annoyance, she
had to remove a stray hair from her tongue. Then it was
his turn, and this time it was from her navel he supped,
the warm caresses of his mouth sending a stab of longing to the hidden place lower down.

Not yet brave enough to approach his sex, she moved
upward and ate cream from his collarbone, relishing the
spicy scent of his neck, which seemed to have intensified since she'd nipped him earlier. *Mon Dieu,* this man
smelled good, better than the aroma of fresh-baked
madeleines emerging from the oven. She didn't think
she'd ever get tired of it.

In rotation they ate cream from each other's bodies
until there was a messy pile of deflated puffs next to the
plate. His cunning licks all over her upper body pitched
her into a state of excited longing. She was even able to
look at his far-from-deflated shaft without hesitation.
The ache in the passage between her legs told her she
was eager to receive him, to find out at last what all the
shouting was about. All inhibitions fled and she was
ready, knees unclenched, for the next stage.

Accepting her unspoken invitation, skillful fingers
parted her lower curls and dabbed cream on her nether
lips, making her squirm deliciously. Then, up on his
knees beside her, he squeezed a blob of cream onto the
tip of that perpendicular rod and gave her an inviting
look.

Her body tensed.

He couldn't be serious. Did people actually do *that*? She'd never heard of such a thing.

Anthony shrugged internally. Judging by the look of alarm on Jacobin's face this was a new concept for her. Another time, then. Apparently that damn French cook hadn't initiated her into this particular intimacy. And Frenchmen were supposed to be such great lovers!

Jacobin didn't seem to be overly experienced in bed, and he found himself pleased by the fact. It would give him very great satisfaction to teach her himself. It was probably just as well. He was so aroused he likely wouldn't last a minute in her mouth. And there was nothing to prevent him from partaking in the feast.

He leaned over and kissed her, tangling his tongue with hers and stroking the tender plumpness of her mouth until he felt that hint of tension disperse and she was melting in his arms, returning his kisses and his embrace with a hum of appreciation. Shifting down the bed with a few murmured words of reassurance, he buried his face in her warmth, reveling in her musky scent and taste mingled with sweet cream and her little squeaks of shock and enjoyment. When he sensed she was close to fulfillment, he raised his head and grinned at her blearily.

"You've never done this before, have you?"

She shook her head, her beautiful eyes bright and big as saucers, the exquisite features imprinted with an expression of awe. She made a choking noise. Good, he'd rendered her speechless.

And he'd better finish the job because he wasn't confident he'd have enough time to do it once he was inside her. Never, in his recollection, had he been so excited in bed with a woman.

Her moans of delight as he licked and sucked her to a quivering climax poised him on the edge of explosion.

Now, he thought. At last. It had been a long dry spell and she was even more delectable than he'd imagined. He was primed to lose himself in her, to sense her shuddering passage clench him tight and bring him to release. Positioning himself over her, he kissed her panting mouth and plunged in.

She let out a piercing shriek.

What the hell?

Bracing himself on his arms Anthony stared at her face. Her look of dreamy satiation had been replaced by shock, ecstatic sighs by a whimper of pain. With a disappointed moan he pulled out and peered down. Dimly he could make out a trace of blood on his cock.

Goddamn it, she was a virgin.

"I'm sorry," he blurted out, too flabbergasted for subtlety, "I didn't mean to hurt you."

"It's all right." She grimaced bravely. "I knew it would hurt the first time. I just didn't know how much."

Remorse plucked at him. Although his acquaintance with virgins was theoretical, he could at least have been more careful. "It was my fault. I would have done things differently if I'd known. I had no idea you'd never—"

"You didn't ask. Why did you assume I was—?"

Bewilderment and guilt fought with the part of him that hadn't caught up to the fact that it wasn't going to get what it wanted immediately.

He interrupted her, his brain oblivious to anything but throbbing frustration. "'Struth, Jacobin! You ran off with the cook. What else was I to think?"

Then he realized what he'd said and watched her expression turn to fury. Shoving him away, she rolled off the bed, seized the plate of profiteroles, and hurled it at his head, accompanied by a flow of what he had to assume were French insults. Her strength exceeding her aim, the missile streaked by its target and crashed onto the floor in an explosion of pastry, cream, and shards of Sèvres porcelain.

"Pig! Brute! Villain!" she shrieked. He was beginning to get the drift. "You *knew*. How could you?"

She looked magnificent, stomping the floor, seemingly unconscious that she wore not a stitch of clothing aside from her stockings and those enticing garters.

If he was ever to fulfill his urgent needs he was going to have to grovel.

"I'm sorry," he said again, kneeling on the bed and trying to look as abject as was possible with a painful erection. "Let me explain."

"Explain!" Hands on hips, she rolled her eyes in disbelief. "You don't need to explain. You think you own me because you won me in a card game."

Ferociously she tugged at the emerald necklace. The torn clasp scored her throat with an ugly scratch and he winced, then winced again as she flung it at him and the stones in their precious metal setting hit him squarely in the face. Her aim had improved.

"You think I'm a *putain*—a whore—just like my uncle did," she yelled.

The accusation stung as much as his cheek did. "I never thought any such thing," he said, desperate to pacify her, "but your uncle told me the cook was your lover."

"And you believed what he said," she said on a sob. "But of course, he's your friend, your gaming partner."

The anger and hurt in her voice penetrated the fog of shock and frustration that swirled in his brain and wrenched his heart. "Please Jacobin, forgive me. I should have told you I knew, but I meant it for the best. Truly I did. Please come back to bed. Let me explain and let me make it up to you. I can make you forget the pain."

She emitted an incoherent howl of exasperation. "I'd sooner make love with a monster. Perhaps I already did." She snatched up her shirt from the floor and pulled it over her head. "I can't believe I ever agreed to go to bed with you. I must have been mad. I knew what you are, you dirty, gambling whoremonger. You are worse than Candover."

While she fumbled under the bed for her drawers and breeches, he summoned a rational argument. "Stop, listen—"

But she cut him off. "I wish Jean-Luc *was* my lover. I love Jean-Luc. He would never have hurt me like you did, you clumsy brute. With him it would have been *perfect*. He may only be a cook but he's more of a gentleman than you. And he's more handsome than you. And he's—he's—he's *taller* than you."

That was too much. He scarcely heard her words. Only the fact that she was talking about size. "Now wait a minute—" he roared back.

"Not even for a second!" she yelled, struggling with a boot. She looked unsure whether to pull it on or beat him with it. "I won't listen to a word. I never wish to set eyes on you again as long as I live."

Concern for her crept up his spine but he was too riled to speak gently. "You can't just leave, you little fool. Think. You could be arrested."

She swung around to face him. "That's right," she spat. "I have nowhere to go. And it's all your fault."

Chapter 18

om Hawkins was a frustrated man. The Bow Street runner had canvassed the household of every guest at the notorious Pavilion dinner, and extended his search to those of every gentleman known to be resident or visiting Brighton at the time. To no avail. Not one of those establishments had recently employed Jacob Léon, or a male French cook of any other name. He still awaited a reply from Paris about the whereabouts of Jean-Luc Clèves, last heard to be working for the Duc de Clermont-Ferrand.

Which left him with the mystery of Edgar Candover's coat, and how it fetched up in Chauncey Bellamy's garden.

It had taken several days for someone at Bow Street to track down the owner of the gentleman's coat that had been discovered in the garden of the Upper Brook Street house. It might have been forgotten altogether had Lady Caroline Bellamy not made such a commotion about it. There'd been no sign of a break-in at the house, neither was anything missing. But Lady Caroline insisted that the intrusion into her garden be thoroughly investigated, and Her Ladyship's father was a duke. Persistent relations of important noblemen had ways of getting their demands met.

A junior runner without much to do was eventually sent to interview the Jermyn Street tailor whose mark the garment bore. And the young investigator had recognized the name supplied by the tailor, Edgar Candover. Or rather the name of his cousin, whose attempted murder was known to all of Bow Street. The information was passed along to Tom Hawkins.

Absent any other leads, Hawkins decided to travel down to Hampshire to interview the younger Candover again.

"Yes, that's my coat," Candover said. "Where on earth did it turn up?"

Hawkins didn't answer. He was the one asking the questions.

"Had you mislaid it, sir?"

"I had. I'm glad to have it back." He reached for it but Hawkins tucked it firmly under his arm.

"I'm sorry, sir. It may be evidence of a crime."

"Good Lord!"

To Hawkins's eye Candover's expression held something beyond innocent astonishment. He probed further. "When and where did you last see the garment?" He waited in silence when Candover didn't respond to the question, then waited some more.

Candover shifted from one foot to the other, uneasy under Hawkins's questioning gaze. "It was taken from me," he said at last.

"Stolen, sir?"

"Not stolen exactly." Candover looked even more uncomfortable. "I don't know whether I should tell you this. It's a family matter."

Hawkins made a soothing noise. "Don't worry, sir. We runners know how to be discreet. If the truth has no bearing on any crime it'll go no further than me. You can count on it."

"The coat was last in the possession of my cousin Jacobin. She left this house wearing it."

"And why would she be wearing a gentleman's coat? That seems an unusual thing for a young lady to do."

"My cousin is an unusual young lady." Candover leaned in confidentially. "I'm trusting you with some information here that would embarrass the family should it get out. The truth is, Jacobin eloped with one of the servants."

Hawkins felt the familiar prickle at the back of his neck that always accompanied an important opening in a case. He kept his voice disinterested. "Did that servant happen to be your uncle's cook, Jean-Luc Clèves?"

"Well, yes. It was."

"A detail neither you nor your uncle felt the need to mention in our earlier conversations."

"Why would we wish to reveal such a shameful fact? It happened months ago. I can't imagine it has any bearing on my uncle's poisoning."

Hawkins didn't enlighten him. If Edgar Candover knew anything useful, Hawkins would get it out of him. Then he'd get back to looking for cooks. Female cooks.

My lord. Please restrict your communications to the subject of confectionery. In the unlikely event, given your lack of appreciation for the art of pâtisserie, *that you wish to request a particular dish, pray convey your requirements through the normal channels and leave a message with Mr. Simpson. I have no desire to speak to you now, or ever, on any other subject.*

Anthony crumpled the latest impertinent missive from his cook—his *cook,* for God's sake—and hurled it at the fire. Naturally it missed and landed on the hearth. Angrily he stamped over to pick it up and rip it into shreds before consigning it to the flames, safe from the prying eyes of the butler, footmen, or housemaids. In the interests of discretion he'd used Jem Webster to carry his correspondence with Jacobin. Three times, he'd written abject apologies, begging for a meeting. Each reply was an unequivocal rebuff, though at least this last didn't contain a torrent of French insults, the meaning of which he could only guess.

It had all been a mistake, and, really, he should have known better.

This was what happened when you let a woman get under your skin. She ended up taking some little thing you'd said or done, mistrusting your motives, blowing it up out of all proportion and then departing in a dramatic snit.

True, some of his behavior might be open to misinterpretation—if you looked at it in a certain way—but the sensible thing was to stop, listen, give the other person an opportunity to explain.

But not Jacobin de Chastelux. She'd made up her mind and exited in high dudgeon, not without saying a few nasty things on the way out.

It was better to put the whole episode behind him, especially since thinking about how she'd looked naked and in a rage made his groin throb. He resolutely thrust aside his guilt at having debauched an innocent. According to all the rules he'd ever absorbed there was only one honorable reparation.

But marriage? He had no intention of marrying anyone, let alone Candover's niece. His stomach churned at the idea of accepting the man as a close family member. And that tender ache in the region of another organ was generated by the same disgust. It must be. His mind snapped shut against the implication that he might *wish* to wed Jacobin.

He was wasting time better spent brushing up on his Hoyle for another bout with Candover. He needed to put aside distractions and get on with the job of avenging his father.

He wrote to Lord Candover, congratulating him on his recovery and inviting him to visit Storrington and sample the confections of his new pastry chef. Enough time had passed since the dinner party for

Candover to have received word of this new culinary talent.

Two days passed, and Anthony hadn't received so much as a glimpse of Jacobin since she'd slammed the door of the Queen's House. He knew she was still in his house—he'd have been informed had she left—but he'd resisted the inclination to seek her out, perhaps encounter her by accident during her daily walk in the park.

Now, it occurred to him, it was only fair to warn her that he had invited her uncle to Storrington. Besides, he needed to discuss the menus for Candover's visit. Otherwise he had no desire to set eyes on her. None whatsoever.

"Simpson," Anthony said when his butler responded to the summons of the bell. "Send Miss Castle to me, please. At once."

"Miss Castle is not in the house, my lord." The man looked rather pleased.

"Where the devil is she? Out on one of her walks, I suppose."

"She did go out, my lord, but not alone. A Frenchman came to the kitchen door asking for her." Simpson's voice managed to combine utter distaste for the country of France and all its inhabitants and something like glee. "They left together."

Anthony tore through the French doors. Beyond the thick shrubbery separating the formal gardens from the park he heard voices speaking in that infernal French. He rounded the rhododendrons to find Jacobin enfolded in the close embrace of the best-looking man he'd ever seen.

Jacobin flung her arms around Jean-Luc as soon as they were out of sight of the house. "I'm so happy to see you, Jean-Luc," she cried in French, almost overcome with joy at seeing his dear, familiar face. With his classical features, slender grace, and golden blond beauty, he was still the handsomest man she'd ever met. But his blue eyes no longer set her heart racing as they had when he'd first appeared at Hurst Park. Instead she felt the comforting presence of devoted friendship. "How did you find me?"

"Ssh, *chérie*. There's no need to cry. Let me have a look at you." He held her at arm's length and looked her up and down critically. "Still beautiful, I see, but no better dressed. Really, you need to do something about your clothes."

An incipient sob turned into a giggle. "Just the same as ever. How wonderful it is to see you! How long have you been in England? And how do you come to be at Storrington?"

Jean-Luc looked grave. "I came to England to find you, to make sure you were well. To find out why you're being hunted for trying to kill your uncle."

"They're looking for *me*? Me, Jacobin?" She gasped in horror.

"No, *chérie*. They're looking for Jacob Léon. They know I recommended you to Monsieur Carême, and a letter came inquiring for me. Luckily, Monsieur le Duc was away from Paris and his maître d'hôtel, Michel, is a close friend of mine. He told me about it and gave me leave to come to England for a few days."

"Oh no! Jean-Luc. You jeopardized your position for me."

"No, *chérie*. Didn't I say Michel was my *close* friend? Besides, Monsieur le Duc loves my *pâtisserie* even more than *milord* Candover. So I drove to Calais and took the packet, an abominable form of transport which should be abolished. It didn't take me long to hear about *milord* Storrington's new *pâtissière*. Your dinner party was a sensation, *chérie*, the talk of London. I'm so proud of you."

Jacobin glowed at his praise. "It was brilliant, Jean-Luc, though I say it myself. I made the basket of eggs and the *vol-au-vent* tower, apricot tartlets, vanilla cream jelly, *gâteaux de Pitiviers*—oh yes, and profiteroles and a timbale of rice with apples and pistachios."

"The sugar basket, eh? You were always better at working with spun sugar than me. But enough of such important topics. We need to concentrate on this little matter of murder. Do you know who would have wished to kill your uncle?"

"Besides me?" Jacobin asked. "I had good reason."

"Yes, but I know you wouldn't have. Even if you were unbearably tempted, poison wouldn't be your method. A kitchen knife to the gut when you were enraged would be more your style. What about Edgar? He will inherit *milord*'s title and estate."

"It's possible." Jacobin shrugged. "But I don't think so. It's the oddest thing. He asked me to marry him. I never thought he cared much for me."

"He knows where you are?"

"No, I met him at a public ball in London. I refused to tell him."

"That was wise. Edgar would tell Lord Candover."

"But I have a better suspect."

Jean-Luc whistled appreciatively when Jacobin described her investigation of Chauncey Bellamy. "This is interesting, *chérie*, most interesting. Bellamy, eh?"

Jacobin grabbed his arm. "You know something! What?"

"*Doucement, ma chère.* In the circles I move in we hear everything about certain gentlemen. And many of these types are English—because they like to come to Paris to indulge themselves. That's why in France my preference is often called *le vice anglais*. Of course, for many years the war kept them away but many, many of them are back now."

"So Bellamy prefers the company of other men. Lord Storrington had an idea that might be so too. Has Bellamy been in Paris since the war?"

"No, it was a long time ago. I only heard by chance because some of Michel and my friends were talking about the old days one evening. An older man, valet to the Prince de Conté, remembered Bellamy when he was a very young man and said he was *fort respectable* now."

"Yes indeed! And married to a woman even more respectable. He'd be desperate to keep the truth a secret. My uncle could have been blackmailing him."

"How can you find out more about this man? Wait a minute." Jean-Luc looked at her through narrowed eyes. "You said Lord Storrington knew something of this? Does your employer know you are involved in this matter?"

She looked away. "Yes. He said he'd help me."

"Look at me, Jacobin." Jean-Luc took her chin in his hand and looked at her with his keen azure gaze. "Does he know who you are?"

"Yes," she said sullenly. "At least, he knows I used to be Jacob Léon."

"For God's sake! He's the man that won you from your uncle. It's bad enough you had to go and work for him. Supposing he finds out who you *really* are? You shouldn't trust him. A man like that could seduce you, or worse."

"I thought he was different," she wailed, her face crumpling. "He seemed kind. Oh! Jean-Luc, I'm so miserable."

He gathered her into his arms and rubbed her back. "*Pauvre chérie,*" he murmured into her hair. "You're not as grown-up as you think. But Jean-Luc is here now. We'll think of what to do. You're not alone anymore."

She sighed into his well-tailored shoulder. It was such a relief to have the comfort of Jean-Luc's unthreatening affection. Not that she could imagine what he could do to help her. And she was reluctant to admit, even to Jean-Luc, how foolish she'd been.

"He does know who I am. He found out. He knows I'm Jacobin de Chastelux."

"*Mon Dieu*, that's terrible! He could turn you over to the authorities. The man is a brute."

Just at that moment the brute crashed through the rhododendrons, ridiculously underdressed for December, hair waving madly in the stiff breeze. Jacobin and Jean-Luc stared at him, clinging to each other as they faced six feet, two inches of furious English aristocrat.

Storrington came to a halt. "Mademoiselle de Chastelux," he said with barely restrained rage. "Despite anything that might have happened between us, I'd like to remind you that you are still in my employ and my servants are not permitted to meet their lovers in the grounds of Storrington Hall." He glared at them, fists tightly clenched, blazing eyes at odds with the stony set of his face. "I expect this man to depart the premises immediately."

Fearing he'd hit Jean-Luc, Jacobin moved protectively in front of the Frenchman and stood firm, arms ready to ward off an attack. Their glances locked, and she tried to hide her fear and hurt under a cloak of defiance. For an instant she thought she detected something like vulnerability in his stormy gaze. Then he looked away.

Without another word he swung around briskly and stalked back in the direction of the house.

Mouths agape, Jacobin and Jean-Luc watched his departure, then Jean-Luc looked down at her with quite a different expression.

"My, my. Things aren't at all as I'd thought. For one thing, *milord* is *very* attractive." His eyes glinted wickedly.

"Oh, really," Jacobin said crossly. "Trust you to notice that."

"Don't worry, he's not my type. And I am most certainly not his. I don't have to look far to find the object of *his* interest. I was frightened for my life there for a moment. I'm very pleased, *chérie*. Lord Storrington would be an excellent match for you. *Très sortable*."

"Nonsense. He'd never so demean himself. He will marry a proper English virgin of good family."

"There's nothing wrong with your family. Michel says the Chastelux are one of the best families of France, and believe me, he would know."

He knew her too well; better than anyone else alive. He read in her face that it wasn't the *good family* part of her last statement that was bothering her.

"Come on, *chérie*. I think you'd better tell me *all* about it."

Hesitantly at first, Jacobin outlined the story of her interactions with Storrington, her indignation gathering steam as she approached the denouement. "And then he said I couldn't be a virgin because I'd eloped with the cook. He meant you, Jean-Luc. He thought we were lovers. And he knew who I was, the rat!" She burned with rage and disappointment as she relived the dreadful moment.

Jean-Luc hugged her again. "And then I suppose you lost your temper and said some things you shouldn't."

"I told him I loved you and I wished you *were* my lover." She blinked back tears. "And it's true, I do. You broke my heart when you told me you weren't interested in women."

He knew her too well to fall for this piece of dramatic exaggeration. "Ah! I cruelly spurned you and ruined your life," he returned in kind. "If only you'd been a boy! Of course, you'd still have been sixteen years old and I have always preferred older men. Let's face it, *chérie*, if anyone's broken your heart it isn't me and never was. Now dry your tears and think about catching your earl. He's the answer to all your problems."

"But he deceived me! He said—"

"Don't tell me what he said. Let me give you some advice. Men will say all sorts of things and tell all sorts of lies, especially when their sexual desires are engrossed. But it doesn't mean they are bad, only that they are men."

She turned her back on him, filled with loathing for the entire male sex, even Jean-Luc. "I can't believe you're defending him!" she said, arms folded defiantly. "He is a coldhearted beast and I never want to speak to him again."

Chapter 19

"I understand you have recently employed a female cook," Hawkins said, unintimidated by Storrington's ferocious stare.

Of all the arrogant noblemen Tom Hawkins had met, Storrington was without doubt the worst. The earl looked at him as though he were a slug who'd announced his intention of trailing slime through his kitchens. Under other circumstances he might have been an agreeable man, no doubt was with his equals. He made no bones about the fact that Tom Hawkins was emphatically not his equal.

"What's that to you?" the earl asked in a voice that would freeze lamp oil.

"Perhaps you are not aware, my lord, that we are looking for a cook in connection with Lord Candover's poisoning."

"I believe my secretary mentioned that inquiries had been made. A male cook if I remember correctly. Mine is a female."

"We have reason to suspect that Jacob Léon, the

cook in question, was a female in disguise." Hawkins watched Storrington closely but didn't detect so much as a hint that the line of questioning troubled him. Apart from disgust at its perceived impertinence.

"My employee is not in disguise."

"Not anymore," Hawkins agreed. "Would you mind telling me how this woman came into your service?"

"If I recall correctly she came from Scotland."

"With references?"

Storrington raised his brows. "Naturally."

"How long has she been with you, my lord?"

The earl waved a languid hand. "Really, I can't be sure. Three or four weeks, perhaps. You may check with my secretary in London."

Hawkins didn't need to. One of his fellow runners had interviewed Storrington's secretary, and Hawkins had seen his notes. Jane Castle had arrived at Storrington Hall the day Jacob Léon disappeared. "How did you discover this young woman?" he asked.

"I don't recall now how her name came to my attention, but we were in correspondence with her for several weeks before she took up her position. It's not easy to find a first-rate pastry cook."

It was interesting, Hawkins thought, that the earl chose to volunteer that morsel of intelligence. His other answers had been as brief and uninformative as possible.

"If you don't mind, my lord, I would like to interview the woman."

"I see no reason for that. Clearly Miss Castle is not

the person you're looking for and I won't have my servants subjected to harassment. You can take my word for it that she had nothing—could have had nothing—to do with the attack on Lord Candover. The very idea is an insult to my household."

"I can assure you, my lord, that the Bow Street runners are not in the habit of harassing witnesses. It would set my mind at rest if I could speak to Miss Castle myself."

Storrington gave him a very nasty look. "Are you impugning my honor, Hawkins?"

Hawkins knew when to retreat. The aristocracy were touchy when it came to their so-called honor, he knew. But there was more than one way to skin a cat. He'd leave his arrogant Lordship for now, but his investigation into Jane Castle wasn't over, not by a long chalk.

Anthony hadn't realized he had such a flair for deception. The hours of practicing a deadpan expression for sessions at the piquet table had helped. He'd done it now: lied blatantly to an officer of the law investigating the attempted murder of a peer.

And all to shield a young woman who refused to speak to him and claimed to be in love with someone else. But when it came down to it, he couldn't let Jacobin be hauled off in chains. He wanted to protect her. He *owed* it to her.

He rang the bell. She'd better damn well speak to him now.

He couldn't believe how pleased he was to see her when she stamped into the library in response to his summons. She glared at him, the cleft chin thrust forward pugnaciously. He'd never found a woman so maddening, so intriguing, so irresistible. He had the oddest desire to laugh. And to sweep her into his arms and kiss her until he extinguished all thoughts of that disgustingly good-looking Frenchman.

A core of insecurity held him back. She'd enumerated in painful detail the reasons she preferred the other man, and objectively he saw they were correct. Clèves was, first of all, an extraordinarily handsome man—and a tall one. Jacobin had never shown any indication of being impressed by his own wealth and position; instead, from their first conversation she'd done nothing but flout Anthony's social superiority. And when she said Clèves, a mere cook, was the greater gentleman, Anthony had to face the humiliating knowledge that she was right. His treatment of her had fallen short of the highest standards of gallantry. An unwonted humility kept him from using physical persuasion to return her to his arms. Fearing rejection, he resisted the urges of jealousy and desire.

And respected the muscles of her upper arms. The fury in her eyes suggested she wouldn't hesitate to use them if he moved even an inch nearer.

She dropped a deep—and ironic—curtsy. At least he knew now where that particular skill came from. "My lord."

He'd risen courteously when she entered the room. Now he gestured her to a chair. "Sit down, Jacobin. And I think the '*my lord*' might go, under the circumstances."

"That wouldn't be correct, my lord," she answered stiffly, remaining where she stood. "I am still your servant."

"Don't be ridiculous. You're Jacobin de Chastelux, a member of both French and English noble families. We've also been lovers." In his frustration he spoke more harshly than he'd intended. "Call me Anthony," he continued more gently. "We're both in the devil of a pickle so we might as well drop the formality."

"I think not, my lord. There's no pickle. We should just forget that evening." She clenched her shoulders in a shudder of distaste.

"We'll talk about that later. The problem I'm discussing now is the minor matter of a Bow Street runner who is looking for a female cook, previously known as Jacob Léon."

That got to her. Jacobin's hand went to her mouth and her expressive eyes widened in alarm. "Are you sure? I heard they were still looking for a man."

"Hm, your precious Frenchman brought news, I see. I'm afraid this man Hawkins is one step ahead of the gossip. He seems to know that Léon was a woman in disguise."

"I must leave at once." Jacobin looked around her wildly, as though prepared to jump out of the nearest window.

"It's all right," he said gently, and moved closer to her. "I fobbed him off. You're safe, at least for the present."

"You did?" She stared up at him with a pinched look, all animation drained from her face. "How?"

"I made up a story about you having come from Scotland and sent him off with a flea in his ear when he tried to argue with me." He chuckled. "I couldn't let him see you, as he wished. I have no doubt he has an accurate description of Jacob Léon. I came over the very haughty aristocrat, I assure you."

"That, I can believe!" Her eyes kindled for a moment, and the return of her natural vivacity pleased him. He hated to see her so downcast and frightened. "I suppose he'll be back," she continued, then gasped, as a thought came to her.

"My God! You'll be in terrible trouble! You lied for me and they're bound to find out."

It felt good to see the loathing disappear from her face. Her concern for him coiled around Anthony's heart like a flame licking dry wood. Longing to enfold her in his embrace and hold her safe, he dared only envelop one of her hands in both of his. And felt gratified when she didn't snatch it away.

"I promised I'd help you. Besides, I can take care of myself."

She wasn't comforted. "Truly, I never meant to get anyone else in trouble. Supposing they catch me. They might hang you too."

"I don't think it'll come to that," he said. "It's damn

hard to convict a peer. I'd have to be tried in the House of Lords, and those fellows look after their own."

"Really? I know nothing of English justice," she said in astonishment. "It wasn't like that in France."

"Even there they've stopped rushing their aristocrats to the guillotine." He didn't add that while he might not fear for his neck, the thought of the scandal, should he be found harboring a wanted criminal, made the traditional English gentleman in him cringe.

"Come," he said bracingly. "We'll just have to find the real villain."

Her face lit up. "I have news of Bellamy! What you suspected was correct. He indulged in an indiscretion in France when he was a young man."

"How do you know this?"

"Jean-Luc told me."

"So that *was* your precious Jean-Luc you were embracing behind the shrubbery." He knew he sounded petty. This wasn't the moment to return to their personal disagreements, but he couldn't contain his jealousy.

Jacobin didn't seem to notice his vexation. She had a way of becoming completely involved in the concern of the moment and was almost bouncing with excitement. "Jean-Luc knows all about these types who prefer men. He heard from his friends about Mr. Bellamy. So you see, we must have been right. My uncle was blackmailing him and Bellamy tried to kill him to keep him quiet."

Not sharing her single-minded fixation on the immediate present, Anthony didn't miss the implication of her statement. No wonder the Frenchman hadn't become her lover when they'd run off together. He felt like ordering champagne.

He happily contemplated an early return to Jacobin's favor, and her bed, if only she would listen to his explanation of his other transgressions. And this time he'd make sure she had no cause ever to leave him again.

"I asked my secretary to find out—discreetly—anything he could about Bellamy's relations with Candover, and his movements around the time of the poisoning." He now felt the urgency of the task, a powerful desire to clear her name and dispel the threat to her. "I'll give him a day or two to report, and if I don't hear anything I'll go to London myself."

For a moment Jacobin felt like hugging him. Then she remembered she still had good reason to be angry. She freed her hand, which had been unconsciously returning his clasp, and stepped back. She could think more clearly without his proximity.

"Jean-Luc thought Edgar might be responsible for poisoning my uncle," she offered.

"Edgar Candover, the heir? Who acts as your uncle's steward?"

She was surprised Anthony knew so much about the family. Edgar wasn't closely related to Lord Candover and spent most of the time in the country, never appearing at London social events. It crossed her mind to wonder how he'd come to attend the ball at the Argyll Rooms. It wasn't Edgar's style at all.

"I don't think it likely that Edgar would do such a

thing," she said. "My uncle has always been good to him. They like each other. And Edgar will inherit everything eventually. Frankly I don't see Edgar having the backbone to kill anyone. He's a very mild man, quite weak."

"I imagine the runners will have investigated him thoroughly, as the obvious suspect. Let us concentrate on Bellamy for now. The other will keep."

"I'm very grateful, my lord, for your help."

"I don't want your gratitude, Jacobin. But I would count it a favor if you'd use my Christian name."

Something in his voice, the way its pitch diminished as he spoke, made her look away. Since she had entered the room her emotions had lurched from anger and defiance to concern and appreciation. Having him as an ally filled her with warm relief. Now the soft note in his voice turned her insides to caramel. Yet there was still much in his behavior to abhor, and she wasn't ready to forgive him.

"Very well, Anthony." To temporize while she resolved her internal conflict, she glanced around the library. It was a very English room, lined with thousands of neatly bound books and furnished in solid oak pieces, totally unlike the gilded French splendor of the Queen's House. She walked over to a bookcase and selected a volume at random. It was a treatise on crop rotation.

"You have a lot of books," she said. "Have you read this?"

He'd followed her and now removed the book from

her hands and placed it on a table. "Jacobin," he whispered. "Please forgive me. And please let me explain."

She felt herself weakening. She eyed him warily but didn't draw back. It couldn't, she supposed, do any harm to let him say his piece. Not, she told herself sternly, that there could be an excuse for his behavior.

"Why?" she said, stiffening her backbone and planting her hands on her hips. "Why did you pretend you didn't know who I was?"

"I truly meant it for the best. I didn't want you to feel any obligation to me because of that wretched wager with your uncle. I assume you know he lost you to me at cards. That was why you ran away from Hurst."

"Of course I ran away! My uncle gave me a choice: you or a brothel. Naturally I chose neither. Why?" she demanded, her rage and hurt bursting from her. "Why in the name of God and all his saints did you agree to such a disgusting bet? Is that the only way you could get yourself a mistress?"

Anthony frowned. He'd never been able to quite explain his acceptance of Candover's scandalous stake to himself. How could he justify it?

"Accepting the wager was wrong," he admitted. "I knew it at the time, but I was furious with Candover. I hardly had time to determine what to do with my winnings"—he placed an ironic stress on the word and cast her an apologetic look—"before he informed me you'd eloped with his cook. But one thing you must believe: I would never have forced you, or any other woman, to do anything you didn't want."

She seemed to accept his sincerity but still looked bewildered. He searched his mind for the answer to her unspoken question, one he'd been avoiding for himself for months.

"I had a half conjured plan to parade you around London as my *chère amie*. I thought having his niece as my mistress would embarrass your uncle, especially if I let it be known to the gossips how I'd won you." He sighed. "It wasn't a well-thought-out plan. Once I met you I doubt I'd even have carried it out."

"What was the other half of the bet, the amount you staked against me?" she asked.

"Twenty thousand pounds."

"So much! Perhaps I should be flattered." She gave an ironic little laugh. "I cost you a pretty penny when I ran off. Shall I apologize?"

"There's no need. Candover paid me the twenty thousand."

Jacobin gave a little jog of excitement. "And we know just where he got it! It all makes sense now. He needed the money quickly, so he went to Bellamy."

"It seems a reasonable conclusion. I was surprised he was able to lay his hands on such a large sum quickly. According to my information he was very short of the ready."

Her forehead wrinkled with suspicion. "How do you come to know so much about my uncle and his finances? I thought he was a friend of yours. And you said you accepted his bet because you were furious. What made you so angry?"

Jacobin could tell he didn't want to answer. "He said something about my mother," he said through clenched teeth.

"I'm sorry. That must have been upsetting." Now that she knew about Anthony's childhood she understood his sensitivity on the subject. "My uncle has a way of finding a sore spot and prodding it."

He turned his back on her and paced over to the window, staring out at the bleak winter landscape. "Candover was never my friend. Quite the opposite. I only cultivated him so that I could lure him into losing his fortune to me. I want to ruin him."

She couldn't see his face but could sense the sadness mixed with suppressed rage in his voice. She walked over and placed a hand on his shoulder. "I can only applaud the sentiment, but why? I know what he did to me, but I can't imagine he had the power to injure you."

"Yet injure me he did, and my family." His hand reached behind him and took hers in a convulsive clasp. He spoke softly so she had to strain to hear him. "He was my mother's lover."

That was the very last thing she would have guessed. "Impossible," she cried. "No one could do *that* with such a disgusting pig."

He angled his head and looked down at her wryly. "Hard to believe, isn't it. Though I have heard Candover wasn't unattractive before he took to eating too much pastry."

Inwardly she applauded his ability to make a small

joke at an emotionally intense moment. "Why do you think such a thing? How do you know?"

He looked away and continued, his voice reflecting inner strain. "My father told me on his deathbed. She and Candover fell in love in Paris, when I was five years old. She was running away to join him when she drowned in a storm."

Jacobin digested this information, squaring it with everything she'd heard about Catherine, Countess of Storrington. She still found it incredible, although a forbidden love affair in Paris would explain the countess's unhappiness afterward.

"She was never the same after they came back from Paris. It was as though she left us then. Her elopement and death merely completed the process. Candover destroyed my father's life and now I must ruin his."

Even as he spoke of his father's blighted life, Jacobin sensed Anthony's revenge was as much for himself as it was for the older man.

"Listen to me, Anthony." She squeezed his hand. "My uncle is a horrible man and I don't care what happens to him. But revenge won't make you feel better. It never does. In France they killed thousands of innocent people out of hatred for the aristocrats and anger at injustice, but it solved nothing. My father always said hate harms only those that feel it."

"Did he?" he asked, glancing down at her. "Perhaps he never had a wrong to avenge."

"My father nearly died during the Terror. Even though he sympathized with the Revolution it wasn't good enough for Robespierre and his followers. They thought my father wasn't fervent enough in his views. And they mistrusted him for his birth. He was imprisoned in the Conciergerie, waiting for Madame Guillotine, when Robespierre fell and he was released."

"How terrifying for you and your mother." The story seemed to have penetrated his preoccupation with Candover's sins.

"For my mother, yes. I was only an infant. But the point is, my father put it behind him. He never resented those who had spoken against him, though he had to encounter some of them in the years that followed. He worked to achieve justice through peaceful means, to bring people together. And he never changed his mind, even though Bonaparte broke his heart when he seized power for himself."

"I'm not trying to change the course of a nation, only to right one injustice. It may be small in the greater scheme of things, but it's there nonetheless. The law can do nothing to punish Candover for my mother's death, so it's up to me."

How sad, Jacobin thought, to see a man who had so much to offer waste his energy on meaningless vengeance.

Hoping at least that human connection—no, affection—might alleviate the bleakness that infected his soul, she continued to hold his hand. They stood quietly for some minutes, then he moved and embraced her from behind, drawing her against his warm, solid frame.

And she realized that his mind—or at least part of his anatomy—had shifted to more earthy matters. How curious to think of *that* at such a moment. It was the furthest thing from her mind.

He nibbled at her ear, and quivers ran down her neck. Well, maybe not the furthest.

"Jacobin," he whispered. His hands were now on her shoulders, and his thumbs gently massaged her nape and shoulder blades beneath the plain neck of her stuff gown. The quivers continued, tightening her breasts and generating heat like a warm pool between her thighs.

"Jacobin." Her name had never sounded better than murmured in those dark, warm chocolate tones. "Come to me again. Meet me at the Queen's House tonight. It will be good."

She didn't doubt the truth of *that* statement, but something held her back from giving in to her own desire. She shook her head.

"Don't say no, please." Mesmerizing fingers were joined by warm lips, raising goose bumps over every inch of her body.

"I can't," she managed to mutter, and pulled away before his nearness could be her undoing. "No."

"Very well. I must accept your refusal, but you can change your mind at any time, and I'll be waiting." He pointed out of the window. "Do you see that urn on the terrace? If you want me, tie something—a handkerchief—to the handle. I'll be watching for it. I can see it from my bedchamber too. As soon as I see the signal I'll meet you at the Queen's House."

"A signal, yes, I see," she blurted out. "I must go."

She fled before she could succumb to the lure of his arms.

Shutting the library door behind her, she stopped and took a deep breath, closed her eyes, and leaned her head against the wall.

She was tempted to forgive him. She wanted to forgive him. She'd preached forgiveness, the lesson learned from her beloved father. She'd urged him to set aside his resentment, yet she wasn't ready to do the same. True, he'd apologized for his deception, but did he really mean it? As Jean-Luc had pointed out, men would do and say anything when motivated by lust. Women too, perhaps. She wasn't at all sure her own instinct to pardon Anthony wasn't driven by a wish to surrender to the bliss of his embrace.

And how could she entrust herself to a man obsessed with revenge, a passion that left a throbbing bruise on men's spirits and could drive them to terrible deeds?

Another understanding tugged at her now she was free of Anthony's distracting presence: that he too had an excellent motive for Candover's murder.

Edgar Candover mulled over the fact that his coat had turned up in Chauncey Bellamy's garden and wondered what it meant. He'd extracted the location from the Bow Street runner in exchange for some information about Jacobin. Nothing important, but enough to keep Hawkins happy. He didn't want the man dashing off and arresting Jacobin for attempted murder.

He knew quite a lot about Chauncey Bellamy, since the man had lost twenty thousand pounds to his cousin at a most convenient moment. Rather too convenient to Edgar's mind. He didn't entirely believe in that card game. Something in Lord Candover's eyes when he triumphantly produced the draft to make good his loss to Storrington had raised Edgar's suspicions. He was certain his cousin had been lying.

Bellamy made a very nice suspect for the role of Candover's poisoner. Edgar pondered what he might do with the information.

"Good evening, cousin," Edgar said, entering the library. "What brings you to Hurst so suddenly?" Candover's arrival was unexpected. Normally he quit Hampshire for London as soon as there was a nip in the air, and rarely returned before the end of the spring season. "I fear you won't be very comfortable here." With Candover's estate stressed by extravagance and ill-luck at the tables, he could no longer afford to maintain two full establishments. Most of the household had been fixed in London for two months.

"I'm only here for a night," Lord Candover replied. "I'm off to Storrington tomorrow."

"Please, cousin, not Storrington," Edgar begged. "The estate can't afford another loss like the last one."

"Don't worry Edgar. I promised I wouldn't play with the earl again. Not that I don't believe I could win." He held up a hand to fend off Edgar's protest. "I'm not going there for cards but for food." He chuckled happily. "Storrington's managed to find a cook who's a genius with desserts. The reports I heard after a dinner he gave in London last week! This woman makes Jean-Luc look like an amateur."

Good God, Edgar thought. *That's where she is.* He knew Storrington had lately acquired a female pastry cook, but when his man had made the inquiry he was looking for a male, and Storrington's servants had refused to tell him anything more.

He was going to have to take a hand in this himself. He was very good at gaining the confidence of servants; they found his manner unthreatening. Hadn't his uncle's housemaid in London told him that Jacobin had been to visit the kitchen? Edgar had given her a sob story about his affection for his missing cousin, and she'd promised to let him know if the staff heard word from her. The girl hadn't known where Jacobin was living, but she'd directed him to that ball at the Argyll Rooms.

He needed to get down to Storrington soon. Hawkins wasn't a stupid man and would no doubt locate a female cook within a matter of days. Edgar had to find her first.

Over the next twenty-four hours Anthony managed to look out of the window at the urn several times. Perhaps a dozen or so. Not more, surely. It was remarkable how often business took him to the library. He hardly had to look for excuses. And of course he had to go to his own rooms, with their view of the terrace, to change his dress for dinner. And to sleep, sadly alone. He refrained from getting up in the middle of the night to look. It was too dark to see anyway (he needed to do something about that). Besides, the urn would still be there tomorrow, unless by some chance a garden ornament thief decided to visit Sussex in December.

No such felon descended on Storrington; morning found the urn in its place, regrettably unfestooned with material of any description.

The arrival of the post offered a distraction. As Anthony had expected, Candover was unable to resist the lure of sweets. He would arrive the next day.

Jacobin must be told about the arrival of the guest, not only because she would be expected to prepare dainties for her odious uncle, but to warn her to keep out of sight.

Anthony felt a certain reluctance to approach Jacobin, whose reaction to the news was unlikely to be positive. And he'd told her things he couldn't have imagined confiding to anyone, with the exception of James. Feeling exposed and vulnerable, he shied away from further discussion of his most private concerns. He'd rather hoped their next meeting would involve her falling into his arms with a bed close at hand and other things than conversation on their minds.

Faced with the prospect of an unpleasant encounter and little hope of anything else, he put off sending for her, dithering around for an hour or so until he saw her familiar gray-clad figure striding into the park.

She sensed rather than saw him coming up behind her and increased her pace. It wasn't that she didn't want to see Anthony. Rather she wanted to see him too much.

His long legs soon caught her. "Jacobin."

"My lord," she said, still walking.

"Not back to that." He sighed. "Could you slow down, please?"

"It's cold. I need to move fast to be warm. If you wish for my company you'll have to keep up."

"I've missed you," he said.

She'd missed him too. She had started to miss him almost as soon as she'd left him in the library and continued to miss him since. She wished he'd leave her alone so she could get on with missing him and not be tempted to do something about it. The mere sound of his voice made her far too happy.

"You saw me yesterday." Her lips twitched with the urge to smile.

"Yes, I did, but I'd hoped to see you again sooner. My garden urn is distressingly naked."

By a miracle. She'd had to restrain herself several times, including once in the middle of the night, from dashing down and tying a ribbon to the handle.

"It has occurred to me, my lord," she said, on the theory that attack was the best defense against her own weakness, "that your hatred of my uncle gives you a strong motive for his murder."

Anthony seemed undisturbed by her statement. "If I'd been responsible for putting aconite in his pudding, don't you think I would have been delighted to turn you over to the runners and see you hang for my crime?"

Jacobin had come up with that argument herself. Every instinct told her that Anthony wasn't a killer.

"You don't really believe I tried to poison Candover, do you?" he asked.

"No," she admitted. "But I do think you're a deceitful louse."

"You are absolutely right."

That slowed her down. She turned to look at his face as she continued to walk at a more measured pace. She read nothing there but genuine contrition. "You should have told me you knew who I was."

"I should have. I was wrong and my excuses were worthless. I'd have done anything to win you, I wanted you so much. And I still do. I can't sleep. I look out of the window at that urn a hundred times a day. I've even invented reasons to enter the house across the terrace instead of using the front door so I can look at the wretched thing again. I can't stop thinking about you." He ran a hand though his hair in the way he had when disturbed about something. His dishevelment made her think of rumpled sheets and him between them.

"I've never felt this way before."

These were sweet words, blurted out without apparent forethought or a trace of design. But his obsession with Candover still disturbed her. She wanted Anthony happy and laughing, as he often was with her, not the dour, supercilious man she'd first known. She'd meant what she'd told him: she was certain that bringing about Candover's ruin wouldn't make him feel any better.

Humor and affection were what he needed to dispel the ghost of his mother.

And she doubted she'd long resist the urge to provide them. During an almost sleepless night she'd admitted to herself that she yearned to return to Anthony's bed.

The decision was made quickly.

She would. This very night. But she wouldn't tell him now. Let him continue to wonder. If, as he'd said, anticipation increased the appetite, then uncertainty must increase it doubly. Then later, while he was changing for dinner, she'd slip out to the terrace and deliver the signal. She'd feel his arms about her again, his naked flesh against hers, and they'd lose themselves in the delight of kisses and caresses and laughter and ecstasy, and he wouldn't be able to think of anything else. She'd drive the thought of her uncle from his head and make love to him until he never thought of Candover again.

He interrupted her ardent imaginings. "I have something to tell you, Jacobin. Your uncle is coming here tomorrow."

It was like being drenched in icy water.

"You'll need to keep out of the way, but that won't be a problem. You'll be busy in the kitchen. You must cook your most lavish dishes for him."

Anthony's trepidation about delivering the news proved justified. She stopped short beside him, and the expression on her face turned from softness to thunder. Her eyes flashed the accompanying lightning.

"You expect me to cook for that swine? To waste the fruits of my art on offal?"

"Think, Jacobin. He'll be so gorged on the fruits of your art he'll agree to play cards again and I'll ruin him. We'll both be avenged." He hoped this appeal to her unfiner feelings would appease her.

He was disappointed.

"*Jamais!* I will never cook for that man. I'd die rather." Her breast heaved magnificently. As always, Jacobin in a rage was a vision to be relished.

"Please, Jacobin. You see, it's your cooking he's coming here for. He heard the reports of your triumph at my London dinner." Play on her professional pride, that was the way to persuade her.

Her eyes were wide with horror. "Now I know why you hired me. I never could understand it when you don't even like sweets."

"That's not true," he interjected hastily. "I love some of your sweets! Little puffy—"

She cut him off with a sweep of her arm. "Don't you dare mention *anything* that has happened between us. The truth is I was bait. A fat, wriggling worm on the end of a hook to lure Candover here and let you enact your foolish revenge. I won't do it!"

"I'm afraid I must insist. Who does it matter who you cook for, anyway? It's quite simple. You merely have to do your job, and finally the man will agree to a rematch at piquet."

Her expression was no longer liquid with rage. It was set in frozen fury. "Finally," she pounced. "Finally, you say. Do you mean he has been refusing to play with you?"

"Yes. He's refused all my invitations until now."

"But he's bitten at the big, fat worm on the end of your hook. You are clever, my lord. But has it occurred to you that he may still refuse to lose his fortune to you?"

He opened his mouth but she cut him off again.

"Of course it's occurred to you. You know all about Candover. You know his stubbornness and you know his weaknesses. You know he can't resist *pâtisserie*. You know he hasn't had a pastry cook since Jean-Luc left. I'm not just bait, am I? I'm a stake. You intend to use me as a bet in another card game with Candover."

Put so bluntly it sounded shocking. "I hoped you wouldn't have to know. There's no chance of me losing," he assured her.

"My uncle is one of the best piquet players in England. When he loses it's at whist with the prince and his friends. His skills at piquet have been keeping his estate from disaster for years."

"I am better. I've spent hours studying the game. He cannot beat me."

"Of course he can. I'm not stupid. I know the luck of the cards can be fickle and defeat even the best player. Do you intend to cheat? To fuzz the cards?"

"Certainly not," he said indignantly. "I'd never do anything so dishonorable. And I have no need."

"You speak to me of your precious honor," she hissed. "Where's the honor, I'd like to know, in using a human being as a stake, as a pawn in your game, not once but twice? I say this to your honor." She spat on the ground.

He'd never seen a woman so angry. For a moment he almost gave in, almost promised not to risk her. Loathing for Candover fought his desire for Jacobin. But the thought of renouncing his long-cherished vengeance was like a sword to the gut. He had to see the game through to the end.

He'd lose her, for sure. She'd leave him now. That's what women did when you allowed yourself to care for them. Like his mother. And his nurse. It was safer not to allow yourself to care.

Ignoring the chill that was gathering around his heart, he wrapped his soul in hatred and assuaged it with the prospect of final victory.

"Shall we discuss the menu?" he suggested.

Chapter 20

She spent hours in the inadequately furnished kitchen, oblivious of the hostility of Mrs. Simpson and her staff, preparing all her uncle's favorite dishes. Except the rose Bavarian cream. She and Storrington had agreed, quite without irony, in the terse discussion that followed her capitulation, that a repetition of that particular dish might upset Candover's stomach.

As she stirred and kneaded and mixed and baked she felt as though her very essence was draining into the motions of her craft and her lifeblood was flavoring the food.

The outcome of the card game didn't concern her. Win or lose, she wouldn't be there to see it. She was leaving as soon as dinner was served.

"I need three more baking trays," she informed Mrs. Simpson curtly. Crashing the metal *plaques* down on the marble slab, she imagined they were his head.

How could he?

Mirlitons and *fanchonnettes*—such pretty names for featherlight pastry frivolities—went into the oven. Bang!

A noble earl. Pah! She'd known truer nobility in the servants' hall. No cook, footman, or lowly scullion would play games with another's life like those noble lords, Candover and Storrington.

She beat violet essence into cream as though it were Anthony's face under the whisk.

Where she'd end up she didn't know. Jean-Luc had given her enough money to pay for her passage to France, and it wouldn't take her long to reach the coast. But people would be looking for her. If she was arrested en route she'd land in jail.

The prospect hardly dismayed her. Nothing mattered but her broken heart.

Fool that she was, she'd fallen in love with him. *Now* she had to realize it. Now that he'd proven himself utterly unworthy of the emotion. And because she loved him she'd acceded to his request, agreed to help him lure Candover to his doom. And after she'd done this for him she'd never see him again. This time there could be no forgiveness.

By late afternoon everything was ready, except beignets and cheesecakes, which must be cooked at the last minute and served warm. She stepped out into the kitchen court for some much-needed air when a familiar voice intruded on her despairing thoughts.

"Well, well, this is a surprise."

Her uncle! She knew he'd arrived at Storrington, but never dreamed he'd demean himself by appearing in the servants' area.

"I came to find this famous cook of Storrington's,"

he said as his beady eyes took in the significance of her cook's apron. "It appears that I have. I suppose Jean-Luc taught you the secrets of the kitchen as well as the bedroom."

That crack had to be pure spite. Candover was surely aware of his former cook's nature.

"It's lucky he did," she retorted. "It's given me something to do so I don't have to depend on your loving kindness."

"What a delicious irony that you've ended with Storrington." His face darkened. "I was shamed when you ran off, you know. I had to renege on a bet and it cost me a pretty penny.

Jacobin shrugged, determined not to show her consternation. "That was your problem not mine. I wasn't yours to wager."

Candover's bulk towered over her, his breathing stertorous and complexion apoplectic. "What else were you good for? I kept you for years. I decided to get some use out of you."

Instinct told her to leave his malicious presence, but there was one question she needed answered if she was to understand the disastrous path she'd been forced to take.

"Why? What did my father do to make you hate him?"

For a moment she detected something like pain shake his fleshy countenance and dull his piggy eyes, then his expression returned to its usual malevolence.

"He stole something from me."

"My father never stole anything in his entire life," she retorted. "He was a good man, the best of men. And even if he did, what has that to do with me?"

"Every time I look at you," Candover said with a bitter sneer, "I see him, right down to that damnable cleft chin. Auguste always got what he wanted because of his looks. He had nothing. No money, no power. But people loved him—women loved him—because he was beautiful. I had everything to offer but my face wasn't good enough."

"You are a ridiculous buffoon!" She might have felt pity for his twisted view of humanity, but she was too angry. "My father had far more to offer than his appearance. He was brilliant, witty, and above all he was a good man. I don't pretend to know what you're talking about, but I can tell you one thing. If you had one iota of my father's kindness, if you had shown even a hint of compassion to a lonely orphan, I would have loved you. And if you treat everyone else the way you treated me, no wonder everyone hates you. There is nothing—nothing—about you to love."

Candover's eyes popped as though his head was about to explode. "That's not true! Edgar loves me. He's like a son to me."

"Edgar knows which side his bread is buttered."

She feared she'd gone too far, that he would hit her. She took a deep breath and tried to calm her racing heart. Satisfying as it was to rail at Candover, she mustn't forget her own immediate danger. He might not yet have connected her with the missing Pavilion cook, but he could do so at any time. Her uncle would love to turn her over to the runners for trying to murder him.

Hands on hips, she stood and looked at him with muted defiance. His own emotions seemed to have subsided, too. He stared back inscrutably.

"Does Storrington enjoy your favors too?" he asked suddenly. "If he knows who you are, then he's been doubly paid, by God."

"I go under the name of Jane Castle," she said evasively. She prayed he wouldn't make the connection with Jacob Léon.

He seemed more concerned with the earl's actions. "Storrington made me crawl." He brooded, seeming to forget her presence. "I had to beg for extra time to meet my obligation. I put up with the humiliation because of the memory of his mother but I haven't forgotten his insolence. It's time to make him pay."

How wonderful! She was now caught in the middle of a grudge match between two men, each bent on vengeance.

"If you want to eat tonight," she said coolly, "I must return to the kitchen."

Candover's expression took on the particular focus that only sweet foods could generate. "What's on the menu?" he asked.

Jacobin thought she might as well indulge his request, given the farcical turn the encounter had taken. "*Gâteau de Compiègne*, with cherries and angelica; small *vol-au-vent*s filled with whipped cream *à la vio-*

lette; darioles; a selection of small pastries; chocolate custard; beignets *à la dauphine*, and *talmouses* cheese-cakes as a warm remove."

Candover nodded approvingly as she enumerated the dishes. "You know my tastes, Jacobin. Perhaps I'll take you back, after all."

Shaken by the encounter, Jacobin retired to her room to gather her scant possessions in preparation for flight. She found the chamber warm; a cheerful fire burned in the small hearth, imparting light as well as heat.

Damn Anthony! He must have ordered it. Simpson the butler would never have lifted a finger for her comfort. Why did he have to do this now?

He was making it hard for her to leave. She collapsed onto the bed and lay flat on her back. The anger that had propelled her through the day faded and she felt only cold misery. But just as the tendrils of warmth from the fire soothed her exhausted body, recollections of Anthony's many kindnesses to her invaded her unwilling brain.

In most ways the noble Earl of Storrington had been far from callous in his treatment of her. Beginning with his assistance to an unknown boy beset by bullies, he'd been—well, noble. He'd given her a job when her circumstances were dubious, to say the least. True, he had an ulterior motive there, but she wasn't the only pastry cook in England. He might have found one with less capacity to cause trouble. And he'd helped her: helped her escape from the Bellamys' garden and used his resources to protect her from the charges of attempted murder. And what he did when he touched her turned her bones to syrup.

In the balance on the other side were his deception and exploitation of her in pursuit of an obsessive drive for vengeance. Major sins, to be sure, but not unforgivable if he would only draw back from the darkness that engulfed his soul. Instinct told her that she could bring him back to sunlight and joy.

An idea sprouted in her mind and took root. She tried to ignore it, but the seedling found fertile ground and grew until it forced itself on her consciousness. In truth she wanted to forgive him, but only if he gave her good reason. If he deserved it. She tried to be calm, to dampen her impetuosity, and to act, for once, rationally and with forethought.

Though the dinner hour was fast approaching and she must return to the kitchen, she made no effort to pack. Instead she extracted something from her chest of drawers, put on her cloak, and made her way cautiously downstairs and out by a side door.

She wouldn't abandon the man she loved to the cold comfort of revenge. She'd offer him one more chance to take another path.

Simpson was taking advantage of a few minutes' peace to enjoy a pipe in the garden, when he heard a noise near the house. It shouldn't be the master or his guest; they were changing for dinner. Peering through an azalea bush he saw a female figure illuminated by the light of an outdoor lantern. It was his master's fancy French cook. And fancy something else too, if he wasn't mistaken.

Whatever airs the woman gave herself, he was still butler here and in charge. She had no business on the terrace, and he looked forward to giving the hussy what for.

But by the time he'd made his way up the stone steps and across the upper lawn she'd disappeared. He examined the area, in case she'd hidden somewhere nearby, and something caught his eye, something pinkish attached to the handle of a stone urn and fluttering in the breeze.

It looked like a lady's garter. Mrs. Simpson was right. The creature was no better than a common slut. He had no doubt of the message the slip of satin was meant to convey, or of its intended recipient. It was no coincidence that His Lordship had ordered the terrace was to be kept lit at all times.

Simpson knew someone who'd be very interested in this piece of intelligence. And would pay for it too.

Chapter 21

The first two bottles of Anthony's best Clos de Bèze Chambertin slipped down Candover's throat as though it were water, but without noticeable effect on the peer's sobriety. The man had an extraordinary capacity for alcohol; Anthony had several more bottles decanted and ready for him. Candover seemed reserved, not fully engaged in his idle gossip about the Prince Regent's set.

Not until the beignets made their appearance as a sweet entremet to the first course did Candover show more than polite interest in the lavish meal. He consumed several of the fried pastries and let out a satisfied sigh.

"As good as I've ever tasted, Storrington," he said, his complexion heightened to a dull puce. "Your cook has an exquisite touch with the brioche." He stuffed another into his mouth, leaving a trace of powdered sugar on his chin.

"I was fortunate to find Miss Castle," Anthony replied, beckoning Simpson to bring in the next course.

He found a certain fascination in examining his guest's appearance, seeking any resemblance to his niece. It was hard to believe that Jacobin, lithe, colorful, and glowing with health and energy, was closely related to the epicure sitting beside him at one end of the long mahogany table. Candover's bulk, scarcely condensed by corseting, spilled over his chair. A roll of flesh squeezed out from the top of his high shirt points and merged with his layers of chin. If there was a cleft there it had long since been smothered in flab.

But Jacobin's chin came from her father, he recalled. He wondered what she was thinking as she worked her magic to lure Candover to destruction. Whether she would ever forgive him.

"Your house is magnificent." Candover was becoming more expansive as he addressed himself to roast goose and cucumbers in béchamel. His eager eyes investigated the other half-dozen dishes being laid out by the footmen. He partook lightly of the savory offerings. "I've always been curious to see it, since I became acquainted with your parents in Paris. I always hoped your late father would extend me an invitation."

Anthony stiffened. For a moment he discerned a challenge in Candover's tone, as though the man were goading him.

"Did we ever speak of the time I spent in Paris?" Candover continued. "I was there for the pleasure of marrying off my sister to an utterly worthless Frenchman. A revolutionary, he turned out to be, would you believe it? He was nearly the biter bit, y'know. Sentenced to the guillotine and rescued just in time. Pity that."

"That must have been a great joy for your sister," Anthony said with a hint of reproof. From everything he'd heard, Candover's brother-in-law, Jacobin's father, was a likable, even admirable man. Jacobin's words about her father and his forgiveness of his enemies nagged at his brain. He tried to contemplate forgiving Candover, who was now filling his plate from the sweet dishes.

"Ah! *Crème française au chocolat.* Chocolate is such an underrated food. It deserves to be used for far more than drinking." Candover's face became ecstatic as he spooned cake, custard, and candied fruit into his mouth. "Magnificent!" He grew redder; perspiration beaded on his pale forehead; he swayed a little in his seat as he ate, as though drunk on sweets.

Anthony began to worry that Candover might not remain conscious for long. He made no move to replenish his guest's empty wineglass.

"Paris," Candover said, suddenly alert again. "We were speaking of Paris. And your mother. I believe we were speaking of Catherine. I think I've told you before, Storrington, how beautiful Catherine was. Everyone was in love with her."

Did the man have a death wish? Anthony wondered, clenching his hands together to prevent them fastening around Candover's elephantine neck. But he'd never given the man any reason to suspect he knew of his affair with his mother. He quelled his anger and turned the subject to trivialities. His time would come.

Candover became more jovial as he sampled each of Jacobin's creations. He was full of praise for the desserts and dropped leaden hints about meeting the cook. "You have a most valuable servant, Storrington. She should be congratulated in person."

Anthony parried the suggestion. "I wouldn't wish to disturb the kitchen now. There's more to come with the remove."

"The artistic temperament." Candover nodded knowingly. "Cooks are like artists, you know. Each has an individual touch with pastry." He popped a morsel between his lips. "Your woman's touch reminds me of my late *pâtissier*, Jean-Luc. He was a genius. As brilliant in his way as Carême. I suppose you wouldn't let your woman—Castle I think you said her name was—come to me?"

The hook was baited but Anthony jerked it aside. "Hardly," he said. "As you rightly say, a good pastry cook is hard to find."

"Yet you take only modest advantage of her talents." Candover stared at Anthony's lightly laden plate.

Anthony nibbled at a *vol-au-vent* that tasted rather unpleasantly of violets. He preferred his flowers in vases. "Quality matters more than quantity, surely?" he asked, glancing at Candover's girth, which he would swear had gained several inches since the start of dinner. "Besides, a good cook is such a boon to one's guests. I'm sorry you weren't present at my recent dinner in London but I collect you were still recovering from your unfortunate illness." He smiled. "I doubt if I'd have the pleasure of your company now had Miss Castle's fame not spread."

Now was the moment to propose a hand of piquet. The gusto with which Candover was devouring pastries suggested that even a hint of using the cook as a stake would lure the man from his self-imposed abstinence from cards. But with the smell of victory in his senses, Anthony couldn't find the words. His mind's eye kept seeing Jacobin's devastated face.

"I suppose you'll want to play cards after dinner," Candover said.

Anthony hadn't had to say it after all.

"I wondered if you'd wish for a chance to recoup your losses," he replied, but with curious reluctance.

Candover grunted. "Did you say there was another course?"

Half an hour later even Candover was sated. He leaned back, his vast stomach distended and causing Anthony a moment's anxiety for the continued health of the matched set of Hepplewhite dining chairs.

"Splendid painting over there," the old glutton said. "Though a trifle gruesome for a dining room, perhaps." He was pointing, not at the famous Storrs Raphael that hung over the mantelpiece, but at a smaller Dutch painting on the wall facing him. Of the many works of art in the Storrington collection, it wasn't the one most likely to draw the attention of visitors, though it had always caused the current earl a certain amusement. It showed an elderly graybeard beset by demons and virtuously resisting the blandishments of a voluptuous seductress: *The Temptation of St. Anthony.*

Anthony wondered who was tempting whom.

The Queen's House was cold and dark. By the light of a single candle, Jacobin drew the curtains before lighting fires, upstairs and down. The last thing she wanted was some nosy servant glimpsing a light and coming down to see who was in the deserted folly at this time of night.

The warmth dispelled the gloom but not her anxiety.

Would he come? Did he care enough—no, forget affection, that was too much to expect—did he *want* her enough to set aside revenge? It seemed an absurdly slender hope.

She'd left the kitchen as the footmen collected the last course for delivery to the dining room. It would be at least an hour before dinner was over, very likely more if the gentlemen lingered over wine. Her uncle always lingered over wine.

To calm her nerves she roamed the house, examining the exquisite appointments and marveling that the late Lady Storrington had shown such indifference to this jewel of a gift. What a nice man Anthony's father must have been, to go to so much effort and expense for his wife, especially if he believed her faithless. What a foolish woman to reject such an expression of love, and neglect her own children. And all for a man like Candover.

In the upstairs chamber she turned her back on the bed, which filled her with mingled anticipation and dread for what she hoped would happen soon, and turned her attention to a large walnut armoire with a double-domed cornice. To her surprise it was filled with clothing. She pulled out a tulle gown, still crisp though its white had faded to palest yellow. It looked to be about her size. At least this time she would be properly dressed.

The simple chemise gown had deep ruffles around the neckline and hem, its only other adornment a gauze sash with a gold filigree pattern. She recalled her mother wearing such garments, which were brought into fashion by her beloved Marie Antoinette. Mama had long resisted the post-revolutionary fashion for raised waistlines, rejecting the new regime's styles along with its politics.

What an odd couple her parents had been, she reflected: her father handsome and glittering as a comet in the night sky, her rather plain mother the model of a staid Englishwoman. What was it like for Mama, she wondered, to be always overshadowed by her husband, to be stranded by political upheaval in a foreign land? Felicity must have had reserves of strength disguised by her prim exterior and which her daughter had never suspected. Like everyone else, Jacobin had been dazzled by Auguste's brilliance and failed to appreciate her mother's less exciting qualities.

She remembered the last time she'd thought about her mother, when she was preparing for her previous meeting with Anthony in this house.

"I'm sorry, Mama," she whispered out loud. "It's not what you'd have wanted but it's what I must do."

Speaking of which, where the hell was he? If he'd heeded the message, surely he'd be here by now. Unless he had the unmitigated gall to think her offer would still be open *after* a session at the tables with Candover.

He couldn't be so stupid.

She lay down on the bed and waited.

"Shall we raise the stakes?"

They had been playing quietly for two hours. It was almost dull. The luck of the cards ran evenly with no extraordinary scores on either side. Anthony, playing with his usual mathematical precision, was ahead, but by only a few hundred pounds. Now he could sense his opponent feeling his age, his weight, and the three bottles of Burgundy and several pounds of sugar he'd consumed.

Candover appeared to ponder the suggestion as he gathered up the cards from the last *partie,* which he'd won by a narrow margin.

This was the moment, when Candover felt confident that the gods of fortune had turned in his direction. Anthony knew better: he didn't believe in luck, only his well-honed skills, diligent study of Mr. Hoyle's treatise on piquet, and hours of practice figuring the odds. There lay the difference between himself and his foe. Candover was a true gambler.

It was time to move in for the kill.

Irrelevantly Anthony found his eyes drawn to the

draped windows. He realized he'd forgotten to check the urn before dinner. Not that he expected any signal from Jacobin now. Or, he had to admit sadly, ever. He could only hope she wasn't packing her bags, having played her part so perfectly this evening. Anthony knew it was her cooking that had lured Candover to the card table. Now he must try and win without risking her. Still, he was tempted to look outside, until he remembered that it wouldn't do any good. For whatever reason he'd elected to hold his final confrontation with Candover in one of the small sitting rooms at the front of the house, rather than entertaining his enemy in the library, his own special sanctum.

It made a curiously tame domestic setting for the denouement of months of planning. Decorated in cheerful shades of yellow and pale blue, the room had been used by Kitty and her companion before his sister's marriage. Now the center of the room was dominated by a card table, opened to its green baize playing surface.

"How much?" Candover asked.

"Shall we say twenty thousand for the *partie*? There seems a certain—artistic justice in the figure."

"Indeed. My slut of a niece cost me a pretty sum. Not to mention my cook."

Anthony burned with anger at hearing her uncle's crude reference to Jacobin. He looked forward to vindicating her too, through Candover's downfall.

"Twenty thousand for the *partie*, you say." Candover made a pretense of deep consideration, but it seemed to Anthony that the man had already made up his mind.

Candover was toying with *him*. "Twenty thousand it is, but instead of money, I want your cook."

It has come down to this, just as he'd intended, and Anthony found he couldn't close the deal. He couldn't get Jacobin's face out of his mind. "I don't think so," he said. "The money or nothing. It doesn't sit well with me to wager a human being."

Candover's great body heaved with laughter. "You weren't so squeamish before. You were ready enough to take that jade Jacobin, damn her! Are you afraid of losing?"

Anthony braced himself against Candover's taunts and fixed the boor with a steely gaze. He remained silent. He sensed that Candover wanted to play. He could outwait him.

"I never took you for a milksop, Storrington. A lily-livered coward afraid to take the plunge." The fleshy face thrust forward. Malice glinted from Candover's porcine eyes. "They say the apple doesn't fall far from the tree. Your father was a weakling too. And your mother was insane."

Anthony saw red. "Have it your way, Candover. Twenty thousand pounds against Jane Castle's contract."

Jacobin didn't know the time, but she must have been at the Queen's House for three hours, maybe four. She had to face the fact that he wasn't coming. She buried her head in the pillows and wept.

Chapter 22

Candover won the cut and dealt first, giving Anthony the early advantage. After five hands he was comfortably ahead, by seventy-three points. It all came down to one deal.

Candover held the elder hand and the opportunity for a big score. Nevertheless, only by a disaster could Anthony lose now. He dealt out the thirty-two cards, two at a time. Twelve cards each and eight in the stock for discards. It took tight control for his fingers not to shake as he picked up his hand and inspected it with an expert glance.

Disaster.

As an elder hand it wouldn't have been impossible. Seven spades, lacking only the king. The king and a small card each in hearts and diamonds. And the seven of clubs. But his opponent would both declare and lead first, giving him the possibility of winning the big bonuses for a pique or repique.

Candover took all five discards to which he was entitled, and Anthony, with the option of only three cards to exchange, assessed his opponent's hand and his own chances.

Unless he picked up the right cards the best he could hope for would be a tie in the match, and then only if he played perfectly. But if Candover held the cards to score a repique Anthony's lead would be wiped out and more.

He gazed at the three cards remaining in the stock. Without improving his hand, he had almost no chance of avoiding defeat. Yet what to discard? His best hope was to pick up the king of spades, which would give him a winning hand. It would be helpful, and probably avoid defeat, if one of those three cards was an ace. And yet he couldn't maximize his chances by taking three discards without losing his guard in one of the red suits. If the gamble failed his loss was inevitable.

Anthony never gambled. He knew the rules: play according to the odds and you'll always come out a winner. And he almost always did.

Almost. That was the crux of the matter. In this case *almost* wasn't good enough. He craved certainty.

He tried to calculate the odds, as he'd done a hundred times. His brain felt thick and dark, like the chocolate custard he'd disdained at dinner.

He fingered the seven of clubs, the one card he could safely do without. What were the odds that a discard of only one would improve his hand? God help him, he couldn't think.

Candover was grinning like a cat who'd found a salmon. He knew what he held and what it meant, as well as Anthony did. With an effort of will Anthony brought his mind to bear on the problem, forced all emotion from his thought process, and concentrated on mathematics.

He knew the answer.

It was unacceptable.

He thought of Jacobin, waiting to hear whether she was about to be turned over to her vile uncle. Although, of course, she'd refuse to go. He'd end up paying the twenty thousand and that didn't matter to him; he'd gladly pay twice, three times as much to save her. But too late he realized that wasn't the point. It never had been. She'd been right all along.

He stood up. Threw the cards on the table.

"I'm sorry, my lord," he said. "I can't go through with this. I regret that I must call off the wager."

"Then I get the cook!" Candover cried triumphantly.

"No," Anthony insisted. "The bet is off."

Followed by bellows of rage and threats of social ruin, Anthony walked out of the room.

He found her in the bedroom. She stood before him, her dress crushed as though she'd been lying down in it, and her eyes reddened. She'd never looked more beautiful. He reached for her, aching for her warmth, aware in the depths of his heart that only Jacobin's touch could console him.

The raised flat of her hand held him off. Her eyes were stormy, implacable.

"So, Storrington. Have you come to deliver me to my uncle?"

"No—"

"Oh, you won, did you? Just as you predicted. I suppose you think that makes everything *magnifique*." She didn't actually spit at him but she might as well have.

"I didn't play, or at least I did but it wasn't the way you think—"

She wasn't listening. She'd worked herself into a fine state of fury and strode around the room, firing off French insults and gesticulating with clenched fists. "*Merdeille!* Do you feel better now, *bâtard*? Has victory made up for all the ills of your miserable life? *Tricheur!*"

"Listen, you little spitfire—"

"You played with Candover and left me out here—alone—for hours. How dare you speak to me? How dare you even try to excuse yourself? So, my lord. Did you ruin my uncle? Are you happy now? All I have to say is take your victory and put it—"

"Stop!" he shouted, grabbing her wrists. "There was no victory."

The words, spoken slow and loud, penetrated her ire. The flailing body stilled and she stared at him, mouth hanging agape in mid-tirade.

"There was no victory," he repeated. "If anything I lost much more than my chance at revenge. I'll most likely be thrown out of my clubs and shunned by most of London's polite society."

"That can't be true. How can they throw you, an earl, out of anywhere? Unless . . . *Mon Dieu*, did you cheat?"

"Not quite that bad, but almost. I walked out of the game holding a losing hand. 'Struth, I can't believe I did such a thing."

She didn't appear shocked, though at least he had her attention. Women just didn't understand these things.

He sighed and let go of her wrists to run both hands through his hair. "I suppose I'd better tell you what happened." He slumped onto a bench at the foot of the bed.

Jacobin perched on the edge of the mattress, but not so close that he could reach her. Once the initial blaze of rage burned off she felt calmer and prepared to listen, though she castigated herself as a weak creature for doing so. He looked haggard and sounded so desolate she felt her foolish heart soften.

"You asked him to play cards?" she prompted.

"Yes. Or perhaps he asked me," he said slowly. "I'm not sure. He was just as eager for the game as I." He smiled at her warily. "Your cooking pleased him excessively."

"I knew he wouldn't be able to resist those dishes, the pig. Go on." She didn't add that Candover had discovered who she was, though she couldn't have said why.

"We played for a while, then I suggested we increase the stakes."

"Did you offer me?"

"No, I didn't want to. I tried to make him play for money but he refused. Then *he* suggested playing for your contract of service."

Her heart thudded. "How much?" she whispered.

"Twenty thousand again."

"Did you agree?" She could hardly breathe.

"Not at first. But then—" He stopped and turned his head aside, and she found it hard to judge his expression. "But then . . . he called me a coward."

Foolish male pride, she thought with returning irritation.

"He called me a coward, just like my father. And he said my mother was mad."

"The filthy bastard! Poisoning was too good for him. I wish he'd choked on a *vol-au-vent*!" Even she could see how unbearably Anthony had been provoked, deliberately so if she knew anything about Candover.

"So I agreed." He bowed his head and hid his face in his hands. "I'm so sorry. I should never have agreed. In my damnable arrogance I thought I couldn't lose." He looked up again and his lips stretched in a smile without a hint of humor. "You were right about that, of course."

"Finish the story," she said gently.

His voice was flat. "We played and I was winning. Then in the final hand, the cards turned against me. The chances were minuscule that I would win. And I couldn't go through with it."

Candover must have been furious. Jacobin had spent her life among French liberals and English servants, giving her an imperfect perspective on the values of the English upper classes. But she hadn't spent all those years in the household of an English gambler without learning about the sanctity of the wager. *A gentleman never reneges on a bet. A gentleman always meets his debts of honor.* The refrain roared through Hurst Park whenever her uncle hit a losing streak and came home to demand Edgar find the money in the estate.

She didn't set much store by Candover's maxims, given his complete lack of any quality she found gentlemanly. But Anthony shared those values. By ending the card game he'd violated every tenet of his upbringing. He'd been wrong, dreadfully wrong, to agree to her uncle's stake, yet he'd atoned for his sin in a spectacular fashion.

"And he called you a coward! He was wrong. What you did took great courage. And you did it for me."

"When it came to the point I found I couldn't risk you."

She jumped up and in an instant was in his lap, cradling his head in her hands and covering his face with kisses. She caressed his head and made soothing noises. His face, which had over the weeks become so dear to her, was drawn and weary. He needed consolation. In fact he deserved it. She kissed him on the lips, stroking the tips of her fingers around his ears.

He seemed to like that, emitting a little guttural sound of appreciation, so she did it some more, and ran her tongue along the seam of his mouth. It opened and welcomed her in while his arms returned her embrace, exploring the curves of her body even as hers moved lower to revel in the muscular contours through super-fine cloth. They kissed deeply and hotly, as though they would devour each other.

"I need you so much," he said softly between kisses, and the desire in his syrup-thick tones matched the swelling of his body beneath her legs. She needed him too. She was in bliss after the dismal hours waiting for him to come, fearing that he wouldn't, in despair because he seemed to have made the wrong choice.

"Wait a minute," she said, drawing back. He gave a moan of protest and moved to recapture her lips. She placed a hand over his mouth. "You made me wait here all evening for you. You might have sent me a message at least."

"I didn't know you were here. I never looked on the terrace until after the card game. I didn't expect you." He hugged her tightly. "Thank you for being here."

It was even better than she'd thought. He'd come to his senses without the incentive of bedding her. He deserved a reward and she was most willing to provide it.

"Come to bed," she said.

Chapter 23

She disengaged from his lap and stood up to look at him, her head tilted to one side, chestnut curls an untidy halo around her roguish face.

Yes, oh yes. Desire surged through him as he followed her to his feet in one smooth movement. She touched his neck cloth, and even that small contact made him think about that hand, graceful yet so capable, touching bare skin. The muscles of his torso quivered.

"Are you going to act as valet?" he growled.

Her mouth curved and he wanted to consume her whole. "If you'll be my lady's maid." The smile broadened. "You're rather large for a maid. But that hint of a beard will play havoc among the footmen."

"And you," he said, holding her by the shoulders at arms' length and scanning her figure appreciatively, "are, for a change, not dressed like a valet. Not that I'm complaining. That style"—he waved his arm in imitation of the curves so delightfully complemented by her frothy white gown—"a new fashion?"

"A very old one. I found it in the wardrobe."

"Turn," he ordered, and loosened the strings gathering the neckline of the dress, untied the sash, and relished the warm silken skin under his fingers as he slipped it down her shoulders.

"Wait," she said, holding the wispy fabric at her elbows and turning again to face him. Her voice dropped an octave. "Hm. I'm a very good valet, I think. Your *cravate* is very well arranged." She patted the elaborate waterfall of starched linen.

"You can't take credit for it. I always tie my own," he whispered. He couldn't be expected to concentrate on playful banter when she was naked almost to the waist. His hand reached out to cup one breast, small but sweetly rounded and soft to the touch, to sense its gratifying weight against his palm. He flicked the strawberry pink tip with his thumb, eliciting a purr from deep in her throat.

She unwound the cloth from his neck and unbuttoned his shirt as his other hand mimicked the actions of its mate. Then she put her arms around his neck and drew his head down for a kiss, and all he could think of was that she was too far away. He crushed her against him and still she wasn't near enough, so he tugged at her skirt, searching beneath it, and his questing hand found . . . a petticoat. And another and another until finally—oh triumph!—satin skin and no drawers.

With an incoherent grunt of approval he used both hands to push aside the layers of material and cradle the firm, soft curves of her bottom. And, wonderfully, she raised herself on tiptoe to rub her core against the hardness straining through his trousers.

"You're not doing your job," he muttered. "I'm still wearing a lot of clothes."

She grinned at him wickedly. "I'm afraid I'm not up to the task. My fingers don't seem to be working properly. I resign." And broke away from him to back onto the bed, where she faced him, half seated, half reclined, supported behind by her elbows, long elegant legs parted and emerging from a sea of white froth.

She was the personification of allure, from the enticing smile on her full raspberry lips to her dainty feet, one bare and delicately arched, the other still partly hidden by a beaded slipper hanging from the tips of her toes. He couldn't resist and made no effort to do so. Urged by the need to possess her, to drive himself into her delectable body and forget every trouble in the world outside the Queen's House, he tore off his shirt and unfastened and lowered his nether garments with unthinking agility; threw himself on her and pulled up her skirts again, intent only on finding the haven he ached for.

Unmistakably, she flinched. With a superlative effort he made himself draw back. He lay beside her on the bed and gathered her into his arms, burying his face in the curve of her shoulder, where vanilla-scented curls tickled his nose. In his own need he'd forgotten her inexperience.

Jacobin was ashamed of herself for revealing her momentary panic. She wanted him as much as he seemed to want her. The logical side of her brain knew there'd be no pain this time, but another part of that organ, over which she seemed to have no control, remembered the shock of their first, abortive coupling.

"I'm sorry," he said through deep breaths. "I'm going too fast. We don't have to do this if you're not ready."

She took his head between her hands and they lay face-to-face on the mattress, inches apart, eyes locked, guilt discernible in his expression. Her first impulse was to deny her reluctance, but she wanted honesty between them.

"I'm just a little afraid," she said softly, "though I know it shouldn't hurt this time. I do want you, very much."

One of his hands, firm and warm, reached between her thighs, and she knew she was wet there as he stroked the spot he'd once driven mad with his mouth.

"I'm glad you're not totally unprepared," he said, "but I was a selfish brute not to make sure. Let's take this slowly. I want your trust as much as I want you. What would you like me to do?"

"I like that," she said, her voice wavering as he continued to caress her.

"What else?"

"I don't know. I don't know much about this."

"Is there anything you'd like to do to me? Any way you'd like to touch me?"

She shivered, some half-formed thoughts tumbling through her mind, but she shook her head. He removed his hand, and she gave a moue of disappointment.

"Let's play a game," he said. "We'll tell each other what we'd like. It can be very . . . arousing, you know."

She didn't know and he must have read bafflement in her face.

"I'll go first. Stand up." He was on his feet and reached a hand down to her. Without another word she obeyed his gesture and followed him to the cherrywood dressing table. He arranged her on the backless seat, her bare buttocks on the velvet cushion, skirts spread about her.

"Have you ever been to the opera?" he asked.

"Once, when I was a little girl in Paris," she replied, puzzled.

"Picture yourself in a box at a theater. The table in front of you is the wall of the box and you're looking out at the crowds in the pit. The stage curtains are drawn, waiting for the performance to begin."

She could see him in the mirror, standing behind her. His lips twitched.

"Tut, tut," he said. "You're displaying rather more than is seemly in public. We'll have to do something about that." He leaned in from behind and, without even brushing his fingers over her flesh, raised the top of her dress to conceal her breasts and carefully tightened and tied the drawstring and the sash. She wanted to cry out, tell him to touch her not cover her up. "That's better. Me too," he added, fastening his trouser buttons.

Their eyes met in the glass, his more blue than gray and glowing sensually. She ached for his hands on her, yet found something erotic in his distance, making her keenly aware of velvet under her thighs while her mind conjured other sensations on her skin.

"The orchestra is beginning to play now and the curtain goes up. You are lost in the music." She closed her eyes, envisioning the scene, the scent and heat of oil lamps, the sounds of the crowds below her mingling with that of harmonious singing. Ever aware of the man standing behind her, and of his voice, the dearest sound in the world to her.

Suddenly she felt cool air at her lower back and opened her eyes. He was leaning over her and raising her skirts, which he tucked into the back of her sash.

"I stand behind you," he continued, low and husky, "and I care nothing for the opera, only for you. I want you now. So I raise your skirts and caress your sweet little rump." He made no move to touch her but her inner passage throbbed at his words, and she leaned forward over the dressing table and involuntarily arched her back, further exposing her bottom.

"Yes, my love. Slide back on the seat and open yourself to my hands as I stroke your silken skin. So smooth, so perfect."

In the mirror she held his torrid gaze, the cool gray

eyes transformed into a stormscape of roiling seas and St. Elmo's fire. And groaned with frustration as he continued to stand motionless.

"Hush, my love. The people in the next box will notice what we're doing if you make a sound. Lean on the padded front of the box and fix your attention on the stage so that I can pleasure you without anyone noticing."

Gritting her teeth, she rested her arms on the dressing table. Who would have known mere words could be so arousing. So frustrating.

"Now I kneel behind you and kiss every exposed inch, run my tongue along the valley between your buttocks, and my fingers tangle in your hair and slide into your hot, wet center to tease you where it feels best."

She'd give him tease! She was going to scream if he didn't touch her soon.

But he used words alone, describing what he did to her with his hands and lips, lavishly praising her response, graphically delineating his own reactions. Words that aroused her to a peak of longing without his laying a single finger on her.

Her breath came in gasps and she was an inferno, ready to explode, to shatter into a shower of embers. Maddened beyond reason she shifted to kneel on the velvet seat, thrust her face into her arms on the dressing table and raised her behind above parted thighs to offer herself to him.

"You're so hot, so wet, so ready for me. And I'm *so* ready for you, hard and aching."

"Anthony," she cried. "Now! For God's sake now!"

"Quiet, love. Not long now. I'm undoing my buttons." She couldn't see or hear anything and feared he was doing nothing of the sort. She was becoming insane with lust.

"Now!" he said. "Now at last I'm inside you, thrusting into you, feeling you warm and slick and tight around me. You're adorable, driving me wild."

He was driving her wild. She was on the edge of that ecstatic tumble into oblivion, but she couldn't quite get there on words alone. She cried out his name in frustration.

"Yes! Yes! Yes!" he shouted in an escalating rhythm. Then with a final cry of triumph he fell silent. And sighed. "That was perfect."

And that was all.

After some moments she struggled to her feet in disbelief. "You can't leave me like this!" she shrieked, slewing around to face him. He was grinning at her, but she was glad to see lines of strain about his mouth, a hint of her own dissatisfaction mirrored in his eyes. And judging by the bulge in his trousers, he was far from done for the evening.

"Fun, isn't it," he said, reaching for her and drawing her into his embrace.

"Fun! Fun?" she fumed. "I'll give you fun."

"Later," he said, still smiling. "Don't forget what I said about anticipation."

He looked so pleased with himself she had to smile back. "You are outrageous. Would you actually do that in a crowded theater. *Have* you ever?"

"The thing about fantasies is that they don't have to be something you'd care to do in real life. The answer is no and no. For a start the box walls are the wrong height and the chairs have backs. Worse still, everything would be in full view of the people in the adjoining boxes, and this isn't something I like to do with an audience. But one can dream." He kissed the top of her head. "Now it's your turn."

"Turn for what?"

"To tell me what you want to do to me. I should think you'd have some ideas after that."

"I most certainly do," she said, her voice rising with the return of a kind of annoyance. "What I'd like to do is tie you to the posts of that bed so you can't move."

"Yes?" he prompted. He didn't seem at all upset at the notion. "Then?"

She recalled their adventures with the profiteroles and cream. "Then I'd cover you with *crème chantilly* over every inch of your body and lick it off, especially"—she pointed at the bulge between his thighs—"*there*. And then I'd leave you before you were satisfied."

He roared with laughter and tightened his embrace. "I adore you, Jacobin, though that's not very kind. At least in my fantasy *you* were satisfied."

"You didn't say so."

"Didn't I? Well, I assure you that you were. And I promise you will be in truth before much more time passes."

She was relieved to hear it and looked longingly at the bed. Any hint of dread had vanished, and she couldn't wait to become horizontal again. He was nuzzling her ear and creating new tremors in her eager body.

"Come to bed," he said.

He was rock-hard and almost dizzy with longing. Seduced as much as she by his own words, he'd had to exert every bit of control he could muster not to make his fantasy real. But this wasn't just any woman. This was Jacobin, the most important thing in the world to him. He wanted, needed, to show her that he'd changed, that his selfish concerns were dust in the wind compared to her happiness. So he hesitated, his ingrained self-confidence dissolved with his arrogance. How could he make it perfect for her?

"Well?" she asked with a touch of impatience. "Should we undress?"

Trust her to not wait for his lead. For a moment he'd made the mistake of imagining her a shrinking violet. Yet she'd never shown a hint of shyness or diffidence. Not his Jacobin. She charged into events headfirst, and he suspected he could spend the rest of his life happily following her.

She ran a hand over his bare chest and rubbed a nipple with her thumb. His cock burgeoned and ached harder, though he wouldn't have thought it possible. "Look at me," she said. "I'm fully dressed and you should be dismissed for incompetence.

"*Mon lapin. Mon coeur,*" he whispered, untying the strings at her neckline again.

"Your French is improving." She replaced her thumb with her mouth.

Without finesse he reached behind her and jerked at the sash. She shrugged the loosened gown from her shoulders, and it fell to the ground with a muslin rustle. Then she set her lips to the other nipple and used her tongue to play with it.

Every one of those damn petticoats had its own tapes.

"I can't untie them," he said helplessly. "You'll have to do it. My fingers won't work."

She raised her head at a quizzical angle. "You are most definitely dismissed." Her lips, the color of new wine but doubly intoxicating, curved in an invitation he had to accept.

"You are rehired," she said, emerging a little breathless from a long, deep kiss. "Despite your shortcomings you have some useful skills."

His answer came in little more than a croak. "I am gratified to have pleased my lady."

And since that particular service had proved acceptable, he cradled her head in trembling hands and repeated it, drawing from her lips and mouth the scent and taste peculiar to her, both sweet and spicy with a faint continuo of vanilla.

Being Jacobin, she didn't remain passive but met his kiss thrust for thrust and drew him closer until the pressure of her peaked nipples against his chest threatened his scanty control. So he drew back, released her, and fell to his knees.

"I have a task to complete," he muttered.

Dispensing with dexterity he seized the waistbands of her petticoats and tore them apart, one, two, three, swept each fine muslin layer impatiently to the floor, parted the chestnut curls revealed, and pushed his tongue through them to find her hot, wet, and swollen. Too soon, it took only a few strokes, she uttered a little cry of delight and exploded in his mouth. He wound his arms about her hips and held her tight to him, his cheek against her stomach, filled with a sensation that felt like joy.

"*Mon Dieu!* Anthony," she said in a strangled voice. "That was wonderful."

"A good servant," he said, looking up to find her eyes round with bliss and a smile that set his heart pounding. "A good servant always endeavors to give satisfaction."

Jacobin rumpled his hair and bent down impulsively to kiss his forehead. "I think you deserve an increase in wages."

Still dazed by her climax, she wasn't sure how she found the words to continue their teasing make-believe but she wanted maintain it. She was learning that Anthony liked to play games in bed, and discovered that suited her very well. But she also sensed this particular charade had a deeper meaning. In playing the servant he renounced their previous relationship. And she thought that in kneeling at her feet and bowing to her wishes he expressed his contrition by his actions, as earlier he'd done in words.

"What is my lady's desire now?" he asked.

"A good servant anticipates his mistress's desires," she replied with a provocative look.

"I believe my lady wishes . . ." He hesitated, then rose to his feet. ". . . to be flat on her back." He snatched her into his arms and tossed her onto the bed, where she landed with a shriek and a bounce.

"Stop!" He made to join her, and she could hardly speak for laughing. "It isn't polite for a servant to wear clothes when his mistress is naked."

"My deepest apologies, madame. The matter will be attended to at once." Apparently he'd recovered his manual dexterity, for it took a matter of seconds for him to shed his pantaloons and undergarments, leaving him deliciously exposed. "I can't take care of my lady when she's so far away."

She beckoned expansively from her nest of pillows. "Approach then, lackey."

Suddenly she was tired of the game. She wanted him in her arms, not at her feet. When more than six feet of masculine muscle, sinew, and skin stretched out beside her, she rolled over to seize him. "Anthony," she cried and didn't want to weep with joy so she kissed him instead.

The linen sheets were cool, crisp, and rose-scented. He was warm and firm with a scent she couldn't have named or described but knew was his alone. She held on tight and took him with her as she returned onto her back, opened her thighs, and wound her legs about his.

And this time it was easy. He slid into her, slick and hard, filling her with joy and a sense of completion she hadn't known she lacked. His endearments gasped in her ear, barely comprehensible but nonetheless sweet, enhanced her pleasure. She experienced a tremendous sense of power. She had rendered this dominating, controlled man incoherent. And of course he'd reduced her to the same state. Her thoughts scattered and she was aware only of mounting excitement as she met his rhythmic thrusts, higher and higher until she again melted into rapture. While hot waves of delight rippled through every inch of her body, he delivered one more almost tormented cry, wrenched out of her and spent himself, then collapsed, his face buried in her shoulder.

Breath gasping in unison, they lay thus for many minutes until she felt her boneless body and shattered mind reassemble.

"That was splendid," she murmured, stretching like a cat as he rolled off her and met her eye with sated gaze. She ran an approving hand over the taut muscles of his stomach. "Can we do it again?"

He removed her hand and held it. "Later. First we need to work out how to keep you from being arrested for murder."

"That Bow Street runner will be back," Anthony said, lying comfortably against a heap of pillows. He tried to ignore Jacobin's hip nestling against his own and concentrate on keeping that hip, and the rest of her, out of jail. "We need to find definite proof against Bellamy."

"How could Bellamy have put the poison in the Bavarian cream?"

"A good question. Tell me how it got from the prince's kitchen to Candover's."

The question obviously troubled her. "The servants from Candover's and other houses bring dishes to the kitchen door after a big dinner and we fill them."

"Who?"

"The cooks."

"Is there any way of telling who filled which dish? Perhaps one of the cooks was bribed."

"I know who filled it."

"Who?" Anthony had a bad feeling about this.

She covered her face with her hands and spoke through a crack between her fingers. "I did," she replied in a small voice.

"Good God! Jacobin!" He sat up with a jerk and looked down at her in horror. "Are you sure?"

"Of course I'm sure. I recognized the coat of arms on the china."

"For God's sake don't tell anyone. We have to pray no one else noticed." He sighed. "Then what? Which of Candover's servants would have taken it?"

"My uncle keeps a very small establishment in Brighton, except in the summer. It was probably his valet."

"Is he bribable? Could Bellamy have paid him to doctor the pudding?"

"It doesn't seem likely. Morgan has been with my uncle for years. He always seemed loyal. He and Edgar's man were the only servants who weren't my friends. The only ones I wouldn't trust."

"Now I think of it, the tale going around was that the valet saved Candover by his prompt actions. Nonetheless, I'll have my secretary see what he can discover." He lay down again and embraced her protectively. He wanted nothing more in the world than to dispel her look of despondence, to make her so safe and happy she'd never leave him.

"Don't worry, sweetheart. I won't let them take you away. I have some influence, with the prince and others." A chill thought struck him. "Not as much as I had, I'm afraid, not once Candover spreads the tale of our card game."

"Will they truly care so much about that?" she asked.

"Gentlemen are supposed to be punctilious when it comes to games of chance." He couldn't even begin to explain to her how badly he'd behaved, as far as his peers were concerned.

She looked distraught. "I'm sorry you had to do that for me."

Gazing at her, he shook his head. "No. Well, yes. For you. But not just for you. For me too. You were right, Jacobin. Avenging myself on Candover was a waste of time. It wouldn't have solved anything. Not that I don't still hate the bastard, but there are more important things in life to worry about." Like the woman beside him in bed, for instance. Especially her. He'd never let her go.

He felt a reawakening of interest.

"I feel much better," he remarked.

"I'm glad. I feel very good too." Her head was tilted to one side, and she looked at him with a suggestive gleam in her eye.

"Lovemaking will do that to you. In fact, it probably has a lot to do with my current good health."

She cocked an eyebrow. "*Vraiment?*"

"Yes, really, Mademoiselle Mischief. It's been a long time for me."

"Since when?"

"Since my father died. I haven't been in the mood. Until I met you. Until the first time I set eyes on you."

"You thought I was a boy when we first met."

"Yes." He grinned. "That was a problem."

Jacobin was delighted. Perhaps he cared for her, though she dared not hope his feelings equaled her own. Still, she thought optimistically, she would work on that. She reached down and found a certain part of him expressed interest in a second bout.

"Hm," she said, imbuing her tone with invitation. "After so long you have much to make up for."

It was some time before either was capable of coherent speech.

"By the way," he whispered a while later, "sometimes fantasies can become reality. I'd be only too happy to indulge yours, with a happier conclusion, of course. And I'd like to do the same to you."

She examined the idea of him tying *her* to the bed and found it not displeasing. Somewhere along the way, she realized, she'd begun to trust this man, as well as to love him.

Less alone than she'd felt since the terrible year when she'd lost both her parents, she curled up beside him like a kitten, and drifted into sleep with a smile in her heart.

In the morning she woke up and found him gone.

Chapter 24

Whoever put the Queen's House in order, removing the Holland covers, putting fresh linens on the bed, dusting and polishing every surface till it gleamed, had failed to wind either of the handsome clocks. Jacobin had no idea what time it was. She looked out of the window to check the position of the sun and found it was snowing. No wonder she felt cold.

Really, she thought, as she dressed in her own shabby garments, he might have lit the fire before leaving. Then recalled that wasn't one of his skills.

Never mind. He had other, more important talents. Her muscles were a little stiff, there was some tenderness between her legs, and she felt wonderful. And starving. Breakfast in bed would have been nice.

She skipped downstairs and found her cloak, bracing herself against a blast of frigid air when she stepped outside. The snow had thickened and a light mantle of white clothed the path away from the hamlet. Even the prospect of asking Mrs. Simpson for breakfast didn't dampen her spirits. She had no illusions that the events of last night—or at least their general tenor—wouldn't be common knowledge in the servants' hall. She could expect all sorts of insolent glances and suggestive remarks.

But this morning she found it impossible to care. She and Anthony would arrange something. He wouldn't be needing her services as a cook anymore, now the match with Candover was over. Perhaps she'd take up his offer of a house on the estate and they could spend hours in bed together.

What that would mean in the long term, she refused to consider. She wouldn't look beyond the immediate concern of her growling stomach. Even Candover couldn't have eaten everything served last night. And if the servants had demolished the lot—she'd noticed their scorn for her didn't extend to rejecting the fruits of her labor—she'd whip up something new. Almond tartlets sounded good.

Humming to herself, she rounded the rhododendrons and almost tripped over the body. The large body sprawled on its back in the pathway, an ugly wound leaching blood into the snow.

Candover. My God!

She knelt and felt for a pulse. Nothing. The flesh was cool, and she was almost certain he was dead. Her mind was numb as she gazed at her uncle's lifeless hulk. She had no fondness for the man and he had surely loathed her, yet she felt no joy in his demise. Maybe he wasn't beyond help. She gathered her scattered wits, just as footsteps approached from the direction of the house.

"Anthony!" she called out. "Help!"

A man emerged through the bush-lined walk. She'd never seen him before. He bent over and felt Candover's pulse, as she had, and swore under his breath. Then rough hands pulled her upright. She glimpsed a scarlet waistcoat beneath the man's heavy coat.

"Jacobin de Chastelux. I arrest you for the murder of Baron Candover of Hurst."

Too late, drat it, and not by very much if he judged correctly. Hawkins cursed the snow that had slowed the last miles of his journey from London to Sussex. He should have left last night, as soon as he'd discovered from Storrington's secretary that wherever Jane Castle had come from, it wasn't Scotland.

At least he had the satisfaction of catching the wench red-handed. In this weather it was hard to tell how long the man had been dead, but he judged it wasn't long.

The girl tried to shake off his firm grip. "Fetch Lord Storrington," she had the nerve to demand. As though he didn't know the earl was in it with her up to his arrogant eyebrows. Unfortunately he was going to have a hard time pinning the deed on His Lordship, even as an accessory.

"Forget it," he said. "His Lordship's left you to face the music alone. He drove to London this morning." Hawkins's leathers had been splashed with icy mud by a speeding carriage that must have been carrying Storrington like a bat out of hell away from the scene of the crime. "You're coming with me to the magistrate."

Mr. John Withercombe, the local beak, was less ac-commodating than Hawkins would have wished. Re-siding two miles from Storrington Hall, he held his neighborhood magnate in considerable respect.

"Storrington's cook, you say." He scratched his head under the old-fashioned wig, and his wrinkled face creased with concern. "I don't think I can let you take her away without consulting him. He wouldn't be pleased."

"I found her leaning over the body," Hawkins re-peated. "And I have ample evidence this wasn't her first attempt. She should be lodged in Chichester to await trial at the next assizes. The Prince Regent himself will be most displeased at any delay in bringing her to justice."

Obviously Lord Storrington's displeasure meant more to Withercombe than the prince's.

"I'll lock her up here," he said stubbornly, "and if Storrington hasn't returned by tomorrow we'll think again." It was the only concession Hawkins could wring from him.

The woman was billeted in the magistrate's lockup while the two men returned to Storrington Hall to look for the murder weapon.

It wasn't much of a jail, at least in the view of one who'd been brought up on stories of the worst excesses of the French Revolution. No massive stone walls; no chains; no dripping water; no jailers clanking bunches of heavy keys; no weeping aristocrats awaiting the tumbrels; no rats. The English, it appeared, didn't have the French flair for drama when it came to incarceration.

It was really quite tame. More like an ordinary room in the domestic offices of a manor house. A narrow bed stood in one corner, and a hard straight-backed chair was supplied for seating. The floor was of rough pine and the walls whitewashed. A canvas bucket in the corner completed the amenities. Jacobin hoped it would be emptied with reasonable frequency. The small window did at least have bars, but they didn't look very formidable. She fancied that with a blunt instrument she might be able to gouge them from the window frame and make her escape. There could be worse places to spend a few hours.

That was how she felt all morning, when she expected Anthony to come and rescue her at any time. She didn't for a moment believe the runner's assertion that he had fled to London without a word to her.

By mid-afternoon she was anxious, but comforted herself with a recollection of his trying to wake her. She'd buried her face in her pillow and refused to move. Sleep seemed irresistible after such an exhausting night. He must have been telling her he had business to conduct that morning.

By the time a servant delivered her a tray of plain but palatable food she was worried. And long after dark, when the single tallow candle had guttered and the absence of all noise told her Mr. Withercombe's household had retired for the night, she lost all trace of composure. She would still have welcomed Anthony's appearance at the door of her prison, but was prepared to greet him with a bang on the head with the slop bucket.

As she shivered through the night on the hard little bed, she replayed the events of the morning and didn't like her conclusions.

Anthony had a prime motive for killing Candover: to keep him quiet about their aborted card game and save face with the London *ton*.

Anthony had traveled the same path to Candover's body that she had, but sometime earlier.

Anthony had disappeared from the scene, leaving her conveniently in place to be seized.

And she'd given Anthony the one piece of evidence that no one else knew about, the piece of the puzzle that would surely have hanged her for the Brighton poisoning: that it was she who had filled the dish from Candover's armorial service with rose Bavarian cream.

Chapter 25

"**I**'m surprised to see you again so soon, Storrington. Delighted, of course. And sorry to have kept you waiting. I collect your business is of some urgency." Lord Hugo Hartley displayed his usual grace, but Anthony thought he looked drawn and pale, lending credence to his servant's earlier excuse that His Lordship was engaged with his physician.

Anthony could have retorted that it wasn't nearly soon enough. He'd been frantic with anxiety at having to wait until late afternoon to be received by the old gentleman. But he couldn't treat the elderly doyen of the *ton* with discourtesy and expect cooperation.

"No matter, sir," he replied politely. "I used the time to attend to another matter."

"How can I be of service this time? More reminiscences of Versailles? I enjoyed our conversation."

"Not this time. I'm anxious to find out about some recent activities of Chauncey Bellamy."

"Bellamy again?" Anthony didn't detect anything in Hartley's face beyond polite curiosity and he was looking hard. "Why don't you ask him. He's almost your next-door neighbor."

Anthony tried not to gnash his teeth. "Unfortunately I discovered this morning that the family left London two days ago to spend Christmas in Northumberland."

"Ah, yes. At Lady Caroline's family estate, no doubt. I don't know why you think I would be able to give you any information."

He had to move carefully with Lord Hugo, though he'd been quite prepared to beat the truth out of Bellamy. "I wish to know about a recent altercation between Bellamy and Candover."

"Candover? I recall you asked about him before. May I be crude enough to ask what affair it is of yours?"

"I believe Bellamy may be implicated in the attempted poisoning of Lord Candover."

Lord Hugo raised his eyebrows. "And you wish to find out if this is true out of a purely altruistic interest in justice?"

"A . . . dependent of mine is under suspicion of the crime. Naturally I wish to see that justice is done. And as I said, I have reason to believe Candover and Bellamy quarreled badly."

"I still don't know why you've come to me."

"My surmise is that Candover extorted a large sum of money out of Bellamy by threatening to expose a secret about him. I hoped, knowledgeable as you are about so many members of the *ton*, that you might be able to cast some light on the matter. If you cannot, I shall communicate my findings to the investigating officer, who will, I imagine, pursue the matter. But things could not then be kept from becoming public, and I should be loath to cause a scandal if it wasn't . . . merited."

"The gloves are off, I see," Lord Hugo said with a cool smile. "I suppose you wouldn't let the matter rest if I were to assure you that Chauncey had nothing to do with the unfortunate event in Brighton."

"No," Anthony replied baldy. "I would not."

"I was somehow afraid of that. Would you be so good as to pour me a glass of sherry? And one for yourself, if you wish. My doctor won't be pleased, but the telling of such a tale requires a douceur."

As he handed the old man a glass, Anthony felt a stirring of guilt. Lord Hugo looked tired and distressed. It didn't sit well with him to bludgeon the truth out of the venerable dandy, but it had to be done, and without delay. Once news of his card game became generally known, Anthony was going to find his influence in London greatly diminished. Lord Hugo mustn't know that his threats of creating a scandal were probably hollow.

"So, Storrington. I'm going to tell you an old, old story."

Anthony sat down and prayed desperately that what he discovered would be enough to clear Jacobin.

"A long time ago in Paris, a young man stopped in the city on his way home from touring the German states. Very dull, the German states, very staid. Just like the young man and, indeed, like his father who had ar-

ranged the tour. But Paris has a way of shaking the sobriety out of a man, especially a young one. This youth
had all his short life fought against certain . . . desires
. . . which were, let us say, socially unacceptable. But in
the heated atmosphere of the queen of all cities he lost
his head and committed an indiscretion. He wasn't the
first to find himself in this situation, and likely no last-
ing damage would have been done. But unfortunately
for our protagonist a certain peer, spending an evening
touring the city's more notorious locations, discovered
what happened. I'm sure I have no need to go into details with a man of the world such as yourself."

Anthony nodded and sipped his wine quietly, suppressing a rising optimism.

"No great harm was done. The young man returned
to London and in a few years made an advantageous
marriage. From time to time over the years he found it
necessary to give some slight financial aid to the peer
who knew his secret, never enough to seriously trouble
a man of fortune such as himself, but annoying, nonetheless. One does so dislike to be obligated."

Anthony could scarcely remain seated. He was ready
to bolt for Bow Street without a second's delay. But
Lord Hugo's story wasn't over.

"Then a few months ago his tormenter made a new
and very large demand, far greater than could be met
out of normal expenses. A sum that would arouse suspicion in any inspection of his accounts. He came to
me for advice. Men with his tastes have a way of doing
that. They see me as something of a father figure, I be-

lieve, though a far more sympathetic father than most of them were born with."

"You advised Bellamy to kill Candover?" Anthony blurted out, smashing the anonymous charade of the narrative and getting straight to the point.

Lord Hugo closed his eyes and shook his head distastefully. "Please, Storrington, don't accuse me of such methods. Candover got his money, but in return he signed a letter confessing to some little peccadilloes that I knew he'd committed over the years. In chess parlance we created a stalemate: Candover would not be able to trouble my friend again without in turn being faced with disgrace. Quite a poetic solution, don't you agree?"

"But the poisoning . . ." Anthony began.

"Clearly poor Chauncey had no need to murder Candover. And I can assure you he never made any such attempt. I see by your face that you are disappointed. But much as I'd like to help Mademoiselle de Chastelux, I can't do it by sacrificing an innocent man."

Anthony could only gape at him. "How did you . . . ?"

Lord Hugo's face lit up with a genuine smile. "I don't go out much these days, but I am lucky enough to have many faithful friends who keep me amused by telling me what's going on in society. Then I have many idle hours to ponder what I've heard. I know a young cook went missing from the Pavilion, a young man who looked very like my old friend Auguste de Chastelux. And I know you recently employed a female pastry cook of surpassing skill. It wasn't very difficult to reach the conclusion that the two cooks were, in fact, one. I'd like to help Auguste's daughter. I asked Candover about her once and received a very chilly answer. Someone should have done something about the poor girl."

"There, I agree," Anthony growled.

"It appears you have the matter in hand. Do let me know if there's anything I can do to help, but you seem a man of considerable resource. And bring Mademoiselle de Chastelux to see me. I'll see what I can do to smooth over any social difficulties that arise from her late employment."

Anthony spent the night at an inn, though without taking much advantage of the excellent bed. He passed most of the nocturnal hours pacing in frustration at the weather. What in London had been a sooty sleet turned to a businesslike snow once away from the human-generated warmth of the metropolis. He wasn't going to be any use to Jacobin or anyone else lying in a ditch.

Added to his bitter disappointment at the loss of Bellamy as a suspect was a nagging concern about that damn Bow Street runner. His secretary had sustained an interrogation by Thomas Hawkins. Discreet as he was, he'd let out the fact that Jane Castle's Scottish origins were news to him. Anthony castigated himself for not writing to warn him.

He prayed the snow had also delayed Hawkins.

Jacobin's heart sank when the key turned in the lock of her jail and the door opened to reveal the runner. He tied her hands behind her back with a piece of twine and conducted her roughly into the magistrate's office.

Her eyes were scratchy with tears and sleep, her gown was creased and her hair loose and tangled. She'd never felt less confident. Raising a degree of pride, she lifted her chin into the air and imagined herself Marie Antoinette, facing the tribunal.

To her dismay Withercombe was alone. No sign of Anthony, who seemed truly to have abandoned her. Disdaining to show fear, she stared down her nose at the magistrate.

"Well, Miss Chastelux," he said. "I trust you spent the night comfortably.

The runner muttered impatiently.

"The accommodations were quite comfortable, thank you," Jacobin said, pretending she was the Queen of France. "And the dinner palatable. I commend you on the excellence of your jail."

Withercombe seemed nervous. "Well, yes. I'm glad you found it acceptable. Be sure to mention it to Lord Storrington."

She couldn't help an inward smile. The man sounded for all the world like an innkeeper. "I shall make a point of it." *If I ever see him again*, she added silently.

"Thank you," he said, clearly gratified. Then responded to a cough from the runner. He picked up a silver-handled gun from the desk in front of him.

"Have you ever seen this weapon before?"

"No," she said.

"Are you certain? It belonged to your uncle, Lord

Candover. His coronet and the letter C are engraved on the stock."

"I suppose he brought it with him to Storrington. There are so many dangerous criminals on the roads these days. The authorities do nothing to stop them." She gave Hawkins a nasty look. "They prefer to waste time persecuting the innocent."

Withercombe looked stern. "This is one of a pair of guns reported stolen from Hurst Park around the time of your departure from that house. It was discovered in the shrubbery near Lord Candover's body."

Jacobin kept tight control over her facial muscles, but internally she quailed. This was bad. Very bad.

"I've never seen it before. I never set foot in my uncle's gun room and I don't know how to shoot a pistol."

"She's hardly going to admit it," Hawkins interjected. Even Withercombe had to see the justice of that comment.

"What were you doing in the gardens at that hour?" asked the magistrate.

"I was going for a walk," Jacobin replied.

"Not busy with your duties?"

"I had prepared many dishes for dinner the night before. I wasn't required that morning."

"Unusual weather for a walk," said Hawkins. "It was coming on to snow quite hard."

"Hm," said Withercombe. "Mr. Hawkins makes a good point. Taking a walk for pleasure in such cold seems odd."

Jacobin shrugged. "I like snow. It's pretty."

Withercombe didn't seem to know what to say to that, but Hawkins was made of sterner stuff. "The servants say your bed wasn't slept in. Where did you spend the night?"

She was saved from having to answer this awkward question by a commotion outside the door, which swung open to reveal Storrington looking ten feet tall in a multicaped driving coat and a tall beaver hat.

"Withercombe," he roared. "What the devil do you mean by arresting my fiancée?"

"I had no idea you were betrothed to the young—er—lady," Withercombe said. "I thought she was your cook."

It was lucky Withercombe was easily intimidated, Anthony thought. Not a bad old boy, but hardly a pillar of strength when it came to law enforcement. Jacobin appeared stunned. He threw her a meaningful look, silently begging her not to give the game away.

"Our betrothal is new," he said. "No doubt Miss de Chastelux didn't wish to say anything before our families were informed and the news made public."

She caught on quickly. "Anthony. How happy I am to see you. These gentlemen believe I had something to do with the death of my uncle. Absurd, isn't it?" Sadness suffused her countenance. "It is tragic that he has been killed, is it not? Who could have done such a dreadful thing? They made me spend the night in *jail* and have tied me up."

He went to her and embraced her. "How terrible for you." The indignation in his voice didn't have to be feigned. "Withercombe, untie her at once. I must take her home."

"Wait a minute," said Hawkins. "I have evidence of her participation in Lord Candover's attempted murder by poison, not to mention that I caught her red-handed, leaning over his dead body."

Anthony had heard what had happened when he reached home, and he'd had time to plan his tactics. He eyed Hawkins with disdain.

"You'd think a cunning murderer would have the sense to run away, not waste time examining the body after the deed was done. Instead you leaped to the dubious conclusion that a young woman of good birth, *my* betrothed wife, had killed her own uncle instead of the glaringly obvious solution that she was trying to help him."

Withercombe coughed. "You did say she was calling for help when you found her, Hawkins."

"She heard me coming and did that to conceal the truth." A hint of uncertainty had entered the runner's voice.

"Withercombe." Anthony addressed the perplexed magistrate. "How long have you known me?"

"Well over thirty years, my lord. And your father before you for almost as many. I had the honor of attending your christening."

"And have you ever known me to be slipshod in my responsibilities?"

"Oh no, my lord."

"Then you know that if you release Miss de Chastelux into my care you can trust me to keep her close and make her available for questioning as the investigation into the murder proceeds. Devoted as I am to my betrothed, I would hardly wish to find myself married to a murderess." He gave a wintry laugh and kept an arm firmly about Jacobin's waist. "Now please, untie her."

The day was won, at least temporarily. Notwithstanding the protests of the runner, another fifteen minutes saw Anthony handing Jacobin into his carriage. As soon as the door closed behind them she flung her arms around his neck, and he held her with fierce gladness.

"You were brilliant!" she cried. "I almost felt sorry for that runner. There's no one like you when it comes to playing the self-important nobleman." For once she seemed to approve of him in that role. He hugged her tightly.

"It's not over yet," he said into her curls. "We'll have to be married immediately. It's the best way to protect you."

She pulled away from him. "But that was a ruse! We're not really engaged."

"Yes we are. We'll be married today."

"I'm not marrying a man who left me alone and didn't even leave me a note."

"How can you worry about something so trivial at a time like this?"

She snorted with indignation. "It's not trivial. I woke up and you were gone and then I found my uncle's body and spent the night in jail and *you weren't there*. Not a single word for twenty-four hours."

He snatched her up and pulled her onto his lap, where she continued to wriggle and make furious noises that made him want to laugh, despite the seriousness of their predicament.

"Listen, little spitfire. I did leave a note. There was no paper in the desk at the Queen's House so I left a note with Simpson at the house that I was going to London to find out what I could about Bellamy. I'm sorry about what happened, but I couldn't get home last night through the snow."

"Oh." She subsided into his arms and snuggled up to him. "Did you find anything in London?"

"Nothing good." He related his conversation with Lord Hugo.

"I'm afraid it looks like we've hit a dead end with Bellamy." He held her closely, feeling her disappointment in her slumping body. "But don't worry, darling. We'll keep looking. And they'll find it damn hard to hang a countess."

She took his face between her hands and looked at him intently. "Anthony, you are gallant to offer, but you can't marry me just to save me from hanging. They'll think you were in it too, and we'll both be in the same fix."

"I'd rather be in a fix with you than without you."

He meant it too, but she didn't seem to hear his words.

"At least they won't know now that you walked out of your card game. Candover won't be able to ruin you."

There was a moment's charged silence.

"I didn't do it," he said.

"Of course not."

"But the thought did occur to you."

She held up her hand, her thumb and forefinger half an inch apart. "Just for a tiny moment the idea might have crossed my mind. But truly I knew you wouldn't have. But I don't understand why you didn't find the body on your way back to the house."

"I went back a different way. There's a route through the woods which no one can see from the house. I didn't want any of the servants to know where I spent the night."

He kissed her and rejoiced in her eager response. It felt so good to have her in his arms again. He'd do anything to keep her safe.

"Let's talk about our wedding," he said.

"We're not getting married."

The argument had hardly begun when the carriage came to a halt. They'd reached the house. The door swung open to reveal another traveling carriage parked near the entrance, an elegantly dressed woman descending from it.

"The devil," Anthony said. "Kitty! That's all we need."

Chapter 26

Although Lady Kitty had been perfectly agreeable during their two encounters, Jacobin was slightly in awe of Anthony's very proper sister. But on closer inspection Kitty didn't look her usual impeccable self. Her hat was plunked onto hair that had clearly been done in a hurry, with several locks sticking out from under the brim, and her traveling redingote was misbuttoned.

"Anthony," she cried, clearly on the verge of tears. "Thank goodness, you're here."

"What the devil are you doing here, Kitty? Does Walter know?" he said, stepping out of his own carriage.

"Be nice," Jacobin hissed. "Can't you see she's upset?"

Kitty stood with clenched fists, ignoring Simpson, who was holding the front door open for her. "I had to leave. I couldn't stand having that woman in my house a moment longer."

Hushing her with a gesture, Anthony pulled Kitty inside. Jacobin followed, receiving an ugly look from

Simpson, who was, she suspected, about to order her around to the servants' entrance. Perhaps it would be for the best. She made to tiptoe off and leave the siblings alone, when Anthony grabbed her by the wrist and hustled her along behind Kitty into a sitting room.

Kitty looked at her inquiringly. "Miss Castle. What are you doing here?"

"She's not Miss Castle. Her name is Jacobin de Chastelux but not for much longer. She and I will be married today and she'll be Countess of Storrington."

A strangled sound, hastily repressed, from the butler drew his attention.

"Simpson," Anthony ordered, "have Lady Kitty's usual rooms prepared, and one of the best chambers for Miss de Chastelux. And then have hot water sent up for a bath."

Simpson left, reluctance expressed in his every movement, and Anthony looked back at Kitty, who had astonishment written all over her face.

"You're going to marry your cook? Why on earth?"

Jacobin thought about denying it, but she was curious to hear his answer.

"Jacobin is the daughter of Auguste de Chastelux, a French nobleman, and her mother was Candover's sister. I won't have you treat her with anything less than complete respect."

"Well, of course not!" Kitty was thoroughly diverted from her own troubles. "How splendid. You must tell me all about it." She turned and kissed Jacobin, who, for once, couldn't think of a thing to say. "I always wanted a sister and we shall have such fun planning the wedding. A big London affair in the spring and you shall come and stay with me first and be introduced to everyone. Oh! This does make me feel better."

"My first object in life, Kitty," Anthony said sarcastically, "is to attend to your amusements. But in this case I must set them aside. As I said before, the wedding takes place today."

"Absolutely not! Whatever will people say? Well, I know what they'll say and it's quite unacceptable. Given your fiancée's recent—shall we say unusual—employment, we'll have a lot of work to do to make things right for her. I know you wouldn't want unpleasant gossip about your bride."

"You're quite right, Kitty." Her words had mollified him. "But unfortunately we don't have any choice."

Kitty's eyes swung unerringly to Jacobin's stomach. "When's it due?"

Given what she believed, Lady Kitty was taking it very well, but Jacobin couldn't let her misapprehension stand.

"I'm not *enceinte*, my lady," she said. Then turned to Anthony. "We'd better tell Lady Kitty what my position is. And, by the way, we're not getting married."

"Yes we are. And it's none of Kitty's damn business."

Jacobin folded her arms and looked at the ceiling. "I won't even consider the matter unless you tell your sister exactly what has happened."

Kitty embraced her again. "Bravo! You know just

how to manage my brother. I can see you two will deal superbly together." She turned to her brother, keeping an arm around Jacobin's shoulders. "Out with it, Anthony. I want to know everything."

Jacobin let Anthony do the talking as he related most of her story, leaving out only the immediate reason for her flight from Candover's house and his own quarrel with Candover.

"This murder charge," Kitty said with a frown at the conclusion of the tale, "you can take care of it, can't you?"

Jacobin was grateful that Kitty didn't think she was guilty. Or perhaps she did, she mentally amended, but didn't care. That made Jacobin feel uncomfortable. At the same time it showed extraordinary loyalty on Kitty's part toward her brother. Anthony's resentment of his sister was clearly not reciprocated.

"I hope so, but it won't be easy," Anthony admitted. "That's why we must marry at once. As Countess of Storrington it'll be far harder for that runner to convince the courts of her guilt. She'll be given every benefit of doubt. And it'll give us more time to find the real killer."

"I see," said Kitty, "that a quick marriage will have to do. But not today. Jacobin must have the complete support of the family. James must be here, and Aunt Margaret too. Write to them today, and I know they'll come at once."

Anthony agreed with some reluctance that Kitty was right. They were discussing which of their cousins might also be persuaded to travel to Storrington, at short notice in winter weather, when Simpson returned to announce that Jacobin's bath was ready.

Feeling tired and grimy after her night in captivity, Jacobin left without argument. She'd deal with Anthony later, when she felt more herself.

"I'm grateful to you for accepting Jacobin without question. This isn't how I ever imagined planning a wedding." Not that Anthony *had* ever mentally planned his own marriage—that was the kind of thing females did—but if he had, it wouldn't have been in such a hole-in-the-corner fashion. And he needed to acknowledge Kitty's backing, though in a resentful part of his mind he felt he'd rather have fought her disapproval.

"Of course I accept her. You're my big brother and whatever you want—in important matters—I will always support. There can be no question about it."

He thought about Kitty's own affairs, the trouble in her marriage that had brought about her precipitous arrival at Storrington. He supposed he owed her reciprocal assistance. He was about to broach the matter when she came and stood beside him and tucked her arm around his.

"I know we've never had the same friendship you and James share—I've often envied it—but you must never doubt my affection for you. But I have to ask one thing. What in the name of heaven were you doing tangling with Candover? He's always struck me as a most disagreeable man. And from your account he treated his own niece very badly. There's something behind this you haven't told me."

Anthony sighed and looked away. "It's because I don't like to talk about Mama."

"Mama?" asked Kitty, all astonishment. "What does Candover have to do with Mama?"

He couldn't think of a way to put it delicately. "He was her lover."

"No! Impossible. I don't believe it for a minute." She looked at him suspiciously. "Does James know about this nonsensical notion?"

"Yes. We thought it was better not to tell you."

"Brothers! Men!" she huffed with an exasperated toss of the head. "What gave you both such an idea?"

"Papa told me when he was dying. She was running away with him when she died."

"That can't be true. You must have misunderstood him."

"No, I didn't. He said she'd fallen in love when they went to Paris, just after you were born, and received a letter from him that day. She was going to join him and was drowned."

"But Mama killed herself. She wouldn't have done that if she was meeting a lover."

"Killed herself?" he asked, flabbergasted.

"Didn't you know?"

"No I didn't. For the simple reason that it isn't true."

"Come and sit down with me," Kitty said gently, and he allowed himself to be led over to a sofa. She took one of his hands in both hers and held it on her knee. "I think I always knew. She was so very unhappy. All my memories are of someone who carried a dark weight on her soul."

"She wasn't always like that. When I was young she was happy. Then you came along and she was never the same." There, he'd said it. The terrible thing he'd always thought about his sister.

"I used to fear that was true," Kitty admitted, "but one day, when I was about thirteen, I think, I told Nurse Bell about it, and she said it was nothing to do with me. That Mama was ill in her mind and that was why she committed suicide. She made me see that a baby girl couldn't have done that to her mother."

"Oh yes, Nurse Bell. You were always her favorite. She never had any time for me." Anthony didn't care that he was speaking like a petulant child. He wanted to shout, to weep, to roar with grief. "You had Nurse Bell. I had nobody once Mama sent Nurse Taylor away."

"Nurse Taylor?"

"*My* nurse." Anthony remembered something he hadn't thought of in years. "It wasn't long after they returned from France and I was crying because Mama wouldn't let me visit her in bed in the morning like she used to. Nurse was comforting me, hugging me, when Mama came in. She started screaming at Nurse, saying she was trying to steal me from her. She told her to leave. And I never saw her again." He was squeezing Kitty's hands, clinging to them as though they were a lifeline, which they were, the only thing keeping him from disgracing himself with tears.

"I'm sorry, Kit," he said, not noticing that he used her childhood diminutive. "I'm behaving as though I was five, not five and thirty."

"Don't worry," she murmured. "I've two boys myself, remember, and I know they feel just as strongly as girls but they're taught not to show it. That was a dreadful thing that happened. You lost your mother and then your nurse, just when you needed her most. No wonder you were angry at me."

He could see that he shouldn't have been. It wasn't her fault. But he couldn't yet admit to her that it had been his beautiful, impossible, beloved mother who had wronged him. It probably didn't matter. Kitty knew.

"If what you say is true, why didn't Papa tell me?" He still couldn't accept that virtually his every action for two years had been based on a false premise.

"It was hushed up because of the scandal. And of course he didn't want us children to know. But Nurse Bell said she'd heard Mama left a note. There was no question that she threw herself into the millstream."

Anthony pulled his hand away and stood up to walk over to the fireplace. He stared at the flames dancing around the logs in the big hearth.

"I've made a fool of myself," he said bluntly. "I've been trying to ruin Candover by winning his fortune from him at cards. And I've done a couple of things I'm deeply ashamed of."

He told her about the two occasions that Jacobin had been used as a stake.

"And she forgave you?" Kitty asked. "I'm not sure I'd be speaking to you under the circumstances, let alone agreeing to marry you."

"She was devilish angry. The second time she only forgave me because I threw in a losing hand and called off the bet rather than risk her."

His worldly sister knew exactly what that meant. "You'd be destroyed if word got out. Let us pray on bended knees that Candover didn't have a chance to tell anyone about it."

"I am concerned about his valet. When I arrived I was told the man was prostrated with grief over Candover's death. I haven't had a chance to speak to him."

"His valet." Kitty thought about it. "There might be gossip, but you could likely carry off a denial against the word of a servant."

"With the *ton*, yes. But I'm not so sure a Bow Street runner will dismiss the tale so quickly. Nor should he, though it's inconvenient for me."

"This is dreadful! Both of you under suspicion. They'll think you planned it together."

"I know. That's why I have to find out who really killed Candover. I have some ideas I must discuss with Jacobin."

He wondered if Jacobin had finished her bath. He longed for her presence, for her company, for her to make him laugh in the face of disaster. And he had to make sure she wasn't serious about refusing to marry him. Although she'd stopped arguing about it while Kitty planned the wedding, she hadn't ever said yes. He knew her infuriating, adorable stubbornness too well to believe her fairly won yet. But he could be just as obstinate, and he wasn't giving in until he had his ring on her finger.

He glanced over at his sister and realized it was with affection. His resentful irritation with her seemed to have dissolved. She was so like his father in appearance, and suddenly he missed that kindly, reserved man. Too reserved, as he himself had been. It was good to talk about one's troubles. Had his father confided in him sooner, he wouldn't have made his confused deathbed confession.

Joining Kitty on the sofa again, he threw an arm around her.

"Enough about me. What's this about you leaving Walter. What about the children?"

She refrained from weeping, for which he was exceedingly grateful, but rested her head on his shoulder.

"I know I can't leave him for good. But having Marabel in the house for days was too much. Then yesterday I particularly asked him to accompany me to call on Sally Jersey. But when the time came he'd taken Marabel off to the City to meet her banker. He didn't even let me know. I only found out from the footman. So I sent down a message that I was unwell and didn't come down for dinner, and he never came to my room to see how I was. This morning I rose and he'd already gone out with her again. I called for the carriage and here I am."

There was no point suggesting that her erring spouse might be guilty of little more than thoughtlessness. He sensed that it wouldn't be well received.

"Poor Kitty," he said instead. "It sounds like Walter is behaving disgracefully. As soon as I can, I'll have a word with him and make sure he knows he can't treat my sister so shabbily."

"I wish to thank you for your graciousness toward me, my lady," Jacobin began when she joined Kitty before dinner. "I cannot seem a welcome addition to your family."

"Nonsense, my dear, and call me Kitty. We are to be sisters, and I'd do anything for Anthony."

Jacobin waved a hand expressively. There was something unmistakably French in her gestures and intonation, despite her impeccable English accent and grammar. It was deliciously ironic, thought Kitty, that her brother, with his dislike of the French, should have fallen so hard for her.

"As for that," Jacobin said, "I don't think so. Anthony believes he should marry me because he feels a duty, an obligation to take care of me, but it isn't necessary. He'll help me escape this murder business and then there'll be no need."

"Have you told him this? I think you'll get an argument from him."

"Your brother is very stubborn, but I'll make him see sense. He doesn't really want to marry me. He needs a nice respectable English debutante who will make a good countess." She didn't look at all pleased at the notion.

Interesting, Kitty thought. *He hasn't told her he's in love with her. Probably doesn't know it himself.* If it wasn't for unfortunate legal entanglements, she'd find the situation thoroughly entertaining.

Since those entanglements must be avoided in the presence of the servants, Kitty led the dinner conversation to the subject of Jacobin's family. Simpson was patently agog with curiosity at seeing a pastry cook transformed into the future mistress of the house. It wouldn't do any harm for him to spread the word that the future countess's birth was irreproachable.

"Tell me how you got your name," Kitty said. "I understand that your father had revolutionary tendencies, but surely the Jacobin party was the most bloodthirsty of the political groups in France at that time."

"Papa used to joke that it saved him from the guillotine, since he preferred the Girondistes. He said he fooled the Jacobins by naming his daughter for them. But in fact the name had nothing to do with them. It was my mother's choice, a family name. The first notable Candover was created a baronet by James I."

Kitty gave the superior smile of one whose family earldom was an Elizabethan creation. She didn't need to mention that James I was notorious for awarding baronetcies in exchange for infusions of cash into the treasury.

"And then his grandson," Jacobin continued, "was made Baron Candover by Charles II."

"Loyal supporters of the Stuarts, apparently." A distressing idea occurred to Kitty. "You're not a Catholic, are you?"

"Oh no. My mother refused to convert and my father cared nothing for religion. I was brought up in the Church of England. We attended the English embassy chapel in Paris, when it was possible."

Thank God! She might persuade the stuffier Storrs relations to accept a cook, even a Frenchwoman. A Catholic would be beyond the pale.

All in all Kitty was well pleased with her brother's bride. There was nothing wrong with her manners, and with her striking looks and witty, confident bearing, she might very well take the *ton* by storm, once she was properly dressed. What she was wearing was impossible. Kitty would see about lending her some clothes after dinner. Luckily they were the same size.

But the best thing was the way Anthony gazed at Jacobin throughout the meal, as though she were a delectable sweet he yearned to devour. He'd made quite a fuss when Kitty had insisted on delaying the wedding for another three days. Anxious to bed her, if he hadn't already done so. Kitty supposed she ought to leave the pair alone and let him work his powers of persuasion on his reluctant fiancée, but she couldn't resist torturing her brother by acting the very enthusiastic chaperone.

Once Simpson and the footman had withdrawn, Jacobin brought up the subject that must be her greatest concern.

"It has to be Edgar!" she said, "He must have killed my uncle. We have no one else."

"It would help if we could place him in the vicinity of either attempt on Candover's life." Anthony said.

"But he was," Jacobin cried, her eyes so wide they dwarfed her face. "How could I have been so stupid? He was in Brighton the night before. That's why I was on the dark side of the square when you saved me from those drunkards. He was standing near the back entrance to the Pavilion and I had to avoid him. I was wearing his clothes."

She hadn't, Kitty realized, heard the whole story of her future sister-in-law's adventures. Jacobin was going to lead Anthony a merry dance. It would do him good.

"And naturally," Anthony chimed in, "he'd be able to introduce aconite into the pudding easily enough. How lucky for him that you were there to take the blame. If it was luck. Are you sure he didn't see you?"

"I don't think he did. Besides, he asked me to marry him. He wouldn't have done that if he wanted me blamed."

Anthony bristled. "You never told me that. When? Before you left Hurst?"

"No, at the Argyll Rooms."

"That puny little man I saw you with. That was Edgar Candover?"

Kitty suppressed a smile. Her brother sounded jealous.

Jacobin was looking at him through her eyelashes.

"Edgar is short, yes. That's why I can wear his clothes. But he's not so ill-looking. I was a little sorry I couldn't accept, but I knew he'd be in trouble with my uncle and he was quite dependent on him. But now, why not? He's Lord Candover and has the whole estate."

"You're already going to marry someone who's suspected of murder. Me."

Anthony's eyes were laughing, and Kitty realized how rare his smiles once had been. It wasn't that he'd ever lacked humor, but his wit had been acerbic. Jacobin had plumbed undeveloped depths of joy in her somber brother.

"Hurst Park is a very fine estate. I was happy there when my uncle was away. Perhaps I'd like to live there again."

"You're not to go near the man. In fact, I'll ride over tomorrow and choke the truth out of him."

"I'm coming with you," Jacobin said.

"No you're not. You will stay here with Kitty."

"No! I want to choke Edgar too."

"Choking is man's work. I'm bigger and stronger."

"I'm very strong. I could choke him just as well as you."

"But I'm bigger. Size matters," Anthony said, with a shake of his head. "When it comes to choking, I mean."

It was, Kitty decided, time for the ladies to withdraw before the pair of them started to make love on the table.

* * *

Kitty was a damnably officious chaperone. She hadn't given Anthony a moment alone with Jacobin before dragging her off to bed. And he hadn't even had the wit to discover which chamber Jacobin was in. He was contemplating the most efficient way to search Storrington Hall's eighteen guest rooms when the door to his own bedchamber opened and a vision appeared. A vision in a nightdress.

"Where the devil did you get that thing?" he asked.

"Kitty lent it to me," Jacobin replied with a giggle. "Do you not find it seductive?"

"If that's what she usually wears to bed I'm not surprised she's having trouble with Walter. He'd never be able to find her."

Jacobin was swathed from neck to toes in ells of white flannel that gave not so much of a hint at the body beneath. True, with her piquant face and gold-tinged curls she looked like a Botticelli angel. But Anthony wasn't particularly interested in angels. A Botticelli Venus perhaps. Now, that was another matter.

"Kitty takes it with her when she travels in case she has to sleep in a damp inn. I thought you'd like it." She examined his face. "No? Never mind. I'll take it off."

She began to raise the skirts, revealing slim ankles and well-formed calf muscles.

"Stop right there," he said, suppressing the urge to dash over and assist her. "We're not yet married and it wouldn't be proper."

"We're not going to be married." Her smile would have melted the resistance of an Essene monk.

"Yes we are, and I'm not going to touch you until you're my wife."

"We'll see about that." With one efficient movement the flannel monstrosity was on the floor and her shapely curves revealed in the candlelight to his delighted gaze. His body reacted predictably, but he forced himself not to move as she sidled to where he stood next to the bed and inserted her hands thorough the opening of his shirt. He clenched his teeth and summoned every scrap of restraint as she stroked his chest in sensuous sweeps.

"Stop," he said, hoping his voice communicated a confidence he was far from feeling. The scent of her hair tickled his nose, and though he tried not to look down, he couldn't avoid a glimpse of rounded breasts that were begging for his caress. "Stop."

She obeyed. For a second. Then nimble fingers dropped to the fastenings of his breeches. When the siren had most of the buttons undone he could take no more. Seizing her around the waist he swung her onto the bed and laid her on the velvet counterpane, using his hands to pin her wrists above her head.

"You're touching me," she crooned triumphantly.

"I'm changing my tactics. I'll show you touching. I'll touch you until you agree to marry me."

"Is that a threat or a promise? Go ahead. I shall enjoy this."

He let go of her wrists and stood up. "Stay there," he said, and walked over to a large double chest of drawers.

"I'm not going anywhere."

He returned and sat beside her on the bed.

"What are you doing?" she asked, eyeing the two long neck cloths.

"Guess."

Her body twisted from side to side but not with any great vigor as he tied the white linen around each of her wrists, then to the bedposts.

"This is an outrage," she said, but she was laughing and made no effort to escape.

She looked so magnificent spread-eagled on the dark burgundy velvet that it was all he could do not to simply take possession there and then. But he had a plan. As a precaution he kept his own garments on. A couple of layers of cloth might be feeble restraints on his loss of control, but they were better than nothing.

"Now," he said, "I shall persuade you to change your mind." He picked up a quill pen from his bedside table and held it by the nib.

Jacobin was enjoying their battle of wills. Lying naked and bound made her feel more thrilled than helpless; in fact the sense of vulnerability added to her excitement. She squirmed with anticipatory curiosity at what was coming next.

The feather brushed her neck and crossed her shoulders, soft as a whisper, then descended the valley between her breasts before rising again to play with her hardening nipples. His attention followed the progress of the quill, his expression assuring her that his desires matched her own. Then he mirrored the movements of the feather with the firmer but still gentle touch of his fingers.

"You're so strong," he said, as the slight roughness of his hands smoothed her shoulders. "Cooking seems too mild an activity to develop such muscles."

"You wouldn't think that if you'd ever broken up a loaf of sugar or rolled out puff pastry."

He grinned and looked so devilishly lovable she would have kissed him had she been able to move. "I can see I'll have to be careful with you. It would be too humiliating to be dealt a leveler by my wife."

"You forget," she said, "that I'm not going to be your wife."

He merely smiled at her again and continued his ministrations, teasing her with hands and feather over every inch of her body save the one that most ached for them. She raised her hips suggestively. Ignoring the hint, he concentrated on the sensitive skin of her inner thighs.

"Touch me there, damn you!"

"Here?" He placed his hand over her mound, but without penetrating her curls with so much as a finger. She shook with yearning.

"Yes! More!"

"Will you marry me?"

"No."

He removed his hand. She clung to her resolve to win their contest but her will was waning. She feared she wouldn't be able to hold out much longer.

He feared he wouldn't be able to hold out much longer. She was writhing on the bed, exhorting him to go where he most wanted to be, and began to cry out in French. That was a good sign. She tended to break into that language when her emotions were engaged. He also noted that she wasn't making any effort to escape her bonds.

"Marry me," he demanded again, his hand on the baby skin of her inner thigh, close enough to feel the heat emanating from her core. He bent over and kissed her on the lips, swallowing the torrent of French curses and plunging his tongue into her warm sweetness in imitation of another act. "Marry me," he managed to mumble for the last time, knowing his control was on the verge of incineration.

"Yes," she uttered in a strangled voice. "Yes, I'll marry you. Now for God's sake untie me. I want you inside me *now*."

Thank God. He tore off his clothes.

"Just pull hard," he said. "The cloths are only loosely tied. You could have escaped at any time."

She jerked her hands loose and grabbed his shoulders, then pushed him over onto his back. She straddled him, then impaled herself on his straining cock, inducing a shudder of relief.

"I was going to agree anyway," she whispered, bending forward so that her lips brushed his ear without stopping the motion of her hips for an instant. "I came to your room to tell you."

He could see that she'd never let him have the last word. Not that he cared a tinker's cuss. He gave himself up to the joy of their union, urged her on as she rained kisses and caresses on his face and chest, sucked on his small tight nipples, and rode him like a wild thing. A natural she was, using instinct to grip his eager cock so he could happily relinquish himself to her charge. And when he felt her inner muscles convulse he released control altogether and joined her in her climax, spilling his seed inside her with a glad shout of triumph.

She slumped on top of him, drained and boneless but not too spent to appreciate the hard body beneath her, a much better resting place even than velvet brocade. His eyes were closed and he looked relaxed and happy. She realized that a core of tension, a kind of suppressed anger that he'd carried since she first encountered him, had vanished. In fact it had been absent all evening. Something had changed him, something between him and Kitty. He was at peace with himself. She didn't want to ask him about it now. There'd be time enough later.

She rolled off and felt her stomach. It was dry.

"When we did this before you made a mess," she said, not knowing exactly how to put it.

He ran his hand over her ribs, then joined hers on the flat plane of her belly.

"I promised before I wouldn't get you pregnant. But since we'll be married in three days I didn't think it mattered anymore."

She worked out the implications, and her mind played with the notion that she might be with child. "I'm glad," she said. "I want to bear your children. And thank you for keeping your word before."

Raising himself onto his elbow he looked down at her. "I did some things that were wrong, treated you dishonorably. I know now that I was suffering a kind of madness—not that it's any excuse. But I want you to know that I do keep my promises and I always will."

Her heart turned over at his serious expression. Drawing his head down, she kissed his forehead like a benediction.

"I believe you," she whispered.

"Anthony," she suddenly asked, curled up in his secure embrace sometime later. "Why do you want to marry me?"

He opened his eyes and lifted his head to look at her. "Why did you finally say yes?"

She couldn't remember now why she'd resisted the idea since it was exactly what she wanted. She'd decided in the course of the day that saying no was just plain foolish. So what if he didn't love her? Was she such a poor creature that she couldn't meet the challenge of altering that fact? And anyway he was adorable and perfect. Not that she had any intention of telling him that.

"Jean-Luc told me I'd be a fool not to catch you, and I decided he was right."

"I could tell he was a man of sense. Any other reason?"

Clearly he was on a fishing expedition and she was in the mood to indulge him.

"Because you're utterly adorable and quite perfect," she said.

A girl could—and often did—change her mind.

His arms tightened about her and he kissed her deeply. Then he gazed down at her with a look in his eyes she'd never seen before, which took her breath away.

"I want to marry you because I love you and wouldn't want to live without you," he said.

Quick work, Jacobin thought in self-congratulation.

Chapter 27

Anthony loved her and they were to be married in two days. What more could she want from life? Though she knew, rationally, that her legal difficulties were far from over, she had every confidence that Anthony, who had left in the early morning for Hurst Park, would sort them out. She spent an enjoyable morning with her future sister-in-law trying on clothes and having Kitty's maid dress her hair in different styles. She'd never experienced much feminine company and found these sisterly activities thoroughly delightful. It was wonderful to think she'd soon be part of a family. James, she had no doubt, would make a charming brother-in-law, and even the imminent arrival of the formidable Aunt Margaret—she who disapproved of colored dresses for unmarried girls—couldn't dampen her exuberance.

"Do you think I should wear this when your aunt arrives?" she asked anxiously, though not-so-secretly thrilled at her appearance in the mirror in a dashing morning dress of burnt orange trimmed in forest green.

"It's gorgeous." She sighed. "I can't believe you want to lend it to me. But I don't want to embarrass Anthony by appearing not *comme il faut* to his aunt."

"Embarrassment is the last thing my brother will be feeling when he sees you in that costume," Kitty asserted firmly. "As for Aunt Margaret, she's not a bad old thing, though inclined to be stuffy. She adores Anthony and is utterly loyal. The only thing that'll truly upset her is that you're being married in such a hurry, and by special license. She knows what people will say."

"What's a special license?" Jacobin asked idly as she adjusted the feather on her bonnet.

"Normally it takes three weeks to be married because banns have to be called in the home parish of both bride and bridegroom. A special license allows you to be married anywhere and at any time."

"I know nothing of English marriage customs. I've never even been to an English wedding. In France it always takes a long time—arranging the contract."

"That's usually true here. I suppose Anthony will deal with the settlements afterward."

"How do you get this license?" Jacobin hoped it wasn't so complicated that it would entail postponing the wedding, or even requiring her betrothed to be away for another day. She was already missing him. "Will Anthony have to fetch it himself?"

"From the Archbishop of Canterbury's office. He picked it up in London the day before yesterday. What's that for?" Jacobin had leaped up at these words and given Kitty an energetic hug.

"Just that I'm so happy and you're so kind to me," Jacobin said.

She almost wept. Anthony had intended to marry her even before her arrest. It set the cap on her joy and made her bitterly regret that she hadn't reciprocated his declaration of love. A tiny, lingering nugget of distrust had prevented her from averring her own feelings. Not that he'd seemed to notice, judging by his attentions, which had lasted most of the night. Perhaps these things were less important to men. But she minded. She desperately wanted to tell how she felt. Now. She wanted to lavish him with affection and didn't know how she'd survive until he came home.

A commotion outside Kitty's bedchamber interrupted their sisterly embrace. The door opened, and a gentleman in a state of considerable agitation burst in.

"Kitty! What the devil do you mean by going off without a word?" he roared, leaving Jacobin in no doubt that she was in the presence of Kitty's erring husband. "I've been looking for you all over London. James told me you were here."

"I'm amazed you even noticed," Kitty responded coldly. "And I'm even more amazed that you could drag yourself away from Marabel."

"Marabel?" A frown wrinkled Walter Thornley's pleasant face. "You couldn't think Marabel and—"

"What else was I to think?" Kitty demanded hotly. "You've hardly moved from her side since Francis died."

"I was just trying to be helpful, and keep out of your way since you were obviously tired of my company."

"It's you who were tired of me! I don't know about horses and dogs and hunting and all the things you're interested in, but *Marabel* does. At least we used to get on in the bedroom but lately we haven't even had that. You haven't come near me in weeks."

Thornley strode over to his overwrought wife and took her masterfully into his arms. "How could you doubt me, Kitty? You know I adore you, and always have. But you're so clever and beautiful and know all about clothes and furnishings and fashionable life and I'm just a dull old country squire. Please come back to me. I don't care how often you redecorate the drawing room, or any other room in the house for that matter. Just don't leave me again."

"Oh Walter!" Kitty burst into tears and returned his embrace with interest.

Jacobin tactfully removed herself from the room.

Anthony decided to ride the thirty odd miles to Hurst Park. It would be faster than driving, given the state of the roads, and he was consumed with impatience to find out about Edgar Candover's movements. As he turned out of the main gate of Storrington, waving to the gatekeeper, another rider joined him and kept pace alongside.

"My lord," Tom Hawkins said, "you're leaving early. I will, if you don't mind, ride with you."

"If you insist. As long as you're going where I'm going."

"I don't much care," said the runner, "but I'd prefer not to let you out of my sight."

"I'm glad you can tear yourself away from the prosecution of Miss de Chastelux."

Hawkins gave a mirthless chuckle. "That'll keep. This morning I'm more interested in your movements. I had an interesting conversation yesterday afternoon with Lord Candover's valet." Then, a sarcastic afterthought, "My lord."

Anthony didn't pretend not to know what he was talking about. At this point he might as well be honest with the man.

"I understand, Hawkins, that you have a job to do and that finding either my fiancée or me, or both of us, guilty of murder would complete that job. But—and I don't expect you to believe me at this moment—it would be wrong. For the simple reason that neither of us had anything to do with killing Candover. That being so, I am anxious to find out who did, as you should be. And Edgar Candover, who has just inherited both a title and an estate, seems to me the obvious candidate." He looked down at Hawkins, whose hack was a couple of hands shorter than Anthony's highbred saddle horse. "I do trust you haven't been so negligent in your investigation that the thought didn't occur to you."

"I thought of it," Hawkins said. "But you can't arrest a man without evidence and I haven't found a single witness who can place the new Lord Candover anywhere near the scene of either crime."

"What would you say if I told you Miss de Chastelux saw Edgar Candover in Brighton the day before the attempted poisoning?"

Hawkins looked thoughtful. "I would be interested, my lord. Though I regret that her testimony might be imputed to self-interest."

"Understandable," said Anthony affably. He'd decided there was no capital to be made from antagonizing the man. "But I'd be happy—and I'd appreciate it—if you'd accompany me to Hurst Park, my present destination, to see what else I can discover there."

Edgar wasn't at Hurst, neither did anyone know where he was. The staff there, who had been questioned by Hawkins before, were polite but reserved. They answered direct questions but didn't volunteer information, until Anthony recalled that Jacobin had lived among these servants and counted them her friends.

"Betrothed to Miss Jacobin?" said the elderly manservant who acted as butler in the absence of most of the household in London. "Why didn't you say so before? What splendid news! I'd be happy to tell you anything I can, my lord."

The floodgates opened. In response to Hawkins's questions—Anthony decided it would be more effective to let the runner lead the investigation—it emerged that Edgar Candover frequently absented himself from the house.

"We assume his absences have always been on estate business but he doesn't keep us informed."

"Where does he go?" asked the runner. "Is he riding around the estate or is he in the habit of being gone for longer periods?"

"It's hard to say," the manservant admitted. "Mr. Edgar—Lord Candover I should say—isn't a demanding gentleman. He often dines away from home so there's no reason for the staff here to keep track of him, so to speak."

"Was he here yesterday morning?"

"Let me see. He dined here the night before but I don't remember when he went out. He was here for dinner last night."

"Would anyone else know when he left the house?"

"Not the house, but maybe the stables. You might ask Josh, the head groom."

Josh was just as unhelpful. He'd taken one of the plow horses over to the blacksmith the day before, and when he returned, Mr. Edgar's horse wasn't in the stables. But whether it had been there early in the morning before he left for the farrier he couldn't say. They were short-staffed and he didn't even have a full-time stable boy. That youth shared duties in the kitchen and would have been making up the kitchen fire and blacking the boots first thing.

It was frustrating to find nothing definite, but Anthony could sense that the runner was intrigued. His features quivered like a terrier after a scent, and he made no pretense of being uninterested in the servants' answers.

"You're more knowledgeable about such things than I, my lord," he said as they left the stables, "but it seems to me the estate isn't in very good heart. I don't know how it speaks to the new Lord Candover's motives, but I think it'd be wise to discover where things are financially. Money," he added, touching a finger to the side of his nose, "is the most common motive for murder."

Chapter 28

By the middle of the afternoon Jacobin was bored and fretful. Kitty and Walter didn't reappear so she'd explored the house by herself, tried to interest herself in a novel, then retired upstairs to change into one of Kitty's gowns. She couldn't wait for Anthony to see her properly dressed, then to throw herself into his arms. She ran downstairs with unladylike haste to see if he'd returned.

Simpson was in the hall, and, not wishing to deal with his barely veiled hostility, she went first to the library, Anthony's favorite room. It was empty. Something caught her eye on the terrace outside: a white handkerchief tied to the handle of a certain garden urn.

He was back!

A hard, icy rain was coming down; it would have been sensible to put on something warmer than the light wool shawl that went with her gown. But, she thought with a shiver of something other than cold, Anthony would soon warm her up. She could hear the roar of the millrace through the howling wind, but a faint welcoming light glowed from the ground-floor windows of the Queen's House. She tore open the door and slammed it behind her, ready to hurl herself at him.

A chill quiet contrasted with the tempest outside. She went through the door from the small vestibule into the main saloon, which was bitter cold and lit by only a pair of candles. As usual it was going to be up to her to light the fire.

"Anthony," she called. "I'm so happy you're back. I have something to tell you."

Silence. Was he teasing her? "Anthony," she repeated.

She moved farther into the room, searching for him in the half light. Unease prickled the back of her neck, dousing her euphoria. She heard, or perhaps only sensed, the air stirring behind her, and a hand touched her shoulder.

"Jacobin." The voice was close to her ear.

She stopped dead.

"Edgar." She could hardly enunciate the syllables. Then slowly turned to face her cousin.

He must have been standing behind the door when she entered the room. He stood there, short, slight, and neat in his precisely tailored garments. And the expression on his face so reflected Edgar's habitual mild amiability that she found it impossible to credit that he was a murderer. It had to be wishful thinking on her part to consider him guilty. Edgar Candover just didn't seem dangerous.

Yet she couldn't think of an innocent reason for his presence at the Queen's House.

"What are you doing here?" she asked. "Did you know I'd be here?"

"Oh yes, cousin." His soft, slightly high-pitched voice conveyed no emotion. "I knew about your signal to Storrington. His butler is a helpful man. He doesn't like you very much, you know."

"Simpson? He knew?" Of course Simpson had found out. As she was well aware, servants always knew everything.

"I understand you're to be married, Jacobin."

He sounded sincere, but it wouldn't hurt to get nearer the door. She fancied she could outrun Edgar if it became necessary.

"Yes, Edgar, is it not wonderful? You must wish me happy." She forced her features into an expression of trust and edged sideways.

"I do. At least I would." His voice dropped a notch and gained a mournful tone. "But, alas, the ceremony won't take place."

"Not take place?" Indignation overcame the alarm she was beginning to feel. "Of course it will. Lord Storrington and I love each other."

Then remembering her last meeting with Edgar, she softened her voice. "I'm sorry I couldn't accept your offer, Edgar. I hope you're not upset." If she could keep him talking she might be able to reach the door. At least he'd made no move to restrain her.

"No, I'm not upset," he said, his dull eyes glowing

with some unidentifiable emotion. "But I'm afraid it's going to be very sad for Storrington when you are found dead."

During the ride to Guildford to find Candover's solicitor, Anthony considered what he already knew of Candover's finances. A large portion of the Hurst Park estate was mortgaged. Yet for some reason there were substantial lands that remained unencumbered. None of the land was well maintained, for every penny of Candover's income had gone to his pleasure with nothing being put back into improvements. And Candover had sold off a great deal of movable property: jewelry, paintings, and a valuable collection of rare books, including several Caxtons.

It occurred to Anthony that some of the land might, in fact, belong to Jacobin. Lord Hugo had mentioned that Auguste de Chastelux had required a large dowry to accept Jacobin's mother, and it made sense that part of that settlement would remain in English property. Given Candover's charming personality, it wasn't much of a stretch to believe he'd withheld Felicity's fortune from his despised niece.

Jacobin would be pleased to discover she wasn't penniless, he thought with a smile. Not that he cared, but given his future bride's fierce independence, he knew she'd appreciate not entering marriage empty-handed. His mind lingered pleasurably over the previous night's lovemaking. What a good thing it was they had to marry at once. His stomach tightened with anxiety about what the solicitor might reveal, and whether it would help clear them both of suspicion.

"Lord Candover's will is quite straightforward," the solicitor said. "Everything goes to his cousin Edgar, the new baron. With the exception, of course, of the portion set aside for Felicity Candover and her issue through the terms of her marriage settlement."

He was right, Anthony thought. And Jacobin would be thrilled.

"Does Miss de Chastelux inherit a good sum from her uncle's death?" Hawkins asked eagerly. Anthony could see the direction the man's mind was taking.

"But presumably Edgar Candover gets more," he said quickly to restore Hawkins's attention to more fruitful fields. "He must have inherited a substantial estate."

The solicitor hemmed and looked at them over his spectacles. "It's a little complicated. In recent years Lord Candover has been what I can only call improvident. But his sister was guaranteed a half share of the income from the property at Avonhill in Wiltshire during her brother's lifetime and the lands in their entirety after his death. And since his late Lordship wasn't able to mortgage them, they represent the only productive part of the estate. The new Lord Candover's inheritance isn't particularly enviable. It will require quite an infusion of money to restore it to prosperity."

So, thought Anthony angrily, Candover has been living off Jacobin's inheritance from her mother for all these years. The man had deserved killing.

"Jacobin de Chastelux stands to benefit considerably

from her uncle's death," said Hawkins. "More so than the male heir."

"Is the property hers outright," Anthony asked, "or does she hold only a life interest in it?"

"If Miss de Chastelux marries, her property will go to her husband, and to her children if she has any. If she were to die unwed, it reverts to the estate."

Anthony saw what that meant, even as the damn runner continued to look triumphant at finding a cast-iron motive for Jacobin to murder her uncle.

"Don't you understand, you dolt, that Edgar Candover had a perfect motive for killing Candover and making sure his cousin was blamed? That way he'd get the whole lot, including the valuable part of the estate."

"It seems convoluted," Hawkins objected. "I prefer the more straightforward motive. Criminals are rarely subtle."

Anthony wanted to shake him. "To hell with what you prefer. It's in Edgar Candover's interest to see his cousin dead before she marries. And she's supposed to be marrying me in two days' time."

"You intend to kill me?" Jacobin still could scarcely credit it. "You killed Candover," she said, "though I don't understand why. And I certainly don't see why you have to kill me."

"I don't want to," Edgar said earnestly. "But it's the only way. If you're alive I'll never get the Avonhill estate. My cousin squandered and gambled away most of his fortune except that one property. For eight years I've held things together getting no thanks and very little respect. But I didn't mind because I knew that eventually I'd get the title and Avonhill. It's the only thing he never mortgaged, and I made sure enough money went back into the land to keep it profitable. It's a snug little place and will suit me. I'm a very modest man. He never told me the estate was your mother's and was to go to you. When I discovered the truth a few months ago I knew he had to die before he spent everything."

Jacobin considered this latest evidence of her uncle's perfidy. "I don't want it," she said, trying to placate Edgar. "You can have it. Storrington has plenty of money."

"I wish I could accept your offer, but Storrington would never let me have it. Once you're married he'll have control over it. You should have accepted my offer while you had the chance."

"You won't get away with it, Edgar. Storrington will hunt you to the ends of the earth, and if he doesn't kill you, you'll hang."

"Oh no. You will be blamed for killing Candover. Your note confessing to the crime will be found near your body. You are going to commit suicide in a moment of remorse."

She looked for a weapon. Edgar wasn't much bigger than she was, and she was strong. A large and ornate vase stood on a side table. Sèvres, she thought irrelevantly, and ugly. She wanted to weep when she remembered the last time she'd smashed Sèvres porcelain in this house. She looked forward to breaking it over Edgar's head.

Though her glance was discreet, he noticed the object of her attention. "Don't even think about it, Jacobin, or I'll shoot you." He was pointing a gun at her, a twin of the pistol that had killed Candover.

"You've been planning it for months, haven't you? My God! You probably even meant for me to be blamed for the poisoning. Did you see me in Brighton that night?"

"I *knew* you were in Brighton. No one ever thinks I'm clever." His voice shook with resentment. "Without me your uncle would have been under the hatches years ago, but I got no thanks for my work. But when you ran off with Jean-Luc, I knew he wasn't any use to you. Cousin Candover didn't know that, all he cared about was Jean-Luc's cooking. He believed you'd truly eloped with him. I traced the two of you to London and found out he'd got you a position in the prince's household at Carlton House. Then I just had to wait my opportunity, wait until Candover was invited to dine. It was convenient that it was in Brighton rather than London. There was always food to be purchased after Brighton dinners."

"So all those words of affection you said to me at the Argyll Rooms were nonsense."

"Oh no, Jacobin. I would have married you then. I used to envy Jean-Luc. For eight years he had all your smiles, all your attention, and you hardly noticed my existence."

Though she'd rather have spat at his declaration, flattery might buy her some time. "I wish you'd told me then, Edgar. I was always fond of you but I had no idea. And now I see how very intelligent you are."

His pale eyes warmed a little and he smiled. "That's good of you to say so, Jacobin." He moved closer to her, and for a moment she thought he was going to kiss her. Vile as such a prospect was, it might give her a chance to snatch away the gun.

Instead he pressed the barrel of the pistol into her ribs. "It's time for your suicide, my dear."

"I'll never write a note," she retorted. "You'll have to shoot me."

"No need. The note's all ready and sitting on that pretty little desk over there. I've had plenty of time to practice imitating your handwriting."

"Anthony will know I didn't write it. There's no paper in that escritoire."

"No matter," Edgar said, unimpressed. "I fancy Lord Storrington will be too stricken with grief to recall such an unimportant detail. Now, lead the way out, please. And don't forget, I won't hesitate to shoot you here if you give me any trouble."

"Out? Why?" Jacobin had an insane notion that Edgar was worried about blood on the carpet.

"You're going to drown yourself in the millrace, just as Storrington's mother did."

"How do you know she killed herself?" Jacobin had learned that fact from Kitty earlier in the day, but it certainly wasn't general knowledge.

"Candover told me in one of his drunken fits. Said he'd driven her to it, boasted of it because he'd fancied her himself and she turned him down. We Candovers don't like to have our wills thwarted," he concluded with a touch of manic and pathetic pride.

She couldn't let him do it to Anthony. Even if she had to die, at least it wouldn't be in sinister imitation of his mother's demise. She'd fight Edgar just to spare Anthony that grief.

Anthony's horse was spent by the time he slid from its back and abandoned it at the front door to rush into the hall. Hawkins, whose lesser-bred nag was slower but had more stamina, was at his heels.

"Simpson," Anthony yelled. "Where is Miss de Chastelux?"

"I haven't seen her this afternoon," the butler replied stiffly.

Kitty emerged from a drawing room. "Anthony," she said in a worried voice. "Jacobin has disappeared. She's not in her room, and we can't find her anywhere downstairs."

Barely registering that Walter Thornley stood beside her, holding her hand, Anthony grasped Kitty by the shoulders. "When did you last see her?"

"Several hours ago." Kitty's tone was sheepish. "Perhaps she went out for a walk." She sounded doubtful, as well she might, given that the rain was coming down in sheets, assisted by a growing gale.

He tore into the library and looked out of the window.

There was one hope. In the half light he could make out something white clinging damply to the urn.

Thank God.

"The hamlet," he said. "Have someone follow me with a heavy cloak and order a bath—two baths—for our return."

His own attire was still sodden from the ride but he gave it no mind. She was likely awaiting him, warm, dry, and *safe* in the Queen's House, yet his anxiety wouldn't be assuaged until he had her in his arms. He ran out of the library door and took the steps from the terrace in leaps.

He could see light in the Queen's House but the door was swinging, wide open. "Jacobin," he shouted at the threshold.

He could hear nothing above the wail of the wind, the creak of hinges, and the thudding of his heart. Something—a movement?—off to one side caught his attention, and he peered into the deepening gloom, to the other end of the lake. She couldn't be out on the bridge, could she?

The bridge, Jacobin thought. It had to be on the bridge. Once they had crossed it, Edgar would push her down the steep slope into the roaring stream. She'd considered her chances of swimming to safety and regretfully dismissed them. She was, at best, a weak swimmer and the water would be icy, the current fierce, and her clothes would weigh her down.

The railing of balusters along the sides of the gently

arched structure was low, no more than knee-high at
most. If she could distract Edgar as they crossed she
might be able to unbalance him and push him into the
water. It wasn't much of a plan but the best she could
come up with. She had the advantage of near darkness
and knowing the territory.

She could feel Edgar's breath on her neck each time
she hesitated on the rain-soaked path, and he pressed
her from behind.

"Keep moving," he muttered.

They were at the end of the bridge now, and she
increased her pace, praying she wouldn't slip on the
three shallow steps that led to the apex of the structure and that Edgar would. At her little spurt of speed,
she drew away from the gun barrel that had been
nudging her back the whole way from the Queen's
House. She listened intently, desperately waiting for
her chance.

It came, she thought. Not sure if she was correct in
sensing a hitch in his walk, a booted foot hitting the
riser of a step, she swung around with all her strength,
slamming her arm against Edgar's body.

She heard a splash—the gun falling into the water,
she hoped—and hurled herself at her cousin. He
slumped onto his rear, arms splayed, his head against
the railing.

"You bitch," he shouted, struggling to rise, but she
was on him now. She grabbed him by the ears and
banged his head against the stone coping, over and
over, beyond caring what she did to him.

Afterward she realized she might have killed him had a pair of strong arms not pulled her away.

"You rescued me again," she muttered.

"I think you rescued yourself," Anthony replied. His tone was steady, even a little amused. But the way he held her close to his hammering heart and pressed kisses over every inch of her face told her all about the measure of his relief. "It seems to have been Edgar who needed rescuing."

She twisted her head to see her cousin, blood oozing from his head, being trussed up by Tom Hawkins.

"You knew I was strong."

"It's lucky I like strong women."

"I love you," she said, and relaxed into his embrace.

Chapter 29

With Edgar awaiting trial for Candover's murder, Kitty had decreed that a hasty marriage was unnecessary and they could wait for St. George's, Hanover Square in the spring. A compromise was negotiated in the form of a Boxing Day wedding at Storrington in the presence of every cousin, distant connection, and miscellaneous member of the *ton* who could be lured to Sussex for the occasion. A surprising number had been ready to change their Yuletide plans at the last minute.

Charming people for the most part, but Jacobin found life somewhat lacking in drama. And excitement. It seemed like an age since she'd been able to snatch more than five minutes alone with Anthony. Being a fiancée was tame compared with the role of a mistress. With the house bursting at the seams, discreet nocturnal passage creeping was an impossibility.

The day before Christmas she excused herself from a ladies' decorating session in the drawing room and crept outside. Through the windows of the library she could see a group of men sitting around with glasses of brandy and spending a thoroughly enjoyable afternoon without the distraction of holly, pine boughs, and mistletoe.

James Storrs glimpsed her from the room and winked at her. She'd already established a friendship with Anthony's easygoing younger brother. She shrugged at him and rolled her eyes. He must have drawn his brother's attention to the window. Anthony looked out at her with a smile that made her heart race.

Quickly she turned her back on him, not without a come-hither glance over her shoulder and a wave of a length of satin ribbon. She was running low on garters. When she reached the London shops she was going to have to get some new ones, in every available color.

It took him a ridiculously long time to extract himself from the masculine gathering. Probably listening to an improper story, she thought waspishly as she roamed around the saloon of the Queen's House. Its rich rococo decor, in marked contrast to the faux rustic exterior, never failed to make her think of France. With a pang of nostalgia laced with sadness, she wished her parents could be at her wedding.

And Anthony's too. She found Catherine Storrington's actions perplexing. Although Anthony had come far in reconciling himself to her death, it would take a long time for him to be truly at peace with her abandonment of him. He had accepted that he would never discover the identity of his mother's lover.

Her attention fixed on the late Lady Storrington's desk, which she recalled had once resided in her boudoir and been brought to the Queen's House after her death. It was an elaborate object, not large, but paneled in two or three different woods and trimmed with ormolu. At a glance it looked like a small armoire, but the front hinged down to form the writing surface and reveal an intriguing nest of drawers, cubbyholes, and little cupboards. Although far more elaborate, it reminded Jacobin of a piece her mother had owned in Paris.

Her mother had told her Marie Antoinette was particularly fond of such desks. In fact the French name for them, *secrétaires*, with its double-entendre connotation of secrecy, had been used by the queen's detractors to suggest that she was using her numerous writing desks to conceal secret documents. With nothing else to do, Jacobin poked around in the piece, opening and shutting drawers and doors to see if there could possibly be a hidden compartment.

Idle curiosity became genuine interest when she noticed that a niche on one side was shallower than its twin. There might be a space behind it large enough to hold a small bundle of papers. Groping inside, she detected a slot, about the size of a sixpence. She inserted a fingernail and pried away the back panel. Something fell out: letters, and a miniature portrait in a gilt frame.

She knew who it was at once, for the face was as familiar to her as her own. Chestnut curls, brown eyes, a firm straight nose, and a cleft chin. A masculine version of herself. Her father.

* * *

Silently she handed him the miniature.

"Is this your father?" Anthony asked. "You didn't tell me you had a portrait of him. You really are very like him."

"I found it in the desk."

His mind grappled with the meaning of her words. "Why . . . how?"

He accepted a letter from her outstretched hand and examined the single sheet carefully. The paper was of good quality but the folds were fragile, as though it had been opened and read many times. The handwriting was unfamiliar, in a foreign style. "It's in French. Will you read it to me?"

She nodded, eyes shining with tears.

"'My dearest Catherine,'" she translated. "'With a heavy heart I write my *adieu* to you. I understand that your duty and devotion to your family must come before our love. You will return to England with your good husband and live once more with your beloved Anthony and the little Kitty. Don't be sad, my love. The thought of your melancholy weighs on my soul. I want only your happiness, and it tears my heart that we can never find joy together. Be happy with Lord Storrington and your precious children whom you love so much. I shall marry Felicity and do my best to be a good husband, for she deserves it. And I shall devote my efforts to improving the lot of my unhappy country, to making my fellow citizens free and happy and peaceful. Have care of yourself, Catherine. And avoid Candover. Although he will be my brother-in-law, I fear his malice and his spirit of vengeance.' "

Tears poured down Jacobin's cheeks and choked her voice. " 'Since the first moment I saw you at Trianon your beauty and loveliness of spirit have possessed my senses. Although our love will never be *consommé* . . .' "

She hesitated. "Consumed . . . or consummated?"

"Consummated, I imagine," Anthony said softly.

" 'Although our love will never be consummated, the very great passion I have for you will never die. On the day of my death I shall hold your image in my heart. *Adieu* my Catherine, my very dear Catherine. I will love you always. Auguste.' "

Anthony's mind was a blank.

"I'm sorry, Anthony," she said, but he was hardly attending.

"Impossible. It's incredible." He tried to think, though his brain felt as though it were stuffed with bran.

He was the handsomest man in France. Candover's words came back to him during their first infamous card game. He hadn't heeded them at the time, but it was the first hint: that Candover had hated his brother-in-law because he'd won the heart of the woman he wanted. It was all there had he thought to look: the clues to a trail of events that led from a visit to Marie Antoinette's retreat at Versailles in 1786 to this moment in this house, built in imitation of the same corner of the French royal estate.

"How could I not have seen it?" he said aloud.

"The truth was there to see had I interpreted things correctly."

Jacobin couldn't believe it. She was standing there, her heart broken, and he was thinking *logically*.

It wouldn't last, she knew. Soon the anger that had long burned over her uncle would turn against her father, then her.

She laid her father's letter carefully on the desk, giving it a last regretful look. Despite the misery the contents had caused her, she hadn't been able to help thrilling at the sight of his handwriting and at the passionate words that had brought him back to her so vividly.

"I shall leave now," she said flatly. "I'll return to Hurst and see my uncle's solicitor. At least I have money. You won't have to worry about me."

His eyes fastened on her. "What the blazes are you talking about?"

"I understand that we cannot be married, and I think it's better if I go at once."

"Go? Go?" His voice rose to a shout and he grabbed her shoulders roughly. "No! You can't leave me. You can't abandon me!" He sounded panicked and held her so hard it hurt.

"But . . . but . . . you can't want me now. My father . . . your mother. You must hate him. You must hate *me*."

He gathered her into his arms. "Hate you?" he asked, so tenderly she felt her senses melt with relief and love. "I could never hate you. I love you."

"I'm sorry," she said again through tears, "for what my father did. For what he did to you."

"He did nothing, and neither did Mama. You read the letter. He sent her back to me and Kitty and my father."

"Aren't you still angry?"

He was thinking about it. She could tell by the way his body stilled, though he held her in his embrace. "No," he said in wonder. "It's gone. She couldn't help falling in love but she could help what she did about it. Her behavior was irreproachable."

"It made her very unhappy," she said somberly.

"I think she was always unhappy in a way, not because of what happened, but because she was an unhappy person. Lord Hugo said something about that, about a hidden darkness. After her separation from your father she succumbed to an illness that was already lurking. She probably couldn't help it."

"Poor lady," Jacobin murmured. Then, more severely, "But she should have tried harder for her children's sake, for your sake."

Anthony released her and walked over to the window. "I was angry with her," he said haltingly. "I never admitted it to myself. It's why I became obsessed with Candover, because I didn't want to blame her. I took it out on poor Kitty too, and she was innocent as a babe. She *was* a babe. But now I can forgive her. Mama, I mean. There's nothing to forgive really. She did her best."

Pleased as she was for him, that he could finally put his mother's treatment of him behind him, she still couldn't fully sympathize with the woman.

"Anthony," she said. "If I die you are not to abandon our children. And if you die I *will not* kill myself."

He couldn't help smiling as he turned to see her standing with her hands on her hips, scowling ferociously. No, he thought gladly. She was made of sterner stuff, his Jacobin.

"Children? Are you trying to tell me something, my love?"

"What? Oh no. At least I don't think so. It's too soon to tell."

He rather hoped she was with child. Especially since they'd be married in two days and the infant wouldn't arrive embarrassingly early.

"I know you'll make a wonderful parent, just like your father." He looked straight into her eyes, wanting to reassure her that he felt no resentment toward Auguste de Chastelux. "He sounds a remarkable man."

"Oh, he was! I couldn't have had a better father."

"You must tell me all about him."

"I'd like to. I think we both had good fathers."

He nodded. His own father had, in his own way, been the best of men.

"Why did he say that about Candover?" he said abruptly. "On his deathbed, I mean. My father said a letter came from Candover, just before Mama . . . died. What did the villain have to do with it?"

"I forgot!" Jacobin exclaimed. "There's another letter." She picked it up from the desk and gave it to him.

He froze when he recognized his mother's hand, and his fingers trembled. It was directed on the address panel to his father.

"'My lord.'" His parents had always addressed each other formally, he remembered. "'Today I received a letter from Candover. Auguste has been executed in France. I cannot bear to live without him in this world. I pray I may meet him in the next. Kiss Anthony, Kitty, and James for me. I love them all but I know I have failed in my duty as a mother. They will be better without me. I'm sorry, my lord. You have always been a good husband, better than I deserve. I commend our children to your care. Your respectful and affectionate wife, Catherine Storrington.'"

An odd farewell, Jacobin thought as he read it. The words seemed perfunctory, almost cold, for all they spoke of love and respect. As though Catherine had already, in her own mind, departed the world when she wrote them.

Her heart ached for Anthony. What a contrast to her father, who, despite the loss of his love, had carried on to be a decent husband, an adoring father, and to make something of his life in his political writings.

"When did your mother die?" she asked.

"August 1794."

"That's when my father was imprisoned. He had taken my mother and me out of Paris for safety, but he returned to testify on behalf of a friend. It did no good. The friend went to the guillotine, and he was arrested. My mother must have got word to my uncle—"

"—who couldn't wait to tell my mother the news. The bastard couldn't resist making her miserable."

"And even boasted to Edgar that he drove her to her death," she added. "He deserved to die. No," she corrected herself, "no one deserves to be killed, but I can't say I'm sorry it happened to him."

He chuckled, a surprising, though welcome, sound.

"Why are you laughing?" she asked suspiciously.

"You always make me laugh. It's one of the things I love about you."

"That's good. I think." Actually she knew it was good. She felt like singing and dancing and leaping with joy.

"Very good." He was moving closer, with a look on his face that managed to be both mirthful and heated at the same time.

She swayed her hips, tilted her breasts up, and eyed him provocatively through her lashes. "What are you going to do now?" she asked huskily.

"Now immediately or now in the future?"

"Either or both."

"Well . . . in the longer term I'm going to marry you and spend a lot of time in bed with you and laugh a lot and eat a lot of little puffy things and have as many children as you wish for and be happy for the rest of my life."

"That sounds . . . acceptable. And immediately?"

"I came here this afternoon in answer to an invitation. I intend to accept it. Immediately."

Epilogue

The Countess of Storrington's
Little Puffy Things

Take plenty of whipped cream . . .

The Countess of Storrington awoke at noon feeling hungry. She rather fancied a bit of French
pastry. She could, of course, descend to the kitchen
and make something, but one of the disadvantages of
being a peeress was not being really welcome in the
kitchen.

At least Mrs. Simpson was no longer there.
Once Anthony had ascertained that the Simpsons'
interactions with Edgar had been motivated by simple
spite toward Jacobin, rather than a more sinister
malice, he'd pensioned them off to a cottage on his
most distant estate. Jacobin's old friend, the cook
from Hurst Park, was now installed in the kitchen

at Storrington Hall. But Jacobin had learned that as mistress of the house her relationship with the servants required a certain formality.

Still, there were many, many superb things about being a rich and fashionable countess.

After a shaky start, Jacobin had been a success with all but the stuffiest members of the *ton*. Edgar's murder trial in the House of Lords became the public sensation of the day. By the time he was convicted and hanged with a silken rope, such being the dubious privilege of a felonious peer, most of the details of Jacobin's past life were public knowledge. All Anthony's family connections rallied round, and a number of older members of society came forward to support the daughter of Auguste de Chastelux, whom they remembered with affection from pre-revolutionary Parisian jaunts. The Prince Regent pronounced himself immensely amused that a countess had been employed in his kitchen and jovially offered to take her back into his service. The *coup de grâce* was an appearance at one of Lord Hugo Hartley's rare dinner parties, where Mr. Chauncey and Lady Caroline Bellamy had been persuaded to join the company. Although a few sticklers might (and did) note that the couple's daughter and niece were otherwise engaged that evening, there were very few people who cared to be regarded as higher in the instep than Lady Caroline. The new Lady Storrington's acceptance was assured.

Among the younger and more dashing, Jacobin was seen as a heroine and amassed an entertaining circle of friends. She'd even conducted a *pâtisserie* lesson for a group of young married women. They'd spent an enjoyable afternoon making French pastries and a terrible mess in the kitchen. She and Anthony had to dine out for the following three nights to let the servants recover.

The single most superb thing about being a rich countess was the earl. It was time, she decided, to issue her daily forgiveness for getting her into the condition that had cut short the season in London and made her so wretchedly ill every morning that she had to remain in bed. He would, to do him justice, have gladly stayed at her side, mopping her brow with cool cloths and holding a basin at the ready. But she'd snappishly sent him on his way when he'd woken to find her retching and offered sympathy.

She would, as always, make it up to him.

Pondering the probable whereabouts of her husband, she climbed out of the ancestral bed, pulled on a lace-trimmed robe, and wandered over to the window for a good stretch and a look at the weather.

The weather was fine and the garden urn exceptionally well dressed. Around its slender neck it sported a starched linen neck cloth tied in a perfect waterfall.

Excellent.

He met her at the door. "Recovered from the journey, I see. Unless it was something else that made you so charming this morning."

She cast him a nasty look, and he laughed.

"Come in," he said. "I have a present for you."

"Diamonds?" she said hopefully.

"I think you have enough jewels for the moment. Something better."

Instead of leading her into the saloon, he opened the door on the other side of the vestibule into what had been an unused storage room.

"Oh, Anthony!" It was perfect. It had a long marble table with an ice trough built in beneath it to keep the surface cold; a huge ice closet; the most modern range and oven; copper pans and molds in every shape and size hanging from hooks. Everything, in fact, that a well-equipped pastry room demanded.

"How did you do it?" she asked, hugging him tightly enough to squeeze the breath from a weaker man. "How did you know what to buy?"

"I didn't, of course. I left it all up to Jean-Luc. He arranged the whole thing before returning to France."

Jean-Luc had been in England recently when his employer, the Duc de Clermont-Ferrand, and his household had made a month-long visit. Jacobin had tried to persuade him to come and work for them, but he refused, he said, ever to spend another winter in the brutal English weather. Jacobin's protest that the climate of northern France was little better fell on deaf ears. Jean-Luc was happy with the dessert-loving *duc* and his friend Michel, the *duc*'s maître d'hôtel. He'd dined *à trois* with her and Anthony one night, and escorted her to a masquerade when Anthony had to attend an all-male political dinner. But Jacobin knew, despite her husband's indulgence, that their old friendship would be forever circumscribed by the barriers of rank.

"I'm hungry," she said. "I'm going to cook something right now."

"Am I allowed to make a request?" Anthony asked.

"You don't need to. I know what you like."

"Splendid. I'll leave you to it," and he left the room.

She happily explored her new domain, discovering flour, sugars, spices, and other dry goods in a cupboard, while the ice chest had a compartment for eggs, butter, and cream. She set water to heat on the stove and assembled the ingredients for *choux* pastry. But after a while she felt lonely. He might have stayed to talk while she cooked. What was he doing, anyway?

She heard a noise upstairs, and her lips curved.

He was lying on the bed when she entered.

"That was quick," he said.

"I have a new recipe for profiteroles. It omits the pastry." She held up a bowl of whipped cream, then produced two strips of cloth from her pocket.

His eyes darkened with the intent look that never failed to make her hot all over.

"I do believe," he drawled, "that I'm about to realize one of my deepest fantasies."

"No," she said, approaching the bed with purpose. "This one's mine."

Author's Note

I've always been fascinated by culinary history, especially old cookbooks. There's nothing more fun than finding a really disgusting recipe and wondering "How could they eat this?" The oldest known cookbook was written by a Roman, Apicius. A highly concentrated fish stock was a staple of ancient Roman cookery and sounds completely vile.

The Regency period gave the world its first "celebrity chef " Antonin Carême, the Wolfgang Puck or Marco Pierre White of his day. Carême cooked for Napoleon, the Bourbon kings, the Tsar of Russia, Talleyrand and the Prince Regent. He also published several bestselling books. His works on pastries and desserts, confections as they were more generally called, laid down the foundation of classic French pâtisserie. When I read Ian Kelly's superb biography *Cooking for Kings* I had to include Carême's tenure at the Brighton Pavilion in a Regency novel.

In the end the demands of the plot prevented the great man's actual appearance in my book. He gets sick so Jacobin is called to pinch hit for him. Carême did in fact suffer from chronic respiratory problems, made worse by the extreme conditions of heat and cold he worked in and constant exposure to charcoal fumes.

I tried to make my description of life in the Prince Regent's kitchens as accurate as possible. The huge Brighton kitchens were Prinny's pride and joy and he liked to show them to his guests. A picture of the main kitchen may be found on my website although, sadly, the crazy palm fronds decorating the pillars were added after my story takes place. As Jacobin discovered, Carême didn't like working with women and he became unpopular with the Prince Regent's staff for not sharing the income from the sale of surplus food. In fact his time in England was an unhappy period in his life and lasted little more than a year.

I wanted to include some of Carême's recipes in *Never Resist Temptation* and had a great time combing through his books. Along the way I found some of the oddities I enjoy. What do you make of a recipe that calls for "about one hundred middle sized lobsters' tails" but gives you the option of substituting carrots? Carrots? The dish is called *Chartreuse à la Parisienne, en Surprise*. Surprise indeed, and not a good one, to get a mouthful of carrot when you're expecting lobster.

Since Carême's English staff complained about the differences between English and French measurements, I compared some recipes in French with their translations in the English edition. In one place the original called for a piece of butter the size of a walnut which in translation became a turnip. Either turnips used to be much smaller or the English liked a lot of butter. Yet classic French cuisine has a reputation for excessive richness.

I've been asked whether I tried any of the recipes in my book. Well, I'm not the greatest baker myself, and Carême's directions lack the exact measurements we're used to in modern cookbooks. How much, for heaven's sake, is a "plateful" of cream? What size plate?

I did think I should attempt *choux* pastry since it features prominently in the story. And I'll admit that though the technique appears not to have changed, Julia Child's recipe was a lot easier to follow than Carême's. You may find an account of my attempt to make "little puffy things" on my website *www.mirandaneville.com* together with additional Carême recipes for dishes mentioned in the book. If you try them please let me know how they turn out.

Miranda

Next month, don't miss these exciting new love stories only from Avon Books

Secret Life of a Vampire by Kerrelyn Sparks

No one can throw a bachelor party quite like Jack, the illegitimate son of the legendary Casanova. But when the party gets out of hand and the cops show up, Jack has some explaining to do . . . if only he wasn't struck speechless by the beauty of Officer Lara Boucher.

Sins of a Wicked Duke by Sophie Jordan

One would think the last place a beauty like Fallon O'Rourke could keep her virtue was in the mansion of London's most licentious duke. Yet Fallon is perfectly safe there . . . disguised as a footman! But how long can her deception last when she begins to desire the sinful duke himself?

Taken and Seduced by Julia Latham

Adam Hilliard, secret Earl of Keswick, lives for revenge, and Lady Florence Becket is the key. But when Adam kidnaps her, they both find far more than they ever desired . . .

Her Notorious Viscount by Jenna Petersen

Proper Jane Fenton knows the danger of associating with a notorious man like Viscount Nicholas Stoneworth, a man who could tempt any woman into certain scandal. But finding her missing brother depends on transforming Nicholas into a gentleman, so Jane must ignore the promise of sinful pleasure in his eyes . . .

At Avon Books, we know your passion for romance—once you finish one of our novels, you find yourself wanting more.

May we tempt you with . . .

- **Excerpts** from our upcoming releases.
- Entertaining **extras**, including authors' personal photo albums and book lists.
- Behind-the-scenes **scoop** on your favorite characters and series.
- **Sweepstakes** for the chance to win free books, romantic getaways, and other fun prizes.
- Writing **tips** from our authors and editors.
- **Blog** with our authors and find out why they love to write romance.
- **Exclusive content** that's not contained within the pages of our novels.

Join us at

An Imprint of HarperCollins*Publishers*

Avai... 331-3761 to order.